BY GREG BEAR

Darwin's Radio (Winner of the 2001 Nebula Award for Best Novel)

Darwin's Children

Dead Lines

Vitals

Blood Music

Moving Mars

and many more

CITY AT THE END OF TIME

CITY AT THE
END OF TIME

Greg Bear

BALLANTINE BOOKS DEL REY NEW YORK

Copyright © 2008 by Greg Bear
Map copyright © 2008 by Casey Hampton
Impossible armillary sphere design copyright © 1984 by Greg Bear

Published in the United States by Del Rey Books, an imprint of The Random House Publishing Group, a division of Random House, Inc., New York.

DEL REY is a registered trademark and the Del Rey colophon is a trademark of Random House, Inc.

LIBRARY OF CONGRESS CATALOGING-IN-PUBLICATION DATA
Bear, Greg.
 City at the end of time / Greg Bear.
  p. cm.
 ISBN 978-0-345-44839-2 (hardcover : alk. paper)
1. Young adults—Fiction. 2. Time travel—Fiction.
3. Seattle (Wash.)—Fiction. I. Title.
PS3552.E157C58 2008
813'.54—dc22   2008006643

Printed in the United States of America on acid-free paper

www.delreybooks.com

9 8 7 6 5 4 3 2 1

FIRST EDITION

Book design by Casey Hampton

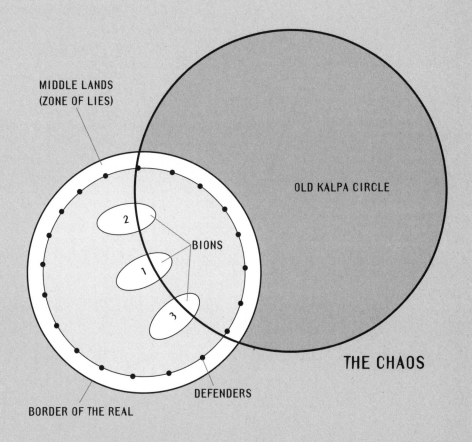

MIDDLE LANDS
(ZONE OF LIES)

OLD KALPA CIRCLE

2

1

BIONS

3

THE CHAOS

DEFENDERS

BORDER OF THE REAL

THE KALPA
AND ENVIRONS

A.

FOURTEEN ZEROS

PROLOG

The Kalpa

Coming to the Broken Tower was dangerous.

Alone at the outer edge of an empty room half a mile wide, surrounded by a brutality of high crystal windows, Keeper Ghentun drew in his cloak against the mordant chill. A thin pool of air bubbled at his feet, and a fine icy mist lingered along the path he had taken from the lifts. This part of the city was not used to his kind, his brand of physicality, and did not adjust willingly to his needs.

Servants of the Librarian came here rarely to meet with suppliants from the lower levels. Appointments were nearly impossible to obtain. And yet, Ghentun had requested an audience and had been summoned.

The high windows gave a panoramic view of what lay outside the city, over the middle lands and beyond the border of the real—the Typhon Chaos. In all the Kalpa, only the tower had windows to the outside; the rest of the city had long ago walled itself off from that awesome, awful sight.

Ghentun approached the nearest window and braced for a look. Directly below, great curves like the prows of three ships seemed ready to leap into the darkness: the Kalpa's last bions, containing all that remained of humanity. A narrow gray belt surrounded these huge edifices, and beyond that stretched a broad, uneven black ring: the middle lands. That ring and all within was protected by an outward-facing phalanx of slowly revolving spires, blurred as if sunk in silt-laden water: the Defenders, outermost of the city's reality generators.

Outside of their protection, four craters filled with wreckage—the lost bions of the Kalpa—swept away in a wide curve to either side and back again, meeting in darkness hundreds of miles away: the city's original ring.

Out of the Chaos, the massive orb of the Witness beamed its gray, knife-edged searchlight over the lost bions and the middle lands, blasting against the foggy Defenders, arcing high as if to grasp the tower—too painful to watch.

Ghentun averted his eyes just as the beam swept through the chamber.

Sangmer, the first to lead an attempt to cross the Chaos, had once stood on this very spot, mapping the course of his journey. A few wakes later he had descended from the Broken Tower—even then called Malregard—and gone forth on his last quest with five brave companions, philosopher-adventurers all.

None ever heard from again.

Malregard, indeed. *Evil view.*

He felt a presence behind him and turned, bowing his head. The Librarian had such a variety of servants, he did not know what to expect. This one—a small angelin, female in form—stood barely taller than Ghentun's knee. He colored his cloak infrared, making the nearest pools of air bubble furiously and vanish. The servant also shifted spectrum, then brought up the temperature in the chamber until finally there was some pressure.

Ghentun bent to give the angelin a primordial speck of dirt, a crumbled bit of Earth's basalt—the traditional payment for an audience. These were the old rules, never to be forgotten. The Librarian and all his servants were liable to withdraw at a whisper of rudeness into ten thousand years of silence—something the Kalpa could no longer afford.

"Why are you here, Keeper?" the angelin asked. "Has there been progress this side of the real?"

"That is for the Librarian to judge. All honor to its servants."

The angelin silvered and froze—simply stopped, for no reason Ghentun could fathom. All the forms had been observed. Ghentun switched his cloak and plasma to slow mode so he might maintain some disciplined comfort. Clearly, this was going to take a while.

Two wakes passed.

Nothing around them changed except that out of the Chaos the Witness's gray knife-edge beam swept three times through the chamber.

———

The angelin finally cleared its silvery shell and spoke. "The Librarian will receive you. An appointment will be made available in fewer than a thousand years. Pass this information to such successors as there may be."

"I will have no successor," Ghentun said.

The angelin's reaction came with surprising swiftness. "The experiment is concluded?"

"No. The city."

"We have been out of touch. Explain."

Ghentun observed sharply, "We do not have the luxury of time. Decisions must be made soon."

The angelin expanded and became translucent. "Soon" could be interpreted as an affront to any Eidolon, but particularly a servant of the Librarian. It was difficult to believe that such beings still lay claim to the honor of humanity—but it was so.

"Explain to me what you can," it said, "without denying the privilege of the Librarian."

"There are troubling results. They may be harbingers. The Kalpa is the last refuge of old reality, but our influence is too small. As the Librarian anticipated, history may be corroding."

"The Librarian does not anticipate. All is permutation."

"No doubt," Ghentun said. "Nevertheless, world-lines are being severed and unnaturally rejoined. Others may have been dissolved. Whole segments of history may already be lost."

"The Chaos has crept backward—in time?"

"Something like that is being felt by a few of the ancient breed. They are our indicators, as they were designed to be."

Intrigued, the angelin reduced and solidified. "Canaries in a coal mine," it said.

Ghentun did not know what canaries were, and only vaguely understood the implications of a coal mine.

"Do any of the ancient breed experience unusual dreams?" the angelin asked.

Ghentun drew his cloak tight. "I've revealed what I can, all honor to the Librarian. I need to make the rest of my report in person—directly. As instructed."

"From Malregard, we watch your breeds crossing the border of the real—violating city law. They seem determined to lose themselves in the Chaos. None have been observed to return. Is your report an admission of failure?"

Ghentun carefully considered his position. "By nature, they are a sensitive and determined folk. I am humble before the Eidolons— I leave those observations to your kind, and seek criticism from the Librarian, if it is due—directly."

Another long pause.

The Witness's gray beam again swept the chamber. As it passed through the angelin, Ghentun observed a lattice of internal process— the highly refined, jewel-like structure of sapphire-grade noötic matter. The angelin oscillated before Ghentun's face. Its lips did not move but its bubble of cold shimmered. "Induce an individual affected by these dreams to accompany you to the Broken Tower."

"When?"

"You will be notified."

Ghentun felt a flush of frustration. "Do you understand urgency?" he asked.

"No," the angelin said. "You can either stay and explain it to me, or carry out these instructions. In seventy-five years there will be an interview with the Librarian. Is that *soon* enough?"

"It will have to do," Ghentun said.

"Peace and permutation be upon you, Keeper."

The angelin darted off, leaving a trail of silvery vectors that quickly summed and vanished. Once, the vector trail of an angelin would have been a glorious thing to behold. Now it seemed pale and constricted.

Reduced fates, narrowing paths.

Ghentun gathered up his cloak and departed Malregard. He had not answered the angelin's question about dreams, because he needed to hold back as much as he could, to be revealed only later—to the central mind of the Librarian himself, he fervently hoped. At any rate, his level of optimism about this whole endeavor had never been high.

The end of all history, of everything human and worthy—consumption in the malign insanity of the Chaos that had been looming for ages—was now upon them.

After a hundred trillion years, it was likely that the Kalpa was beyond saving.

FATE SHIFTERS

PART ONE

TEN ZEROS

CHAPTER 1

Seattle

The city was young. Unbelievably young.

The moon rose sharp and silver-blue over a deck of soft gray clouds, and if you looked east, above the hills, where the sun would soon rise, you saw a brightness as yellow and real as natural butter.

The city faced the coming day with dew cold and wet on new green grass, streaming down windows, beaded on railings, chill against swiping fingers.

Waking up in the city, no one could know how young it was and fresh; all had activities to plan, living worries to blind them, and what would it take to finally smell the blessed, cool newness, but a whiff of something other?

Everyone went about their business.

The day passed into dusk.

Hardly anyone noticed there was a difference.

A hint of loss.

———

With a shock that nearly made her cry out, Ginny thought she saw the old gray Mercedes in the wide side mirror of the Metro bus—stopped the next lane over, two car lengths behind, blocking traffic. The smoked rear windows, the crack in its mottled windshield—clearly visible.

It's them—the man with the silver dollar, the woman with flames in her palms.

The bus's front door opened, but Ginny stepped back into the aisle. All thoughts of getting out a stop early, of walking the next few blocks to stretch her legs and think, had vanished.

The Metro driver—a plump black woman with ivory sclera and pale brown eyes, dark red lipstick, and diamonds on her incisors, still, after a day's hard work, lightly perfumed with My Sin—stared up at Ginny. "Someone following you, honey? I can call the cops." She tapped the bus's emergency button with a long pearly fingernail.

Ginny shook her head. "Won't help. It's nothing."

The driver sighed and closed the door, and the bus drove on. Ginny took her seat and rested her backpack in her lap—she missed the weight of her box, but for the moment, it was someplace safe. She glanced over her shoulder through the bus's rear window.

The Mercedes dropped back and turned onto a side street.

With her good hand, she felt in the pack's zippered side pocket for a piece of paper. While unwrapping the filthy bandage from her hand, the doctor at the clinic had spent half an hour gently redressing her burns, injecting a big dose of antibiotics, and asking too many questions.

Ginny turned to the front of the bus and closed her eyes. Felt the passengers brush by, heard the front door and the middle door open and close with rubbery *shushes*, the air brakes chuffing and sighing.

The doctor had told her about an eccentric but kind old man who lived alone in a warehouse filled with books. The old man needed an assistant. Could be long-term. Room and board, a safe place; all legit. The doctor had not asked Ginny to trust her. That would have been too much.

Then, she had printed out a map.

Because Ginny had no other place to go, she was following the doctor's directions. She unfolded the paper. Just a few more stops. First Avenue South—south of the two huge stadiums. It was getting dark—almost eight o'clock.

Before boarding the bus—before seeing or imagining the gray Mercedes—Ginny had found an open pawnshop a block from the clinic. There, like Queequeg selling his shrunken head, she had hocked her box and the library stone within.

It was Ginny's mother who had called it the library stone. Her father had called it a *"sum-runner."* Neither of the names had ever come with much of an explanation. The stone—a hooked, burned-looking, come-and-go thing in a lead-lined box about two inches on a side—was supposed to be the only valuable possession left to their nomadic family. Her mother and father hadn't told her where they had taken possession of it, or when. They probably didn't know or couldn't remember.

The box always seemed to weigh the same, but when they slid open the grooved lid—a lid that only opened if you rotated the box in a certain way, then back again—her mother would usually smile and say, "Runner's turned widdershins!" and with great theater they would reveal to their doubting daughter the empty interior.

The next time, the stone might stick up from the padded recess as solid and real and unexplained as anything else in their life.

As a child, Ginny had thought that their whole existence was some sort of magic trick, like the stone in its box.

When the pawnbroker, with her help, had opened the box, the stone was actually visible—her first real luck in weeks. The pawnbroker pulled out the stone and tried to look at it from all directions. The stone—as always—refused to rotate, no matter how hard he twisted and tugged. "Strong sucker. What is it, a gyroscope?" he asked. "Kind of ugly—but clever."

He had written her a ticket and paid her ten dollars.

This was what she carried: a map on a piece of paper, a bus route, and ten dollars she was afraid to spend, because then she might never retrieve her sum-runner, all she had to remember her family by. A special family that had chased fortune in a special way, yet never stayed long in one place—never more than a few months, as if they were being pursued.

The bus pulled to the curb and the doors sighed open. The driver flicked her a sad glance as she stepped down to the curb.

The door closed and the bus hummed on.

In a few minutes the driver would forget the slender, brown-haired girl—the skittish, frightened girl, always looking over her shoulder.

Ginny stood on the curb under the lowering dusk. Airplanes far to the south scraped golden contrails on the deep blue sky. She listened to the city. Buildings breathed, streets grumbled. Traffic noise buzzed from east and west, filtered and muted between the long industrial warehouses. Somewhere, a car alarm went off and was silenced with a disappointed chirp.

Down the block, a single Thai restaurant spilled a warm glow from its windows and open door.

She took a hungry half breath and looked up and down the wide street, deserted except for the bus's dwindling taillights. Shouldering her pack, she crossed and paused in a puddle of sour orange glow cast by a streetlight. Stared up at the green slab wall of the warehouse. She could hide here. Nobody would find her. Nobody would know anything about her.

It felt right.

She knew how to erase trails and blank memories. If the old man turned out to be a greasy pervert—she could handle that. She had dealt with worse—much worse.

On the north end of the warehouse, an enclosure of chain-link fence surrounded a concrete ramp and a small, empty parking lot. At the low end of the ramp, a locked gate barred access from the sidewalk. Ginny looked for security cameras, but none were visible. An old ivory-colored plastic button mounted in green brass was the only way to attract attention. She double-checked the address on the map. Looked up at the high corner of the warehouse. Squeezed her finger through the chain link.

Pushed the button.

A few moments later, as she was about to leave, the gate buzzed open. No voice, no welcome.

Her shoulders slumped in relief—so tired.

But after all she had been through, no hope could go unchallenged. Quickly, she probed with all her strength and talent for a better way through the confused tangles of outcome and effect. None appeared. This was the only good path. Every other led her back to the spinning, blue-white storm in the woods.

For months now she had felt her remaining options pinch down. She had never pictured this warehouse, never known she would end up in Seattle, never clearly foreseen the free clinic and the helpful doctor.

Ginny pulled the gate open and walked up the ramp. The gate swung back with a rasping squeak and locked behind her.

Today was her eighteenth birthday.

CHAPTER 2

Jack Rohmer's body was thirsty. Jack Rohmer's body was tired.

Up one street and down another, the bicycle carried the slender, dark-haired young man with hardly any guidance. An occasional push on the handlebars, an uncaring flex of the shoulders, tongue poked through slack lips, brown eyes staring ahead—all that and the steady, monotonous pedaling told both the world and the bike that Jack Rohmer had gone blank.

Slung over the back fender, a saddlebag full of hammers rattled in the dips.

By itself, even a young body is interested not in adventure or novelty, but in continuity. It prefers not to make important decisions. A casual turn, leaning into a curve, the slightly startled avoidance of cars and other obstacles—these form the sum of the body's abilities, given the absence of its owner. It is the wakeful brain that is restless.

In an hour, Jack's body had traveled miles from his intended destination. Had there been hills, no doubt by now the body would have slowed and taken a breather. But along the level streets in this harbor district of warehouses and factories, rolling over rough asphalt and brick paving, it was more trouble to stop than to go on.

The bike swerved around a rut.

A truck came out of nowhere and bellowed. Jack's right eye twitched. The driver waved a ham-sized fist out the window. Jack rode on, oblivious. The truck roared through the intersection, missing him by inches.

Streetlights buzzed pinkish-yellow beneath gathering clouds. Jack's feet pumped arched cycloids at a reduced rate through the shadows.

Three miles per hour. Then two. One. The bicycle became unstable. The body dropped a leg. The leg landed early and he hopped and snagged the toe of his shoe, bending it back.

"Ow!"

The body had had enough.

Jack returned—above the neck. Panic crossed his face. He slid off the slim leather seat and jammed his groin down on the bar. That re-united body and soul in a painful instant. He tumbled and lurched up on both legs before the bicycle collapsed.

One foot plunged through the spokes of the front wheel.

"Ow! Damn!"

His voice echoed from corrugated doors and high, flat gray walls. Stunned, he caught his breath and looked around—he was alone, no-body had witnessed his predicament. Gingerly, he rubbed his aching crotch, then gave his watch a confused glance. He had been absent for an hour and five minutes. He remembered almost nothing.

There had been a high window and darkness; the most extraordinary darkness, filled with a blinding, knife-edged gray light and *something* watching.

Over the roof of a warehouse he saw tall stacks of empty blue, brown, and white steel containers marked with the names of shipping companies. Somehow, he had pedaled deep into Sodo—south downtown—almost in sight of the docks and their huge red-painted cranes.

Something skittered under a row of big Dumpsters.

Jack pulled his foot from the spokes and inspected the old running shoe and torn sock. The wheel was ruined but his leg was barely scratched. He lifted the bike and turned it around, ready to roll it back the way he had come.

A soft chirrup in the shadows—another scrape—and something long and low scuttled between strapped bales of cardboard boxes. Jack's eyes went wide. For a moment he thought he had seen a snake—a snake with pliers on its tail. Curious, he walked toward the piles, bent over, and lifted a soggy layer from the concrete.

A staccato tapping vibrated a wide, flat bale on his left. With a gri-mace, he jerked the bale aside and let it flop over—just in time to see something long and shiny black, with many legs, and tail pincers the size of a lobster claw, scurry into a hole in some metal siding.

Jack leaped back with a yelp.

He thought he had seen an earwig as big as his forearm.

In the next hour, as he pushed the wobbling bike beneath the high-arching free way, as the sky turned dark and drizzle soaked him to the skin, he half convinced himself that what he had seen near the docks was the shadow of a rat, not a giant bug.

He returned to the third-floor apartment, replaced the bike's wheel, stowed it in the storage locker, changed out of his wet clothes, and ate a quick supper of canned chili. Burke, his roommate, had brought up a stack of mail before going to work. Burke was a sous chef at a fancy steak house. He worked six days a week until midnight and came home smelling of steaks, wine, and brandy: the perfect roommate—seldom there, and Burke left him alone.

Jack moved stuff around the apartment to keep Burke's memory fresh—if he rearranged things, Burke did not try to rent out his room. He sorted through the stack. Nothing but bills, all in Burke's name.

With returning confidence, Jack stood in the middle of his small bedroom and practiced juggling three of his four rats, along with two hammers. The rats took this with accustomed patience, and when he returned them to their cage, they squeaked happily. He fed them. They were bright-eyed. Their whiskers twitched.

Satisfied his reflexes had not been affected, he packed the hammers back in a lower dresser drawer, blinked to adjust his eyes, and watched the drawer fill in with bowling pins, Bocce and billiard balls, bricks, and rubber chickens.

With some difficulty, he managed to push the drawer shut.

Just two weeks ago an attractive older woman, Ellen Crowe, had invited him to her house on Capitol Hill. Food—conversation—sympathy. Jack was used to the attention of older women.

He felt the stiffness of her note in his shirt pocket, pulled it out, and rubbed his finger over the silver curlicue design on fancy cream board. The card carried a second invitation to dinner, no date specified. *When you're ready*, Ellen had written. On the back, she had neatly penned the phone number of a free clinic.

Perhaps he had told her too much over the shrimp risotto. He rubbed the card again, feeling for misfortune and feeling none—not from the card, not from Ellen.

Sitting on the back porch, he tracked a receding V of identical gray and brown porches under low, rapid black clouds, sipped a cup of chamomile tea steeped from a thrice-used bag, and listened to the steady rain. Jack had come to think he was finally happy. Poor, but that didn't matter. Now a real worry clouded his cheer. He was blanking out too often. He had even mentioned it to Ellen Crowe.

And he was seeing things. Giant earwigs.

He balanced the second hammer on one finger, tossed it, and caught the flat of its handle on the tip of his thumb, where it stayed with hardly a wiggle.

Jack laid the hammer on his lap and sighed.

"Tomorrow I will visit a doctor," he announced, and pulled up a woolen blanket. When the wind wasn't blowing, he liked to sleep on the porch. For a moment he stared at the blanket's felted fibers, magnified them in his mind's eye, saw them hooked to each other every which way, packing off in all directions. Life was less like the felt and more like a bundle of cables, crammed up against other bundles with hardly any distance between. Some cables were short. Some ran on for ages. All hooked up with others in ways few could predict. But Jack could feel those hookups, those points of crossing, long before they arrived.

His eyes grew heavy. As the sky darkened, he napped right there on the porch, cradling the hammer in his lap, under the blanket. His sleep was deep and normal. He snored. For once, oblivion.

His legs slumped, but the hammer did not fall.

Jack never dropped anything.

CHAPTER 3

Wallingford

Something huge slammed the beggar into the low, wet gray brush. He rolled on his side and stared up at the flat steel panel of a big green garbage truck. The truck's diesel grumbled and belched black smoke. The driver poked his bald head out of the cab. "Hey, freeloader! Get a job!"

The blow had left the beggar with a knuckling throb in his gut. His head hurt, too. He couldn't remember his name, only that he'd been running from something painful and ugly. That much sang like a tuning fork in the middle of tangled thoughts—

He had stretched, reached out too far.

Trying to escape.

The beggar decided that the garbage truck driver wouldn't act so cocky if he had actually struck a pedestrian—even a freeloader. Nothing had hit him. He was just *here*, lying unexpectedly by the side of a road, one booted foot stretched to the curb, the other bent almost to his butt—owlishly observing a line of traffic backed up at an intersection.

His thoughts came together like a puzzle—but something rose up and tried to blow them apart again, something sharing the tight volume behind his eyes . . . another mind, scared, resentful.

The beggar expertly crushed this companion as he would an insect, and focused on important details. First, where was he? A thick branch snapped and he crunched deeper into the brush. He felt a bundle dig into his back—knapsack, coat, sweatshirt, plastic bottle. Part of him—the part he was trying to suppress—still remembered stashing them there. He felt like a half sweater, somehow mated to another half, the yarns two different colors and everything in the middle—in between—unraveling. What would he be doing in any better world, stashing clothes and water in the bushes?

His left arm came into view, the dirty green coat sleeve crusted with what looked like snot.

The garbage truck turned left and rumbled on. He knew the area—a street fed by an off-ramp from Interstate 5, near Forty-fifth. Once, he had driven it every day to get home, turning at this very corner.

But these cars looked wrong.

He got to his feet, stiff and sore. His stomach throbbed with a snaky, coiling pain—something this body was used to. That shook him. *This* body. *Chronic pain.*

Two names circled like prize fighters, until one punched the other down—sheer experience and stubbornness winning out over dismay and indignation. A whimpering inside, then—silence.

None of it felt right. Something had gone wrong.

I am Daniel.

I am Daniel Patrick Iremonk.

The snake did flip-flops. He whirled and was sick in the bushes. He refused to look at what came up.

Other cars whizzed past, their designs sleek, bubbled, chopped—slick magazine parodies of the cars he knew. Their drivers stared in disgust or did not see him at all—eyes on the upcoming turn.

This was scary—*Daniel* was frightened. The other fellow was beyond caring. Not too strong to begin with, he had quickly been beaten down into a set of mud-colored memories. It had never been this way before. Of course, Daniel had never tried to jump so far. *Look around. Maybe you haven't left the Bad Place after all.*

Daniel—Daniel Patrick Iremonk—had always escaped—jaunted, that was the word he used—long before the situation went totally sour. That was his talent. He had never before waited for things to get so awful. *Make sure it isn't still after you—the dust, slime, scrambled books, the hundreds of cryptids—all the impossible things happening at once, and everyone staring at you, like you've walked into a horrible, hushed surprise party.*

They drag you in, lock the door, start with the nasties . . . fun and games . . .
I need *to remember, I really do—but I don't* want *to.*

Daniel wiped his mouth and rotated slowly, orienting himself. Sunshine, clouds, mud from recent rain. Across the street stood a wide, blocky beige building, three stories tall—condos on top, shops on the bottom. He knew it well. Minutes ago, it had been a run-down hotel.

Cars burped and jerked to a stop again as the traffic light changed.

Usually, when he jaunted—willed himself from one strand to another—only one thing or a few subtle things were different: the circumstances that he wished to change. Daniel had never moved into a version of himself that had gone so far downhill.

The window of the nearest car rolled down and an elderly woman smiled and held out a one-dollar bill. A whiff of gardenia and stale cigarettes curled out with the warm air. He blinked but did not move.

The elderly woman scowled and pulled in her arm.

The light turned green.

The beggar shoved his hands into his pockets, allowing this body to show him where the important things were—the motions its muscles made every day. Filthy fingers clenched a wad of cash. He withdrew a plastic bag containing a tight roll of ones, a five, and some change.

On the opposite corner stood a woman in layers of sweaters and vests and a long skirt over faded jeans. Her fuzzy, cherry-cheeked doll's head poked up from a smudged collar. Her arms and legs resembled a bundle of sticks wrapped in felt. She clutched a sign asking for money, but ignored the one driver who had stopped and waved a dollar bill out the window. The driver honked. She seemed to wake up, snatched his money, and the car veered right to merge with the traffic on the freeway.

Cheap bastards. Dollar bills. You eat nothing but burgers and hot dogs and feel your gut rot.

Daniel wasn't wearing glasses, but even across the intersection, he had clearly made out the denomination. He felt the bridge of his nose, cringing at the touch of his grimy fingers. No creases—no mark where glasses had ever perched. This body, whatever its problems, boasted decent eyesight. In every strand Daniel had visited, he—and all the other Daniels—had been plagued with miserable eyes—but good health. Fingernails—on these hands, worn and encrusted, but not bitten to the quick. All Daniels bit their nails.

Except for the money in the bag, his pockets were empty. No wallet. No ID.

The dirty woman turned to stare at him. But she was not scary—not part of the awful, silent party.

He felt an urgent need to get to a bathroom, but where? No Porta-Potties in sight. He thought he knew where he lived—a dozen blocks or so west, in Wallingford—but doubted he would make it, given the snake twitch in his bowels. Still, he had to try. The last thing he wanted was to fill his pants during his first hour in a strange new world.

He reached back, grabbed the knapsack, coat, and bottle, and took off at a run, having *jaunted* just far enough that the WALK sign flashed without the push of a button.

Several cars braked, almost hitting him—but none did.

One thing's the same. I still have the knack. Better living through physics.

He broke into a jerky, knee-slamming run.

CHAPTER 4

Seattle

The clouds filled in and rain grayed the pavement. He liked this city. It reminded Max Glaucous of London, where he had been born and where as a boy he helped catch and sell songbirds—plentiful bullfinches, hardy goldfinches, delicate linnets sweeter than canaries.

Glaucous still likened himself to a bird-catcher—a plump, finicky bird-catcher. He had spent most of his life moving in the night across England and the United States from city to flyspeck town to city again, casting his net and waiting with infinite patience for the rarest, the most correct sort of feathery morsel; unwilling to snare and deliver to his employers just any bird, for that would be unworthy of his craft—and could also bring a fatal conclusion to his long and benighted existence.

His employers sometimes stationed two or more collectors in the same region, the same city. Place and privilege did not matter to them. And then it behooved him to find and eliminate the competition, usually not a difficult task; so many had been recruited lately, and rarely did Glaucous encounter anyone with his experience.

And so here he was, answering an ad in a newspaper—not *his* ad— striding up Fifth Avenue as if he had any business going out by day: a short, broad, hard-packed man of indeterminate years. He wore a salesman's gray suit over a plain white shirt. A black tie cinched his thick neck like a noose. Sweat beaded on his pale, pocked face. He paused in the shade of a long theater overhang and removed a kerchief from his pocket. His hands were thick and strong and he curled his fingers to hide scarred knuckles. The air was cool but the day's low deck of clouds had opened a fissure, and he did not like the sun. Its warmth and glow on the wet street reminded him of things lost—among them, his capacity to have regrets. The brightness shone into his small black eyes and illuminated spaces in his head like gaps in a shelf of old books.

Nostrils flared in his broken, pudgy nose. Eyes half closed, handkerchief back in its pocket, hands resting on a slender black hook-cane, Glaucous saw as on a magic lantern scrim the old donkey cart stacked high with nets and wicker cages and hung with baskets of heavy iron stars, to weight the nets; the call-bird linnet, muzzy in its small wire coop on the board beside the old crookback catcher; spring's early morning dark draped over the streets like a towel over a cage. Young Max's teacher and only family grimaced and plotted which fields to visit and how far to roam. That time of year they usually traveled to Hounslow for bullfinches.

He had listened to his crippled master's soft words while tying the ropes, stumbling about half asleep on the broken cobbles. He rode the bouncing tail of the cart, staring pig-eyed at violet dawn.

Later in the day, on the journey back to London and the waiting shops, Max plucked gray and brown feathers from the nets and balanced the flap-riot baskets, their hundreds of cheeping new captives slowly but steadily falling quiet, bunching like chicks and squeezing shut their frightened eyes. Many of the birds succumbed to shock before ever they were cooed by sentimental housewives. It was his job to pull the dead and dying and toss them to the hedgerows or the gutters. Sometimes, in town, sleek brown rats humped and danced between the cart's wheels, and feasted.

In a stuffy basement room, the crookback trained Max to pipe bullfinches, using shrouds and starvation to subdue the new birds, then exposing them to call whistles that sugared the dismal air, with brief shafts of sun and food as reward. In this way, he taught the little creatures by rote to trill London's most popular tunes.

The bird-catcher had died of consumption after sixty pain-filled years. Before the catcher's estranged son kicked Max out of the small angled hovel they called home, Max had freed the last of their stock—raised the wicker doors and shooed a week's glean into smoky skies. His final act of charity.

Glaucous had last visited the old crookback's favorite birding grounds after the opening of the Hounslow Barracks train station, curious but saddened to see the once familiar fields covered over with lanes, yellow brick houses, small gardens. After all these years so much had changed, yet things were much the same for him; still hunting and delivering young creatures to self-assured gents and their Lady. But this Lady—the Chalk Princess—was no mere woman.

The morning air was much the same, anyway.

Pocketing his kerchief, Glaucous sucked flame into a small pipe, flipped the match, and left the awning's shade. He walked south, away from the shining wealth of blue-green glass, red and gray stone, concrete and steel—away from the bustle of young office workers and closer to the haunts of those with empty eyes and outstretched hands. All cities the same, rain or shine—prosperity and wealth pressing down on blinding need.

Glaucous took a professional interest in some of the dwellers that stood or squatted like dusty dolls on the sidewalks—scammers, jongleurs, sharps, the gypsy draggle of every big city. He paid particular attention to the young ones. Some of these could be Chancers or Shifters, unaware of their low-grade talents—but still of interest, especially if they began to dream.

Unlike London, at a brisk walk one could actually cross downtown Seattle east to west in less than an hour, working the streets—though he preferred to sit in his apartment and wait. The bird-catcher's patient facade, so deceptively like repose.

He found the gray Mercedes in a dingy pay parking lot, its rear windows golden with smoke, the dash littered with twelve receipts, one for each day. Sharp fingernails had clawed paths through the soot near the door locks. So it was true: the Chandler and his incendiary partner were in town.

Turning east, Glaucous paused to stare at building numbers, until he found the entrance to the Gold Rush Residential Hotel. Here he stopped, tapped his cane, and let out his breath in a low, contemplative moan. Beyond the heavy glass door, pinched between an Oriental antiques shop and an abandoned secondhand store, the hotel's narrow lobby proffered a dusty, coffee-colored hospitality. Thick paint smothered undecorated walls and lay dirty and cracked over plaster moldings. Two square brown couches and an old chair waited vacant and worn around a cigarette-scarred black table. The table carried stacks of *The Stranger* and *The Seattle Weekly*, cut bundle-strings dangling.

A middle-aged clerk ambled out of his retreat behind the desk and checked out Glaucous, who nodded pleasantly, as if they had met before. "Do you have a Mr. Chandler in residence?" he asked. "I believe he's expecting me."

The clerk scowled. "Use the house phone or just go on up," he said.

London—barbed nest for all its poor fledglings—had soon pricked young Max into a burly squint, low, lashed, and ugly. After the death of the bird-catcher, the twelve-year-old, dumped on the streets once again, proved himself a fair hand at penny-toss and cards. Hunger and inexperience led to street fighting, where he acquired scarred knuckles, puffed ears, and three bends in the bridge of his nose. In a music-hall riot, one hard roll down a flight of stone steps dealt the final knock to his bulldog physique, stunting his growth at five-four. Few would tangle with such a glowering brute, and so within a few months he secured work as a bodyguard for well-heeled gents possessed by hungers that would not be sated: cards, whoring, the Fancy. The things and events he now witnessed and the deeds he was called upon to perform were more awful than any he had seen as a bird-catcher's boy. Clients, associates, and their enemies came to refer to him by a variety of epithets: dandyshield, bonesmith, batbreak, fistfolly; cane snipe, johnny-brute. In two years he learned to keep his mouth shut and skim what he could while his employers lolled senseless with drink or drug.

During Max's last stint as a batbreak, his then-master lapsed into the croaking and squeaking of a paretic. Max was instructed by a private nurse how to fit the master's ruined face with wax and tin parts, to fill fissures and replace lost bits while the syphilitic grotesque whistled his stinking breath through vacant nose holes.

Soon Glaucous found himself once more at liberty, the master's house boarded, the last drib of wealth wasted on quack nostrums. Nothing left, nothing gained. And yet . . .

Glaucous was becoming aware that he might possess an unusual talent. He hardly believed in it; rarely used it. Yet within a week of being ousted, on the streets again, freshly charged by hunger, he had no other option. He honed his gift, and in the close-knit world of the Fancy, quickly acquired a reputation—a dangerous one. At the heel of one of the "ton," an ability such as his was tolerated, but on his own, Glaucous was of no use to anyone but himself, and so, no use whatsoever.

A gentleman of noble blood, his ancestry within hailing distance of Westminster, caught Glaucous "cheating" at cards. The gentleman's toughs corralled the remorseful, ugly young man. The gentleman ordered him transported to his country estate, caged like a dog.

There, Glaucous was confined to a series of basement rooms, heavily padlocked, each larger and a little brighter than the last. The housekeeper eventually assigned him to a plump, foppish man named Shank, either to punish for the gentleman's amusement or to discover and refine whatever genuine talent this rough lad might have. And so it was done.

In time, Shank informed the young tough that there was a name for his crude ability. Glaucous was a natural-born Chancer. "Else a pug like you would been crushed in the streets and died ere now," he explained. "Some call it luck, others fortune. We know it here as Chancing, which is great *Will*, consistently applied to random circumstance to guide favor—for your gentleman and for him alone, of course."

Under Shank's guidance, Glaucous made coins land as desired, reordered cards without touch, directed the plunk of a silver ball on a spinning roulette wheel and the tumble of wooden spheres in a rolling cage. Their handsome and noble master was not himself a gambler, but recognized that many of that persuasion would extend favor and even cash for the company of such a lad in the clubs of the day.

And so Maxwell Glaucous's lot improved, while the company he kept declined in character, if not dress and station.

————

Glaucous picked up a copy of *The Stranger* and lucked it open to the classifieds. There it was . . . the ad, but not *his* ad. He dropped the paper on the table and took the hotel stairs with silent footsteps.

On the second floor, he sniffed and reached out his hand, searching for retrograde fluxes. Two more flights to go. On the fourth, Glaucous paused by a fire door, tested its hinges for squeaks, then pushed. Beyond lay six rooms, three on each side of the hallway, and at the end a milky window reinforced by steel wire. The light from the window quivered. Light resented Chancers, and now there were two in close proximity.

Glaucous brushed the knob of the first door on his left. Harsh music competed with the grating voices of overgrown children—*television*. Quiet as a cat, he crossed the hall and felt the opposite door. Room empty but not silent—not to his questing fingers. Someone had allowed himself to be murdered. The knots of bad luck still vibrated with a singing whine.

Glaucous slid down the hall. Behind the next door, he found what he was after: soft, steady breathing, comparative youth—the Chandler was less than a fifth his age—and strength, but profligate and poorly managed.

Again his nostrils quivered—this time at a smell like candle smoke. This had to be the Chandler's partner—a veiled woman, very dangerous. Glaucous leaned in and heard the flip of a coin—a Morgan silver dollar, judging by the muted ring as it bounced off the room's thin carpet. The Chandler was practicing. The dollar landed heads. Anyone could do such a trick, but he was not counting the coin's spins. He was drawing down the coin's lines. From different heights—including a ricochet from the ceiling and another from a wall—the dollar always landed heads.

Glaucous matched his breath to the man's. He also matched other rhythms: pump of blood, drip of lymph and bile. He made himself a shadow.

Squatted back to the wall, eyes shut.

Waited.

———

Shortly after his last visit to Hounslow, at the height of his employment as a gambler's companion—his fame beginning to spoil prospects—the noble gentleman had informed him it was time to move on. Glaucous's gambling days were over, in London at any rate, and probably across Europe.

"You should try Macao, young friend," Shank suggested, but then added, in a low voice and with eyes averted, that a special appointment might be arranged—if he desired, at long last, a secure and permanent position.

Glaucous had long since grown leery of the streets.

As if in a dream, he went where Shank directed—down a pinched and filthy road near the market in Whitechapel—and at the end of a blind alley, met an odd, twisted man, small, pale as death, and musty as a wet mop. The mop-dwarf fumbled him a card embossed with a single word or name: WHITLOW. On the other side, an appointment had been scrawled in pencil—and the warning:

This time, forever. Our Livid Mistress expects her due.

Glaucous had heard incomplete and confused reports of this personality in his travels. Reputedly the leader of a small cadre of men with exceptionally dubious reputations, she was whispered about, but seldom if ever witnessed. She had many names: our Livid Mistress, the Chalk Princess, the Queen in White. No one knew her true business, but it seemed a singular ill fortune invariably found the creatures sought by the men and women in her employ—ill fortune, and something referred to as "the Gape," to be avoided at all cost.

Now at liberty for the first time in a decade, and suffering from a perverse curiosity, Glaucous took the train and then walked to Borehamwood, and there was met by a young-looking fellow with a club foot and waxy smooth skin, narrow nose, wispy ghost-blond hair, and deep blue eyes. He wore a tight black suit and gave his name, last name only.

This was Whitlow.

Whitlow carried a silver-tipped black lacquered cane and a small gray box with a curious design on the lid. "This is not for you," he told Glaucous. "I have a meeting with another later this day. Let's move on."

Out of Glaucous's memories of that meeting—a palette reduced to dim grays and browns—he recalled unsteady nerves and embarrassment at his ill-fitting wool suit. (Shank had insisted he return all his master's fine clothes. "What monkey owns his livery, I ask you?")

Whitlow shared a tot of brandy from a silver flask, then escorted him up the hedgerow drive to the main house, a mouse's holiday of neglect, one wing caved, rooms filled with roosting pigeons. Whitlow gained entry using a huge old key, then, with quiet humor, pushed Glaucous down a hall littered with broken furniture and the bones of mice and cats, arranged in rings and whorls, toward a special sort of room where, Whitlow said, none had lived or visited for several hundred years. Such rooms—difficult to find these days—best suited the closest servants of their Lady, who—he explained in a whisper, opening an inner door— ultimately paid their bills.

Whitlow locked the door behind Glaucous.

After a time of stuffy silence—long enough to feel pangs of hunger—Glaucous was joined, through no door he could detect, by an insubstantial being—a gentleman, judging by his soft voice and odor or lack of same. This nebulous figure, wrapped in a deeper cloak of shadows, never assumed definite form or size. Judging by the tapping of his hands around Glaucous's face and shoulders—fingers like batting flies—the gentleman might have been blind. "I never go anywhere," he whispered. "I am here always. *Here* moves where I need to be. I am called the Moth. I transport and recruit for our Mistress."

He spoke for what seemed a long time, his voice suggestive, modulated, indistinct. He spoke of books and words and permutations, and of a great war—greater than any dreary combat between imagined heavens and hells. "*Our* hells are real enough," he said. "And our Mistress controls them all." This Lady, he said, sought *Shifters* and *dreamers*. Chancers, properly instructed, were ideal hunters and collectors. The

Moth handed him a crust of bread, dusty with mold, then tapped Glaucous's temple with a flitting finger. "If you serve well, you will never lack work," came his muffled words. Apparently, having come this far, no refusal was permitted. "We pay in more than coin. Time no object. Different birds, different cages, Mr. Glaucous. Listen close, and I will pipe you all the songs you need ever sing."

After some hours, the door opened, spearing the room with a broken shaft of sun. Glaucous blinked like a mole. Whitlow reappeared to usher him out. Behind, the room keened a wretched, pain-filled sound like none he had ever heard, and reclaimed its emptiness: spent.

Back on the hedgerow drive, dazed and exhausted, Glaucous asked, "Will I meet ever the Mistress?"

"Don't be a fool," Whitlow admonished. "We never hope for that. The Moth is bad enough, and he's less than the tip of her pinky."

———

For the next hundred twenty years Glaucous traveled from city to city across the United Kingdom, and then the United States . . . working as a diversion in carnival pitches, card parlors, side shows . . . always seeking, keeping a low profile, and wherever he went, posting ads in newspapers, ads that never varied except for an address, or later, a phone number— .

Always asking the same question:

Do you dream of a City at the end of Time?

———

Glaucous kept deathly still. He could feel any vibration along the boards and beams. All was quiet. There would be no visitors for the next few minutes.

The collector behind the door—endlessly tossing his silver dollar—had failed in certain courtesies. He had not alerted Glaucous to his presence, nor had he shared information. He was poaching.

Glaucous rapped a callused knuckle on the door, then fluted his voice, young and uneasy, the same voice he had used on the phone to answer the Chandler's ad. "Hello? It's Howard. Howard Grass."

The slender man who opened the door held up his silver dollar between thumb and middle finger. His pupils were large, black, and steady. He presented a cold, surprised smile—and then a superior grin. "Mr. Glaucous. How nice to see you."

Glaucous knew the signs of a Chancer about to strike. There was no time to lose.

In the slender man's fingers, the head of the crowned silver woman on the Morgan faced north. Glaucous rolled up one eye, drew down a contrary strand, bent it sideways—and the head faced south.

The Chandler's heart also flipped, instantly filling his chest with blood. His fingers twitched and he released the coin. Falling, the stamped ounce of gray metal landed flat on the carpet—eagle side up. His face turned sickly green. Silent, he toppled facedown, stiff as a plank, and covered the coin.

Also tails.

In the bathroom, the veiled woman began to shriek. Without the Chandler, her talent and passion flowered unchecked. Fire shot from around and under the bathroom door. Glaucous lent his assistance.

She achieved her heart's desire.

———

That afternoon, wrapped in melancholy, Glaucous sat in his warm apartment, shades drawn, the only light in the cramped living room focused on a phone sitting on a table next to his chair. Behind the closed door to the bedroom, his own partner, Penelope, sang in a low, childlike voice. Around her song flowed a steady buzz, like an electric bulb about to go dark.

Glaucous's eyes turned sleepy. An hour before, he had eaten a spare lunch—an apple and a piece of wheat bread with three thin slices of salami. In those first days in London, it would have been a feast.

He stared at the phone in its oblong of golden light. Something was stirring. He could feel a strong tug on the triggering thread that announced prey. Always before, his employers had informed him of a new rule, changes in the game. This awareness was arriving without warning. Perhaps there had not been time.

Had he made a mistake, eliminating the Chandler?

Reaching out, he could feel as many as three small birds in his vicinity—almost certainly three—though one seemed odd, not what he might have expected. Of the other two, from long experience, he was sure he knew their habits, their concerns and fears, their needs.

A darker air was arriving. Max Glaucous could feel it in his light, lucky fingers. Long dreaded, long awaited—destruction, followed by freedom—an extraordinary conclusion to his troubles.

Three sum-runners.

Whitlow will join us. And the Moth. They cannot do this without me. Finally—my reward.

And my release.

CHAPTER 5

Wallingford

Trying to contain his churning, liquid misery, Daniel walked spastic. The sidewalk, old and gray and cracked, presented a rolling course of uneven obstacles. He leaned to the right on Sunnyside Avenue, grimly determined to make it home. He was ashamed. Daniel had always been the driver of his own soul, in control on the highways and byways of the fibrous multiverse. Now—he could barely keep from fouling his pants.

The neighborhood had not changed so much that he could spot the differences. In truth, he had never closely observed the houses more than a few doors away from his own. In his present hurry, there was no time to put together a catalog of obvious changes.

The sun slanted. This sick new body wore no watch and carried no keys; despite Daniel's patting and thrusting, he could not find a key in all those pockets nor in the knapsack—but both he and his new body agreed, as they approached the concrete steps, the peaked porch roof and square tapered pillars, *this* was where they lived, *this* was where they hung whatever shingle they owned.

His house. The same house. That much was the same, thank the powers that be.

Whatever powers care to take credit for any of my madness. And what about the sum-runners?

The lawn stood high and brown and overgrown with weeds. He climbed the steps from the street and jerked himself around the side yard to the rear, glancing back—apparently not used to entering the house by daylight—a furtive peer, then a scarecrow scramble through waist-high jungle to the back. The old rosebushes that had once belonged to his aunt were no longer in evidence, and—he noticed this as he made a horseshoe around the rear porch, trying to decide where he might have hidden a key—*there is no key*—

The windows had been papered.

The body remembered, so he went down on his knees—oh, how that made the snake twitch!—and pushed at a basement window, then skinnied himself through, stood on a box, and clambered to carpeted concrete floor—splish-splash, carpet soaked, the whole basement stinking of mold and mildew. The power was turned off. In the dark, he shambled up the basement steps, struck his shoulder against a first-floor wall, and fumbled his way by touch into the bathroom.

He pushed down his pants and found the toilet. The pain made him scream. He almost passed out.

Daniel slumped against the wall, his elbow cushioned by the toilet paper in its wooden holder.

————

Half an hour later he leaned forward and his hand found a candle stub on the bathroom sink. A match, a matchbox. He struck the match and lit the candle, then stripped down and took a cold shower—letting the body do what it knew how to do.

One foot out of the shower-tub, he fumbled for a filthy towel. Looked at himself in the medicine cabinet mirror. Eyes sunken and dull. Gaunt, straggling hair, skin sallow beneath a tangled, matted beard.

Years of getting most of his calories from alcohol.

He heard a new, rough voice come out of that ruin of a mouth, between those rotten teeth—

"Oh—my . . . *God*."

This was not Daniel Patrick Iremonk—not any sort of Daniel. This time, he had shoved himself into a body not even remotely his own. He had jaunted into an entirely new game—revealing a new and staggering aspect of his peculiar talent.

He was in another man, living another man's life.

FOURTEEN ZEROS

CHAPTER 6

The Kalpa

Seventy-five years had passed since Ghentun had met the angelin in the Broken Tower—less than a blink for a great Eidolon, but a lengthy span for a mere Mender.

The Keeper walked unseen over the bridges connecting the three isles, the foundation plateaus that rose above the flood channels and supported the stacked Tiers; up the lifts and stair cores of the fifty-floor blocs of niches, as he did almost every wake, studying his charges, the ancient breeds, as they worked, moved about, talked, worried— escorted their wide-eyed children, fresh from the crèche—prepared foods purchased in busy markets, harvested from meadows and fields beyond the two broad flood channels, known as Tartaros and Tenebros.

In all the Kalpa, only the Tiers still had seasons worth observing— births and deaths, children delivered from the crèches on high, aging breeds relieved of their burdens by the Bleak Warden, their primordial mass recycled into new children, and a few—wanderers all, instinctively tuned—selected by the Keeper to be trained, equipped, and sent out into the Chaos to become marchers. A rhythm of interest now only to him, it seemed—but also, he hoped, to the Librarian who had planned it all ages before. Great Eidolons could so easily forget . . .

The chronological weather had calmed of late, and time was ticking along with such cheer—allowing actual days of sequence, when memory functioned almost as designed—that some in the Kalpa felt the old ways and rules might be returning. That was unlikely. The great reality generators were faltering, usually by tiny increments, but sometimes by leaps and bounds. Terrifying intrusions—streaks and smears of the Typhon's nightmare void, breaking through to the Kalpa—were more frequent. Dozens of Ghentun's breeds—most vulnerable, living as they did at the city's foundation levels—had been destroyed or gone missing.

Something in the Chaos seemed to be hunting.

In the dark before wakelight, within a loud shout of the Tenebros bridge, teams of referees were sleepily clearing and roping off a fallow meadow, preparing for the games the breeds called little wars. Invisible—though not without some effect on the breeds around him—Ghentun made his way through the gathering crowds. He found a good vantage on a hillock, drew up his legs, and sat. Soon enough he would be on the move again.

Another game was in play—grander and much more dangerous, not just to the breeds, but to Ghentun himself—but at the end, they might find the key to defeating the Typhon. In the meantime, the citizens of the Tiers did their best to live as they always had—bravely, foolishly, wisely. They were hardy folk. Whatever the circumstance, they found their amusements.

———

The skirmish on the meadow was going splendidly, most agreed. The traditional engagement had begun while mist still draped the mounds and grasses. Five hundred breeds—divided equally into four tribes—began their contest at the sound of the judges' horns, great jagged blats that echoed from the high, bright ceil.

Jebrassy—strong and dashing in armor he had made from purple keel-husks—sallied out with eight pickets in like garb to assess the chances of breaking through on their opponents' left flank, and there was a lovely, knock-all fray in dense fog as they met other pickets.

All along, as he fought—giving many more blows than he received—Jebrassy had the uncomfortable sensation he was being watched. From the corner of his eye, wisps, puffs, interruptions in the fog that hollowed and twisted and vanished—distracted him. He did not fight as well as he wished, and perhaps that was fortunate, considering the damage he was already doing.

Jebrassy and his fellows—Khren and the others—took to their combat with spirit, swinging their stravies with such conviction that few challenged them, and many lodged protests with the judges who glumly wandered in to intercede.

The older warriors squatted with narrow, discouraged eyes. The good days were gone, they said, shaking their heads. Some felt the contests were not violent enough—others, that mercy and honor had been forgotten. They seldom agreed about much.

Through morning and into evening, the war resumed, mounted with shouting and cursing and singing of martial airs, bluster, batting, torn hair, and flying spittle, until the ceil dimmed to brown and welcome tweenlight fell over the breathless, bruised combatants.

The seniors loved to watch fights, as long as not too many were hurt—and Jebrassy's crew was pushing that tolerance to the edge. Many groaned and limped away—and many more grumbled on the field and off.

Jebrassy, by his own estimation, retired from the din in full glory, head bandaged, arm wrenched. In camp, he was dosed by a stolid medical warden, a drum-shaped machine with stubby lift-wings, now folded. Though almost faceless—just three off-center glowing blue eyes in an oval head—the wardens always seemed saddened by such goings-on, but performed their duties without chide or complaint.

Sometimes, it was said, in the broad dark ports high in the walls or in the ceil, overlooking the meadows and fields, the Tall Ones, masters of the Tiers—in the naive conception of the breeds—watched these lovely little engagements and made judgments that would be taken into account when the Bleak Warden came to snip your final hours and fly you to the crèche. Some even claimed—though Jebrassy highly doubted it—that the Tall Ones walked among their favorite fighters, and if they were not doing well, clouded them in mist and flew them away . . .

But he had fought to his satisfaction, thumping and being thumped, and so be it; he was willing to be profane and think in other directions. That somehow made things better. As the warden finished its patient ministrations, Jebrassy looked up past the gleaming, off-center eyes, squinted at the mellow browns and greenish-golds of the tweenlight ceil, and wondered what the Tall Ones really thought of such idiocy. He had never known anything but the Tiers, of course, and that irritated him. His spirit felt crushed beneath that vast, rounded roof. He was an adventurous fellow, filled with ambition to exceed the sight lines shared by those around him—short, flat lines, mostly, though long enough in the fields to suggest the mysterious Wide Places some whispered about, where one could see forever.

Standing beside a makeshift stand displaying sweet chafe and tork— intoxicating juice fermented in heavy jugs—an elderly male breed waited while the warden applied a last twist of bandage. Jebrassy stiffened. The warden apologized in flat, sympathetic tones, but the ointments and glues were not what caused him pain.

A time of parting had arrived. The elderly male, Chaeto, was his second per—his male sponsor. A stocky fellow with the full spiky beard of a breed soon to make the acquaintance of the Bleak Warden, Chaeto and his partner Neb had taken Jebrassy in after his first sponsors vanished. They treated him well, yet Jebrassy had brought them little but grief.

Chaeto approached and stood by him, eyes gray with inner turmoil. They acknowledged each other with finger-taps to their necks, Jebrassy first, as required. Jebrassy then stroked the old male's extended palm.

The gesture brought little solace.

"You did well out there," Chaeto said. "As always. You're a fighter, that's sure." He cleared his throat, then looked aside. "Not many more seasons we'll have to raise young breeds. Mer and I think you'll benefit no more from our instructions. Already you pay no heed to our pleas."

Jebrassy stroked his per's palm again, apologetic supplication. They had affection, but neither could sidestep what the old breed was about to say. "You're determined to stick with your toughs, aren't you?"

"My friends," Jebrassy murmured.

"You still talk of wandering off to die away from the Tiers, without benefit of the Bleak Warden?"

"No change, Per."

Chaeto looked up at the last glimmer on the ceil. "We're taking in a new one. Can't have you spread ... your plans ... to a fresh umber-born. Can't have that in your mer's niche. We've done our best. It's the winding road you've chosen. You'll go on now without us." Chaeto withdrew his palm, leaving Jebrassy's finger suspended. "I moved out your stuff. Mer's broken up, but new young will mend her."

The elder touched Jebrassy's neck one last time, then turned and walked off with the limp he had acquired over the last few years. The wardens, having paused as if to listen, went about their repairs to the rest of the injured. The other breeds turned away—little or no sympathy for Jebrassy's plight. He had delivered too many thumps and jabs.

Chaeto had likely told the high toller of their home level. The high toller would ban him from the neighborhood—even though there were vacant niches.

He was on his own. He would never see either of his sponsors again, except by accident—perhaps in a market—and even then, they wouldn't acknowledge him. He was what he thought he had always aspired to be—a free breed. And it hurt far worse than any of his slight wounds.

Jebrassy got to his feet and looked around for someone, anyone, with a generous jug.

———

After the field had been cleared—seven injured, none seriously, a disappointment for the more bruise-happy breeds—the walls of the nauvarchia grew high in the Tenebros, between the inner meadows and the first isle, and water gushed into the sinuous shallows. Brightly decorated boats were hoisted and rowed out, and a different set of breeds fought a rough-foot, sink-all sea battle. Those who had fought earlier—and could still walk—gathered along the wall and ate, drank, cheered, and complained, until hardly any had the strength to move. The wakelight dimmed to gray dark. The walls fell and the waters drained. The battered boats were lifted and rolled away, and the spectators who had drunk too deep and could not move were tented by their friends. The rest limped and strolled back over the meadows and fields—waved off by crop-tenders if the fields contained produce. A robust few danced and sang with their last energy across the bridges to their blocs on the three isles, happily convinced that the little wars were fine things, perfect for keeping the ancient breed amused and healthy.

———

Jebrassy pushed himself from the littered wall, winced at the tug of his bandages, steadied himself—he had consumed a fair volume of tork—

and realized only then that he was being watched—and by someone he could actually see.

He turned with what he hoped was dignified grace to meet the sharp, half-critical gaze of a glow—a pretty young female. She wore an open vest and flowing pants whose colors revealed that she resided in the middle bloc of the second isle—as had Jebrassy, until now.

The glow approached. Her hair was short and lustrous in the fading light, her eyes fixed and penetrating, so full of intent that he wondered if her mer and per would emerge from the milling crowds and retrieve her, or request an immediate testimonial from the sponsors he no longer had.

That would be awkward.

Jebrassy met her gaze with puzzled dignity until she came within a few inches, sniffed him, and smiled. "You're Jebrassy . . . aren't you?"

"We haven't met," he said, mustering all the wit he had left.

"They say you like to fight. Fighting is a waste of time."

He half stumbled over an empty jug. "Is there anything else worth doing?" he asked, steadying himself.

"We have three things in common. The first is, when we dream, we stray."

She could not have shocked him more—or come closer to wounding him. Jebrassy had told only Khren, his closest friend, about the straying. His frown turned to dismay, then genuine distress and embarrassment, and he looked over his shoulder, blinking at the crowds as they walked in chattering clusters up the ramps and off the field.

"I'm drunk," he muttered. "We shouldn't even be talking." He started to walk off, but she looped her arm under his and tugged him to a stop.

"You didn't let me finish. I want to leave the Kalpa. So do you."

He regarded her with inebriated wonder. "Who told you all this?"

"Does it matter?"

He smiled. He practically leered. This might turn out to be a mischief after all—two reckless youths, left to their own devices. The glow's expression did not change, except for a disgusted flip of her lashes.

Taken aback, he asked, "What's the third thing?"

"If you want to know," she answered, eyes glinting in the last of the tweenlight, "meet me by the Diurns just before next sleep. My name is Tiadba."

Then she turned and ran toward the ramps and the bridge—faster than he could follow, drunk as he was.

CHAPTER 7

As light ebbed and shadows gloamed, Ghentun arranged his notes—he kept them in a pouch beside a small green book—and strolled through the lower floors of the first isle bloc.

Moving still unseen from niche to niche, he wrote in Puretext with a flower finger he willed to be tipped in soft silver, feeling affection and sadness as he monitored the most recent generation of ancient breeds to be delivered.

Ghentun's mind wandered. Before becoming a keeper, he had been a student of city history—and like all historians in the Kalpa, that meant he knew very little about a great deal. What he knew—but had never seen—began with a blanket of smooth utter blackness, sprayed with trillions of stars: the Brightness. Something less than a memory now, and little more than a dream.

Across its first hundred billion years, the cosmos expanded until its fabric stretched thin, opening voids wherein dimension had new or no meaning. Galaxies became distorted, burned out, wrinkled away.

Space itself was aging, decaying—some thought dying.

For longer by far than the Diaspora that had flung humans to the fringes of the universe, they survived in the last tight islands of artificial suns, surrounded by a great and growing emptiness. This became the status quo. The early universe was seen as feverish and squalid, abnormal.

The Age of Darkness became wreathed in the dignified mantle of a sedate if dwindling maturity—watched over by a gerontocracy of immortals, all convinced of their unsurpassable wisdom.

For a few, however, these scattered islands in the abyssal dark were not enough. A minority—not sane, yet certainly not suffering from a deathly complacency—expressed a willingness to journey on, to leave behind the warmth and light of the remaining stars. They were denied, or worse—overwhelmed, quashed, all but exterminated. A handful managed to escape, to sacrifice all they knew, and to make the adaptations necessary to survive in the cosmos's last frontiers: the crumbling wastes, dejects, and desponds frayed out over a radius of three hundred billion light-years.

Out there, in the Far Dark, to the amazement of the gerontocracy, new technologies proliferated. Bold explorers discovered how to take advantage of the once deadly seams and rifts, squeezing huge stores of energy and sustenance from what most had thought a barren, decrepit desert.

Those last few pioneers did more than survive. Ever resourceful, they learned to live and prosper and multiply as never before. Empowered, they eliminated or absorbed their oppressors.

They built countless empires.

The Age of Darkness was followed by the Trillenium—the greatest period of growth and learning in human record. Zeros stacked upon zeros. Histories were made and lost like the guttering of an infinity of candles. All strangeness was joined, and all life, human and otherwise, was accepted and improved upon, redefining the very idea of humanity and leading to triumph upon triumph, rebirth after rebirth.

No matter that the universe was growing ever weaker and thinner. In its prolonged throes, it fed its young handsomely—until humanity's farthest flung descendants encountered the first evidence of the Typhon.

It took a billion years to gather conclusive proof of the Typhon's existence—a rapid few millions of years for it to be analyzed and vaguely understood. By the example of its very perversity, it generated a wealth of new mathematics and science—and new ways of going mad.

Nothing like the Typhon had ever been observed. Neither a place nor a thing, the Typhon spread by scavenging aging universes. Some labeled it a pathology, an infection, a parasite—a violently aggressive membrane of change. Others claimed it was a younger, undisciplined creation infiltrating the ruins of the old.

Where the Typhon grew, worse than silence reigned. The knots of this universe were undone: geodesics failed, sightlines achieved fractal terminations, information swallowed by so many varieties of singularity—collapse, estoppage, endvols, countercepts, twistfolds, enigmachrons, fermion dismays—

And it grew faster than signals could convey, tearing through the aged matrix, eating up the rotting fabric, creating regions not of darkness—those at least were familiar—but of inconsistent, lawless misrule.

It was said that anything could happen there. Perhaps more accurately, it was widely reported that *everything* happened there.

This, even the hardiest and most stubborn of all Earth's children—the last wave of the Diaspora—could not tolerate. This, they could not fight. Most succumbed.

The mind-numbing vastness of their reduction defied historical measure. Survivors who still cherished their terrestrial origins finally retreated to the ancient home system, where humanity—its offspring, hybrids, and manifold allies—now cowered in the fastness of old Earth, living under the dwindling light of a rekindled sun and surrounded by the last few dying planets.

Those who had transformed themselves into new kinds of mass and energy were forced to live together, in very reduced circumstances. Difficult times followed—thousands of centuries of pointless violence: the Mass Wars.

Outside, the Typhon raged—and gained.

———

In a way, the Kalpa's last chapter had begun over a million years ago, when the City Princes of the twelve cities of Earth had commissioned Sangmer the Pilgrim to find and retrieve a former citizen called Polybiblios from the realms of the Shen—beings who claimed never to have shared ancestry with anything remotely human. Sangmer had crossed the last tracks of free cosmos to the sixty suns of the Shen, found Polybiblios living and working on the greatest of the Necklace Worlds, and carried him back between the threatened wastes, bearing knowledge he had gained from long study with the Shen.

Sangmer also brought back to Earth a most unusual being named Ishanaxade. Some said Ishanaxade was the last of her kind, rescued and protected by the Shen, left to her own progress for a few million years and then given new form by Polybiblios. All the legends of those times—and they varied widely—agreed that Polybiblios adopted Ishanaxade, calling her his daughter, and that on the return journey, or shortly thereafter, she was betrothed to Sangmer, who was richly rewarded for his perilous and timely journey.

Along Sangmer's return path, the last of the ancient worlds met their doom. The sixty suns of the Shen were consumed by the Chaos—a fate the Shen themselves seemed content to accept.

———

The City Princes took a risk, bringing Polybiblios into their circle of rule—but the cities of Earth had grown desperate, watching sun after sun swallowed and transformed. They hoped that Polybiblios, with his Shen training, might be able to keep the Chaos at bay—and upon his return, he did indeed design the suspension that for so long protected the sun and planets.

The Shen had taught him well.

All surviving humans owed Polybiblios not just their lives, but their sanity. Yet no human could know the limits of his invention. How much had he learned on the far side of that dying sky . . . ?

The suspension blocked Typhonian misrule—but only inside an oblate zone that reached just past the groaning gray ball of stone and ice that had once been Neptune. Beyond the suspension, light stopped as if glued to a page, matter dissolved like blood in water.

Earth, little more than a cold cinder, was now thought to be—had to be—sufficient. There would be no recovery of the lost light-years. So ended the dominance of living, thinking beings in the cosmos.

Some called it a final golden age—life's long arrogance finally tempered by the incomprehensible.

Scant years later, the Chaos pushed through the suspension and sucked up the sun and the other worlds, then threatened the last twelve cities of Earth. The suspension was pulled tight, severely weakened, almost destroyed. Yet even now the Mass Wars continued. The City Princes—noötic Eidolons all—forced conversion upon all but one of the cities. Those who did not agree fled a thousand miles across the cinereous desert to Nataraja.

Both history and legends were sketchy about the ensuing age. These things were accepted by most, though sequence was vague:

Nearly all but Menders and Shapers—the engineers and underclasses of the Kalpa—were made of noötic mass, far more convenient, reliable, and powerful. But Polybiblios was still primordial. To better understand and control him, the City Princes forced him to convert as well—making him a Great Eidolon like themselves, which they must have considered a tremendous honor. In return, the City Princes vowed not to interfere with his strange, Shen-inspired researches. But conversion did not make Polybiblios more tractable or sensitive to their concerns. If anything, he became more distant and reclusive, speaking only with Ishanaxade through his new Eidolon parts—angelins and epitomes.

He moved into the tower that rose a hundred miles above the first bion of the Kalpa, and continued working.

In time he became known as the Librarian.

———

The Librarian soon specified that a new class—or underclass—of citizens be made of primordial matter, a whim assumed to have implications both philosophical and personal. The City Princes now completely controlled Earth's supply of this ancient stuff—the last in the universe. They usually released their stores in small quantities to replenish the few remaining Menders and Shapers who served them, and for ritual exchanges between Eidolons. Somehow, the Librarian persuaded them to allocate to his control a much larger supply.

Without specifying their intentions, the Librarian and his daughter began to fashion their first prototypes of ancient humans. Since histories of the early Brightness had long since been lost, their designs were conjectural at best. Some scraps of ancient data suggested that early humans could not live without being surrounded by leaping and flying insects— and so, insects and arthropods were designed and incorporated as well.

Ishanaxade oversaw the opening of the lowest levels of the Kalpa's first bion and the repositioning of the foundation piers that divided the ancient flood channels, creating three islands. Upon completion of the empty blocs and the landscaping of the primitive but eerily attractive meadows—overarched by a false sky that divided time into bright and dark, wakes and sleeps—an allotment of primordial matter was moved from the holdings of the City Princes. The first of the ancient breeds began their hidden lives.

But the Librarian's plans were interrupted.

The Chaos pushed in again. Ten of Earth's last cities were consumed—transformed, played with, tortured. Their former citizens even now haunted the vast broken deserts, parodies and playthings of the Typhon—monsters beyond the imagination of even an Eidolon.

Only the Kalpa and Nataraja remained. And then communications between these two cities were severed.

The Astyanax of the Kalpa, the last City Prince, lost what little faith he still had in their erstwhile savior. Ishanaxade was exiled—or left the Kalpa to go to Nataraja—though none could say why, and none even knew whether Nataraja still survived.

From the Tower, Sangmer studied the new configuration of Earth—and crossed the freshly roiling Chaos to find his wife. He was never seen again.

A terrible conflict now broke out. Some believed the Librarian vented his wrath at the Astyanax for banishing his daughter. He reduced power to the suspension. Four of the Kalpa's seven bions were surrendered to the Typhon. In return, the Astyanax sterilized the Tiers and ended the first population of ancient breeds—those nurtured and taught by Ishanaxade.

The Tower was almost destroyed—broken in half. But the Librarian survived. And it finally became horrifyingly clear that the last humans, whatever their shape or construction, whatever their philosophy or ambitions, could no longer fight.

Under extraordinary pressure from his fellow Eidolons, the Astyanax conceded.

Joining forces with the Kalpa's finest minds, and using more than half of the city's resources, the Librarian reconstructed a much smaller, more concentrated ring of reality generators—the Defenders—and thus pushed back the Typhon one last time.

Exiled it beyond the border of the real.

Most believed Nataraja and its rebels did not survive.

After Sangmer's final pilgrimage and disappearance, the Astyanax banned all attempts to leave. The outward windows of the last three bions were sealed shut—all but in the Broken Tower, still the preserve of the greatest and most curious Eidolon of all.

Work on the Tiers resumed, with a new, redesigned population of ancient breeds set in place of the old.

A young Mender of no special distinction, Ghentun was summoned to Malregard, interviewed by angelins, and chosen to be Keeper of the Tiers—and that was that. There was no contest, no list of applicants.

Like many of the young Menders of that era, he had converted to noötic mass—fashionably giving up his gens inheritance. Yet to accept the position of keeper, the Librarian's epitomes insisted he must reconvert—he must become primordial again.

In the process, something went wrong. While retaining his knowledge of history, he lost all personal memories. The old Ghentun vanished; the new was born. Yet how could he have regrets? Mere Menders did not question the decisions of Great Eidolons.

Sometimes, when Ghentun watched his breeds sleep, they would shiver with a strange resonance, as if listening to death-cries out of the deep and broken past—sensing their compatriots, made of the same ancient matter, flesh of the same flesh, crawling along their mashed and bundled fates, until they reached the severed ends—and fell into the dimensionless maw of the Typhon.

As they had been designed to do. *Canaries in a coal mine.*

Proving—if true—that the Tiers were not the idle toy of a demented Great Eidolon, but the one last, true chance to save their tiny scrap of universe.

———

Finished with his inspection, Ghentun ascended in secured lifts through the outer thick walls to the source of all breeds, the crèche, high above the Tiers.

At the outer circle of the crèche, the Keeper made his signs of respect before the fluid, light-absorbing draperies. Beyond lay the Shaper's rotating nurseries, where hundreds of new-made breeds slept in quiet rows, awaiting their nativity—should it ever arrive. The curtains swung wide and a golden light spilled over, warming the Keeper's skin. He had always enjoyed seeing where his breeds were formed, nurtured, and subliminally instructed through infancy, then prepared for transport to the Tiers by the umbers—slender grayish-brown wardens, low and swift.

Several of these umbers met Ghentun beneath the wide sweep of the Shaper's pallid caul. Two escorted him through the caul—proceeding without escort might subject him to unpredictable fields and pressures—and higher still, between green curtains of gel and tall, eerily still cylinders of primordial ice—into the lambent mist of the vitreion, the Shaper's inner sanctum—where machines could not go.

Here, on natal pads arranged in counterrotating spheres, the golden glow intensified. Spin-foundries like frantic bushes—all silvery vector-curves and whirling branches—surrounded and refined a dozen half-formed infants, their motions so rapid Ghentun could not track them at his highest frequency.

The last Shaper in the Kalpa, the crèche's mistress of birth stood on six slender legs beside an elevated natal pad. At Ghentun's approach, her small head popped up from a radiance of dark, field-wrapped tool-arms. Shapers and Menders had long since parted ways in physical appearance. She acknowledged his presence, then finished imprinting an early layer of mental properties into a small, quivering thing covered in fine white fur, its large eyes tightly shut, though its lips moved continuously, as if it might awake at a whisper.

The Shaper put away her kit and joined Ghentun on a walk through the prototypes annex.

"I'm not sure what more can be done," she said as they slid between the history pallets, on which were suspended most of the second-stage proposals for the inhabitants of the Tiers—a sobering record of extended development, indecision, and failure. Ghentun himself had made a number of significant mistakes early in his tenure.

He transferred his notes to the Shaper, who read them with several of her many eyes.

"No instructions. No *orders*," she complained.

"Am I to make last-minute improvements—if they *are* improvements—at my own discretion? We've already given a few the capacity to reproduce—outside my control. That's dangerous enough—though it increases their sensitivity. If we make them any more sensitive, they'll tremble at a breeze—and die of stress. And if we make them any smarter, they'll die of boredom." She made a small whirring sound of irritation. "One could hardly call all those *books* amusing."

Ghentun touched the outline of the single book in his bag. "They're smart enough," he said. "The Librarian wishes to examine an exceptional specimen." He projected an image—a young male breed, bristling with aggression. "I saw this one first when they were sport-fighting along the fallow meadows. And once, I caught him staring in my direction as I walked past, almost as if he could see me."

The Shaper thrust two arms forward, grasped the image, spun it, and let it go. It flew off and faded to nothing. She had an aversion to images. "His name is Jebrassy. I tuned him a bit hot. He's a born marcher—he'll join one of your suicide groups soon enough."

"Reproduction?"

"He's one of the new maters, if some fertile female will have him—which I doubt. He rings like a bell—even on the natal pad, something came to him, took his voice, and changed him. A strong dreamer, I suspect. The breeds call it straying—blank eyes, vacant stares, troubled sleep. Puts off the others." The Shaper regarded Ghentun with a slant of her three mid-distance eyes—accusing, amused, impatient. "Do *you* stray, friend Ghentun?"

Ghentun did not dignify this absurdity with an answer. "This one seems right. I'll confer with Grayne, arrange something . . ."

"Grayne? She's still with us? Now there's a piece of work. One of my finest—just goes on and on . . ."

"She's a sama now, and march leader."

"She was so fine in her youth. Shame on us all, sending our pretty children into that wasteland. I've never been proud of my labors here, Keeper."

"No one else requires your talents, Shaper."

She acknowledged as much. "The Librarian should be pleased. These breeds vibrate to the slightest trembling of the lines. While the Eidolons ride their endless circles of amusement, trying to ignore the obvious—down here, the breeds have become exquisitely sensitive to something I can't perceive—though I do wonder. Perhaps it is the past . . . twisting, knotting, in agony. Am I right, Keeper?"

Ghentun did not answer this, either. They both knew it was likely—and the main reason for the existence of the Tiers.

"Yet wake by wake the generators fade—and the Chaos has no patience," she said. "How long until you get the Librarian's attention?"

"Soon," Ghentun said.

"There's no pleasing Eidolons. I've known that all my long life. If the Librarian's still not happy—" The Shaper reached into Ghentun's bag, swifter than he could think, and lifted out the green book with fingers so strong they threatened to crush it. "Archaic little treasure. You've stolen this from your sama," she accused.

"Her predecessor, actually."

"Enlightening?"

"It's in breed-text. It changes whenever I read it—so I assume it's not for our eyes."

"Then why bother?"

"Curiosity. Guilt." Ghentun made a short grumble—Mender embarrassment, Mender humor. "Aren't you curious what the Librarian has in store for them?"

The Shaper simply snorted. "We could start over. Improvements are still possible." She seemed unwilling to give up her work, however much its results, or its cruel necessity, scratched at her sympathies. "What do you think we have, a few thousand years?"

"I doubt it," Ghentun said. He motioned for her to return the book. Reluctantly, she did so, with finger-marks pressed into its binding. Slowly, resentfully, the book began to heal itself.

"This is our last crop," he said. "It's these breeds, or nothing."

CHAPTER 8

First Isle

"Do you think I'd tell a *glow* your secrets?" Khren asked, and from his shocked expression, Jebrassy instantly knew his friend's guilt.

They both lounged as casually as their present mood allowed in Khren's niche, surrounded by colorful and meaningless prizes from the skirmish—captured pennants, two padded but heavy stravies, marked with curling leaves on which were scratched wishes for luck and strength—and a magnificent jug of tork that Khren had won in a bet on the nauvarchia.

"What else did you blab?" Jebrassy asked. He and Khren had known each other since being delivered by the umbers, fresh out of the crèche.

"She was curious. She asked questions. I answered. She has her ways, you know that."

Jebrassy narrowed his eyes and smiled. "You fancy her?"

Khren lay back and gazed at the ceiling, irritated that this pairing might be thought unlikely. "Of course not. I've got my eye on another."

Jebrassy had yet to meet this other, or even hear her name.

"If she were anything to me," Khren said, "I would have told her a youth march is nonsense and dangerous besides. It's already got *you* disinherited."

"What could I ever inherit *here*?" Jebrassy asked.

"There's nothing wrong with *here*," Khren said. "We made out pretty well in the skirmish. Why fight if there's nothing to fight *for*? And it looks like you attracted the attentions of a fine glow—by showing off your muscles and dealing a few good thwacks. All very intellectual and rebellious, I'm sure."

"We have no protection against anything the Tall Ones want to do to us. We're toys, nothing more"

"I prefer to think of us as *experiments*," Khren said, and then shrugged, having brushed up against the zenith of his philosophical abilities.

"What's the difference?"

"Ancient breed, ancient quality. If we're experiments, we'll exceed all the others, and they'll reward us for our courage by liberating the Tiers. Then, we can go anywhere we like—even the Chaos, if that's worth a visit. And nobody knows if it is."

"It is," Jebrassy said. "I'm sure of it. I've got my sources . . ."

Khren lifted his small ears, showing mild amusement. "So learned."

"Well, I do." Jebrassy had worked his way around to the second point of contention. "Why did you have to tell her about my straying?"

"I didn't volunteer. She asked—as if she knew already. She's very persuasive." His voice fell off and he gave Jebrassy as lewd and suggestive a glance as his broad, chiseled face allowed.

"Unlike me, she still has sponsors," Jebrassy said. "I doubt she'll talk with either of us again."

"Ah." Khren got up and poured himself another tumbler, then flumped back into the cushions—without spilling a drop—and examined the color of his drink in the warm light of the ceiling.

"I don't need a partner," Jebrassy said. "I need to get out of here and see how things really are, beyond the gates."

"You haven't *seen* the gates," Khren said. "You can't even describe them—all that out there is just empty words and names. Even if you believe the stories, nobody's ever gotten that far and come back to tell, and that says something."

"What?" Jebrassy said. "If we shame the wardens, and they tattle to the officers, those who escape the Tiers but get caught are handed over to the Bleak Warden? Or put in cages for the Tall Ones to enjoy?"

"That sounds pretty cruel even for Tall Ones," Khren said.

"I *hate* being ignorant! I want to see things, *new* things. I hate being *taken care of*."

With this outburst, the air between them settled a little and Khren returned to his accustomed role—of being a sounding board. In truth, Khren found Jebrassy's plans intriguing—he regarded them with a fascinated mock horror, as if, having played them over in his own mind, he had reached an impasse—a wall beyond which he could not foresee making any personal decisions. Khren at times seemed unwilling to believe that these plans meant any more to Jebrassy than they did to him—intriguing but empty talk.

"What did your visitor leave behind the last time?" Khren asked, savoring a final drib of tork. Jebrassy had kept his friend company in drink through two previous tumblers, but no more—he needed a clear head for tomorrow. For the meeting he knew couldn't possibly happen.

"He's a fool," Jebrassy muttered. "Helpless. He knows nothing. An *aaarp*." He belched to emphasize that degraded status. The concept of insanity did not exist among the ancient breed. Eccentricity, whims, and extremes of personality, yes, but insanity was not part of their mix, and therefore no one accused another of having lost touch with reality—except as a vague concept, an uncomfortable joke—suitable for belching.

"Well, did he tell you anything more?"

"I wasn't there. When he comes, I go. You know that."

"The drawings on the shake cloth."

"They never make sense."

"Maybe your visitor has met *her* visitor, and that's how she knows so much about you."

"You've talked with him. You know him better than I do," Jebrassy said, slumping deeper into the cushions.

"You—he—could barely talk at all," Khren said. "He looked in my mirror and made *sounds*. He said something like, 'They got it all wrong!'—except slurred. Then he—you, your visitor—just stumbled over and sat right where you are now, and closed his eyes—your eyes—until he went away."

Khren waggled his finger. "If that's what straying is all about—better you than me, mate."

TEN ZEROS

CHAPTER 9

Seattle, South Downtown

To pass the long gray time, as the rain patted and blew against the sky-light over the shadowy, high-ceilinged room, Virginia Carol—Ginny to her friends—paged through a thick, sturdy volume called *The Gargoyles of Oxford*, by Professor J. G. Goyle, published in 1934. *And was Professor Goyle's middle name Garth, or just plain Gar?*

The remains of a half-eaten sandwich, still in its waxy wrapper, awaited her attention on the bare brass table beside a high-backed reading chair. She had been hiding in the green warehouse for two weeks, waiting for an explanation that never seemed to come. Her fright had faded, but now she was growing bored—something that two weeks ago she would never have thought possible.

The pictures in the gargoyle book were amusing—leering, perverse figures designed, scholars said, to scare off evil spirits—but what caught her eye was a grainy photo embedded in a chapter on the university town's older buildings. On the inside of a stone parapet high in a clock

tower, someone had clearly incised, in proper schoolboy Roman majus-
cule, cutting through a centuries-old black crust of grime and soot:

DREAMEST THOU OF A CITIE AT THE END OF TYME?

And beneath that, *1685*. Another inscription below the date, presumably a name or address, had been vigorously scratched out, leaving
a pale brown blotch.

Conan Arthur Bidewell pushed through the door at the far end of
the room, carrying more books to be returned to the high wooden
shelves. He observed her choice of reading. "That's a real one—not one
of my oddities, Miss Carol," he said. "But it does reflect unpleasant
truths." His cheeks were sunken and thin wisps of hair covered a leath-
ery, shiny pate. He resembled a well-preserved mummy, or one of those
people found in bogs. That's it, Ginny thought. And yet—he's not exactly ugly.

She showed him the picture. "It's like the ad in the newspaper."

"So it is," Bidewell said.

"This has been going on for centuries," she said.

He peered through his tiny glasses. "Far longer than that." Under his
arm he carried two folded newspapers—*The Stranger* and *The Seattle
Weekly*. He laid them out on the reading table. One paper was a week
old, the other from the day before. Sticky tabs marked ads in the classifieds. The ads were almost identical.

> *Do you dream of a city at the end of time?*
> *There are answers. Call—*

Only the phone numbers were different.

"Same people?" she asked.

"Not to be known. Though in our neighborhood, I believe where
once there were two, there is now only one. But soon there will be
more." Bidewell stretched and cracked the knuckles of his free hand,
then ascended a tall ladder that rolled along a high, horizontal track fastened to the cases. The track extended over doors and a boarded-up
window, all the way around the room. Bidewell replaced the books he
had been studying, his thick corduroy pants hissing as he bent and
straightened his spindly legs.

"They've been looking for people like me, all this time? They would have to be very old," Ginny said.

"Some still survive and do their work, if we should call it that. There are so many foul currents in these young, deep waters. Were you followed here?"

Perhaps deliberately, he had not asked this question until now. Whatever his peculiarities, Bidewell seemed sensitive to her fears.

Ginny still did not want to remember the Mercedes, the coin-tossing man, the burning woman. "I think so," she said quietly. "Maybe."

"Mmm." Bidewell finished fitting the books back into their gaps and descended the ladder, making small chuck-chuck sounds with lips and cheeks. From the last rung, he glanced over his shoulder and squinted at the broad milk-glass globe light hanging from a bronze ceiling fixture. "I should be changing out those bulbs, shouldn't I?"

"The ones who place the ads, who scratched this . . ." She tapped the picture from Oxford. "Are they human?"

Bidewell nodded quickly, like a bird. "That particular inscription was carved by a schoolboy, on the dare of another schoolboy . . . who was paid by an older man. But to answer your question, most are human—yes."

"Why don't they die?"

"They have been touched," he said. "Their lives improbably extended. I'm sorry. I don't mean to be obscure."

Ginny was still not clear on these details—not even clear on whether she would just leave Bidewell's warehouse, abandon any hope of explanations—in due time, in due time—and take her chances outside.

At the age of sixteen, Ginny had begun to experience periods of abstraction. When walking, riding on a bus, or just before sleep, she would lose a snip of time and memory. After these lapses, she sometimes experienced a lightness of heart, a sense of returned affection not otherwise found in her erratic adolescence. Other times she felt a suffocating sense of dread, of loss—along with a bad smell of something beyond burning, and a gritty, dusty, bitter taste of something beyond decay.

At the same time, she became aware that she could will herself into different situations—though her efforts often seemed to backfire. Since losing her family, Ginny had persisted in making wrong moves—as if determined, at any fork in the road, to take the wrong path.

Never quite certain how she accomplished any of this, she began to read books about parallel worlds—and found them fascinating but un-satisfying. She did what she did, but still without explanation as to why and how she could do it.

She had told no one about her ability—until Bidewell took her in. Only last week, listening to her story, for once the old man had opened up enough to render an opinion. "Sounds very like someone lost, en-slaved, in the Chaos. Whatever that may be, not to be known, not to be known."

He had pinched his lips between two thin fingers and reiterated sev-eral times that he could only guess, he was no expert.

Exasperating man.

"What *do* you know, Mr. Bidewell?" Ginny blurted, slamming shut the heavy book. The clap echoed from the ceiling.

"Call me Conan, please," Bidewell encouraged. "My *father* was Mr. Bidewell."

"And how old was *he* when you were born?"

"Two hundred and fifty-one," Bidewell said.

"And how old are you?"

"One thousand two hundred and fifty-three."

"Years?"

"Of course."

"That's impossible."

"Improbable," Bidewell corrected, pushing up his small glasses and lifting the spine of another book close to his pale blue eyes. "Many things are conceivable, but impossible. Many more are conceivable, yet not probable. A very few are inconceivable—to us—yet still possible." He hummed to himself. "Moving stacks does wonders. Look what we have found, dear Ginny—volume twelve of the complete works of David Copperfield. The Dickens character, you see—who was actually a writer. Not the magician—though it would be interesting to meet *him*, sometime. I wonder what his dreams are like? A few choice questions . . . My dear, if you have time, could you check for a small fault on page 432? This print is tiny, and my eyes are not what they used to be."

He held out the book.

Ginny stood and took it from Bidewell's outstretched, gnarled hand. She was tiring of this constantly mutating nonsense—how could fic-tional characters write a book, much less fill a set of twelve or more vol-umes?—yet she felt safe here. A bitter contradiction.

She remembered when Bidewell had first lightly clasped her fingers, welcoming her to the warehouse and provoking—at once—a shudder and an odd sense of comfort.

"What sort of fault?" she asked.

"Anything, really—a typo, misspelling, lacunae, rivering. We must note the fault—but we must not make any corrections, or try to hide the apparent defects. They could be more important than thou canst know, young lady, to that Citie. Whatever and wherever that Citie may be."

———

Another week passed, and Ginny's restlessness grew. She could feel the foul currents Bidewell had spoken of—and something even more alarming. The river up ahead—her river—seemed to come to an abrupt end. She could not tell how far ahead—weeks, months, a year. But beyond that—nothing. Bidewell refused to tell her more, and most of their conversations ended with his crackling, "Not to be known, not to be known!"

Bidewell's warehouse was home to over 300,000 books. Ginny estimated the numbers on the shelves by quick count, and the numbers in the boxes by quicker calculation. Besides the two of them, seven cats called the warehouse home, all polydactyl—with many toes, and two with what appeared to be little thumbs.

These two were black and white. The smaller, a young male just out of kittenhood, silently padded up to her as she sorted and read, and rubbed against her ankles until she picked him up, placed him on her lap, and stroked him. Warm and loose-rubbery beneath soft fur, with a blaze on his chest and one white paw, he purred approval until she stopped, then leaned up on her chest and tapped her chin with a wide paw. She felt a light pinch.

He would not share any of her sandwich when she offered a bite, but instead, as a kind of hint or example, lay at the foot of her bed that night an intact but very dead mouse. All the cats were independent, and seldom responded to her chit-chits and here-kitties, but during the long nights, she would find one or two or sometimes three on the end of her cot, feet curled under, eyes slitty, watching her with warm, rumbling contentment. They seemed to approve of Bidewell's new visitor.

The cats, of course, were essential to the safety of the warehouse. Bidewell did not consider mouse-nibble edits at all helpful.

Time passed a little quicker after she met the cats. Curled one after another on her lap, they even made up for Bidewell's suggested reading list: he put aside, near her worktable, a stack of books on mathematics, physics, and several texts on Hindu mythology. Three of the books on physics seemed more advanced than she thought science had progressed so far, discussing faster-than-light travel as if it were a fact, for example, or detailing five-dimensional slices and cross sections of fates in space-time.

Next to these he placed five books with mostly blank pages—which he referred to as "culls." Ginny examined the culls carefully and discovered that each had one letter printed on one page, and nothing more—page after page of pristine blankness.

Whatever mysterious things happened in libraries and bookstores and among the stacked boxes in publishers' warehouses, it seemed that the mostly blank books were least interesting to Bidewell. "They are at best nulls, voids, spaces between keys. At worst, they are distractions. You may use them for your diary or as notebooks," he said, and then glanced at the other stack. "Those are for your education, such as it must be, and limited as we are."

"Are *they* defective, too?" she asked. "Should I look for the errors and mark them?"

"No," Bidewell said. "Their errors are natural, and unavoidable—the errors of ignorance and youth."

Ginny, in her few years of formal schooling, had always enjoyed math and science—coming to an easy understanding of problems that bewildered her classmates—but had never thought of herself as any kind of nerd. "I'd prefer a television or a computer with an Internet connection," she said.

Bidewell shuddered violently. "The Internet is a frightful prospect. All the world's texts . . . all the world's hapless opinions and lies and errors, mutating endlessly, and why? Who can ever keep track or know? It is not the incredible magnitude of human folly that interests me, dear Virginia."

She was hardly a prisoner, yet no matter how often she approached the door that led outside, she could not bring herself to pass through. The tension in her head and chest became unbearable, yearning and fear swirling until her stomach knotted. She could not go outside again—not yet.

"Why are you keeping me here?" she cried one morning, as Bidewell carted in another load of boxes filled with books. "I'm sick of it! Just you and these cats!"

Bidewell snapped back, "I do not keep you here. Wherever you go, I'm sure you will find your way home—by the long route. That *is* your talent. The cats might miss you." And then he walked off, knees snicking, and shut the white warehouse door with its oiled groan of counterweights and pulleys.

Ginny kicked at a crate, then turned to see the smallest cat sitting on the floor, watching her with complacent curiosity.

"You've got everything you want," she accused.

The cat's tail thumped a sealed box. He stood on his haunches and vigorously scratched the cardboard, leaving a catly symbol, like an X with an exclamation mark. Then he marched off, tail high and twitching.

Sometimes he even nibbled the corners of the books on the worktable. Bidewell didn't seem to mind.

——

With the appearance of the girl at his wire gate, Conan Arthur Bidewell had experienced three sharp emotions: irritation, exhilaration, and fear—the last, at his age, almost indistinguishable from joy. The air was thick with change. The girl's appearance was after all no more miraculous than the condensation of a drop of rain from a moisture-laden cloud.

Yet now he knew: the work of many lonely years was coming to fruition. Why *not* joy, along with the inevitable palpitations of coming danger?

For too many decades, far too many, he had been lost in his books, charting the statistics of improbable change. What could be more desperate or more futile? Waiting for the sum-runners to sow their flowers and produce a new family for him and the warehouse. And now—

Bidewell had long been noting the changes in the literary climate. More and more significant finds were being sent his way, from all over the planet. (Pity they could not reach out to other planets! For similar events must be happening Out There, as well, puzzling other scholars— if they were as vigilant.)

The moods of his books had darkened and clouded over. *This is the way the world ends—not with a bang, but a misprint.*

He had noted other changes in the neighborhood—a decrease in mice and an increase in cats. The warehouse contained two more cats than it had before the girl's arrival. They seemed to get along well with Minimus, his favorite. No doubt they all belonged to Mnemosyne—in their independent way.

And now Bidewell and the cats had a girl to keep them company, an unremarkable girl mostly, moody, guarding her emotions, as well she should. She was in a precarious situation. She believed she was eighteen years old. Bidewell knew better, but did not have the heart to tell her. Let them all discover the truth when they came together, for inevitably— despite the predators that searched them out and suppressed them, much as the cats reduced the warehouse's population of mice—there would be others. Their time had come.

A time of conclusions.

Ginny had survived a downward spiral and a terrible shock. He saw that she needed to recuperate and so did not load her overmuch with chores. The girl performed her jobs well enough. She opened boxes and weeded through the least promising collections, and was becoming a discerning reader, no surprise, considering her origins. She might eventually be of real help, but Bidewell wondered whether they would have the time for her skills to develop to where she could make a real difference.

The work in the warehouse proceeded, though he already knew what he needed to know: that the past was responding like a barometer to a tremendous decrease in pressure. So little past remained, and hardly any future.

What one thought one remembered was not a reliable guide to what had actually occurred—not anymore.

History truly was bunk.

CHAPTER 10

Seattle

A busker must satisfy all of his customers. To women, he must be young, charming, and funny; an amusement hiding a brief yearning. To men, he must appear ragged and clownish—not a threat despite his youth and good looks. To children, he must be like one of them—if they could only sing and dance and juggle hammers and rats.

Jack was making decent money, about twenty-eight dollars in three hours, deposited by members of his occasional audience into a floppy canvas hat planted on the sidewalk outside the downtown Tiffany's.

Today, as he had for two years, Jack was working with live rats. They were used to his tricks and he never dropped them—never. The rats may not have relished flying through the air, twisting their tails and heads, beady black or pink eyes flashing, seeing in spinning succession sky and ground and Jack's hand, but there it was; they were gently caught and gently tossed, and then they were fed, and there was always something interesting to look at through the mesh of the cage as they groomed themselves. Rats had led worse lives.

By four o'clock the crowds fled the concrete canyons, on their way home, so Jack packed up the cage and impedimenta, hung them on the front and back fenders of his bike, and began the long haul out of down-town, up Denny to Capitol Hill.

He was reluctantly on his way to the Broadway Free Clinic. First, he made a stop at Ellen's house. Her small gray bungalow was perched be-hind a slender garden topping a three-foot-high retaining wall, up two flights of concrete steps. She was still on a day trip out of town, so he found the key she had left hidden for him and stashed his rats high in the rafters of the old single-car garage, away from prowling cats.

Jack could be very handsome. He had made himself only slightly handsome around Ellen. Her longing was a puzzle—not motherly, not lustful—not entirely. He liked the attention. It made him feel rooted. She might remember him for weeks at a time—unlike everyone else. Still, he moved some small things around in the living room.

She had recommended the free clinic. "Even buskers need check-ups," she had said.

He thought about last week's dinner. Ellen had set the table with fine silver, crystal, and antique china, and served up salmon in berry glaze with rice and buttered fennel root. She had regarded him with a pecu-liar mix of longing and caution when she thought he wasn't looking, and he'd tried to reward her approval—without being too open.

She was not a hunter—not a spy. But vigilance was essential—espe-cially when he felt safe.

As she'd asked, he brought in her mail, sorted and dumped the recy-clables, then checked the moisture in her aspidistras and an indoor lemon tree by the broad front bay window.

Jack lingered for a few minutes, staring through the window across the street, and noted the distance between streetlights; wondered what the view would be like at midnight, in almost complete darkness, or better yet early in the morning, with all the lights off and just a glimmer of dawn. He could almost see it—the picture swam before him, this time overlaid by something else that could not and certainly should not have been there. The houses across the street seemed made of glass, and through them he spied a plain or desert, black as obsidian, studded with huge, indistinct objects—alive in their way, but full of hatred and envy, unforgiving.

With a groan, he closed his eyes, then shook his head until the after-noon light returned—and quickly drew the drapes.

———

The clinic waiting room was full. The doctors were dealing with seven moms and their sick children. Jack enjoyed children, but when they were not well or otherwise in real need, they made him feel uneasy, in-adequate. With averted eyes, he listened to the coughing and snuffling, the crying, the fighting over toys.

He tapped his fingers on the wooden arm of the chair, beating out the same bouncing song he hummed under his breath when he juggled—more a series of tuneful grunts.

An elderly man stood as his name was announced and deposited a *Seattle Weekly* on the center table. Jack picked up the tabloid, flipped past the media reviews—he did not much like movies or television—and lingered over the articles on clubs and live music. Always looking for a few good tunes.

He was halfway through a formal analysis of a new fusion-Ska-grace band when the words on the page shifted left. His head whirred. Some-thing seemed to hover before his eyes: a cloud of large winged insects, il-luminated by a brilliant beam of light. Then they blurred and slipped off, smudging into the paintings on the clinic walls—past the chairs, the little children's corner filled with toys.

A small fish tank bubbled away near the reception desk.

The bubbles froze.

The clinic fell silent.

He could see, but what he saw was skewed—rotating this way, then that, around a center point that expanded and changed color from red to blue to shades of brown and pink.

Then he looked directly into another pair of wide eyes, staring with an expression he could not read. He could not make sense of the face— too many contours—but there was nothing frightening about it. Somehow, he knew that this person was gentle, concerned, interested in him.

More than interested.

Behind the face, a receding tunnel opened onto artificial brightness. He became aware that his own face was foolishly slack, lids heavy.

He was dreaming again.

———

The face: flatter than he was used to, pug nose tipped with pink hairs, thick reddish fuzz reaching to her cheeks, tiny ears.

As one set of biological opinions took over from the other, he found the face attractive, then more than that—beautiful. A hint of concern and sadness became attached to his desire.

His own hair felt different—bunched back, spiky and short, more furry bristle than hair. He tried to take control of his lips and tongue, but it was not easy. Whatever sounds he made were bound to be garbled. He fumbled at his ears with questing fingers. They felt like hot button mushrooms.

The female with the flat pink nose wiped his forehead with a slender hand. She spoke again. *Gabble, gabble, gabble*, but pretty. She might be reciting poetry—or singing. Colors in his vision ran riot. He could not tell whether she was blue or brown or pink. Then, like a picture coming into focus, he acquired one frame of language and dropped another, colors became natural, and speaking was easier. Command of his body—at least of face and mouth—became more confident.

"You're back," she said. "How wonderful. Do you remember me?"

"I don't . . . think so," he said, well aware neither of them was speaking English, nor any language he had ever heard before.

"What do you remember?"

He looked at the curved ceiling. Large winged insects—bigger than his hand, with shining black cylindrical bodies—hung upside down, crawling. Each had a letter or symbol on its back. They moved into parallel, seemed to want to form rows—and thus make words. He could not read the words. Still, everything around him was real—absolute, with a solid, repeatable feel.

"This isn't a dream, is it?" he asked.

"I don't think so. Not on this side."

"How long . . . ?"

"You've been twitching for a while. Less than a . . ." She used a word he could not capture and hold, so it slipped away.

"Where am I?" he asked.

"I don't mean to be rude, but there is a protocol. We made it up. Your body-mate is a little . . ." Another word, embarrassing in whatever context it might have had. "He left you a message, which I have improved upon. To inform you of where you are, and what not to do."

He could not turn his head, so she raised a square black cloth covered with glittering red and yellow writing—a *shake cloth*.

"I can't read," he said.

"I'll read it for you."

"My name is . . ." But he had already forgotten who he had been and where he had been . . . before he was here. He tried to stand up, but his body tingled and he fell back.

She touched her ear and then her nose in sympathy. That was like smiling, maybe. "Never mind. Let's try this first. You appear to come from a time very far from this one. If you are real, and not a trick of the Tall Ones, then you should be taught some facts."

She turned the square and read the glittering words.

"'Welcome, polar opposite! I have been going astray of late, and assume you are the culprit. There is little to tell you, other than what you plainly see; I am of the ancient breed, poor enough and adventurous. If you are from the immediate future, please do not leave evidence of our fate; I prefer not to know. If you are from the past, then all I can say is that clocks no longer keep the time. Still, life is happy enough—if you stay humble. Otherwise, the Tiers can be cruel. If you are from the immediate past, and want to walk around, take care of my body—and do not dally with any attractive glows you might meet.'" At this, the female's face became wreathed in dimples and curves. "'You may amuse yourself by fighting in the skirmishes.'"

"No, you won't," the female added, glancing at him. Then she continued, "'There have been changes since you were here last. We're going on a march. And that's all I know. But I hope to know more.'"

The female looked up, hopeful. "That's all he managed to set down," she concluded. "Does it make sense? We'd like to know all you can tell us, of course—anything you want to tell us."

She was obviously concerned about his reaction to the message, which was already fading in his thoughts. *I've seen her before. But was that "before" before—or after—this?*

No sequence.

Remember, Mnemosyne!

"I'm confused," he managed to say, his mouth numb again. "If I stay here . . . for a while—I'll need to learn. Could you teach me?"

"That would be my delight," the female answered. "Though you rarely stay long. Are you from the future, or from the past?"

"I don't know. Is this . . . the Kalpa?"

"It *is*!" she cried out in delight. "The Tiers are inside the Kalpa, at the bottom, I think. We are very humble. You *do* remember!"

"Only some things . . . I remember *you*."

"We've never met, until now," she said, with pretty concern. "But Jebrassy has told me about you . . . a little."

"What's your name? Wait . . . it's Tiadba, isn't it?"

She was even more delighted, but puzzled. "Did he tell you that? What's your name?"

"I don't know. This is where I go when I stray, isn't it?"

"Where you go, and whom you visit. But where do you come from?"

"I don't remember. It's all mixed up."

Tiadba showed concern. He could see that, but the way her face made expressions, the way her cheek and jaw and lip muscles moved, was strange . . . Strange and lovely. She had such tiny ears and her eyes were large, almost like the eyes of a . . .

Another word lost.

He squinted at the ceiling. He could almost read what the letterbugs were spelling out. Insect pets that spelled out words. "What are they doing?" He tried to lean forward, get up, stand again. Too fast, too much. His eyes lost focus and his vision skewed. Shutters seemed to clack and close around him. He did not want to leave, not when he was on the brink of learning more, with this beautiful female to help him. He had been so lonely for so long!

He tried to reach out, but his hands wouldn't move.

"I'm falling. Hold onto me," he said, angry that his lips were so thick and clumsy.

"Try to stay, try harder!" Tiadba grabbed his hands, his arms. She was surprisingly strong. But all sense was draining from his head and

body and limbs. The last thing he saw was her face, her eyes—brown—
her flat, expressive nose—

Jack's awareness squashed down to a fuzzy point, something
whirred and snapped—the point expanded—vertigo turned into blurs
of light—and he was back.

He blinked at the fish swimming in their tank, listened woozily to
the hum of the waiting room's heating system. Tried to hang onto what
he had experienced—especially the face, the female, and the letterbugs,
a weird idea—fun, actually—but by the time he realized where he was,
everything slipped away except a sense of panic. Someone was in desperate trouble.

Here, there—now, then?

That urgency faded as well.

Jack looked around. The families had been reduced to a lone mother
in a sari and her sleeping infant. An elderly couple had taken seats
nearby. Embarrassed, he looked at his watch. He had blanked for thirty
minutes. Somehow, he had kept turning the pages.

He folded the newspaper and put it in his satchel.

The attending nurse stood in the door to the waiting room. "Jack
Rohmer? Dr. Sangloss will see you now."

CHAPTER 11

First Avenue South

Ginny pushed a handcart stacked high with boxes down aisles formed by
more boxes, having caught the knack of steering with the single long
handle, like a backward toy wagon—anticipating the turns, working
everything in reverse. These boxes arrived two days ago and had been
dumped unceremoniously on the warehouse's cold but dry loading dock,
beneath a corrugated tin overhang. So many boxes—where did they all
come from? Where did Bidewell get the money to send out all his scouts,
buy all these books, have them shipped from around the world?

More mysterious still, *why?*

She pushed the handcart to the sorting table in the same corner as
her sleeping area. She had walled off her bed with crates and boxes.
Books do make a room.

The warehouse was heated, fortunately—everything maintained at a steady sixty-five degrees, and dry. Bidewell may have been mad, but he did not collect just to collect, then allow his items to mildew and spoil.

As Ginny unloaded the boxes, Bidewell stepped in through the rolling steel door that led to his library and private rooms. In the same dark brown suit he always wore, his ancient body made a gentle question mark against the door's dingy whiteness. He paused, then took a shuddering breath, as if lost in weary contemplation, perhaps of a job never to be completed; work beyond anyone's power to finish.

He turned his head slowly and said, "These are all paperbacks?"

Ginny noticed for the first time that this was true; she'd been working on autopilot for the last hour, letting her thoughts go as she repeated the mechanics and motions. "So far," she said.

Bidewell clasped his hands. "Books produced in quantity seem to enjoy mutation, especially in the great piles that modern publishers stack in their vast warehouses. Packed together, compressed, unread— they reach a critical mass and start to change. A symptom of boredom, don't you think?"

"How can books be bored?" Ginny asked. "They're not alive."

"Ah," Bidewell said.

She spread the books out on the table in stacks five high. All of them had been printed in English; all were less than twenty years old. Many were in sorry condition; others appeared brand-new, except for browned paper and the occasional chipped or dinged corner or spine. They smelled musty. She was coming to hate the smell of books.

Bidewell approached. Ginny never felt threatened or afraid in his presence, but all the same, could not help thinking that he needed watching.

He studied the stacks she had made. Like a dealer of cards, he worked through them, fanning the pages of each book with his thumb, lifting them to his nose to sniff, barely glancing at what was on the aromatic pages. "Once a text is printed, there are no new books, only new readers," he murmured. "For such a book—for such a text, a long string of symbols—there is no *time*. Even a new book, freshly printed, stored in a box with its identical compatriots—all the same—even that book can be old."

Ginny crossed her arms.

Bidewell suddenly showed her a toothy smile: wood-colored teeth. *George Washington's choppers, but these are real—and they look strong.*

"Everything old is *bored*," he said. "Hidden away in great piles of sameness, lives and histories laid out, unchanging—wouldn't *you* play a little game, given the chance?" He stared up the aisles between boxes and shrugged, then blew his nose with a crisp, bubbling hoot. "A letter flipped, a word changed or lost—who will ever know? Who even looks or cares? Has there ever been a scientific survey of such tiny, incremental deviations? What *we* are looking for is not the trivial, the commonplace, but the product of permuted genius: the book that has rearranged its *meaning* or added *meaning* while no one was looking, no one was reading—and most fascinating of all, the book that has altered its string of text across all editions, throughout all time, such that no one can ever know the truth of the original. The variant becomes the standard. And what this new version has to contribute—that must be interesting."

"How could you ever find it?"

"I remember what I read," Bidewell said. "In my lifetime, I have read a lot. Within that significant sampling, I will know if anything changes." He waved his long fingers over the table and sniffed. "These are of minor interest. They have varied individually, a letter here, a letter there. Their variations are intriguing, perhaps even significant, but of little use in the time left to us."

"Sorry," Ginny said, petulant.

"Not your fault," Bidewell said. "Like me, books can be tedious." He winked. "Let's get through this shipment by eventide. Then, we will order in takeaway."

With an impenetrable look of severity, Bidewell stalked away through the aisles to the steel door and closed it behind him, leaving Ginny to her endless task of sorting and stacking.

She opened the next box on the handcart, pulled out a paperback, and lifted the pages to her nose. The odor of rotting pulp made her sneeze.

CHAPTER 12

The nurse weighed Jack and guided him to the doctor's cubicle, a small gray and pink space. She took his pulse with expert fingers, then wrapped his wiry arm in an inflatable cuff and pumped it up to measure his blood pressure.

A few minutes later the doctor entered and closed the door. Miriam Sangloss was in her early forties, slender and strong-jawed, with short brown hair. She wore a white lab coat and a gray wool skirt that fell below her knees. Black socks with pumpkin-colored clocks and sensible black running shoes completed her wardrobe. On her left hand, he noticed, she wore a garnet ring, at least two carats.

She flashed a knowing flicker of a smile and looked him over with sharply focused brown eyes. "How's our rat man today?" she asked. He wondered how she knew—perhaps Ellen had told her.

"Fine. Losing bits of my day," he said. He hated to admit to being sick. Being sick meant he was losing his touch. Soon he would become slow and wrinkled and stooped-shouldered and no one would want to watch him perform. "Going blank," he added.

"For how long?" Sangloss asked.

"How long am I blacking out?"

"How long have you been losing bits of your day?"

"Two months."

"And you're how old—twenty-five, twenty-six?" She turned the page of the chart on her clipboard. He wondered how she had put together so many notes.

"Twenty-four," Jack said.

"Much too old. Stop it right now."

"Too old for what?"

Look at you. Handsome as a young devil. Strong and agile. Fit. You don't get sick. You live life on your own terms. You always will—we expect that of you. So what's really *wrong with you?*

He could almost see Dr. Sangloss's lips moving, telling him that, but she hadn't spoken aloud, of course. It was all contained in the long look she gave him. Over a brief sigh, she bent her gaze to the tablet and said, "Tell me what you experience."

"It's probably nothing. I drop out for a few minutes or as long as an hour. Two or three times a day. Sometimes I'm fine for a week, but then it happens again. Last week I rode my bike on autopilot all afternoon. Ended up near the loading docks."

"No bumps or bruises?"

Jack shook his head.

"Any recent trauma, lapses of judgment, odd behavior—hallucinations?"

Again, no.

"You're sure?"

He looked at a poster on the far wall—a medical artist's rendering of a male head in profile, cut in half, framed and mounted beside a corkboard. The poster reminded him of learning how to swallow and disgorge Ping-Pong balls and small oranges. "A kind of dream. A place. A mood."

"Any smells or tastes or sounds before or after these episodes?"

"No. Well—sometimes. Bad tastes."

"Mostly just the lingering sensation of a forgotten dream. Is that it?"

"I don't know." To her skeptical gaze, "Really."

"No drugs? Marijuana?"

He solemnly denied this. "Cuts back on my timing."

"Right." She inspected his left hand, spread the fingers, stared curiously at the calluses. "Any family history of epilepsy? Narcolepsy? Schizophrenia?"

"No. I don't think so. I don't know much about my mother's side of the family. She died when I was twelve."

"Did your father smoke like a chimney?"

"No. He was large—fat, really. He wanted to be a stand-up comedian." Jack gave her a squint.

Sangloss waved that aside. "We should do a follow-up. No insurance, correct?"

"Zero."

"Street entertainer's union? Teamsters?"

Jack smiled.

"Maybe we can get you a pro bono appointment at Harborview. Would you show up if, if I arranged that?"

He looked uncertain. "What, like a biopsy?"

"MRI. Brain scan. Petit mal epilepsy usually occurs in children, drops off at puberty. Kids can have dozens of small seizures each day, sometimes hundreds, but rarely lasting more than a few seconds. That diagnosis doesn't quite fit, does it? Narcolepsy—possible, but that doesn't fit, either. Has anyone seen you black out?"

"I just did, in the waiting room. I kept turning pages. Nobody seemed to notice." He pointed to the chair, where the *Weekly* poked out of his jacket pocket.

"Ah." She shined a small bright light into each of his eyes. "Phone number?"

"I beg your pardon?"

"Your phone number, for the appointment."

He gave her Burke's phone number. Dr. Sangloss wrote it down on his chart. "I'll ask Dr. Lindblom to get you into Harborview. Do this—for my sake, if not for yours, okay?"

Jack nodded solemnly, but his eyes were elusive.

Sangloss brandished a tongue depressor. "Open wide," she said. When he could not talk, merely issue round vowels, she said, "I saw you downtown three weeks ago. Does anyone complain when you juggle rats?"

"Awm," Jack said. She lifted the wooden stick. He poked his mouth square between two fingers, then released it, letting it flop loose, and smiled. "Some. They pet the rats. I show them how I handle them."

"What else do you juggle? That's alive, I mean."

"I used to juggle a kitten."

"Really? Why did you stop?"

"Got big. I gave him to a friend. Not many cats like to be juggled—that one was special. And I had a snake, once. Snakes are tricky."

"I bet." Sangloss made more notes.

Jack clamped his jaw. "What's wrong with me?"

"Nothing obvious," she said. "Keep a little notebook handy. Record each episode—frequency, sensations, aura, whatever you can remember. They'll ask at Harborview."

"All right."

"And stop tossing your rats, okay? Until we figure this out."

———

Dr. Sangloss finished her clinic hours, said good-bye to the receptionist and the nurses, then locked the doors, turned down the heat, checked the taps in the bathrooms and the lab, briefly inventoried all the locks and security cameras in the pharmacy, and stood for a moment, looking around the front office. The clinic served many different kinds of patient. Not all were responsible.

The office was quiet, the street outside the half-shuttered window deserted. A light wind sent a whistling note through a crack some-where. An old, drafty building.

She walked down the hall to her small rear office, where she filed a few folders and unlocked the lower desk drawer. As she plucked out her cell phone, she felt a chill—strange, since the old furnace had just fin-ished its final blast of heat for the evening.

Almost strange enough to make her open the book that Conan Arthur Bidewell had given her, with instructions never to read it, or even to carry it in her hands for very long. Bidewell was an odd man but a compelling one—and he paid the clinic's bills.

Five years' worth.

Tonight was the fourth anniversary of their first meeting at the green warehouse down in Sodo. Green warehouse, green leather binding on her small old book, half hidden by textbooks and journals on a metal shelf.

She stared at its short, cracked leather spine, imprinted only with a number on the nub—*1298*. A number, or a date.

What would she learn if she *did* read it?

Dr. Sangloss jerked loose from the book's spell and punched in a number on her phone. A woman answered. "Ellen? Miriam. I've exam-ined your young man. No doubts. You have his address, don't you? . . . Not implying a thing, dear. I'm sure we'll all feel motherly. Say hello to the Witches. I don't think I'll make it tonight. Might spook the poor fel-low. Let me know what they think."

CHAPTER 13

Wallingford

The living room windows were covered in plastic. Someone—perhaps the real owner, years before—had tried to remodel and given up. Lath and plaster had been pulled out, old paper-wrapped wiring lay in bent, ragged coils. The roof leaked and water warped the wooden floor, seep-ing down to flood the basement.

The house had been deserted long enough for a homeless beggar to find his way in and set himself up in crude comfort—no heat, no power, nothing but running water left on for the gardeners who no longer came. The beggar had added a few sticks of furniture and a mattress, probably snuck in with exhausting effort during the night.

When he could stand up without retching—for the first time in days—Daniel searched the house all over again.

And this time . . .

In a hole just behind the upstairs bathroom sink, he found a carton tied with string. He cut the string and poured out the contents. A battered wallet flopped on the cracked tile floor, driver's license visible behind a yellowed plastic window. The photo confirmed that this body had once belonged to a man named Charles Granger, age 32 at the time the license was issued. Another shake tossed out sheets of typing paper, a black marker, and a blunted pencil.

A small, dense gray box, taped to the bottom, fell out last—and he knew this was what he'd been looking for all along.

His sum-runner. The sometime stone.

The box was the same, with the same sigil carved in bas-relief on the lid: a circular design with interlinked bands or hoops wrapped around a cross. How likely was that? Another connection between Daniel and Charles Granger. He did not try to open it—not yet. With a low whistle, he put it in his pocket, then flipped through the papers. Random scrawls, odd symbols—terrible handwriting, yet familiar, in its way.

Too close. Very spooky.

Where was Granger now, the previous occupant of this heap of a body—lost, pushed aside, bumped out of the nest? Just another victim. And what about all those other strands, all the world-lines he must have crossed—the myriad densely bundled fates between Daniel Patrick Iremonk and *here?*

No Daniel in this strand. Only someone living in his aunt's old house, someone who writes things down in odd symbols—

The closest I could find.

Just not me. *Why?*

The box was the crucial connection. Had Charles Granger been a jaunter as well? *Charles Granger is at the end of his rope. The box knows. It brought you here.*

He riffled the papers, stuffed them back into the carton, then closed it up again.

Outside, the wind picked up.

Daniel stood, joints popping and cracking. Something wasn't right.

Something wasn't finished. He had found the box—*a box*—but Daniel Iremonk had never kept his sum-runner in a cardboard carton—too obvious.

He had hidden it behind the brick fireplace.

Daniel felt along the bricks and found a loose one near the baseboard. He scraped it back and forth, pulled it out, knelt down with a grimace, and reached into the opening.

And found a *second* box.

As if working through instinct, he placed both boxes side by side. They were identical in appearance. He puzzled them open. The stones lay in their velvet-cushioned interiors, sharing the same orientation.

He removed them and held them in his hands, inspecting their distant red eyes. They refused to twist—and refused to fit together. Two identical pieces of a puzzle.

He returned the duplicate stone to its box, closed it, and dropped it into the cardboard carton, then covered it with Charles Granger's papers.

Best to keep no more than one on his person, and hide the other—as a backup.

———

The sounds of traffic on the arterial that ran past the northern corner of the old house—a regular hum and wet swoosh—should have been soothing, like freshets down a watercourse. But Daniel could not find peace. He could not sleep. He lay twitching in the torn sleeping bag on the wooden floor in the middle of the rear bedroom. Little electric flashes raced through him, as if his heart were being tickled by the frayed end of a low-voltage cable. Things kept popping up in memory—impossible things he could never have personally witnessed. Each little jolt came with its own bill of lading, a sense of personal loss that left him weaker and more confused.

Even before he arrived here, Daniel had often felt as if he were a knot tying up all the loose rope-ends of time. Far too much responsibility.

Time does not rush along as a point; it smears out like the passage of a brush a minute or an hour or a week wide, sometimes a month—a brush made of fate-laden fibers, painting different pictures for different people.

Knowing this gave Daniel an advantage—he could *feel* his way across the width of an hour, a week, a month. Anticipate something unpleasant? Make a left turn instead of a right, find a door opened instead of closed, elude bad fortune—and if something came up that seemed unavoidable, jaunt to a very close but slightly skewed, just slightly improved world—a strand without that particular impediment.

That had been his method, until now.

He had made his way from fate to fortune to fate, closing his eyes and *squeezing* himself loose . . . always joining up with alternate versions of himself, so little different that no one could tell there had been a change—a strange cuckoo landing in nests no doubt occupied by other cuckoos.

Daniel never spent very long in one strand. He had started his killing early on—sacrificing others to enhance his fortune—desperate, as if he needed many more chances to get where he needed to be and do what he needed to do. It might have been those betrayals—those metaphysical murders—that had brought him low and thrust him into the middle of the Nasty Silent Party—that diseased, broken strand, surrounded by so many other rotting worlds.

An infinite supply of fortune had passed through his hands, and now, apparently, he had sucked the wellspring dry. He sometimes wondered if he had killed the entire universe.

But no. There were worse things than Daniel Patrick Iremonk out there, waiting to get in.

———

Perhaps the puzzle boxes had been there all along, unguarded—and Granger had found them, but didn't know what they were or what they carried.

Poor kind of shepherd.

A pile of bottles had grown in a corner of the kitchen—Night Train, Colt 45, Wild Irish Rose. Even on Daniel's home strand, those same brands and bottles had lined the shelves in corner markets, leering landmarks of the constancy of human pain and sin. Cheap booze, common to all strands . . .

His mind raced as much as this mind could race, a sluggish pile of gray matter poisoned by years of alcohol, drugs, and disease. The nipping, coiling snake in his gut.

Daniel jerked up from the mattress, batting at his arms. His skin was convinced it was infested with tiny bugs. *Punishment for sin? Bugs in your skin.*

He walked into the living room and pulled aside the brown paper taped to the window. Outside, the dark streets were relieved by street-lights, each illuminating a blurred ellipse on the sidewalks and grass.

A car drove past—*shush* and *whoosh* of wet pavement—its head-lights intensely blue.

For two days now, barely able to move, he had been reading—pulling newspapers and magazines out of recycling bins under the kitchen sink, trying to find out how much time he had—how much time they all had in this world before the signs multiplied, the cryptids started proliferating, the books spilled over with nonsense—and the dust and mildew began taking hold.

> *Brer Rabbit ran so fast*
> *Skip right out o' his skin,*
> *Had ter push 'nother rabbit out—*
> *And climb—*
> *Back—*
> *In.*

He let the shade drop and pulled up a lone dining room chair in the middle of the floor. The chair legs scraped on the uneven boards like the cry of a hoarse old woman.

What else was different about this world? Besides the desperate minus of Daniel Patrick Iremonk . . .

You tell me what's different, Brer Rabbit.

Whar you fum?

Daniel's home had also been called Seattle.

Classic Seattle. Wetter and grayer than this one, if that was possi-ble—less populated, not nearly as much concentrated wealth. A friend-lier city—more face-to-face communication, neighborhoods sticking together—kids didn't spend endless hours glued to computer screens, locked in artificial worlds—more grounded; a world he remembered as more suitable, more right, yet he had never fit in. Always looking for a way out, an excuse to leave, and finally he had found both, to his infinite and probably short-lived regret.

Right out o' yo' skin.

Finally, in his teens, he had put that name to what he was doing: jaunting. Crossing the strands of varied fates—traveling in the fifth dimension for advantage. Playing Monopoly without moving around all the squares: squiggling around the game board, or digging down *through* stacked boards.

The rich got richer because they were rich, but the poor got poorer because they had to stick to the rules, they could not burrow through the game like a Monopoly mole, or jump sideways—like a rabbit.

> *Now, dat rabbit, some rabbit,*
> *Brer Rabbit, my, how he could jump!*

Also in his teens, he had decided it was time to study up on what he was actually doing, and that eventually led him across the freeway to an old Carnegie library on the corner of Fiftieth and Roosevelt—still there. In the soft glow of great hanging saucer lamps of bronze and milky glass, listening to rain patter against the high windows, Daniel had studied popular science books by Gamow, Weinberg, and Hawking, and finally came across P.C.W. Davies, who had taught him about special relativity, singularities, and universal constants.

A man named Hugh Everett had created the Many Worlds interpretation of quantum mechanics, and two Davids—Bohm and Deutsch, very different in their thinking—had taught him about the possibility of multiverses. Daniel had then conceived of branching realities, four-dimensional cosmoses arranged side by side, in a way, across a fifth dimension . . . a thick rope of world-strands.

John Cramer, a professor at the University of Washington, had speculated about retrocausality—particles reaching back to reconcile their present with the past—which Daniel could feel happening inside his gray box—though he had no idea what it meant.

As he got older and acquired a little savvy (you couldn't jump backward and stay young, and you certainly couldn't jump forward—just "sideways," "up," or "down"), he imagined himself a kind of athlete. How *often* could he jump—and how far, with how much sense of direction or accuracy?

How could he improve his situation the most?

Where would he finally land, measured on the Money-Love spectrum?

That got him into a frustrating tangle. Trying to end up with more money, he soon learned that improved circumstance required more personal effort, not less—and his base personality was not good at *keeping* lots of money.

And so he tried improving his life at the expense of another's—predatory jumping. (And wasn't that where his talent had been all along? He had seen it so often—Daniel doing better, Joe Blow not so good, whereas Joe Blow had been doing okay before the jump—but he could never *prove* it, not with any rigor—and maybe he didn't want to know for sure.)

Daniel was never deliberately cruel. He didn't enjoy hurting people. He was just a man with a nervous tic for fortune—but no knack for ultimate design, no fashion sense for fate. *Maybe I'm a lot more screwed up than poor, sick, scrawny Charles Granger. After all, I pushed him out.*

Right out o' his skin.

He would need to make another move soon—and how could he do that? He didn't even know how he'd ended up in Granger, except that they shared versions of the same house, proximal to the same stones.

Standing on the corner, staring at drivers—even in his worst times, those last days when the shadows began closing in—he had never been so isolated. He had to start reaching out, checking the pulse and mood of real people with real emotions.

The night was lonely—scary lonely. Being alone seemed less attractive than it had ever been before—because now Daniel was certain of two things.

This world was nearing its end. And this body was dying.

CHAPTER 14

Capitol Hill

Ellen Crowe had company when Jack returned. The clink of wine-glasses and female voices in the dining room revealed that Ellen's book group was in session. They called themselves the Witches of Eastlake.

He looked at the invitation on the card. He had forgotten it was tonight.

Jack opened the garage door as quietly as possible and was up on the stepladder bringing down the cage when Ellen called from the rear porch. "Hey, stranger. Don't be shy. Are you hungry?"

Jack walked back. His rats sniffed the air, fragrant with cooking. "I don't think your friends would like me barging in," he said.

"It's my house," Ellen said.

He gave her a weak smile. He *was* hungry—he had not eaten since breakfast, and Ellen was a fine cook.

Jack sat on a stool in the kitchen as Ellen pulled a tray of game hens from the ornate black and chrome gas oven. The roasted birds smelled delicious. The rats clustered at the front of their cage, noses twitching.

She forked one of the birds onto a plate on the counter. Mushroom stuffing, Jack noted. "We've already eaten. Help yourself to salad. There's wine in the fridge."

"Am I going to sing for my supper?" he asked.

"Anything but that," Ellen said.

Shoving a napkin into the collar of his black T-shirt and floofing it out like an ascot, he struck a pose with upraised knife and fork. Baggy pants held up by red suspenders, hair wild and black and face thin, high cheekbones and large liquid eyes, Jack flaunted his formidable lack of dignity. "What are you reading this month?"

"An Oprah book. You wouldn't like it."

He sniffed.

Ellen sniffed back. "Enjoy. There's canned dog food for the rats in the fridge. I'll introduce you during dessert."

Jack pruned up his face. He did not know what she was up to. Some sort of test—or bizarre revenge?

"*Relax*," she whispered, her expression fierce, and pushed through the door into the dining room. The door swung back with a light breeze.

Jack found the dog food, spooned some into a dish, and delivered it with a flourish to the cage. "Fill your bellies, my sweet little rodents. No more flying. And maybe no more food for a long, long time." The rats considered the likelihood of game hen and the food actually at paw, then, resigned, fell to nibbling.

He sat at the counter and opened the newspaper he'd filched from the waiting room. He paged through the classifieds, seeking something—he could not remember what. But there it was in the middle of the last page: the message his eyes had read and remembered while the rest of Jack's mind was elsewhere. Frowning, he touched the short ad—very short.

Then he stopped eating and shifted uncomfortably on the stool. Glanced at the screen door leading to the back porch. Something outside, waiting? No . . .

When he resumed eating—the food was too good to ignore—he kept glancing at the ad, until he tore it out and stuffed it in his pocket.

The rest of the paper he stuffed into Ellen's recycle bin, under the sink.

———

The talk through the kitchen door sounded cheerful, raucous in a feminine way, and after several glasses of wine, more directly truthful. The postprandial effects of good warm food had loosened Ellen's guests.

Ellen thought they were ready. She served dessert. Then she pushed Jack through the door and stood beside him, one hand high and bent at the wrist, the other at waist-level, like a couturier showing off her new line.

Across the long oak dining table, the two older women fell silent.

"I've told you about Jack," Ellen said. "He works the streets. He's a *busker*."

Her guests stared, then exchanged veiled glances, as if there was so much to say but no way they would ever be caught saying it—not in front of their hostess. In their forties or early fifties, both looked as if more exercise and sun might do them good. Granny glasses, silk pantsuits—the redhead wore rhinestone-studded denim—fine manicures, and fashionable hairdos. Jack quickly sized them up: wealthy street marks, incomes over a hundred K per annum. One perhaps a lesbian—did she know? Under normal circumstances, he would happily separate them from as much money as he could get away with.

For their part, Ellen's guests regarded Jack with stiff civility—a too-young male of suspicious dark good looks in their female fastness, invited, to be sure, but *why*?

Jack groaned deep in his throat, then bowed. "Ladies," he said, "thanks for the wonderful food. I don't want to interrupt." He tried to retreat through the kitchen door but Ellen jerked him back by his elbow.

The women looked to her for guidance. She lowered her hands and folded them, demure. "Jack's a friend," she said.

"What sort of friend?" asked the eldest, older than Ellen by at least ten years.

"What does Ellen mean, 'work the streets'?" asked the other, the redhead, pleasing enough in her plumpness. "What's a *'busker'*?"

"It's from the French, *busquer*, to seek, like a ship trying to find its course," said the eldest. To her, Jack was a sand grain, a small sharp point of irritation.

Ellen gestured like a teacher, *Tell the girls.* For a hot instant he did not like her at all.

"I'm a showman," Jack said. "I do magic and juggle."

"Does it pay?" the redhead asked.

"Sometimes," he said. "I get to keep bankers' hours."

They did not return his smile—though the redhead's lips twitched. And what was *he* to Ellen, *really?* she seemed to ask. Such a skinny young man!

The eldest glanced around the table with wide eyes behind thick glasses. "Can you show us a trick?"

Jack instantly assumed a dancer's restful pose. Bowed his head as if in prayer. Lifted his hands, fingers to thumbs, as if to snap castanets. The ladies watched for some seconds. Tension built.

The (probable) lesbian scraped her chair and coughed.

Jack raised his chin and met Ellen's eyes.

"I don't do tricks," he said. "I invite the world to dance."

"Tell us how you do that, Jack," Ellen murmured.

All three women looked around the room with nostrils flared, like lionesses smelling blood. He did not like this kind of attention. His patience reached an end.

"That's it," he said. "Thanks again, but I'm done. Here's my *trick.*"

For a tenth of a second—no time at all—the dining room fell under a muffled blankness, like stuffing your ears with waxed cotton. The crystals on the chandelier quivered. All six of the flame lights behind the crystals sizzled out.

"I'd like to ask—" the redhead began, but Jack pointed and lifted his eyebrow, and she looked out the window. Simultaneously, on the narrow street in front of Ellen's house, two cars mated with a grating slam.

The walls shuddered.

All three ladies jumped and exclaimed.

"Was that thunder?" the redhead asked.

Ellen hurried to the front door. For the moment, they had forgotten about Jack. He shoved through the kitchen door, lifted his rats with a swoop—they flattened on their haunches—and fled down the porch.

As he pedaled along the back alley, he could feel a familiar stiffness creep up his shoulder blades. Ellen shouldn't have done that. That went beyond pixie—it was cruel, like introducing Peter Pan to Wendy when she could no longer hope to fly. Worse, he had moved so far off his line of good consequence just to arrange an exit that it might take days to jump back.

And who knew what could happen during that time?

As he coasted down a hill, Jack felt totally exposed.

CHAPTER 15

First Avenue South

That night, Ginny and Bidewell dined on take-out Thai food—what Bidewell insisted on calling "takeaway." He rarely cooked. There was no kitchen, only a hot plate and the iron stove where he kept a teakettle. The refrigerator held only white wine, cat food, and milk for tea.

Bidewell expertly wielded chopsticks. They had already discussed his years in China, searching for certain Buddhist texts and trying to escape from Japanese soldiers in some war or another; Ginny had not listened closely.

From the main storage room in the warehouse, they heard a bump and cascading thumps—a stack of books falling over. Ginny pointed with her chopsticks. "Your cats?"

"Minimus is the only one who pays attention to my books."

"Other than me," Ginny said, then added, "They seem to go wherever they want."

"All my fine Sminthians stay *here*," Bidewell insisted. "Like me. The warehouse is all they need."

"*Sminthians?*"

Bidewell pushed a classical dictionary her way. "Homer. Look it up."

Bidewell was cleaning away the paper plates and boxes when Ginny asked, "Why do you let the cat—why do you let Minimus—knock things over? He might hurt the books."

"He doesn't *hurt* them," Bidewell said. "Some cats are sensitive to the spiders between the lines." He slid shut the flue on the stove to stifle the fire inside.

"What the hell does that mean?" she asked to Bidewell's retreating back. He smiled over his shoulder, then vanished into his sleeping quarters, beyond the library and the warm stove.

———

That evening, Ginny found a small, thin brown book on her table. It told a peculiar story.

THE SCRIBES' TALE

Near the end of the eighth century, on the island of Iona in the Western Hebrides, off the coast of Scotland, a monastery protected many of the great manuscripts of antiquity from waves of intemperate history breaking over Europe and Britain.

In the abbey, monks copied and illuminated manuscripts and prepared for the day when the classics would again be spread to other abbeys, castles, and towns—and to the universities which were even then being dreamed of, centers of text and learning that would shine light from the past on a world buried in darkness.

Within these stone walls, copy rooms had been set up, dimly lit by tallow candles and on occasion by oil lamps, where apprentices were taught the craft of faithful reproduction of old manuscripts gathered by monks and collectors from around the ancient world.

Books were being invented to replace the antique scrolls, bound volumes being more easily read and carried, and more durable.

It was claimed that this copy room was the most faithful and accurate of any in Europe, and the apprentices—as they grew older and more expert—were celebrated beyond their station, and thus acquired pride. And this pride took the form, so the legend tells us, of a spider that plagued the copyists one cold winter, as they wielded with gloved hands their pens and brushes. Candles warmed the gelid ink in its tanks, and the monks' meticulous strokes froze upon the paper before they could dry. (Indeed, to this day, some of these manuscripts bear letters with a special inky sheen—freeze-dried.) There was not fuel enough, neither brush nor wood nor dried seaweed, charcoal from the mainland, nor dung from the island's cattle, to warm the abbey.

Despite the cold, the spider—so the copyists informed the abbot—became visible first as a moving spot in the corner of ink-weary eyes, a blur that zipped across the pages, leaving delicate, inky trails. Errors began to creep into the copies, as these apparitions distracted the monks. And no sweeping or blessing improved the situation.

The spider soon became bold and lingered upon the vellum, lifting its forelegs and spreading its palps in defense as it was brushed aside or hit with a pounce-bag. It always disappeared without a trace—only to reappear on another page, at another copy-stand.

For weeks this apparition—or natural nuisance, none could say which—haunted and befuddled the monks. Some claimed it was a pagan spirit sent to devil them and increase error in our sin-stricken world. Others, usually skeptical, still found it hard to believe so tiny a creature could survive the chill without infernal assistance, the fires of hell being almost a tempting prospect through early spring.

And so it went until the heather lost its sere and budding leaves poked forth green and red from bush and tree. It was February, and the island's hard winter was passing early with rain and storm into glorious days of golden sun. Monks took a break from their work and gathered seaweed from the white beaches to fertilize their gardens and small farms. Balmy breezes danced through the abbey, coaxing the chill out of old stone and dank earth. Grass pushed high and green, and the making of vellum and fine parchment resumed as the calves and lambs were born.

The winter's copies were brought out and displayed to the air, to dry away mildew, and the abbot examined them in the brightness of the abbey garden, his weak but loving eyes vigilant for errors, blemishes, anything that might make them unacceptable to clients present or future. (For many books were stored in the abbey's stone tower library, against the future demand of a world reborn.)

And so the abbot was the first to discover that one copy in an entire run of manuscripts bore in its margins a scrawled, clumsy, and unsanctioned poem, thus:

> *Between the lines*
> *A bogey walks*
> *Eight legs, eight eyes.*

Letters will flee
Ink will be smeared
Till it be born
In ash and dread,
Wolf's eye red,
Seen by the Three;
Who spare the mite
That words make flesh
Five lost, reborn.

The abbot ordered this abomination pumiced, and yet within hours the ink on the offending page returned, stubborn and bold. The master of copyists stripped the page, carried it to the trash heap outside the stone walls, and burned the offending vellum, intoning prayers of exorcism before spreading its ashes over the bones and offal.

But neither spider nor poem would die. Someone had copied those lines, with subtle variations, on scraps of vellum and wood and even on shards of pottery, no one knew how many times, and pressed them into the chinks between the abbey stones and elsewhere. In old structures and homes across the island the copies would continue to be found, now and again, until the Vikings arrived. But before the Vikings, manuscripts from Iona became less and less trustworthy, until copying was stopped and all newer copies were either burned or stored under lock and key, for none could be sure that *all* copies back to the beginning were not tainted, the minds of even expert readers being imperfect to the task of total recall of so many pages.

The abbey was closed and the most valuable and beautiful books transported elsewhere.

No one knew what the poem meant, yet for years, scholars claimed the spider and its errors could be removed for good, if that secret were to be discovered. Who were the three, and why did they live in ash and dread, and what apocalypse would resurrect just five corpses from their graves? (For some versions had as the final line, "Raising five dead.")

And why all the concern, why the whispers and stories and frantic efforts to shrive and cleanse? For it was after all only an eight-legged bogey, tiny though fierce; none had been bitten or in any way injured by its journeys over the copied words. And those manuscripts had likely not passed through antiquity unchanged, having been scribed by so many diverse hands through the centuries, in different languages and different nations; even in Saracen lands, where error must be the rule.

Some—heretics no doubt—still insisted that the spider was a servant of God and simply marked with its legs the proper corrections, based on memories of errors it had witnessed long before.

But doubtless God would never have assigned such a task to loathsome vermin.

Ginny closed the book, frowning deeply. That did it. She'd had enough of Bidewell and his obscurities.

Ignoring her fear, she pulled back the steel bars, undid the bolts, and tugged open the door to the loading dock. The night air was cool and damp and smelled faintly of exhaust. Only a few cars traveled this way after six. Rain had passed several hours before and now the evening sky, still bright with dusk, was clear and intensely blue.

Ginny stepped onto the ramp and stared up with hungry, grateful eyes, as if she could fold and stash away the entire sky, keep it beside her always . . . not a book in sight, anywhere.

She examined the shadows in the small, empty parking lot. Nobody watching. Stiff, still not sure what she would do, she walked like a marionette down the ramp to the open gate, jerking her head to look up, look back.

A few more feet, a couple of yards . . .

Time to regain her strength, her resolve—to do what she was born to do. She had lost all confidence in her ability to walk between raindrops. Why had she ever come here in the first place? The clinic—the doctor—she couldn't think clearly, her ears were buzzing so, and her heart felt as if it might explode in her chest.

They never give up, you know. Once you make that call, they're always waiting.

She murmured, "I wish I could fly away. *They're* keeping me here."

You're keeping me here.

"Just walk!"

Down at the corner, beyond the long, dark warehouse wall, a stoplight turned green, yellow, red, then green again. The sky darkened. The street was deserted.

The air smelled fresh and empty.

For the first time in two weeks, she searched for a more fortunate side branch—sent ahead her ethereal feelers for the nearest, safest parallel, a colder, fresher stream.

Something interrupted her concentration. She looked down. Minimus wound between her legs, tail like a soft finger against her calves. The cat looked across the road, then butted her ankle.

The thin man with the silver dollars, the smoky female. Are they still out there?

"You don't know anything," Ginny said. "Don't you *ever* want to get out?"

The cat bumped her again. Things weren't so bad—they were friends. Did they not share mice, did she not have those elegantly marked boxes of books to investigate?

She pushed the gate open and sidled through.

The feelers upriver reported back: no fresh streams left, not for her, not for anyone. She had to stay on this island of peace or face again the horrible thing, the spinning, swallowing, impossibly white, impossibly *female* thing to which the pair had tried to deliver her. Tears streaming, Ginny turned to go back in. Then she heard music from miles away, flowing gently south on the breeze.

Come out and play.

Her fingers let go of the gate. One backward step and she stood in the middle of the sidewalk, arms spread like wings. The gate tapped the lock. The lock snicked shut.

Minimus remained behind the wire.

Whoever Ginny was, wherever she was, *this* was the act that had always defined her: getting out, leaving, turning onto a different path, whatever the danger.

The cat watched with round deep eyes.

"I won't be long," Ginny said. "Tell Mr. Bidewell . . ." And then, flushed, laughing at how silly that was, she wiped her eyes and ran north, following the faintest, most enticing music she had ever heard.

———

Bidewell kept an old swayed cot in one corner of his private library. The girl had ignored his advice. There was nothing he could do but wait.

She was more important, far more powerful, than he was—in her way, perhaps now the equal of what was left of Mnemosyne.

He closed his eyes.

The closest thing to love he had ever known—this search for evidence of the ineffable, the track of the mother of all muses, the one who reconciled—who kept the universe in trim. Now slowly being strangled, fading, unable to fulfill her functions.

Haunted across the ages by a hideous shadow.

Bidewell moved through his ritual preparations for sleep, stretching as far as his old muscles would allow, popping joints in spine, shoulders, hips, with grim satisfaction, then slowly lying down, waiting for his pains to negotiate and settle into accord.

A furious scrape and scuffle interrupted his meditation. Between meows and hisses came a clacking and flipping and several sharp chirrups. A cat was chasing prey around the boxes—not a bird, surely, unless it had plastic wings.

Minimus appeared atop a high box against the dark outer wall and jumped to snare something the size of one of Bidewell's pencil cases—something that made an effort at flight, and failed.

Both cat and catch tumbled behind the boxes with a thump. Triumph was invariably followed by delivery. With delivery must come congratulations and reward, a snack. This was their compact, cat to man, man to cat. Bidewell rose to retrieve the box of kibble he kept on a high shelf, away from boxes. He had learned that lesson several times, having to clean up after a sick cat. Minimus, whatever his finer qualities, loved to gorge. Yet he never ate anything that he caught.

A few minutes passed. Bidewell sat at a small desk reserved for gentle reading on sleepless nights, and turned on the old brass lamp. Here, he kept a compact edition of Butler's *The Way of All Flesh*, which, with its acerbic rejection of the mundane, he found suitable. This worn volume, of course, had a pair of concluding chapters not found in any other edition.

Just as Bidewell seated himself, Minimus padded out of the darkness and leaped to the table carrying in his mouth a glistening, jeweled creature. The old man drew in his breath and pushed back his chair. The cat threw him a sidelong look, dropped his catch, and squatted.

The creature—a kind of insect, though ten inches long and with too many legs—had been shocked into immobility. It slowly flexed its long body and shivered a pair of shining wing cases the color of polished dark oak. On the wing cases—part of its natural design—the insect bore a single, ivory-white mark, like a symbol, or a letter in an alphabet Bidewell did not know. It cocked its large head, like a cicada's, and its compound eyes glinted with brilliant blue highlights.

Minimus had done the insect no visible harm, but its movements were feeble. Docile even in distress, it gathered up enough energy to cross to the edge of the desk, where it paused like a clever toy, cocked its head again, and chirped.

Watched closely by both man and cat, it turned and approached a close-packed row of boxwood pencil cases decorated with large Egyptian hieroglyphs.

Minimus licked his paw.

The insect sidled up to the nearest case, then, with a hiss, dropped into an attitude of conformity, of fulfillment—and was still.

The insect was dead.

The cat lost interest and jumped to the floor.

Astonished, Bidewell traced the white symbol with a bony finger. "Not from any time I know," he said.

His texts, hundreds of thousands of them, were acting as a kind of lens, focusing the improbable and retrieving from not so far away, perhaps, those things that would only become likely across a greater fullness of time. A fullness now deteriorating, coming apart in sections—jamming and mixing histories in alarming ways. If nothing more were done, the future would drip-drop into their present like milk from a cracked bottle.

They could reach the end of their meager supply of time within a few days or weeks, and then: confusion, nightmare, loops of repetition; the final surprising, unpredictable dribbles of false opportunity and hope.

Terminus.

Perhaps he was in such a loop now. But the appearance of the girl— the wayward young woman, keeping him moody company—proved he was not. There was still one opportunity, one chance to forestall the inevitable.

She would return. The stones would gather.

All his life he had been anticipating and preparing for this occasion. He felt fear—of course. And a kind of joy. There was real and immediate work to do—connections to make, teams to assemble, children to protect—blessed children. Surely they would come to him like a new family to replace the old, the ones that had failed or vanished—children pushing up now like spring flowers, and so improbable! Better by far than any volume of deviating text.

And of course the predators were here as well.

FOURTEEN ZEROS

CHAPTER 16

The Tiers

Jebrassy felt little regret as he crossed the bridge over the flood channel to the long roads. Having time to himself, time to think, was like leaving a stuffy, crowded niche.

Beyond the end of the bridge, out in the fallow meadows, two small wardens were hunched over, wings folded, inspecting something in the dirt. Jebrassy scratched the side of his head and glanced sideways. A curtain of pale fog shrouded whatever drew their interest. He seldom saw this style of warden in the Tiers—small, glistening gold bodies—and they certainly never engaged with breeds.

But he knew what they were investigating—the remains left by an intrusion. He wanted to turn aside, but instead squinted through the fog—trying to see the half-imagined, shifting figures, invisible masters of the Tiers—the Tall Ones. Jebrassy felt a sting of shame. He was nothing to them—less than a pede to the farmer who loaded it with packages and baskets for market. The teachers taught only what the Tall Ones wanted them to teach—not what any of the breeds actually needed to know. How he hated them all!

There was an old sama in the market—he had visited her once already, just to give voice to his questions: Why did time in the Tiers—the cycles of wakes and sleeps—vary so? What was outside the Tiers, if anything, and why didn't marchers ever return? Questions the teachers never responded to.

Why am I straying?

The sama would not carry tales to others—unlike Khren.

———

It was growing late, she said; she wouldn't have much time. She gave no name; samas never gave their names, often moved between isles and levels in the Tiers, their niches unknown, untraceable. Nobody paid them—they performed their work for food left over in the market, telling fortunes, leading prayers, treating minor injuries—the wardens took care of anything more serious. They were generally poorly dressed, often dirty and smelly, and this old female was no exception.

She drew up the blankets around her narrow market stall—consultations with samas always took place in an awkward crouch, blankets raised to block the light and prying eyes—then she pushed aside her crusted bowl, squatted before Jebrassy, and thrust a thin bright stick into the dirt between them. The stick lit up her brown face and made her experienced black eyes gleam like broken glass.

Her questions, as always, were blunt. "Did your sponsors kick you out because you fancy yourself a warrior, hanging with punks—or because you are straying?"

Jebrassy leaned forward and splayed his fingers on the ground. Samas could ask whatever they wanted—they were *outside* normal expectations. "They aren't my true sponsors. Mer and Per were taken."

"Taken, how?"

"A nightmare came." This was a euphemism; Jebrassy was ashamed to use it.

The sama did not show any sign of understanding—it was not her job to understand. Who could understand what happened during an intrusion? "How sad," she said.

"The new ones sponsored me for a few hundred wakes. Then they got tired of me," Jebrassy said.

"Why?"

"My rudeness. My curiosity."

"Where do you sleep?"

"Sometimes, under a bridge. Other times, I hide out in the clusters on the flood channel walls."

"The old Webla neighborhood? High up among the false books?"

"Nearby. Lots of empty niches. Sometimes I stay with a friend." He tapped his knee. "I find shelter."

"Has anyone ever spoken to your visitor, the other?"

Jebrassy lifted one finger, yes. "My friend tells me about him, sometimes."

"But you don't remember what was said."

Two fingers circling, no.

"Do you know others who stray?"

His hairline flexed. "Maybe. A glow I've just met once. She . . . she wants to get together later. I don't know why." Jebrassy let that thought hang between them.

"You have no value?"

"I'm a warrior, a vagrant, no family."

The sama hooted low amusement. "You don't understand glows, do you?"

He glared.

"You say you're unworthy. But not because you stray. Why, then?"

"I want to know things. Earlier, if I couldn't join a march, I thought I would fight the Tall Ones and escape the Tiers."

"Huh! Do you ever see Tall Ones?"

"No," he said. "But I know they're there."

"You think you're special, wanting to escape?"

"I don't care whether I'm special or not."

"Do you think this glow is dim?" the sama asked. She hadn't moved since they squatted and started talking, but his own knees hurt.

"She doesn't look dim."

"Why do you want to meet with her?" She scratched her arm with a filthy fingertip.

"It would be interesting to find someone—anyone—who thinks like me."

"You're a warrior," she observed. "You take pride in that."

He looked away and drew back his lips. "War is play. Nothing here is real."

"We get delivered by the umbers and we learn from our sponsors and teachers. We work, we love, we get taken away when the Bleak Warden comes. More young are made. Isn't that real enough?"

"There's more outside. I can feel it."

She rocked gently on her ankles. "What else do you dream about? When you're not straying."

"The intrusion that took Mer and Per. I saw it. I was just out of crèche. After, the wardens made me sleep for a while, and I felt better, but I still dream about it. I thought it had come for me, but it took *them* . . . doesn't make sense."

"No? Why?"

"Intrusions come and go. The wardens put up shades and fog, clean up, and it's over. Teachers just keep quiet. Nobody knows where the intrusions come from, what they're doing here—even why they're called 'intrusions.' Do they come from outside? From the Chaos—whatever that is? I want to know more."

"What more is there to know?"

Jebrassy got up.

The sama rocked. "I don't offer comfort. I fix letterbug nips, pede pinches, sometimes I fix bad dreams—but I can't help *these*."

"I don't want comfort. I want answers."

"Do you even know the right questions?"

Jebrassy said, too loudly, "Nobody ever taught me what to ask."

Outside, the noise of the market dwindled. He heard a plaintive whine—a hungry meadow pede tethered in a stall, waiting for its tweenlight supper of stalks and jule.

The sama poked out her wide lips and fell back from her squat, then stretched her legs and arms and let out a deep, sighing breath. He thought his visit was over, but she did not draw aside the blankets that curtained the booth.

"I'll go," he said.

"Quiet," she advised. "My legs hurt. I'm wearing down, young breed. Not too long before the Bleak Warden comes. Stay a bit longer— for me." She patted the ground. "I'm not done trying to riddle you. Why come to a poor old sama?"

Jebrassy sat and gazed uncomfortably at the thatched roof. "This glow, if I get interested in her, and she in me . . . it won't be right. She has sponsors. I don't."

"Did *you* approach *her*?"

"No."

The sama pulled a sachet of red jule from her robe, wrapped it, and tied it with chafe cord, making a broothe for steeping in hot water. "Drink this. Relax. After you stray, take notes. Do you have a shake cloth?"

"I can find one."

"Ah—you mean, steal one. Borrow one from your friend, if he has one, or from the glow, if you see her again. Write it all down and come back to show me."

"Why?"

"Because we both need to know what questions to ask." The sama stood, drew back the blankets, and let in the failing gray light from the ceil. The market was closed and almost empty. "Perhaps dreams are like flapping a shake cloth—you erase all the words you didn't choose. Young warrior, we're done, for now."

She pushed him out of her stall.

A very young glow, fresh from the crèche—tiny red bump still prominent on her forehead, swad-boots wrapped around her tiny feet—stood before a shuttered stall, feeding a hungry pede. The pede curled its glossy black segments around her ankles, wriggling its many legs. The young glow squirmed and looked up at Jebrassy with an expression of tickled delight.

He touched his nose, sharing the moment.

To take a partner, inherit or be assigned a niche, live in the Tiers in silent contentment, ignoring things you couldn't understand . . . sponsor a young one . . .

Why want more?

He had seen how much the intrusion concerned the wardens. None of this was going to last long, he could feel it in his bones.

———

On his way to the Diurns, Jebrassy stopped, peered at the ground, then knelt to examine the quality of the gravel that lined the path. Until now he had never given much thought to the substances that made up his world. He compared the gravel to the material used in most of the bridges, asking himself how this stony stuff differed from his own flesh, from the crops in the fields—and from the flexible stuff of the wardens, which he had had a number of opportunities to feel as he was being hauled away from one or another altercation.

Gravel, crops, flesh—not the same as the exposed isles beneath the Tiers: silver-gray, neither warm nor cold, but strangely neutral to the touch. Yet that silver-gray stuff constituted the foundation and the walls and probably the ceil, the limits of his world.

Again, Jebrassy needed desperately to know more—to understand. In that regard, he differed from nearly all the breeds he knew, so much so that he wondered if there had been a mistake in his making, if the umbers had dropped him on his head after hauling him out of the crèche.

Stork.

He shook his head sharply at that unknown word, that difficult memory of a sound.

You're delivered by the umbers—they're like storks, right? They leave you under a cabbage leaf.

"Shut up."

His bare feet took him farther down the path.

You're like an animal in a zoo. But you don't even know what a zoo is. Why are they keeping you here?

Jebrassy did not *dislike* his visitor, and certainly did not fear him, but these residues offered no answers. When Jebrassy strayed—when the visitor took over—typically, nothing happened, as Khren had pointed out.

"I don't know what you are," Jebrassy growled under his breath. "But I wish you'd *go away*."

He stood by the bridge, looking over the still and covered meadows market and the beginning of the long roads which fanned out to the far limits of fields and walls surrounding the Tiers, their neighborhood—half a day's brisk journey across, overarched by the ceil, the curtain wall, the moist wall, their vertex at one extremity—and the long round wall opposite—most difficult to reach, but under and through which ran the flood channels.

Sometimes the teachers referred to the round wall as the outer, and the other two as inner.

All of them—limits.

Barriers to curiosity.

CHAPTER 17

The wardens had spread mist and black curtains around the site of the intrusion, at the outer perimeter of a field of chafe sprouts in the shadow of the Moist Wall. They now hovered, awaiting Ghentun's inspection.

Behind the curtains, an irregular section of the chafe field measuring about a third of an acre had been turned into fine snowy crystals, primordial matter converted to something different, deadly or useless: the hallmark of the Typhon, perverse, even malevolent. In the middle of the crystals, a male breed—a farmer, judging from his stiff scraps of clothing—had been carelessly rearranged.

The farmer had still been alive when the wardens found him.

"Did you kill this one?" Ghentun asked the lead warden.

"He was suffering, Keeper. We summoned a Bleak Warden and terminated him. No one has touched him since."

The Bleak Warden itself—slender, with a red thorax and shiny black lift-wings, now lay deactivated beside the farmer. White crystals cluttered its frozen, bent limbs. It would have to be disposed of, along with the body, the soil, and all else that the intrusion had touched.

Ghentun glanced toward the straight road that led from the unused inner precincts—the Diurns and the apex bridge—all the way across the meadows and fields to the narrowed, arched haft where the first isle absorbed the Tenebros flood channel. A few breeds were still about in the tweenlight. All of them avoided the fog.

In the seventy-five city years since he requested his interview with the Librarian, Ghentun estimated he had lost over two thousand breeds. These invasions into the lowest levels of the Kalpa were now occurring once or twice every dozen sleep-wakes. Most seemed to target breeds—those who saw, who perceived, in the oldest ways. More often than not, the wardens investigated and drew their conclusions without his presence, but Ghentun was beginning to doubt their accuracy. He could not discount the possibility that the wardens were being manipulated by the city officers, Eidolons loyal to the Astyanax, who in all these thousands of centuries had paid little attention to the Tiers.

In the Kalpa's higher levels and more prosperous urbs, the reality generators seemed better able to protect the vast majority of citizens. Intrusions rarely occurred there, but perhaps it was because the Chaos had no interest in Eidolons. Still, the more intrusions there were in the Tiers, the more danger there might be for the higher urbs—real, metaphysical danger, and political danger for the Astyanax.

Once the poor farmer had been removed, the whited soil was scraped and stored in sealed containers by small gray wardens. As before, the containers, the victim, and all the wardens who had touched them—tainted by that contact—would be locked away in the vaults deep below the flood channels. Ghentun had visited those vaults several times during the past century. They had been unspeakable in their fermenting, noxious morphing.

"We will have to *export* this one, Keeper," the lead warden confided as Ghentun knelt beside the contorted body. "The vaults are nearly full."

This was almost too much for Ghentun to bear. The tainted evidence of the intrusion would have to be shot out into the Chaos.

CHAPTER **18**

The tweenlight had turned tawny gold, ushering in flat wispy clouds and the muddy shades that came before a sleep. The lowering flush of light was so diffuse and universal that Jebrassy cast only a faint hint of shadow. Everything around him—old and abandoned—seemed lost in a smoky dream.

The Diurns lay flush against the curtain wall, accessible by a long and sometimes treacherous hike past the end of the abandoned Apex Causeway where it connected the tips of the three isles—the plateaus that supported the stacked Tiers. The curtain wall, in turn, ascended three miles to the overarching ceil, upon which the lights and darks of wake and sleep played out in endless, faded procession, as they had for tens of thousands of lives.

All this fell within one sweep of his eye from where Jebrassy now walked along the causeway. He also glanced from side to side to make sure there were no screeches or wardens waiting in the shadows to nab sleep-hikers. The wardens were particularly vigilant after an intrusion.

Behind him, the causeway stretched more than a mile toward the bridges that had once carried the old neighborhood's traffic over the Tartaros, the larger of the two channels that separated the blocs. Four slender, twisted spires flanked the conclusion of the causeway, five hundred feet tall and needled through with fluted pipes that, it was said, had once produced deep and awesome sounds—music. Whether the spires were original to the Diurns or had been added later was unknown—there were so many tottering, muddled layers of old breed construction here, contributing to the dangers of the entire precinct, which had long ago been condemned and blocked by debris and screech sentinels. Most of these had themselves long since collapsed, failed, or were simply forgotten, and were no longer necessary, since few of the ancient breed felt the urge to come here. There was enough faded grandeur in the inhabited parts of the Tiers to satisfy anybody.

At the apex where the Curtain Wall met the Moist Wall, spread an amphitheater that could once have seated thirty or forty thousand of the ancient breed. As a stripling, Jebrassy had been here twice, demonstrating his bravery or at least his persistence—climbing the debris, evading the few sentinels that were still active, making his way down the dirt-encrusted, sloping aisles between the risers to the gallery, a roofed labyrinth that stretched for several hundred yards to the proscenium.

The Diurns were visible from several points in the gallery where the roof had fallen. Jebrassy, working his way once more through the stone maze, speculated as he had before that this might have been the site of old initiation rituals, and was certainly not part of the original construction. Even upon his first visit, the labyrinth had proved simple enough to solve—a left-handed maze with a distal twist, made easy by ages of decay.

Is the glow testing my resolve? Poor test.

Retracing the path he had taken before, still clear in memory—any adventure, however disappointing, was etched deep—he came to a huge gap in the gallery roof. This rewarded him with an unobstructed view of the Sounding Wall, a name that meant nothing to him—a mottled gray expanse hundreds of feet high, blank but for eroded holes and corroded extrusions where large things had once been set or fastened.

A few more minutes of climbing and threading the last of the gallery's barriers brought him to the base of the amphitheater's Sounding Wall, and from there it was just a snap until he stood in the immense, glimmering shadow of the curved Wall of Light.

Jebrassy took a moment to catch his breath. The immense screen was streaked and crusted top to bottom with dust and soot—not from smoke, but from the accumulated miasma of thousands of generations of living beings. At the far end, an ornate and partly collapsed partition of stone and masonry—its highest remnant still towering hundreds of feet above the gallery—had left a pile of rubble that spilled onto the proscenium and the lowest sweep of the amphitheater, where all the seats had long since been stripped or rotted away. Clearly, many ancient breeds had tried to solve the mystery of this place—or to use it for their own purposes, adding their own masonry structures. Most of their efforts, like the original, had come to ruin—even greater ruin, since, Jebrassy thought, it wouldn't take much to scrub the screen, rebuild or replace the seats in the galleries, and restore at least the outward appearance of the original design.

But no one now living could match the endurance and ingenuity of the Wall of Light's original builders.

And who were they? Tall Ones?

"I don't know," Jebrassy murmured to the residue's soft question. "Be quiet."

High above and beyond the amphitheater, a breeze across the pipes embedded in the four spires blew a low, breathy chuckle, like hundreds of amused voices.

The Diurns themselves were just left of the screen—three merging ellipses, each over a hundred yards across, on which various displays still labored, it was said, to tell the time in ways that no one alive could fathom, even if anyone could have read the moving and broken and scattered lines of symbols within each ellipse.

This was the only theory that had ever made sense—that the Diurns had once been a huge timekeeper, attached to the side of an even larger public and ceremonial display that had ages before fallen into disuse.

To the right of the Diurns, the immensity of the Wall of Light— a thousand feet wide and half that in height—still gleamed with softly passing gleams, haphazard attempts at images, all repeating at hourly intervals, broken by faults that no longer even attempted to flicker, but hung dark and dead.

The Diurns had looked thus since the earliest times known to the ancient breeds.

Jebrassy leaned back as far as his neck would allow, to take in the whole of the screen, then turned swiftly and stared out over the amphitheater, as if to glimpse forty thousand ghosts—the citizens who had once sat or stood there, transfixed by what must have once been a magnificent gathering place, a crowded exchange of stories.

This theory grew in him as he absorbed the setting through older, presumably more sophisticated eyes: that once information and gossip had been shared communally, thousands attending at once, receiving instructions, warnings, and (possibly) news about events in the Tiers—headlines and banners, visions of the world beyond the Kalpa, now denied.

Just a guess, but it felt right.

The inner voice expressed no opinion.

The ruins, with their grime and patina of age—common in the abandoned precincts behind the Tiers—conveyed their own special message. Along with the flickering quality of time itself, the intrusions, and declining populations—evident from empty niches and long-deserted neighborhoods—the architectural decay proved that whatever the Kalpa might once have been, it was no longer in its prime.

The Tall Ones were getting weaker. The long bondage of the ancient breeds might soon come to an end. Then, all who wished could pass under the round wall, through the pumping stations at the outflow of the flood channels, walk beneath the arches and through the gates, cross the border of the real, into the final freedom of the Chaos . . .

A beautiful dream.

The shuffle of Jebrassy's feet as he padded back and forth, glancing high at the vague, fragmented words . . . these small sounds bounced back from the walls with portentous distortions.

A loud crack and rumble to the left of the screen announced another fall of masonry. Large stones and pieces of rusted metal rolled and thumped in a dusty sift at the far side of the gallery. The whole prospect angered and frustrated him—lost knowledge, failed communications, pretenses to educating the masses . . . like all the false books that taunted breeds who searched the deserted hallways of the high levels in the Tiers—endless shelves, their titles fascinating, when he could read them. But none could be pried loose. He had tried thousands of times since childhood. The books were solid, cold, useless.

If we're toys or tools, he thought, nobody much cares anymore what we do or think. Maybe they don't even care if we live or die . . .

He did a slow dance, listening for the echoes, and touched his nose at this folly.

Better folly than boredom and safety.

"Hello!"

The single word drifted high and leaped back, acquiring a spooky rattle. Jebrassy turned to see a shadowy female perched on the edge of the proscenium.

She stood up in the dim light cast by the screen.

Jebrassy let out his breath in a relieved grunt.

"What did you think I was?" Tiadba asked.

"You're late."

"Nice dance. Why did you come here—just because I asked?"

"I've been here before," he said. "It's no big deal. Do I get to ask questions, too?"

"Certainly."

"Breed females like sturdy, normal men with sturdy, normal attitudes. What makes you different?"

Tiadba strolled along the base of the screen, skirting the piles of rubble. "Not all of us have slow blood," she said. She looked down at something by her feet, stopped, and sucked in her breath. Her shoulders tensed.

Jebrassy joined her. She had found a shriveled body—a young breed, probably male. It lay curled in the rubble, covered with dust and flakes of crusted veneer that had drifted down from the screen.

Tiadba knelt to brush the dead breed's clothing. "Some of us go seeking . . . a few dozen each generation, troublemakers, disturbers of the peace," she said. "Not even the Bleak Warden found this one. You and I could end the same way. Does that frighten you?"

Jebrassy twirled two fingers clockwise.

Tiadba did the same, agreeing. "It might frighten us," she said firmly, "but it wouldn't stop us."

"You still haven't answered my question."

"Some say we're toys or pets. I know we're more important than that. We're the end of a long experiment. That's why we stray. The Tall Ones want us to."

"And how can *you* know—how can you be sure?"

"If I show you, you must make three promises."

"You like things in threes, don't you?"

"Triangles are stable. Females seek stability—you said so yourself."

Jebrassy drew his brows together.

"You must promise you will never tell another."

"And?"

"You must promise you will use what you learn to guide all our explorations—not just your own. You will not seek glory alone."

This smarted. He had hoped to do just that. "And?"

"You must not go on a march by yourself or with anyone else—not right away. You will consent to be chosen—or you will stay in the Tiers."

"Nothing is worth that. I'd . . ." He shuddered. "I'd go mad if I thought I couldn't leave."

The desperate slant in Tiadba's eyes told Jebrassy that he had made a serious mistake. "Go on, then," she told him. "I'll stay here and follow a little later. We shouldn't be seen together. When I get back, I'll alert the wardens about this poor explorer."

Jebrassy turned and sat on the edge of the proscenium. What could she possibly offer that would be worth such sacrifice, such slavery?

"There *is* going to be a youth march," Tiadba said to his back, her voice carrying an odd quaver. "It's being assembled very carefully . . . not quickly enough. We're all impatient. A lot of preparations have to be made. But soon, it will happen."

Jebrassy had heard rumors of groups handpicked, trained, sent down the flood channels. Rumors were all he had ever heard.

"There's a plan, a leader," Tiadba said. "Someone we trust."

This had the ring of truth. He had always wondered how anyone could survive in the unknown outside the Kalpa without training, supplies, or equipment.

Tiadba sat next to him, startling him again, her movements were so quiet and graceful. She glanced left, eyes half lidded in peaceful drowse. With a little shudder, she moved closer and leaned her head on his shoulder. Her touch was electric. His heart thumped and his hands warmed.

"You won't lie," she said. "And you'll never let us down."

"How can you be so sure about everything?" he asked, trying to be abrupt.

"Because I know you. We've met before," she said. "Don't you feel it?"

He got up, shook out his arms, and started to walk away. "Too many promises, not enough in return."

Tiadba ran after him, wide-awake, lifted his hand, then pulled on his fingers—hard. "Promise!" she demanded. "You *know* you must."

"Let go!" He tried to break free, and she grabbed his shoulders with a small shout. They began to roll across the dusty stage. She was stronger—females of the breed could be that way, wiry and sweetly scented. That scent was their greatest weapon. It made him much less willing to fight.

"Stop it!" he shouted as she held him down on the floor. Her face pressed close, eyes intense. They had covered their clothes with dust.

She frowned so hard that he wanted to look away in shame. "Don't be stupid. Promise! You know you will." Then, in a harsh whisper, lips almost touching his . . ."*Promise!*"

"Give me something, give me hope," he said, his voice resentful and raw. "Promise *me* I'll go on the next march!"

She rolled off and got to her feet, brushing her clothes. "I'm not the one who chooses."

"You say we know each other—but you obviously don't know me at all."

Tiadba placed her hands together and tipped her fingers against her forehead, eyes closed.

"You're taking advantage," he said. "You pick on lonely outcasts . . . you're like a pretty bunch of chafe shoots held out for a pede, to lure them into the fields." He pulled down her hands and stared directly into her eyes. There *was* a connection—he could not explain it, and that angered him more. He let her go.

"If you're so bold, why haven't you run away on your own?" she asked. "What's stopping you?"

He blustered, "Someone has to watch for wardens. I agree with one thing—it takes *planning*."

"What if I tell you about the difficulties, just a little about what's involved?"

"You'd betray your people?"

"I trust you."

"You shouldn't. I'm not responsible."

"Is that what your sponsors tell you?"

"My mer and per are gone," Jebrassy said.

She drew up close again. She was nothing if not persistent. "I know," she said.

"An intrusion took them."

"I know."

"How do you know?"

"Because you spoke with our leader in the market. But before that, I told her about you. She gave me permission to meet you here."

This rendered Jebrassy speechless. That a sama—a healer and listener—would betray his confidence as easily as Khren was almost beyond belief.

Almost. Time itself was changing, there were so many intrusions—and the wardens weren't acting the way they used to. He could almost see the Tall Ones walking among them. Why should he trust anyone or anything?

Tiadba felt his distress and again lightly gripped his shoulders. "I'll tell you as much as I know. You don't even have to promise. It's that important."

"Did *she* tell you to say that?"

"No," Tiadba said. "My risk."

Jebrassy rolled his head in misery. "I don't know who I am or where I'll end up. That's why I went to a sama in the first place." He shuddered.

Tiadba struggled to find her next words. "Two names. Tell me what they mean. I'll tell you one name, and you tell me the other."

"Names?"

"Ginny," she said.

Jebrassy backed off. Before he could stop himself, he said, "Jack."

She looked at him, triumphant—and scared. "Two funny, ugly names," she said. "Not from the Tiers. We *know* each other, Jebrassy. We know each other from somewhere else. It's as if we've known each other forever. I've never felt that with anyone else." Her eyes crossed with the intensity of her emotion. "Some wake or another, one of us will be in very bad trouble. I think I will be the one who needs you. And you will come for me."

Jebrassy groaned and got down on his knees, suddenly weak. It was true. He could feel the intensity of grief already—the knowledge that he would have her, that he would be faithful and bond to this female, and that he would lose her far too quickly.

Out of sequence.

Out of control.

Our lives are not our own.

"It doesn't make any sense," he whispered.

She knelt in front of him and they placed their foreheads together, hands on each other's temples. "Promise me the three promises, and I'll share—I'll show you."

The visitor—a useless residue inside of him—seemed to kick up in his head, trying to force him to make a decision.

Jebrassy stroked her cheek.

They swore in the way they had learned as children, repeating the words to each other over and over, until both had them precisely memorized.

Tiadba then whistled a short tune of sealing.

It was done. Jebrassy had no idea what had just happened. His eyes slowly focused. Tiadba had moved off and stood nearby, staring up. She pointed to an open half cup pushed out from the far right-hand edge of the screen, tiny in comparison to the total span, like a private box seat, but with the worst view of all. "See that?"

"A bump. It's always been there. What about it?"

"They used to call it the Valeria," Tiadba said. "It's where they organized and controlled the shows. I found a way to get up there, from behind the Wall of Light. Would you like to see?"

"It's full of dirt, right?"

"I cleaned it."

He struggled to steady his voice and recover his attitude. "Might be interesting . . . but why so important?"

"The big screen is broken," Tiadba said. "But up there is a *little* screen. Up there we can connect to a catalog of the shows they used to put on in the Diurns. I've watched a few. I think they tell a history. Not ours, exactly. The history of those who were here before us."

"I still don't know how that can help the marchers."

"Aren't you curious, just a little bit? To see things no other breed has seen, nor anyone else, for millions of wakes? To learn how we came to be here, and . . . maybe . . . why? We're so ignorant," she sighed. "And that . . ."

"That's the third thing we have in common," Jebrassy said. "You should also know I'm impulsive. Some say I'm stupid, but I'm really just stubborn. And I care too much."

"Four, five, and . . ."

"Six things we have in common?" he finished.

She drew herself up, standing just a little taller than Jebrassy, not uncommon among the ancient breed. "If the wardens find us, or learn that we know . . . I think they would stop us. They would give us up to the Tall Ones. Understand?"

He nodded.

"Come with me, then. Part of the old gallery fell down a while back, right next to the proscenium."

Jebrassy followed for about fifty yards, and then clambered after her into a darkened pit formed by the walls of a masonry chamber whose roof had collapsed. A small hatch hung open in the base of the proscenium, still partially blocked.

"Are you afraid of tight places?" Tiadba asked as she removed a few stones and bricks.

"I don't think so," Jebrassy said. "As long as there's a way out."

"Well, here's a tunnel. It stretches behind the screen for quite a ways, and then there's a narrow shaft going up. I think there was a lift nearby—but it's not working. To go up there, we have to climb a tiny spiral with lots of tiny steps."

"Show me," Jebrassy said.

Gleeful, Tiadba took his hand and tugged him forward.

TEN ZEROS

CHAPTER 19

Seattle

Ginny had followed the music for miles and now, her long hike finished, she stared up in awe at what she had found: a wide banner painted in red and black circus letters, announcing LE BOULEVARD DU CRIME.

A collision of sounds filled the air—hurdy-gurdies, calliopes, electric guitars, flutes and trombones and trumpets—a screeching but melodious wreck of noise that ascended in triumph to shimmer the clouds in the starlit sky.

A wide smile crossed her flushed face.

"Hey, pretty lady!" shouted a crimson and blue clown balancing a huge nimbus of white hair. "Join the Busker Jam! Certified insane, we am! We're better than Fair, we're not even there!"

The clown led a toothy, grinning monkey that stalked with anxious delicacy on yard-long stilts.

Busker Jam filled several long acres of grass and gravel overlooking the glinting obsidian waters of Elliot Bay, marked at the northern end by a big grain elevator, flanked on the land side by gray and brown apartment buildings and condos, and tapering at the southern end into a sculpture garden—now closed—and a lot filled with a churning puzzle of parking cars. Red and yellow tents flapped and snapped in a light breeze. Food trucks and trailers clustered near the parking lot.

A veering, snaking line of performance rings of all sizes poked up between the food trailers and the grain elevator, each distinctively labeled: THÉÂTRE-LYRIQUE, CIRQUE OLYMPIQUE, FOLIES DRAMATIQUE, FU-NAMBULES, THÉÂTRE DES PYGMÉS, THÉÂTRE PATRIOTIQUE, DÉLASSEMENTS-COMIQUES, and so on, stretching out of sight.

Ginny had never seen so many *artistes*—clowns, musicians, acrobats, magicians, and of course mimes—and she wanted to laugh and cry at once. It was so much like the girlhood she could not remember, but wanted with a desperate ache to return to.

————

As Jack rode along the bike path, searching for familiar faces, jauntily swinging his front tire to keep a slow balance, he spotted a practice circle, and within the circle: Flashgirl, the Blue Lizard, Joe-Jim, and other old friends warming up for a turn in the rings.

Hundreds of patrons milled about in clumps, laughing, applauding, oohing and aahing, dropping bills and change into boxes and hats. It looked like a clink-paff night for his friends and colleagues. Buskers called a good show clink-paff—the sound of coins falling into thick piles of bills.

In the first ring, T-square—dressed in a flame-red leotard—arranged three firepots and a circular roller-coaster-style ramp for his unicycle. On his head he wore a bright blue T-square jutting above a huge pair of wing-tip glasses studded with rhinestones. During his act, he said not a word, simply doing acrobatics on the unicycle and riding through brilliant and startling flashes of fire from his pots. Jack knew what the marks did not: that T-square would soon set his hat on fire and require the assistance of a prestationed shill—his daughter, a savvy and quick nine-year-old who would extinguish him with a spray of foam from a chrome-plated canister.

Needing no ring, Somnambule the Sleepified worked a series of startling card tricks, then struck a frozen pose, leaning into an imaginary wind with kerchief flying and hat about to blow off his head—cradling his cheek against nested hands and snoring until the next act began.

He winked as Jack cycled past. Jack tipped a salute.

Flashgirl did not use fire, but in her yellow and orange jumpsuit, with sultry countenance and angry, superfeminist patter, everything else about her was inflammatory. Her routine consisted of juggled illusions with knives and wands, frenetic dance, and jabbing verbal assaults on male members of the audience—whose sexist attitudes she blamed for the failure of her magic. Nearly everyone laughed; she was good. Not once had Jack seen Flashgirl actually anger an audience member. Still, at forty-five, she was slowing down. He thought from the sag of her shoulders and subtle gasping as she danced that her lifelong habit of smoking might be taking a toll.

Still, buskers worked sick or well—he hoped she was just fighting a cold.

Jack knew where to find the performers' zone, at the end of a short path winding up to the small changing trailer, marked off by stakes and ribbon. The moon-shadow of the huge grain elevator dominated this end of the park, and here, half in lunar shade, Joe-Jim squatted on a big white bucket, eating fruit salad from a plastic tray. He spotted Jack, and for a moment gave him a blank look.

He doesn't remember.

Then something seemed to connect—to click in his head—and Joe-Jim waved his fork. "Brother Jack, back on track!" he called, spraying bits of orange.

"Whom do I address tonight?" Jack asked, shaking hands busker-style, with a sharp clap of palms and a hook-and-wriggle of three fingers.

"Tonight we are Jim. Joe's on vacation in Chicago. Be back in a week. Calls me every day to check in."

Joe-Jim's routine was to perform acrobatics with an invisible partner—mime in the middle of the air, to all purposes, and at his best, he astonished. He was only a few years older than Jack but looked older, and also looked as if he had not been eating well. His eyes were haunted, his high cheeks were dark yellow, and both cheeks and chin bristled with two days' growth of beard.

One of his wrists had been tightly secured with a dirty Ace bandage. A lateral cut, Jack guessed—not a serious attempt.

"Why aren't you jamming?" Joe-Jim asked. He insisted on being called by both names, whoever was actually present. Few in any audience could know that whichever character, Joe or Jim, performed on any given day, was half of a genuine split personality.

"Rats went on strike," Jack said.

"Feeling our age, the rats and I," Joe-Jim said. "Not good times, Jack." The perennial pessimist, Joe-Jim pulled out a pack of cigarettes and tapped one into his palm. "Keeps the demons at bay," he said, and lit up with a squint.

"About those demons," Jack said. "Seen any lately?"

"No more than usual." Joe-Jim pulled up another bucket, inviting Jack to sit. The acrobat-mime had suffered through a lot—muggings, broken love, weeks and months in and out of institutions. Jack suspected he had at most a year or two before the streets and poverty—and the demons—snatched what was left of his health. Busking was a hard life.

"Do you ever run around empty?" Jack asked. "Moments when both Joe and Jim have left the building?"

Joe-Jim blew out a coil of smoke. "I couldn't do my act with *two* invisible guys. Why?"

"Just asking," Jack said.

"No, but it bugs me when we fight. I can't get the invisible guy to do his part." He smiled slyly. "You're about to say, I've adapted rather well."

"You've adapted rather well."

"*I* certainly think so. I could never work in a cubicle, with my mates wondering who would show up day to day." He dropped his cigarette half smoked on the grass and ground it down with his slipper heel. His features grew stiff. "Heads up. Here comes the shadow that walks like a man."

A tall, emaciated anatomy wearing a top hat and formal attire—the suit split equally black and white top to bottom, the back adorned with a metallic blue skeleton—sauntered toward them, his gait that of a zombie Fred Astaire. His face was white and his eyes were ringed with black, and he radiated a deadly gloom.

He ignored Joe-Jim but homed in on Jack with hungry precision.

"Back off, Sepulcher," Jack said, rising with fists clenched.

Joe-Jim looked away and inward.

Sepulcher pinned Jack with his sharp, deep eyes—famished, but not for food. "How's your father, Jeremy?" he asked, his voice as resonant and lost as a bull in a cave.

"Still dead," Jack said. He had changed his name years ago—everyone knew that.

"I'd forgotten," Sepulcher said. "Always good to forget unpleasantness. Then—I saw you, and it all came back."

Sepulcher never seemed to attract much of an audience or make much money. Some on the circuit had speculated he was a rich eccentric with a really bad act, which consisted of standing still for hours on a street corner, his eyes following people as they walked past—and occasionally letting loose with a whistled dirge.

Some buskers—the worst of a generally good lot—were actively creepy.

Sepulcher's real name was Nathan Silverstein.

"I worked with your father, Jack," he said. That was a fact. Silverstein and Jack's father had worked as a comedy team fifteen years ago.

"I remember," Jack said. He turned to say good-bye to Joe-Jim, but Sepulcher grabbed his shoulder in a vise of sharp, bony fingers.

"I didn't want to come here," Sepulcher growled. He sucked in his cheeks and dropped his thin white-lined brows. "These people *hate* me."

"I wonder why," Jack said.

"But you, young son of an old friend, *you* have something I need."

Jack looked down. "Let me go, or I'll break your arm."

Sepulcher let go, but his white-daubed digits flexed. The index and thumb made a space, three inches. "This big. Dark, pitted, shiny. Burned by time. A crooked black rock with a red eye. *They* want me to find it."

Jack stared the man down, his teeth grinding.

"To pay a debt," Sepulcher added. "You have it, I know you do."

Jack shook his head. "Haven't seen it, Nathan," he said. And that was true, in a way.

His father and Silverstein had split up after a few months, despite drawing decent crowds in small comedy theaters across the Midwest. Sepulcher had been different back then, but Jack never liked him.

"That rock . . ." Sepulcher seemed unable to finish his thought. Jack knew he needed to leave, or there might be a ruckus—so he said good-bye to Joe-Jim, then, giving Sepulcher a wide berth, walked quickly to his bike.

Sepulcher stared after him with forlorn conviction—Jack could actually feel the man's eyes like little needles in his neck. "That was *my* rock, Jack! Your father stole it from me! My life has been a misery ever since!"

Other buskers had gathered. Slowly, deliberately, they encircled Sepulcher, whispering, prodding, quietly urging him to move on.

Jack pedaled south.

The whole night was going sour.

———

Ginny walked in a happy daze. She had always loved circuses, street acts, magicians—had always wanted to have a birthday party on a great, sprawling lawn, with minstrels and dancing dogs and jugglers—and she could almost pretend, here it is, here I am, under the stars—my magic moment.

Here I am, finally happy and whole.

And then she noticed the compact young man on the bicycle, riding south along the asphalt path, glancing back over his shoulder. Skinny but well-toned, muscular forearms prominent beneath a striped short-sleeve shirt, swirling black hair, dark eyes intent, not scared but wary.

She stood transfixed. Her arms started to shiver. She wanted to run after him, ask who he was—but he stood on his pedals and sped up, leaving behind the long stretch of tents and rings and the banner that announced LE BOULEVARD DU CRIME.

She knew him.

They had never met.

She ran after, crying, "Wait!"

The bicyclist didn't stop. He vanished in the lights and shadows along the waterfront, under the star-pricked southern sky.

CHAPTER 20

Queen Anne

Jack's roommate, Burke, had not returned. After the run-in with Sepulcher, he needed company—someone other than his rats. Outside, seagull cries blew through the open window, discussing an offshore storm.

The weather would soon turn miserable.

Hastily consumed game hen and the glass of red wine rolled like lead in his stomach. He held his hand to his lips for a belch that refused to come, then reached into his pocket for the classified ad. Unfolding and smoothing it, reading the simple question over and over, he wondered what to do. Whom to trust.

Everywhere he went, he had the weird feeling he was being followed. Somebody—everybody—thought he was *special*. Jack did not want to be special. He wanted to continue with the life he had led for years now, since his father's death.

Since the funeral. Since finding among his father's few effects the box that sometimes contained the melted, curiously shaped stone with the red eye—and sometimes did not.

Harborview. Doctors. Needles. Putting my life in other hands.

In his bedroom, a futon lay bunched up against the wall. A restless night. Most of his nights had been restless lately. He flopped down.

"Not a city, exactly," Jack muttered in the darkness. "A refuge. A fortress. The last, greatest place on Earth."

A rat rolled and squeaked, eyes closed, raised front leg twitching.

"And I wouldn't call it dreaming."

Brows furrowed, he studied the phone number. Better than a visit to the doctor—if the ad meant anything, but of course it didn't. It was wrong on all counts. Not a dream, not a city—and what about at the end of time?

Even thinking about calling the number made his head hurt.

One thing was clear. His time of freedom, of avoiding major decisions, was over. As an aid to finding a better fate, he could focus on the western corner where the ceiling met the walls, all those angled lines suddenly bending and coming taut—he could visualize a stranded cord stretching to infinity, or at least a vast distance, vibrating as if alive, singing to him—he could spend days, weeks, trying to unkink the knots formed while he was caught up in a wind of misfortune—

Or he could trump it all and make his decision *right now*.

He covered his eyes with his hands, miserable. Definitely losing the last of his marbles. Dropping them one by one, watching them roll down the sewer grate—out of control.

His foot kicked out and hit the old steamer trunk where he stored the fragments of past acts, history—his mother's and father's worldly goods.

The stone.

He kicked the trunk again, to offload bad energy.

All the rats watched, awake now, still but for their whiskers. "I know, I kno-o-ow," he soothed.

Time to connect past moments—to see if the rock was in its box. Magic box, magic rock—except that Jack knew magic had nothing to do with it.

Memory is the secret. But I don't always remember—

He stood and reached for the latch on the trunk lid. To open the trunk all the way, he had to lug it out from the wall. He braced to do so. Something behind the trunk caught his fingers. Distracted, he reached back, trying to remember what he had put there—and pinched out a thin black portfolio. The portfolio measured thirty inches wide and eighteen inches high, and had been secured with a twist of dirty linen.

He untied the knot—he was very good with knots.

The portfolio contained nine or ten drawings on thick sketch paper. They somehow looked familiar. At first glance the topmost sketch might have depicted the elongated bows of three ships crossing a wavy black sea, like ocean liners in old posters. But the jutting bows were curvaceous and massive and the sea was really mountains, he decided, so the three objects weren't ships at all. They had to be huge—dozens, maybe hundreds of miles high.

Someone—not him—had sketched suggestions of detail inside the curves, thin lines and blocks of shadow. A narrow tower or mast rose from the central and most prominent of the three shapes. Definitely architecture, not ships.

He pushed aside the first sheet—it made a rippling hiss—and examined the second with pursed lips. This one he did not like at all. Rising behind a smaller scale rendering of the three objects, touched with crayon, pastel, pencil, and watercolor, an oblate orb stretched across almost the entire page. The orb was rimmed with deep red fire but its center was a waxy crayon black, heavily layered. When he held the drawing at the right inclination, such that it reflected no light, the center of the orb became an eclipsed eye with tiny darting flames instead of lids and lashes. And all around the orb, what could be seen of a sky gave the startling impression of rotten, ripped fabric—a fantasia of dark colors and textures highlighted with multicolored squiggles.

He could easily imagine the squiggles glowing like neon signs.

No way his roommate had done these. Burke had absolutely no talent in that department—or any other, except being a sous chef, which was talent enough to earn a real living, unlike busking.

Jack tried to look away from the pages, but they held him with a stomach-churning fascination. He had seen these things before; he knew what they were. So . . .

What were they?

He closed the folio with a broken laugh, tied it, and restored it to its place behind the trunk. Then he shoved the trunk against the wall, hard.

"Who else lives in this room, besides me?" he asked.

CHAPTER 21

The Green Warehouse

Ginny tossed on the cot, winding the blankets and sheets. Like a coward, with nowhere else to go, she had returned to the warehouse. She doubted anyone other than Minimus had even noticed she was gone.

"I *almost* know his name," she whispered, then took a deep breath, let it out slowly, puffed her worries in a cloud that rose to the roof and wisped through the cracks to spread in the high night air.

Her eyes stared up at the old skylight, not seeing the pale moon through the clouds. As she twisted, making small, tight whimpers, the moon cast her face in a ghostly glow; she was far away, pupils dilated, pulse rapid; far away and frightened.

She was not asleep. She was not awake.

This time Ginny had not pushed her host from the body's perch, but shared it. Tiadba had only the vaguest notion that somebody watched through the same eyes and listened through the same ears.

There was too much else happening for this to be important.

Gradually, Ginny—not in control, unable to direct the shared eyes— pieced together that Tiadba was in a broad gray place, walls, if any, far away or behind, and at her feet, a shallow sea of dust sparkled and groaned beneath her bare feet as she walked.

Tiadba was lost in gloom. The adventure meant nothing—all their training, their plans, nothing now.

The group had joined several Tall Ones. A deep, musical voice spoke on Tiadba's right.

"There's little time. You'll pass through the gate when you're fully prepared. Nobody leaves without proper training and tools."

Tiadba looked up at the speaker, wrapping his long, strange face in her own fear and frustration. She wore a silvery mask to protect against the dust that rose in low puffs from their feet. She was part of a group of thirteen, nine of them ancient breeds. Their escorts or guards: four Tall Ones who would accompany them as far as the border of the real, and then deliver them to the Chaos.

The nine and their escorts hiked beneath a high, dark gray roof—while the walls behind receded to a thin line. The effect was disconcerting—a huge flat space, dimness above, and nothing all around but the boundless, dusty plain.

How long would it take to get to where they were going? And where was that?

The oldest Tall One produced a trill that Tiadba interpreted as humor. "Breathe through the masks," he advised. "There's nothing poisonous, it's just old, precious dust—older than you, older than any of us!" He was at least twice as tall as Tiadba, with long, graceful arms and legs, a short, broad, pearl-colored face finely lined, and large brown eyes, spaced on each side of a broad, flat nose without apparent nostrils. (Ginny tried to remember if the Tall Ones were human—Tiadba seemed to think they were, though distantly and nonspecifically related.) He wore a tight black suit covered with close-spaced reddish piping that seemed to rearrange itself every few seconds—disconcerting.

Their own clothes—except for the masks—were what they had arrived in: dun-colored pajamas.

Tiadba (and Ginny, in turn) was beginning to realize just how naive they all had been. *Who's deceiving whom here? Did Grayne know, before she handed us over—before she died?*

And Ginny could sense that Tiadba was still recovering from a nasty scare, accompanied by sorrow—the grief still burned. Something had happened back in the Tiers, something outside of Tiadba's experience.

A bit of Tiadba's backmind became acutely aware of Ginny's presence. *You! Go away. Or keep still and be quiet!*

———

Ginny's eyes fluttered, and for a few instants she again saw the warehouse, the skylight—again felt the presence of boxes and crates stacked out to the walls. The cot's brown blankets bound her like a shroud; she stared up like a wild thing, neck corded.

Elsewhere, time was flowing—she was neither here nor there. She could only vaguely remember where she had been, and who—a lost name, three notes of a much longer tune she could not recall.

Then, her eyelids fluttered and drooped. Her breath became shallow and quick.

Her body settled.

She was away again . . .

———

They had crossed the plain of sparkling dust. Ahead, a silvery cluster of rounded buildings, like soap bubbles made of moonlight, rose from a pedestal surrounded by rivulets of that same dust, blown into low dunes and meanders across a depthless black floor.

"Nothing here is real," said a young male trudging close to Tiadba. His name was Nico. They were all more than weary; they no longer had the full brightness of the ceil over the Tiers to guide them. Their world had expanded immensely—and most of it was ugly, barren, strange. Tiadba looked around at the nine, her nine.

You—inside me. This could be a dangerous time. We're a broken team. I don't know what we're going to do.

Ginny still did not have the wherewithal to respond. She felt loosely attached; what Tiadba saw seemed to wobble and tunnel away, like an image at the end of a long pipe.

Ginny was little more than a poorly connected rider, jostled by her host's thoughts, even by the pounding of her heart. She could not speak, could barely even watch.

The sheets grew tighter, she was falling off something somewhere . . .

———

The group climbed a ramp to the pedestal and kicked off what they could of the dust on their feet and calves. Tiadba knew their names, tried to repeat them under her breath, as if introducing them to her guest.

She was thankful she was not the one doing the straying now; like Ginny—whose name she could not speak or make sense of—her memory of the lapses was minimal. *You're not going to push me aside, are you? That would be awkward for both of us. We could die.*

The group entered the closest of the silvery bubbles. Inside, arranged on transparent racks, suits of armor twinkled and flashed at their joints with false fire. Split helmets draped the shoulders. They were like wet suits but segmented, thick and tightly ribbed—

You dive, in water? Don't distract me now! Please—

Ginny, embarrassed, wanted to withdraw, but could not—like a loose tooth hanging by a painful nerve, neither in the jaw nor out, she was buffeted by Tiadba's emotions—yet knew that Tiadba's upper mind was still only vaguely aware that something was different. In essence, Ginny was being counseled—rebuffed—by her host's housekeepers, the organizers and tenders of a body's everyday needs.

And when she was gone, Ginny knew that these same tenders would sweep away the short shallow irritation of her presence . . . As her own tenders and housekeepers did when their roles were reversed and she played host. So strange! Such a thing to know!

If only she could keep from forgetting, she could bring back these experiences, think them over while she was awake, fit them into all the other puzzle pieces—and perhaps complete a picture.

So little of it made sense.

The bright suits—dull red, pastel yellow, ethereal green, nine different hues—fully occupied Tiadba's awareness, as if she could see nothing else. She had been told of these marvels at the base camp, but only recently—only just before the march across the dust plain in the gray cavern. These were the devices that would help keep them alive in the Chaos, beyond the border of the real . . . and as such, they were outside the experience of any of the ancient breeds in the Tiers. How wonderful, to learn of them; and how disturbing to be told why they were necessary!

Tiadba had long since realized that their plans and hopes for adventure had been more than naive. The Chaos was not sanctuary, not freedom—it was endless peril. Even the Tall Ones seemed to forgo speaking of it unless it was strictly necessary.

What they had experienced before arriving in the flood channel—the sorrow, compounded by the shock of displacement and the grief—was only a hint of what lay outside the Kalpa.

Yes, they were going—finally they were going on a march—but at what risk, at what cost? And who could be trusted, after all these things not told of, never explained?

Go away now! I have to focus . . .

The last thing Ginny could hold onto, like a slippery rope, before the housekeepers swept her up and broke her loose—

Tiadba's hope: *We* will *meet again. You know that, don't you?*

Out of sequence. Everything jumbling, dreams and life contorted.

Where is he? Is he still alive? You know! Tell me!

But Ginny did not know.

Why haven't we heard from him?

———

Ginny fell off the cot and hit the floor in a tangle of blanket and sheets. Sweat soaked her nightgown. Desperately she tried to hold onto what she had seen and heard, but the vision melted like a sliver of ice under the intense heat of waking.

She let out a tight shriek of frustration.

Minimus leaped up from the floor and rubbed against her feet, then sat and watched her untangle and rearrange the bedclothes.

Whatever she had seen, wherever she had been, in any rational sequence, might have come before the . . . the *what*? The lapses that left her with such an awful sense of terror and oppression.

The bad, endless times to come.

CHAPTER 22

University District, Seattle

What are they dreaming? How long until they can't sleep at all?

Daniel closely watched the morning commuters in their cars—when he could see them. In this world, so many hid behind tinted windows, as if shy or afraid. Faces fixed straight ahead, eyes flicking, avoiding his gaze, some reading his sign and smiling—waving—others shouting words of abuse—good people, smart, but they didn't stop and give him money; a very few, and these he felt the most sorry for, rolling down their windows and offering spare change or a few dollars—and the rest don't see him, will not see him, oops, now the traffic is moving, it's too late—would've offered something, sure do feel sorry for you poor folks down on your luck . . .

And how long until they were *all* down on their luck? Fortunes run out, world-strands gummed together and gathered like dried tendons from a corpse, waiting to be trimmed . . . short stalks in a dead bouquet.

For a moment the road was empty, the corners quiet—he could hear the wind blowing through the thin brush and young alders crouched back from the side of the road. Rain had fallen fitfully all day. It soaked through his coat—soaked his moth-eaten thrift-store Pendleton and woolen long johns, his socks squished in his shoes—never wear costly shoes, make sure you smirch your coat and outer garments with dirt after you clean them, rub the dirt into your hands and your fingers—a little diluted mud dripping as you take their few coins and fewer bills . . .

To keep eating, Daniel Patrick Iremonk played along, for now.

A small Volkswagen drove up—yellow, familiar, they had had Volkswagens like this in his world, before the darkening and the cinder-grit dusting, before his precipitate flight. Behind the wheel hunched a plump young man with cherry cheeks, pushed-up nose, and short, thick black hair. The young man wore a gray suit coat, sleeves too short, over a pink striped shirt—a salesman, Daniel guessed. Not much money in the bank, lots of debt, but he kept his car clean and his clothes pressed.

Daniel held up his sign.

> *Bad Times Got ME*
> *A little Cash for food?*
> *God Bless You!!!*

Daniel could freeze the light on red for five or six minutes at a time—drawing out the stop until the drivers got nervous, until they rolled down their windows and offered a payment of cash to *get moving, get this show back on the road, my God that's a long light!*

Cars were backed up all the way to the freeway.

On the opposite corner, Florinda—the lean brown woman—stood like a bundle of twigs, holding her own misspelled message on its dog-eared square of brown cardboard. She rarely looked at the drivers—a bad corner, traffic always moving.

Florinda was in her late forties, face draped by long strands of felted hair, a chain smoker whose habit got her stuck in less desirable locations—she just had to pause every fifteen minutes for a puff, and inevitably she lost her best spots to more aggressive panhandlers.

The light hung on endless red. Frustrating, time-eating, finger-drumming crimson.

The salesman glanced resentfully at Daniel. He was a mouth-breather, Daniel observed—jaw slightly agape, lower lip flaccid. Daniel could not see his eyes—they were shaded from the slanting light breaking over Wallingford.

The salesman finally leaned forward and scowled, then rolled down the window, shoulder jerking with the effort. "If I give you money, will you let me through?" he called.

"Sure," Daniel said, stooping. He needed to see the man's eyes.

The head dropped lower as the man reached into his pocket, plump fingers pushing under the seat belt's hard, square buckle.

Daniel could only hold the light a few more seconds. Too long and the traffic engineers in the city figured something was wrong—sent repairmen and sometimes cops. He'd had to abandon this corner twice because he held a red too long—messing too obviously with all these small fortunes, tiny fates.

"Here," the driver said, holding out four crumpled dollar bills. "Billy Goat Gruff. Just don't ask any questions, and don't eat me."

Daniel stuffed the bills in his deepest coat pocket. Their eyes met, the driver's underslung, blue, direct—Daniel's steady, wide, washed-out.

A little spark hit him in the base of the spine.

"Bad dreams," the driver confessed. "You?"

Daniel nodded, then swung out his arm, and the light changed.

The prelude before the flood.

He could feel that hideous tide already lapping up on the fresh beaches of this world. The first sign—refugees like himself, crippled storm petrels, crawling onto the shore, gasping, wings broken, desperate.

And then—

Bad dreams.

There were ways of gauging how long he had—of measuring the remaining days, weeks, months. He had become an expert at predicting the storm surge.

Daniel folded up his cardboard sign and waved across the intersection at Florinda. "I'm done for the day," he called.

"Why quit now?" Florinda asked. "Lunch crowd from the U."

"You want it?" Daniel's spot was prime—left side of the off-ramp, driver's-side windows.

"Not if you're just going to bust my chops when you get back."

"I'll be gone the rest of the day. Back tomorrow morning. Don't give it up to some other bastard for a smoke."

"I'll hold it," Florinda said, with a surprisingly sound grin. She still had all her teeth.

Daniel missed having good teeth.

He wrapped his sign in a plastic garbage bag and hid it in the bushes, then walked up Forty-fifth, passing Asian restaurants, video stores, gaming parlors—he paused before a used bookstore, but it sold only best-selling paperbacks—hung a left on Stone Way, passing apartments, a fancy grocery store . . . more apartments, condos, plumbing fixtures, hardware.

He descended the long, gentle slope to Lake Union.

Daniel had begun his search three days ago by taking a bus to the downtown library—not the old library he was familiar with but a huge, shiny metal rhomboid—scary. Differences were at once frightening and reassuring. He had come such a long way—that was a good thing. It was also a sad thing. He had left so much behind.

The downtown library did not carry the book he was looking for, and none were available through interlibrary loan.

Despite an excessive amount of wear and tear, with less liquor and better food Charles Granger's body had regained some strength. It took Daniel less than thirty-five minutes—joints aching, heart pounding, hands trembling—to reach Seattle Book Center.

A block and a half from the Ship Canal, on the east side of the broad street, three bookstores shared a single-story brown and gray building. In Daniel's previous world, there had also been bookstores here—a confluence he didn't give much thought to, considering the greater changes he had witnessed.

He paced beside the storefront, darting glances through the half-silvered windows. Art books stood in uneven ranks, spines facing inward, anonymous when viewed from the street.

He set the glass door's bell a-jingle. The owner was instantly on alert—street person walking—but not alarmed. Seeing someone like Daniel—as he now appeared—had to be a common occurrence across the freeway from the university, where so many homeless youngsters and street people hung out . . . Down and out.

Common folk.

Daniel swallowed, sized up the owner: a stocky man in his late fifties, of medium height, with a slight stoop, long hair, and experienced, quiet eyes—calm, slightly bored, self-assured. "Can I help you?"

Daniel worked to keep his voice from shaking. Like everything else subject to corruption, libraries and bookstores scared him—but that wasn't what gave him the shakes. He had only recently weaned this body off its daily medicine, a liter of Night Train and sixty-four fluid ounces of Colt 45.

"I'm looking for a book on cryptids," he said. "Unusual animals, long thought extinct, or never known to exist. New species. Monsters. I have a title in mind . . ."

"Shoot," the owner said with a wary smile.

Daniel blinked. He wasn't used to being received with familiarity, on such short notice. He studied the owner—too perceptive. Scouts, collectors, could be anywhere.

Or, the owner was simply responding to a customer who knew about books. The community of book people was used to eccentrics.

"Signs," Daniel continued, trying to subdue a twitch in his left eye. "Portentous signs hidden in strange animals. Lost in time or place."

"A title would help—that's not a title, I take it?"

"I don't know what the title will be . . . here. The author is always Bandle, David Bandle."

"B-A-N-D-L-E?"

"Correct." Daniel's throat bobbed. His forehead was damp from the strain of this extended interaction.

The owner did not seem fazed. "I remember a book on cryptozoology by someone with a name like that . . . *Travels in Search of Hidden Beasts*, I think," the owner said.

"Could be," Daniel said.

"Don't have it. I can do a search online."

"That would be kind. Most recent edition. How much . . . would it cost? I'm not wealthy." This body was not used to smiling—bad teeth, worse breath. He succeeded in drawing parenthetical creases around his lips.

"Oh, thirty bucks. Good reading copy. It's not very old, is it?"

"Perhaps not. I wouldn't know," Daniel said.

"Down payment of ten dollars. The rest when I get the book in. Probably take a week or two. Address?"

Daniel shook his head. "I'll come back." He removed two smudged fives from his pocket and placed them in neat parallel on the counter. *There goes dinner.*

The owner smoothed out the money and wrote up a receipt. "I always liked those sorts of books," he said. "Adventure in faraway places, hunting down creatures that time forgot. Wonderful stories."

"Wonderful," Daniel agreed, and pocketed the receipt.

"We have a good collection of deep-sea books, just in. Beebe, Piccard, that sort of thing."

"No, thank you." Daniel backed out of the store with a half bow and a short wave of his right hand. *Very good*, he assured his new body. *A good beginning.*

He had come to trust Bandle. Bandle's report on cryptids had given him essential clues years ago, in another strand, another lifetime. Bandle cataloged sightings of animals that could not exist—sea serpents, half-human beasts, earwigs bigger than rats. Any of those could be indicators. Variations, permutations—warnings—all collected into one authoritative text.

But as he walked along, Daniel suspected he would not be coming back. Something about the way the owner had examined him. It was probably dangerous at this late date to even inquire after Bandle.

Ten bucks—wasted.

———

Daniel stood on a steel-edged curb, blinking at the bright clouds and the low autumn sun. Such a lovely world.

You are what you leave behind.

His grandfather had once said, visiting him in prison, *Where are you going, young man? Is there anything you will not do to get there? Eventually, you leave so much behind, you show up before God and you're as empty as your damned puzzle box—you're so empty it's not even you anymore, and heaven doesn't matter.*

Daniel began to cry.

FOURTEEN ZEROS

CHAPTER 23

The Tiers

The passage had been made for someone smaller than either Jebrassy or Tiadba. Once, green circles spaced every few yards must have provided illumination, but they no longer gave even the feeblest light.

Crouched over, then down on hands and knees, they crawled in darkness through the dank tunnel, nothing visible ahead and only a shrinking spot of dimness behind. After a longer time than Jebrassy cared to think about, they still had not reached the vertical shaft.

Tiadba said, "Don't you hate the way time changes? One day, it's short—the next day, it's long. Makes me feel like we've been crawling since we were born. Even here. You'd think at the Diurns—"

"How long was it for you, the last time?"

"I don't know," she said with a small chuff. "Wait. I think it's just ahead." She shuffled forward quickly, and then he could see an outline of her legs and feet as she stood. "Come on. The steps begin here."

The light was weak—dropping from far above, he guessed. "This takes us up to the—what did you call it?"

"The Valeria," she said. "I don't know where any of the names come from. They don't sound like breed speech, do they? The steps are tiny. It's best to curl up and crawl around—wrap your arms and legs around the center of the spiral. Then . . . just hump and slither."

That was easier for her than for him. Another endless time drew them along, *slithering* and on occasion trying other forms of ascent, crouching and taking mincing steps—bumping his head. Tiadba seemed in good humor. His admiration grew, especially as her scent filled the enclosed space.

"Look," she said. Her hand, a barely visible paleness, brushed over a long chink in the smoothness surrounding the stairs. "Look through this gap and tell me if that isn't a lift shaft."

He saw a kind of railing running vertically up a parallel shaft, brighter and wider than the one they were climbing; but no sign of a lift car.

"There's so much we should be curious about, but aren't," Tiadba said from above. Her voice diminished. She had increased their distance; she was thinner, taller, a little stronger . . .

"Don't leave me behind," he called out, only half joking.

Time stretched. His head hurt trying to understand how long it had been. Then a kind of panic set in, and he squeezed against the steps—the surrounding cylinder of wall—with all his strength, until his joints popped and he could feel his flesh bruise. His breath came in husky drags and he felt as if he were dead but still seeing, still hearing . . . feeling his own flesh rot away.

"I'm there!" Tiadba called. "Hurry up. It's small, but there's room for two, if we squeeze."

Eyes searching for light, Jebrassy clamped his jaw and quickened his crawl. Soon he wriggled into a short horizontal corridor, then pushed forward and through another hatch, into an open booth—the rounded half cup of the Valeria.

"Careful—not much room," Tiadba told him.

He stood, brushing against her, then slowly peered over the lip of the cup, down hundreds of feet to the littered and dusty stage below. He could make out the curled-up corpse in the rubble. Looking up with equal caution, not to get dizzy and fall out backward, he saw the last of the wakelight from the ceil, even less convincing at this altitude.

They had spent their whole life within a stage set, he thought . . . for the entertainment of a cruel and uncaring audience.

With a deep breath, he squeezed around beside her and looked down at the control seat and console. Above the console, a screen barely two hands wide had been set flush against the wall, and below that, a surface with dozens of bumps of various colors.

Above the screen, six glassy lenses glittered like insect eyes.

The single seat before the console would have fit a man half his size. Tiadba risked toppling as she squatted and set her butt on the rim of the cup. Both stared earnestly at the gray blankness on the small display.

"This one doesn't work, either," she said. "It took me a couple of trips to learn how to look into the black things. Sit close, and I'll finger up a catalog. I've only seen one or two entries. I didn't want to watch any more, alone, because I'm not sure these old memories, the records, are going to last. Two observers, two memories . . . much better."

Jebrassy stared earnestly at the shining black beads. "I'm looking," he said, perching in a half squat beside her. "I don't—"

She raised her hand and bent his head to the proper angle, and he jerked as bright images flooded his eyes. He could see nothing else. The effect was immediate and startling—scenes flew past so quickly he couldn't make sense of them; intense, sick-making. "I'm going to throw up," he warned.

"You'll get used to it, and it's worth the headache, too. I'm still learning how to look properly. If you want to hazard a guess about all the knobs and bumps, go right ahead."

"What if we accidentally erase the records?"

Tiadba shrugged. "I doubt they'd let anyone here have that sort of power."

Jebrassy felt a surge of interest. Ever above the thought of leaving the Kalpa soared the need to know what he was, and what his place might be. No one had yet been able to tell him that, though since childhood he'd been convinced that in the ancient places, in the depths of the walls—even in such illusions as the ceil, and the false bookshelves high in the blocs—there were clues.

More than clues . . .

The story, complete and convincing.

Justification for all he was doing.

"This seems to slow the parade," he murmured, fingers prodding a dimple. He found that with some practice he could push the dimple to the right or the left. And then he realized that it was not his finger changing the speed, but the way in which he looked at the racing images—the way he darted his attention one way, then the next. Concentration, focus, the flick of an eyelid or facial muscle. The display was controlled by expression more than fingers.

The quickstep parade of scenes slowed to a crawl. Each part of the parade was itself another parade, but moving at relatively normal speed—three-dimensional representations somehow all visible, one through another: visible, dense, and real.

"Getting used to it?" Tiadba asked, pressing her shoulder against his.

"No," he said, but he was—sort of. "How do you choose?"

She patiently explained what she knew. The combination of the floating sense of other-reality and Tiadba's voice was hypnotic. After a while Jebrassy realized he was as fascinated by the sounds she made as by the panoramas they were accessing—which, after all, seemed nothing more than surveys of places within the Tiers, many of them already familiar.

All of the programs were devoid of citizens. They revealed only empty places, deserted spaces. The effect was spooky, like peering into a dead city—or visiting the Diurns themselves.

"The person who operated this was smaller," Tiadba said, and then added in a bare whisper, "But the operator wasn't expected to be any brighter than you or me . . . or very different in shape. They must have been people like us, but they were allowed to see these things, and to know some of what was happening to them. We aren't—not anymore. I wonder why?"

"But there's *nothing* happening," he complained. "No people."

"Be patient. This is just one dimension of search."

He pulled back from the lens to study Tiadba. The attention did not embarrass her, but it did annoy—and she took hold of his stubby ear and gently swung his head back in line.

"There," she said. "We're back to the Diurns themselves. Now watch."

She made adjustments. The pictures and places suddenly came alive. This utter end of the Tiers—the bridges, the causeway—was filled with thousands of people dressed as if attending a festival—far more colorfully dressed than any of the ancient breed, whose clothes tended toward drabness.

Whatever had captured the pictures seemed capable of being everywhere at once.

"They're all *rich*," he said.

"Move in close," she suggested. "Look at their faces."

Together, they swooped low over the crowds, then picked out several individuals. They were definitely not of the ancient breed—not only smaller, but slighter, more delicate, with longer noses, more sharply defined facial features—particularly chins and ears, the ears being quite large, shaped like little wings—their skin pallid, almost waxy, yet vibrant. The crowds behaved in a choreographed fashion, quite unlike the sustained bumping and crowding, elbowing and bobbing, he would have expected from the ancient breed.

"Who were they, do you think?" Tiadba asked.

"The Tall Ones had other toys before us," he said doubtfully.

This angered Tiadba. "We are *not* toys, I told you," she said. "And neither were they." She frowned, struggling to voice her concept. "Maybe they're our . . ." These ideas were so embarrassing. "What's the word—these might have been our *ancestors*."

Confined within the cup-shaped booth, they watched the processions until their muscles cramped, and then took turns standing and stretching. Inevitably, this brought them into even closer contact. Each brushing touch, and especially each press of flesh, was electric.

"There's no way of knowing anything about them," Tiadba said, blinking, "unless we can learn their language, read their writing."

He squeezed back against the wall, trying to examine his companion in the dim light. She had a ghostly aspect now, the spill of light from the lenses shining against her round chin and full cheekbones, glinting in her beautiful eyes.

"To cross the border of the real, you need training and equipment," Tiadba said. "Clothing, machines, things we've never seen before. You can't just go out on your own, or you'll die."

"Who gives the clothes and machines?"

"I don't know."

"How many marches has the sama put together?"

"I don't know that, either."

"Is she working with the Tall Ones?"

Tiadba shook her head again.

"Who gets to lead and get all the glory?"

"None of us knows."

Jebrassy sucked in a deep breath. It was not nearly as simple and direct as he had hoped. Finally, he squeezed down beside her. "All right," he said. "I'm ignorant. I admit it. What's this sama's name?"

Tiadba pretended to concentrate on the lenses. "This must have been a kind of celebration," she murmured. "Maybe they're getting ready to send out their own marchers. It's so different now. But you can tell—they're going down into the flood channels . . . The channels are clean, there's no debris—all the walls are covered with dwellings. So many people living in the Tiers! Why did it change?"

Grudgingly, Jebrassy looked again.

"There's a door, opening to a lift—a working lift," Tiadba said. "Maybe they're getting ready to send a gift to the Tall Ones—you know, to speed the marchers along."

Jebrassy saw all this. Crowds carrying on their shoulders platforms loaded with food, cages full of letterbugs—no different from the ones breeds still kept as pets. And books. He awkwardly zoomed in closer, to see the titles on the spines, but could not read them—the symbols were old, like those on the backs of the oldest letterbugs, and the words they formed made little sense.

"There are still books like that in the walls—on the upper levels," he said. "Can't pull them out."

"I know," Tiadba said with a lift of her brow, an air of mystery.

The procession crossed the channel and stood before the far wall of the channel, where a large door opened, otherwise invisible. They passed the goods through, the gifts—and the books. Tiadba flicked her cheek and the scene pulled back to a diagram, a three-dimensional drawing or map.

Their impossible point of view now soared high above the flood channel, passed through the wall, then the ceil, following a glowing dot on a vertical red line—the lift—higher and higher through constructions of dazzling complexity, presumably the upper parts of the Kalpa, now as transparent as glass, far above the three isles of the Tiers.

Jebrassy saw for the first time their place in things. Three large rounded structures, like great smooth humps, placed side by side—the central hump pushed forward into a walled enclave, open to the . . . But from this perspective, he could not see the ceil. Maybe this new perspective put them *outside* the Kalpa. Maybe outside there *wasn't* a ceil.

Their view drew back even farther, and swooped up. The dot traveled along the red line through the rounded top of the middle hump—was that the Kalpa, or were all three humps called the Kalpa? He realized then how huge the whole must be—hundreds of times larger than the Tiers themselves, with the Tiers at the very bottom. Now his head truly hurt.

The dot slowed and stopped at the base of a tower. The viewpoint continued up the tower's length, but the dot signifying the gifts from the Tiers remained at the base.

The tower stood as far above the limits of the Kalpa as they had already traveled from the basement level of the Tiers. And at the top: the tower ended in an abrupt, ragged peak, as if something had snapped it in half.

"The sama calls this Malregard," Tiadba said. "Have you ever heard of the Broken Tower?"

"In children's stories," Jebrassy said, his breath coming hard, tears in his eyes. He had just passed above and beyond the knowledge of anyone he had ever met, of his sponsors and of their sponsors . . . as far back as he could imagine. "Malregard," he repeated. He tried to swing his point of view to see what surrounded the Kalpa—the Chaos, presumably—but there was only a misty blueness.

"The sama says that means 'Evil View,'" Tiadba said. "Makes you wonder what's out there." She watched his face.

"If you get to go on the next march . . . Would I go with you?"

"I don't choose who goes or doesn't go."

"This sama . . . she decides?"

"She tells us the decisions."

He rubbed his face with his hands and shook his head, overwhelmed. "We're being played with. No Tall One would ever trust breeds with so much. I need to think," Jebrassy said. "You can go back to your niche."

"I can't leave you here. They're waiting on the causeway."

"Who?"

"Some of the team. Now that you know, you can't just go back and tell others. We couldn't risk that."

Jebrassy was beginning to experience the same panic he had felt in the narrow shaft of spiraling steps. "You're the bait. I'm the fool. They'll kill me if I don't go along."

Tiadba looked genuinely shocked. "Breeds don't *kill* each other."

"Except by accident—in a little war, maybe. How unfortunate. That's why your sama selected me—because I'm bold, reckless, likely to die or go missing—like that poor fool down there. Was *he* your last candidate? What did he do wrong?"

"You're being dreadful," she said.

"I'm thinking out loud."

"We'll be spending a lot of time together," Tiadba said quietly. "The teams require each participant to have a partner. Don't you feel it? We're already partners."

"What I'm feeling isn't that clear-cut. Something goes wrong, that's what I'm feeling."

Tiadba swung her arm out to the Diurns. "Who can be sure about anything? What if an intrusion takes us? What if time stops?"

"I don't think . . . I don't think we would even feel it," Jebrassy said, but his hair crawled at the possibility—and whatever it was that lay just on the edge of his memory.

The things that could—that *would* go wrong, even if they never ventured into the Chaos.

TEN ZEROS

Every day, Daniel's memory lost a little color and depth, until thinking about what had gone before became like looking at a faded negative or an impression in wet sand. Charles Granger—all his ingrained habits and instincts, and the ever-present pain—was gaining strength, a steady tide lapping up over a beached intruder.

Daniel opened Granger's carton and lifted out the marker, the blunted pencil, and several sheets of paper. He spread the sheets over the warped wooden floor, avoiding the damp spots, and examined them critically. They were covered with writing—crazy writing mostly, symbols arranged without apparent meaning, rows of repeating words with one letter changed in each word—and numbers, lots of numbers.

Charles Granger had been an occasional poet, but he had also been a thinker and logician—possibly even a mathematician. There was strange order to his scratchings, though Daniel could not reconstruct that order.

The stones knew how to pick them. And when to demand a change—perhaps.

Daniel flipped the sheets over. Some were blank. The time had come to reconstruct his life and thoughts before the last jaunt. He could record this in the blank spaces that remained between Charles Granger's own ramblings. *How appropriate.*

But making this brain, this body, lift the pencil and work with him was far more difficult than finding room between Granger's lines. Whatever Granger had been trying for, the task—the problem—had overwhelmed him. He had been ripe to be replaced, yet already too ripe to be worth replacing.

Daniel smiled grimly, but did not show his teeth.

Still, in the wet darkness, with the candle gleaming on the fireplace mantel and another candle on the floor in a jelly glass, illuminating a fanned circle of pages . . .

Daniel began to write. The crabbed script gradually smoothed, became more like his own. There was only so much he could take control of and re-form in the time remaining.

Granger's time, and the time left for this world.

He frowned in concentration as he wrote: *Granular space. Locality emphasized.*

And then a series of equations. Not so different from Granger's scribbles after all; from reading Richard Feynman, Daniel had picked up the trick of creating his own mathematical notation. No one else would know what the symbols meant.

> All fates have become local.
> Space-time has been breaking up/breaking down. The universe is being digested, curdling like spoiled milk with nasty, rotten whey in between—geodetics shortened, jamming up. Chords (cords?) and fundamentals. Light crosses the membranes, and gravity, but material things cannot pass.
> Not yet.
> That's what I see

He wrote three more equations, long and inelegant, filled with conceptual lacunae. Trying to quantify and formalize these ideas—trying to make them consistent, useful, to make predictions, was more than difficult. Even when healthy it had been damned near impossible for him. His hand was growing tired—his head hurt. His stomach hurt.

He needed to reconstruct what he had written just before the nightmare descended. There were certain theories beyond the reach of his equations—not yet quantifiable, but for that reason, in their own way more true. More useful.

The map is not the territory.

Quickly, fighting Granger's crabwise style, Daniel managed to remember and record this much:

Fundamental: world-lines can be bundled into larger fundamentals. Below the fundamental are the component lines, which can be elevated to fundamentals by observation; and below these, the harmonics and polyharmonics—which defy observation under usual circumstances, but which rise to prominence in the decaying multiverse. We usually access harmonics and polyharmonics in meditative, imaginative, or dreaming states—but they do not usually rise up to absorb our fundamental line of progress.

Yet they contribute. They fill in the sum-runners. All stories, all things.

Fundamental Observers arose in the early multiverse, to fix and shore up the most efficient results of sums-over-history, and to refine the self-propagating nature of the multiverse and create logical simplicity.

They are "intelligent" in a selfless way, but as they do not create, merely justify and refine, they can't be considered gods.

Fundamental Observers like Mnemos . . .

His thoughts suddenly boiled over and steamed off in a crater field of pain and agitation. He dropped the pencil and slammed his fist on the floor, until the pain let up again. He had been trying to remember a name, something to do with memory, apparently . . . Not a god.

A muse.

He struggled to retrieve the pencil, and forced his trembling fingers to scrawl more words before they faded completely:

Sums-over-history.
Lines, cords, braids, cables, fundamentals . . .
Fates.

All the possible pathways a particle can take—or a human—an infinite number, spread out through all space and time, weak where improbable, strong where probable—all, in the end, collapsing into a single, energy-efficient path, the most resourceful and simplest world-line.

No more. Efficiency is turned on its head.

The rules are broken.

He looked up, lips and jaw slack despite the display of rotting teeth. He could no longer make sense out of what he had just written. He had to act quickly.

He had to find a more fortunate strand, a place where Granger lived a stronger, healthier existence. For days Daniel had been reluctant to even make the attempt—had shrunk from it with a dreamlike recollection of infinite loss and horror, remembering only vaguely what had propelled him out of his self, his home, in the first place—what had sent him flying like a gull from a hurricane.

———

Dusk fell over Forty-fifth Street as he stalked west into the fading light, marching to the origin of the long shadows, head still spinning. He stopped at the last used bookstore in the area—he had investigated all the others to exhaustion—and now he paced in front of the storefront, the last window display, dusty and unorganized.

Following the ache in his gut, he crossed the threshold and tripped the door's hanging bell.

The owner, a small, plump woman with white hair and a round face—like a toy granny made of dried apples—got up from her stool and came around the waist-high glass case that served as a counter, making sure he knew she was vigilant. The bookstore cat—orange and fat—looked up from its bed by the cash register and stretched.

The register sat on one end of the case, in which books of value—more value than the cracked-spine romance novels and best-sellers that made up the store's stock-in-trade—had been arranged in proud display: a volume of Richard Halliburton's travels; Nancy Drew mysteries, with dust wrappers; an old Oxford Bible bound in scuffed leather.

Daniel's gaze moved slowly to the last volume in the case, propped on the far right of the bottom shelf: a thick trade paperback. The title and author, in faded red letters, were almost invisible, but he squinted and read: *Cryptids and Their Discoverers*, by David Bandle.

He took a deep breath and closed his eyes. He could almost see the book through his eyelids, glowing like a coal. Bending over, he tapped the glass case with a dirty finger. "How much for that one?" he asked.

"I don't bargain," the apple granny said, still suspicious. She made no move to open the case. "Do you have money?"

He did—nine dollars from standing by the freeway until his back knotted, his legs went numb, and his head turned to clay. His breath smelled like gas fumes. "Some. I hope it's not too expensive."

"It's a first edition," the apple granny claimed, her eyes like blue flints.

"How much?" Daniel persisted.

"Probably too much."

"Could you look—please?"

The owner wrinkled her nose, shrugged, lifted the lace shawl from her shoulder, and slid open the back of the case. Stooping with an expressive grunt, she drew out the book and straightened, clutching it to her bosom.

Daniel had never seen Bandle's volume so thick. The gray stratum of plates was as wide as a finger.

Lifting her glasses, the woman opened the cover with plump, dry fingers. "Fifteen dollars," she said.

"I have nine. I'll pay you nine."

"I don't bargain," she repeated with a sniff.

Daniel afforded the woman an apologetic, tight-lipped smile. "It's dusty. Looks like it's been there awhile."

She squinted at the date penciled below the price. Something relented—a little stiffness went out of her. "Do you *really* want this book?"

He nodded. "A childhood favorite. Takes me back to better days."

"This book has resided in my special case for precisely three years," she said. "It's dusty, but I've never seen another copy. I'll let you have it for fifteen."

"Nine is all I have," Daniel said. "Honest."

She leaned back. Her eyes wizened to piggish slits. "You're the fellow begs up by the freeway, aren't you?"

It seemed that everyone knew Charles Granger. Daniel smiled wide, showing all his teeth—uneven, brown, and cracked—and coughed out a fetor.

The owner's moment of compassion instantly faded, but to get him out of the store, she sold him the book. And all it cost was all the money he had in the world.

———

Back in the dark house, he carried the book into the living room, where he sat with a groan on the broken cane chair, every bone grinding, and studied the spine. Such a fat edition, larger by far than any he had owned before. Sitting hurt too much, so he stretched out on the floor to read by the light of a candle—then pushed up to elbows and knees, and finally, crouched and rocked slowly on a cushion in the corner.

Now he had *the* book, rich and full of detail—bloated, he thought as he thumbed the pages—and he could examine it in his own good time, if he dared. If there was any time left. This was progress of a sort, if learning bad news, *very* bad news, could be considered progress.

And the news was awful indeed. Inch-long fleas. Prehistoric mammals found in New Guinea. Real Bigfoot scat and Bigfoot hair found in Canada and analyzed—DNA proof that the old gentleman was real, a distant offshoot of human beings.

He studied the listing index, skipping to the middle.

> *Flying nightmare in New Jersey Pine Barrens; wingspan of two meters, species unknown, perhaps dragonfly.*
>
> *Garden of Eden, in New Guinea; three hundred new species found there, fifteen new species of lemur, including fist-sized Gliding lemur.*
>
> *Giant true rats, weighing fifty kilograms, found in Borneo.*
>
> *Gigantopithecus, skull located in museum collection in Vienna; ten-foot-tall gorilla. Living specimens sighted in Cambodia?*
>
> *Hairy fishes, found with mammal-like hair follicles . . .*
>
> *Homo floresiensis, human relative one meter tall; used fire, tools. Hunted pygmy elephants with tiny spears.*
>
> *Human-faced crabs in Thailand and Sri Lanka, back of shells bear remarkable likenesses of faces of drowning victims.*
>
> *Hymenoptera: bees learn to use sign language in their dance.*
>
> *Indigo bat (size of eagle) found in Mexico.*
>
> *Kua-Nyu, squirrel-rat species extinct for eleven million years, discovered in Laos.*

Quran frogs, Iraqi marshes, croak "God is Great" in Arabic, with abbreviated suras readable in dorsal skin markings.

Sea scorpions (eurypterids) found off Madagascar; length, three meters; allegedly extinct for hundreds of millions of years, largest invertebrate ever. Natives prize their flesh, sweet and fragrant; claim to have hunted them "since time began."

He flipped to the beginning of the list.

Aepyornis captured in Tasmania; flightless bird twenty feet tall, eats goats, sheep, lays eggs size of two basketballs.

Then down:

Cathedral termites; exported around nation with woodchip debris from hurricane-ravaged Gulf Coast; build nests shaped like Chartres, Notre Dame.

He let the book flop shut, his hands trembling. Cryptids and Lazarids—hidden beasts, and beasts suddenly and unexpectedly resurrected by the thousands from the distant past. The listing index by itself ran for a hundred pages. Given his past reckoning that roughly half of the reports in Bandle were substantially incorrect or falsified, he estimated that there were still over a thousand reliable listings, twice as many as before, when the darkness and dust closed in and he had been forced to flee.

Unlikely things were gathering like shadows around a guttering campfire, ringing in the bright, rational, scientific world he had always valued—and doubted. He would need to find allies. Allies . . . and if at all possible, another host. A new body, stronger, healthier. Younger. He thumped his head against the wall, feeling the snake in his guts coil as if angry at this disrespect.

He could not do it alone; he doubted he had the focus and strength of will to leap so far again, and what was coming would be worse than before.

He opened the book to the introduction. Bandle wrote:

This latest edition incorporates well over five hundred new listings, a greater increase than any past edition, gathered in a period of just three years. This brings up a very nonscientific question: Has someone opened a door to the past, jamming us all together—extinct beasts, impossible beasts, unlikely and yet too real?

Soaked and racked by fever, Daniel reached the physics building on the University of Washington campus at three the next afternoon. He searched the ground-floor directories, then began his hunt through the hallways, peering at nameplates outside office doors, looking for the one fellow who might understand, the most vulnerable fellow he knew— and the most curious.

An old friend.

CHAPTER 25

Capitol Hill

Penelope seldom emerged from her bedroom, and Glaucous never intruded unless it was strictly necessary. The low, constant buzz and his partner's gentle murmurs of control and consolation told him all he needed to know. What lay beyond that closed and locked door was not safe, even for him.

Perhaps the hardest task he faced most days was keeping his partner happy. The changes within Glaucous were subtle, but Penelope had lost so much over the past thirty years, not just the lure of her femininity—her beauty and her youth—but the last feeble spark of her intellect, as Glaucous had shaped her into the wondrous, compliant tool she now was.

Glaucous flipped out the *London Times* he had bought at the newsstand on University Way, sucked his cigar with slit-eyed satisfaction, and read through the headlines. A large black leather lounge chair supported his relaxed, chunky torso, one short, thick leg bent at the knee, slippered foot on the floor, the other leg propped on the ottoman— small, precise toes twitching slowly as he read.

In over a century and a half, he had acquired an eye for many sorts of patterns—economic, political, philosophical, even scientific. The instincts he had learned as a Chancer and companion to the rich and ambitious still served him; over the decades, he'd laid up riches. One had to be prudent. All employers failed in the end—failed their employees and usually failed in their manifold endeavors, leaving one without means. Unless one was prudent. Unless one recognized patterns and knew what to do with them.

Ashes dropped to his silk jacket. He flicked and smeared and brushed them with thick fingers thatched with curly gray hairs to the first knuckle and beyond and around that hair, calluses of varying size, density, and shape, which no doubt Mr. Sherlock Holmes would have enjoyed analyzing. Glaucous had in his long life earned a living in so many different ways—accumulating scars from cock spurs, dog bites, rat bites, the nicks and marks and slams of human teeth. Bites—and strikes.

Fighting had also cocked his nose and thickened his ears.

Perhaps most interesting to a consulting detective: layered on the tips and sides of his fingers like tree rings were the calluses of a mortal man's lifetime of the concealing, switching, rotating, and rolling of coins and cards. And he no longer possessed fingerprints; had lost them before the turn of the previous century.

Decades of waiting in the half-dark had added fat all the way up his pink and pale olive arms, across his rolled back and thickened hips and legs. So many reminders of use and abuse, scars never quite fading. How much longer could it go on? Still wheezing along, his body an engine blessed with incredible fortitude, but his breath shallow, conserved; he might live forever, but he had been smoking for decades and his lungs were not happy, no, quite clogged, in fact.

There might soon come a time of purging and revival—no more vices, long weeks of hiking and exercise, eating little, smoking not at all, clearing his tissues of the dross of the last fifty years—a monkish process which he loathed on general principle.

Might, but he doubted it.

Glaucous's life had been extended by misdirection and cheat—and of course by the Mistress's touch. So much history, so much insight, and for what? He saw himself as the ugly main exhibit in a museum of oddities. When would Maxwell Glaucous be cut loose, his fortitude excised, gift withdrawn as a condition of unemployment?

The room was dark but for the light that shined directly on the creamy paper now creased over his lap. The phone had been silent all day, and before that there was nothing but crank calls from the curious and the rude, the drunken, the bored, and the unsound of mind—his usual correspondents.

Still, he knew the patterns. There was a reason Maxwell Glaucous had come to the Northwest and settled in Seattle. He could feel all the ripples in the local human ocean, like the passages of tiny, sharp-prowed boats through the general swirl and stir of mismanaged destinies.

Seven years of travel across the continent, driving endless miles beside his solitary and unlovely partner . . .

His eyelids slumped. He was slipping into his morning nap. He would awaken in a few minutes, refreshed and alert . . . but for now, there was only the drowse, an overwhelming need for a brief swim across Lethe. The buzzing in the bedroom, the silence of his own stuffy room, the soft comfort of a leather chair. He stared vaguely at the black phone on its stand, watery gray eyes turning in toward the bulbous nose, vision blurring . . .

Both eyes suddenly shot wide and his spine stiffened. Someone had brushed the front door to their apartment.

He could see or imagine knuckles lifted, poised—and then a sharp rap, followed by a quick, deep voice, like gravel rolling at the bottom of a muddy stream, "I know you're in there, Max Glaucous! Open to me. Old times and old rules."

Glaucous expected no visitors.

"Coming," he said, and rose swiftly to his feet. Before answering, he rapped lightly on Penelope's door.

The buzzing stopped.

"Someone's here, my darling," he said. "Are we proper?"

CHAPTER 26

University District

"I don't know you. I don't know anyone by that name," Fred Johnson said to the wasted, sick-looking man leaning on his porch.

"I understand," Daniel said. "I know *you*, though—or someone a lot like you." His voice was rough and shallow. He was exhausted after his hike from the university.

The former Charles Granger rose two inches taller than Fred Johnson, who stood about five-ten, including a shock of black hair arching back from a high forehead. Johnson looked up at his unexpected visitor with as much patience as Daniel could have expected from any man, under the circumstances.

"I need a few minutes to explain," Daniel said. "You probably won't believe me, so I'll leave after I'm done, but I thought if anyone might understand, it would be you. I'm glad you're still here. That's pretty amazing, actually."

"You looked me up in the phone book, right?"

"I went by the university," Daniel said. "Maybe all physicists stay the same, in all possible worlds. Maybe physicists tie up the important threads." He held out his long arms, pulled back dirty sleeves, and grinned, showing rotten teeth.

Johnson looked him over, trying to hide his disgust, and decided he was not a threat, just peculiar. "I don't *do* a lot of physics," he said. "Tell me what you need. A little money?"

"It's not about money. It's about knowledge. I know things you'll want to know."

Johnson snapped his fingers. "You're the guy off the freeway. The beggar." His expression reverted to contempt. "Don't tell me you're shaking us down in our houses."

"I need someone to listen. Someone who might know what I'm talking about. You can help me figure out whether it's going to happen—or more likely, when."

Johnson's cheeks were pinking. Impatient, irritated, more than a little concerned. Feeling protective of someone else in the house, someone important to him.

"Most people don't know what the indicators are," Daniel said. "But things in this strand are definitely going wrong."

Johnson screwed up his face. "If you don't want money, we're done. I don't have a lot of time."

"None of us do, Fred."

Johnson lowered his voice and glanced left, toward the kitchen. "Get off my porch."

Daniel tried to read this reaction—the words were strong, but Johnson was not a violent man. Daniel knew he couldn't afford to be punched in the face or hauled in by the cops. He wasn't at all well. At the very least, he needed a hospital, a good doctor—and at the most—

He needed Fred.

A woman walked up behind Johnson, curious—younger, late twenties, with reddish-blond hair cut short, high cheeks, a long chin, fresh-looking, pretty. "Who's come calling, honey?" she asked, and put both hands on Fred's shoulder, sizing up Daniel.

Daniel blinked aside tears and tried desperately to focus. "Mary," he said. "My God, you *married* him. That's different. That's great."

Her eyes changed instantly. "How do you know us?" she asked, voice hard. "Close the door, Fred."

"Mary, it's *me*, Daniel." His knees buckled and he leaned on the doorjamb.

"Jesus," she said. "He's going to be sick."

Sliding slowly, trying to hang on, Daniel said, "Just get me some water, let me rest. I know it's crazy, I might be out of my head, but I know both of you."

"I sure as hell don't know you," Mary said, but she went to fetch some water while Johnson helped prop Daniel up.

"Why'd you pick our porch, buddy?" Fred asked. "You don't look good, and you sure as hell don't smell good. We should just call an ambulance—or the cops."

"No," Daniel said, emphatic. "I've been walking all day. I'll go away—after we talk, please." He reached into his big jacket pocket and brought out the Bandle. He fanned the pages. "Look at this. Cryptids. Lazarids. So many. It won't be long."

Mary returned with a glass of water. Daniel drank quickly. She had curled her right hand into a fist and he couldn't see a ring. "I won't make a mess. Mary, I'm so happy to see you . . . are you two married? Living together?"

"None of your business," Mary said. "Who the hell are you?"

"I'm your brother. I'm Daniel."

Mary's face turned red and her brows wrinkled. Her eyes went flat. She was no longer pretty. "Get out of here," she demanded. "Goddamn it, get off our porch."

"You better move along, buddy," Fred said. "What the lady says."

"Something must have happened," Daniel said, looking between them, his vision fogging. "What was it? What happened to *me*?"

"If you mean my *brother*, he died when he was nineteen years old," Mary said. "And good riddance, the bastard. I'm calling the police."

CHAPTER 27

Mr. Whitlow had changed considerably across the long century. To the young and desperate Max Glaucous, he had once been friendly enough and kind in his stern way. In those faded brown days, Mr. Whitlow (Glaucous never learned his first name) had been a tidy but conservative dresser, slight in stature but with a good, strong voice; physically strong as well, for all his apparent middle years.

And of course that club foot, which still didn't seem to slow him down.

Now Mr. Whitlow's face appeared pinched and pale in the hallway's yellow light, and his eyes loomed large and black as a moonless night. He wore a tight gray suit with a narrow collar, white cuffs, links studded with large garnets, narrow black shoes. He had cut his glossy black hair straight across, and the white flesh of his neck skinnied above an awkward and hastily knotted bow tie. He carried a fedora now rather than a bowler, and stood at the front door with an air of nervous submission, lips wormed into an angular smile that pushed up his high cheeks but somehow did not pinch his eyes, giving him the look of a ghost-train maniac.

"Do you remember me, Max?" he asked.

"Mr. Whitlow," Glaucous said. "Please come in."

His visitor did not enter, even as Glaucous stood back. Instead, his wide eyes slowly surveyed the room beyond.

It was Shank who had referred him to Mr. Whitlow, and Whitlow who introduced him to the Moth—the elusive blind man in the old empty manor in Borehamwood, outside London. The blind man had approved him for service to the Livid Mistress.

"I am here at the behest of Mr. Shank," Whitlow said. "He informs me you have recently arrived, and already you have flipped the heart of one of our operatives."

"Ah," Glaucous said, feeling his body go gelid. The Mistress's implied disapproval could do that to the strongest of men. "I have never been punished for weeding our fertile ground."

"Circumstance changes," Whitlow said. "You have reduced our company in a crucial time."

"I work my territory alone, Mr. Whitlow," Glaucous restated with low dignity. Slowly, he was coming to realize the dreamlike impropriety of this meeting, and what that might signal—that his intuition had been correct. A noose was being cinched. Otherwise, why reveal so much? For now he knew that Mr. Shank still lived, still worked, and still found favor with the Chalk Princess—despite his apparent absorption in the most dreadful Gape that Glaucous had ever experienced, that dark day of August 9, 1924, in Rheims.

"There are discreet ways to make inquiries," Whitlow said.

Glaucous knew he was being toyed with. "I have worked unsupervised for nine decades. I speak with my employer only when there is a delivery. My last delivery was several years ago, and there was no mention of change."

Penelope watched through the crack of her bedroom door.

Sensing Glaucous's quiet anger, Whitlow still refused to enter. Hunters always visit with caution, approach with deliberation. His smile had not changed, however. Glaucous wondered if the elder collector had become a marionette—a dandled sacrifice to hostility—not that he had ever witnessed such a thing, or even heard of it. But nothing could be ruled out where their Livid Mistress was concerned.

"How has it been for you, my boy?" Whitlow said, his throat bobbing.

"Fair to middling," Glaucous said. "And you, sir?"

"Brambles, thorns, and nettles," Whitlow said. "So many have been recalled, and yet . . . here we are. Have you visited the home country?"

"Not for years. Built up, I hear."

"Unbearably. We have lived too long, Max."

"You're welcome to come in, if you wish, sir. My partner is under control."

"Kindly spoken, Max. I will make my report, issue my invitation, and then we will be done for today." Whitlow grinned. His teeth were mottled ivory perfection. "It is good to know you are well. Refreshes so many memories."

"Indeed, sir."

Whitlow drew himself up and his smile crackled and straightened. "We have all been brought here—*all*."

Glaucous quickly calculated how many that might be—based on years of speculation and observation. Dozens, certainly, perhaps hundreds.

"I am told little beyond that," Whitlow said, "but I trust we are now clear how important your territory has become—fortunately for you. We have reports, and so do they."

"They?" Glaucous asked. Penelope cleared her throat from the other room—listening behind the door.

Whitlow solemnly shook his head. "We have both kissed our Lady's hem, and our Lady's hem sweeps close. How much do you already know, young Mr. Glaucous—sly nimrod that you are?"

Glaucous's small eyes grew wider, though no match for Whitlow's. "Is it over?" he asked, his throat dry.

"Terminus is a possibility."

"Are the sum-runners here?"

"I am told, and feel, that a quorum will soon occupy our time. I beg of you, young *shikari*: do not remove more colleagues. Your thread is mine, and mine is wound inextricably with the Moth's, our great conveyer. We are united in one fate."

Whitlow bowed and backed away, never letting Glaucous out of his sight. "Must hurry on. Many hockshops to visit."

"Indeed, sir."

"Close and lock the door, Max," Whitlow said. "Let me hear the dead bolt shot home."

"Of course," Glaucous said. "Apologies." He closed the door, latched it, and listened for the familiar, off-center *punk-thump* of Whitlow's step as he hastened to the stairs.

Even then Max's fingers twitched to do the old man a mischief.

CHAPTER 28

Wallingford

After four hours of talk in the living room—preceded by a bowl of chicken broth, a glass of milk, and a glass of red wine, all of which Daniel gratefully accepted—Mary pulled her husband aside in the hallway to the kitchen and whispered harshly into his reddening ear, "What in *hell* are you doing? The man's sick—he's been stalking us, he thinks he's my brother, for God's sake—my *dead* brother."

Fred was clearly chagrined, but could not contain his enthusiasm. "All true—but you should listen to what he's been saying. I'm writing it down. He may be the most brilliant man I've ever met."

"What's so brilliant?"

"Fourier transforms—phi of k and r—maximum deviations from zero-energy states of overlapping discretely variable systems . . ."

"Crazy talk."

"Is it?" Fred pulled back, indignant. "He's feeling better, Mary— your soup is pulling him through. He's had a hard time since he came here."

"*Came* here? To our house?"

"Crossed over. He's relaxed, he's just getting started explaining to me—this could be something big."

"He's talking about *alternate worlds*, Fred."

Fred made a wry face. "Nothing new to physics. And that may *be* crazy, but it's the math—he's either read unique stuff or done the work himself, ideas and solutions I've never heard of. Some of it's even more brilliant than Sütō's solution for minimum total energy. Consider an infinite lattice of branching and debranching lines, each capable of producing another lattice—you'd think that would be totally intractable, but the secret is, the branches *don't last*—they sum to the least energy and greatest probability, the greatest efficiency . . . He said something so utterly brilliant it was *stupid.* He said, 'Dark matter is stuff waiting to happen.'"

Mary observed her husband over tightly folded arms, her lips growing thinner with each passing word.

"He wrote down some equations. Sure, it's alternate worlds—but it's also the most efficient states of protein motion and interaction, stacking solutions for sand and salt crystals, perhaps even distributions and probabilities for sparticle production in high-energy accelerators. Mary, if you don't like it—just please *butt out.* Go read or bake bread or something. The man's a gold mine."

His wife's eyes went round. "Have you even asked him why he knows so much about us?"

Fred's nostrils flared. "You won't like the answer."

"Try me."

"He knows what happened before Daniel died—some of the stuff you've told me. I didn't prompt him—he volunteered."

"That wouldn't be impossible to learn."

"Have *you* told anyone about how you sprayed silver paint all over your terrier when it bit you?"

Mary glared, and tears came to her eyes.

"Right," Fred said. "He knows about your older brother. He knows what your father was like."

Mary's face took on a yearning pain. Worse than not believing was not wanting to believe. "Does he know how Daniel died?"

"That wouldn't be logical."

"*You* must have told somebody," she said, working up to anger.

"I never told anyone. Take it to the bank, Mary—he *knows* about you and your family, but not much matches up after he died—after Daniel died, I mean. This Daniel—he didn't die. And in his world, we never got married. Even if it is a delusion, it's brilliant. I won't say I'm convinced—but I do need to listen. Please, Mary." He gently squeezed her rope-taut forearm. "Maybe he'll just tie himself in logical knots and we can boot him out, or call the cops and hand him over."

She seemed to soften, but it might have been exhaustion. "I could ask him some really hard questions. He'd fail, you know that."

"He gets agitated when you're around. Sad and energetic. His health isn't the best."

Her shoulders sagged. "How much longer?"

"Could go all night. He can sleep on the couch—it would be a luxury compared with what he's used to. Please, Mary."

The look she gave him—hurt, puzzled, angry—he mirrored in his own features, but his eyes were fixed, examining. This made it clear to her that Fred was going to be stubborn.

"Find out who he really is," she murmured. "He's lying. He's crazy. And even if he were my brother—you know I wouldn't talk to him. Daniel was an unbelievable bastard. That's why John killed him—to save the rest of us. To save *me*. You remember that, don't you?"

"Sure," Fred said too quickly, and patted her shoulder. "But like you keep saying, he can't be your brother, right? Why don't you get to bed and let me handle him?"

"I don't want him under our roof. He scares me, Fred."

"He's scaring me too, honey. With how smart he is."

She climbed the stairs to the upper bedroom, leaving Fred in the hall, staring at the prints he'd made from photographs Mary had taken in Geneva and Brookhaven—where they had lived and where her father had worked, twenty years ago. The remains of a spiderweb draped from one of the prints, shadows of silken lines drifting apart and rejoining in a draft of heater air flowing down the hall.

Fred followed those shadows, separating and coming together in rippling cycles, until his eyes blurred. Then he hurried to continue his talk with the stranger sitting in their living room. But first he stopped in the bathroom and dabbed a fingertip of Mentholatum under each nostril.

Daniel or Charles—whoever he might be—stunk to high heaven.

———

The evening progressed to morning, and to drinking—soda water for Daniel, Scotch for Fred. Fred was enjoying a half-drunken fever of speculation. "How could you end up in someone else's body? Did you transfer your soul—is there such a thing as a spirit that can be passed on?"

"I don't know," Daniel said. "It's never happened to me before." *Not that I'd remember.*

"Something to do with these world-lines?" Fred asked, his face flushed. "Could we develop an equation to describe it?"

Daniel watched him closely. "Perhaps," he said.

"One world-line is severed—cut free—and flies around, and connects up with the closest similar world-line," Fred said. "Like splicing DNA, or wires in a cable—I don't know how, just a metaphor. What do you remember from your past?" he asked, frowning sharply at the sudden importance of this question.

Daniel looked around the room and shrugged. "Less and less," he said. "Some of it is pretty foggy."

Fred planted his elbows on his knees and slowly spun the glass of Scotch. "Until now, you've relied on the memories of varieties of yourself—but you can't do that anymore. You can't take all your physical memories with you. This body—it's not you. You're coasting on the bump of memories from the transfer, and they're fading."

Daniel agreed.

"Exactly," Fred said, enthused by his own ingenuity. "If any of it's true—then it logically follows."

"I've been writing things down," Daniel said.

"My wife—if you are Daniel, I mean—my wife could supply important memories from your past. Not that such an arrangement would make up for all you've lost—but it would be better than nothing."

Daniel lowered his gaze, suddenly worried that this intelligent man would think his way through to the final solution—what must inevitably happen. Fortunately, Fred seemed more interested in theory, not threat—not actual danger.

"How many people have this talent?" Fred asked.

"I'm not the only one."

Fred's eyes gleamed. "If other world-lines are being eaten up, destroyed, or changed—maybe people like you are migrating here. Escaping from other, eaten-up world-lines. You could tell how close your own line is to being destroyed by counting the people like you, when they start arriving. If you could find them. I mean, how many would actually confess to displacing other people and taking over?"

"Makes sense," Daniel said.

"You look dragged out," Fred said.

"I am."

"It's late. We need to talk more about those Mersauvin solutions. Why not stay here? A couch can't be worse than an abandoned house."

"Generous offer," Daniel said.

"Well, I'm intrigued," Fred said. "We'll continue tomorrow—after my classes."

"Let's sleep on it," Daniel said. "We'll get together later."

FOURTEEN ZEROS

The Tiers

Their first evening in Tiadba's niche, the lovemaking was brief, promis-ing—not what Jebrassy had hoped for. They fell back into attitudes of patience—waiting for what, they could not know. The ceil outside the open end of the niche darkened from gray to blue-black. Small lights gleamed in the darkness, beautiful, familiar—unreal.

Eventually, at her gentle prodding, Jebrassy spoke more of his stray-ing—his suspicion that whoever entered him in dreams did not come from the Kalpa, did not stay long, and left little evidence of his nature. "I think he could be from the past."

She watched him across the pads and coverlets she had arranged for their tryst.

"But I don't know anything for certain," Jebrassy said. "He could be from the future—or maybe he's a messenger from the Chaos."

"Mine's from the past," Tiadba whispered, eyes wide with mystery. "She doesn't know how we live. But wherever they're from, I think they know each other."

Under her direct gaze, Jebrassy burrowed into the coverlets in confusion. In muffled tones he said, "I've written a message. If he should take over while I'm here . . . with you . . . show it to him."

Tiadba dug him out and lay next to him, and both looked through the open end of the niche at the velvety black roof of their world.

"How is it possible?" Tiadba asked. "What's happening out there? Why do they keep us ignorant?"

———

They left the far tip of the third isle and crossed to the grocery fields. The ceil flushed orange and dimmed to gray at the horizon, signaling the onset of sleep, but the fields were still active with red and black pedes gathering ripe fruit. These pushed along on parallel blurs of dozens of active feet between the tight rows of bushes and low, wide trees. Every few dozen yards pede tenders clucked and whistled, announcing the location of pickup baskets and carts.

A single warden, stubbed glassy vanes thrusting from its smooth gray thorax, hovered between the road and the edge of the closest grove. It hummed to itself and ignored them as they passed—just as Tiadba had predicted.

The pedes climbed arched trellises beside the baskets and dropped their loads with trills and pirrips of satisfaction. The tenders gathered the baskets and rolled the carts to the huts where packers and cooks put them up for the next day's meals. This way, the ancient breed in the Tiers fed themselves—though the pedes did the sowing and most of the pruning and hauling.

A mile and a half from the distribution center, Jebrassy and Tiadba left the road, now a worn dirt path, and hiked across acres of fallow ruts not yet sowed with a new crop, through the thin forest that surrounded all the farms. A short time later they arrived at an elevated slab piled high with worn farm machines and utensils, broken or outmoded long generations before. (Jebrassy was sure the pedes had not always done the greater share of gathering—these machines, rusted and caked with age, might have once performed such tasks.)

Making sure they weren't followed, Tiadba gave him a leg up, and he handed her in turn onto the slab. From there, she guided him through crumbling boxes until they came to a bare hole in the middle of the slab—perhaps four miles from the bloc where they both lived. They descended a peculiar ladder way—rungs arranged in a spiral along a deep shaft with an odd bend that, after twenty yards, turned the shaft into a level tunnel, still equipped with rungs but more suited to large pedes than to breeds. It brought them downward and across to a part of the Tiers he had never heard of—a storage area long abandoned, and apparently now used only for such clandestine meetings as these.

Tiadba informed him—her face shining with excitement at the conspiracy of it all—that the wardens never came here. "That grove warden ignored us. Don't you think that's odd? We were out where we shouldn't be, near dusk."

Jebrassy admitted that was odd.

"Some think they've been ordered to stay away. Some think we're *supposed* to do what we're doing."

Jebrassy did not disagree—out loud. But he was full of disagreeing thoughts. He wanted to be defiant—not to fit into anybody's plan.

And when they actually arrived at the small round room, lit by three ancient, greenish lights that shined on the circled faces of the chosen marchers—he felt like a fool. A fool for love.

Tiadba was an utterly marvelous glow—no doubt about it. But her stubbornness was more than a match for his own. She thought little about his feelings, but always about the Goal—that is, *her* Goal. And her Goal, right now, above all things—including his love—was the march. She had literally roped him into this meeting—tied a rope around his waist before they left the middle Tiers, in case he fell as they descended the ladder way, and even now tugged him forward to sit with the group around the perimeter, waiting for the leader—the elderly sama whose name was Grayne.

The circle focused on the waiting dimness at the center.

"She never disappoints," a young male confided to Jebrassy as he and Tiadba pushed back and huddled shoulder-to-shoulder with the others. Jebrassy wondered if the breed was referring to Tiadba, and was prepared to take offense—but it soon became apparent he referred to Grayne herself, the old female.

They all squatted, then fell back and sat against the wall, and soon Jebrassy felt a cold, ancient oppression—he did not like this place. Whatever his enthusiasm for joining a march, all the mystery and concealment struck him as contrived.

"Strange place," he whispered to Tiadba. She acted as if she hadn't heard. "There could be chairs, a table."

"We never leave signs," Tiadba said, and the young male beside him nodded agreement.

"If the wardens never come here—why worry?"

"It's the *form*," the male said, giving him an irritated nudge. "It's the way the march is always done."

"It wouldn't be my way," Jebrassy muttered.

"What would *you* do?" the male asked, his face clouding. He leaned forward to catch a glimpse of Tiadba's reaction, but she was studiously ignoring the whole exchange—and that irritated Jebrassy even more.

"I'd go out there by myself, or with a group of people I know and trust. Well-trained."

"And who would lead?"

"I would."

The male chortled. "Where would you get your equipment?" he asked.

"He doesn't know anything about the equipment," Tiadba said.

"Then why bring him? We're almost ready. This is supposed to be an experienced group."

"Because Grayne requested it." Only a partial truth.

The male thought this over, then, with a shrug, asked, "What's his name?"

"Jebrassy."

"The fighter?" The young male bumped Jebrassy's arm again, this time with his elbow. "I've seen you. My name's Denbord." He pointed to two other males. "That's Perf and Macht. We're friends. We wanted to fight—but the march is more important."

The others, not yet introduced, touched their noses and glanced at one another in accord—fighters were to be pitied, however amusing fights might be.

"Quiet," Tiadba said. "She's coming."

The circle had left a gap near the tunnel entrance. The air was sharp and close. Jebrassy began to sweat.

A small female entered, nearly a foot shorter than Tiadba, elderly and stooped: it *was* the sama he had met in the market. She moved slowly and carefully, using a staff, and two younger females in gray long-shirts and slippers followed, carrying baskets. Fruit was passed— tropps, not yet ripe but full of juice, and dried chafe for chewing. The group refreshed itself while the old female squatted in the middle of the chamber, the dark eyes in her worn, plain face searching the circle until they came to Tiadba—her lips softening their hard line—and then to Jebrassy. She gave him a firm nod.

One of the younger females brought up a short stool, on which Grayne sat with a sigh and completed the inspection.

Is this a trick? She can't be a march leader. She's so old—why hasn't the Bleak Warden come for her? Jebrassy felt his face tighten into a frown, and forced himself to relax—he did not want to reveal any more than he had to.

"Twenty have been chosen," Grayne began. "Four from this group, sixteen . . . elsewhere. The Kalpa is forever—but we are *new*. We are *youth* and *newness*. We are not pets, not toys—we are hope, kept bottled until needed. And now the cap is pulled—we *are* needed. No one else in the Kalpa has the will to cross the Chaos."

"No one else," the group intoned.

"We send our marchers through the gates, across the border of the real, into mystery—to find our lost cousins and to free ourselves. What's *out* there, beyond the Kalpa?" Grayne asked softly. "Does anybody really know?"

Jebrassy shook his head, his eyes held by her black, intense glare.

"Do you?" she asked him directly.

"No."

"And so we all give up to mystery, to the unknown, to save ourselves from suffocation. Are you with us?"

"Yes," Jebrassy said.

Grayne studied him, then got up from the bench, reached into the pocket of her robe, and produced a small bag. The old sama walked around the chamber, handing out little square tabs to everyone—except Jebrassy.

"We'll meet one more time before the march. Everyone will go now—except the fighter. And Tiadba."

Tiadba helped Grayne along the pipe to the surface. Jebrassy followed. The three of them stood there for a moment, while Grayne's breathing slowed. "Everything you know is wrong, young fighter," she said.

The others in the group had already spread out over the rutted fallow field and then down the path through the low groves, slinking past the solitary and unmoving warden, its vanes glowing a faint and pulsing blue in the darkness.

The pedes had curled into glinting, twitching bundles in the near dark, to conserve heat.

"I know I'm ignorant," Jebrassy said, keeping his voice low. "But I'm not stupid."

Grayne reached out and took Jebrassy's jaw in her strong, knobby fingers. She twisted his face toward her, eyes darting. "Tiadba tells me your visitor knows nothing of the Tiers, or the Kalpa. Where do you think he comes from?"

Jebrassy did not pull away. "Tiadba probably knows more about him than I do."

"Never mind," Grayne said, and shivered in the cooling air. "Let's walk."

———

The sama's niche was humble enough—she dwelt in the lowest tier of the third isle's main bloc, within a kind of support column, surrounded by ancient, silent machinery—great hulks of smooth hardness, lumbering, dark, and unrevealing of the tasks they had once performed.

The niche's furnishings were equally humble—a few dun-colored blankets and cushions, a small box where she kept her food—and a larger box, equipped with a finger lock. She offered them water and they sat quietly as she touched the box, opened it, and removed—

A book. A real book, bound in green, with letters on its spine and its front cover. It was the first real book—loose and whole—they had ever seen. Tiadba let out her breath as if someone had knocked her in the stomach. Jebrassy kept his expression under tight control, unsure once again what either of these two females were up to—perhaps no good. Perhaps they were part of a trap laid by the Tall Ones to entice foolish young breeds . . .

His mind raced through confusion after confusion, and then he looked at Tiadba—and realized that she was as entranced as he.

Grayne clutched the book to her bosom and stepped slowly toward them. "I love these dangerous, impossible things above all else in the Tiers," she said, holding it out in both hands and opening it for their inspection. "Isn't it lovely?"

Jebrassy longed to hold it, but did not dare reach out. The cover had been worked with flowers of types unlike any he had ever seen in the produce fields, placed around a design that attracted his eyes immediately— a cross circled by interlaced, apparently whirling bands.

Tiadba glanced at him. He nodded. This design was familiar— though they had never seen it before.

"Is it from the shelves in the upper Tiers?" Tiadba asked.

"Those books aren't real," Jebrassy said. "I've tried to pull them out. They're just decoration."

Grayne circled two fingers over the book and pursed her lips, blowing out her cheeks with a snorking whuff. "Miles and miles of temptation and futility. A curiosity, I think, that we instinctively love books, yet can't have them, can't read them, can't do more than look at their spines, cemented into those awful, wonderful shelves." She solemnly laid the book on a small table between them. "Touch it. It's very old, very sturdy—it's been waiting to be of use for many thousands of lives. You can't harm it."

Tiadba had tears in her eyes as she lifted the book and smelled its cover. "Can you read it?" she asked Grayne.

The sama held up one finger—yes. "Some of us have translated pages. Many pages."

"How?" Jebrassy asked.

Grayne beamed. "Of all my strange instructions and duties, I love this part most of all. There is a secret so wonderful that no one will believe you if you tell them—so don't bother.

"Once, when we were quite young, my crèche sisters and I made up a game. We climbed to the upper Tiers, then ran along the impossible shelves. We laughed and leaped and pulled at the unmoving spines, top shelves, bottom shelves, one up, one down, center shelves . . . tugged on the odd, unyielding volumes for hours, laughing and leaping and failing and falling, and laughing some more. No one expected we would ever succeed, but we believed, as children will, that if we felt so attracted to them, if there were so many children's stories and legends about books, there must be some truth behind them—something behind the tantalizing spinebacks."

Grayne squatted slowly, in private her movements more obviously painful. Jebrassy wondered if he would live long enough to feel that sort of pain. *She's the oldest breed I've ever seen . . .*

For the first time, he caught himself thinking that a visit from the Bleak Warden might be a blessing—not a thing to be feared.

"I wasn't the first to find it—our first loose book on the shelves. It was my best friend, Lassidin—full of curiosity, fastest of all my sisters. A spark among glows, you males say. To me, she was a flame . . ." Grayne closed her eyes. "The Bleak Warden claimed her long ago. But she was the first to solve that riddle, watching, in her brightness, always watching, all the time seeing things we did not, puzzling it through, running, leaping, tugging . . . until she got it right."

Grayne lifted a crooked finger and hooked at empty air, reliving the moment. "Lassidin grabbed a spine . . . just the right spine—and before our eyes she pulled down a book. That surprised her so much she fell and landed on her butt. The book flopped open on the dusty floor, revealing a page covered with letters from an ancient alphabet—some familiar, most not. All of my crèche sisters—there were four of us, families could be larger then—gathered around the book and looked, afraid to touch it. Two ran away. Lassidin and I somehow gathered up the courage to take the book to our family niche, where we hid it from our mer and per. At first we told no one. And when we returned to that spot in the Tiers, where the gap had been—we found another book in its place, as false and unyielding as before. We wondered if we had been dreaming, and rushed back to our niches—where Lassidin had placed the book in this old box, with its finger lock.

"By the time we returned to the upper levels, a few wakes later, Lassidin had solved the puzzle of the shelves, and the shelves rewarded her—us—for cleverness. We pulled down the second of many, which we then retrieved and hid away with the first."

"How many?" Tiadba asked.

Grayne tightened her lips and touched the stiff fur on her nose. "More than one," she said, a faint smile on her lips. "Fewer than a dozen."

"Who loosened the books? Why let anyone look at them?" Jebrassy asked. "I thought the Tall Ones wanted to keep us ignorant."

"A sophisticated question from our young warrior," Grayne said. "I don't know the answer. Some say, however, that a great and powerful citizen, far above the Tall Ones, created these shelves to honor his daughter—long dead or missing. They may not have been intended for us at all. At any rate, in time the Bleak Warden came for my sisters, but never for me." She looked up. "I am the guardian of Lassidin's box, and all the books we plucked from the walls—all the books we were allowed to find."

Tiadba turned to the next page in the green book. Her nose drew up in fine wrinkles and she pushed her chin forward. "I can't read it. The letters are too different."

"They are old. A few are still familiar."

Tiadba followed the lines with her fingers, then said, "Here's one. And another." Delighted, she showed Jebrassy.

"My crèche sister Kovleschi was meeker and did not chase the shelves with us—but she knew of antique letterbugs, marked on their wing-cases by such letters. We visited the families who kept and prized them, and there we studied the way they formed words—and compared how younger bugs with different, newer symbols formed the very same words."

Letterbugs could live many breed lifetimes, and were often passed down for generations.

"In time, we were able to piece together a syllabary, and from that, a beginning dictionary. But even then we could read only a few passages. There are still so many that mean nothing to me. Though I've memorized them . . . as many as will hold still. They seem to change, you know."

Tiadba handed the book to Jebrassy. He, too, examined the first page—and his brow shot up. " 'Sangmer,' " he read, drawing his finger under one odd word. "Is this about *Sangmer?*" Sometimes the teachers told frightening stories to breeds who had misbehaved, some involving a traveler named Sangmer, who died after he strayed beyond his neighborhood.

"Perhaps I haven't been so foolish after all," Grayne said, eyes twinkling. "Most of our books speak at many points of Sangmer and Ishanaxade. They were partners, and not always happy ones. A tempestuous pair. What little we can read tells us that ultimately they both vanished in the Chaos."

"And what do the other books tell?"

"More puzzling still, they speak of things no breed can understand. Of the aging of the world outside this one, and of the decline of all-powerful rulers . . . and how they were forced to retreat to the Kalpa.

There is even a brief history of the last years of what seems to have been a shining brightness in an open *sky*, something called the 'sun.'"

"I'd like to read that," Jebrassy whispered. "I'd like to read them all." He looked around as if afraid that Grayne, the niche, the box—these real books—might just vanish in a puff.

With her staff, Grayne pulled the box toward her. "These were *our* books. They were meant for us alone, to guide us. You will find your own books—and they will accompany you to places we could never go. Perhaps they will even finish the great story." She narrowed her eyes, near exhaustion.

Tiadba seemed stunned, but she took the book from Jebrassy— pulled it from his grasping fingers—and handed it to Grayne, who returned it to Lassidin's box.

Grayne closed the cover and locked it. "This will be the last march," the old sama said. "Out there you will go, utterly ignorant, unless you find your books and learn how to read what they contain. You will tell those stories to your fellows. Every march has its stories and instructions. Those are the rules."

"Whose rules?" Jebrassy asked.

Grayne ignored him. She removed her cloak, revealing thin, bowed shoulders under a smooth black gown, and handed it to Tiadba. "The sisterhood made this, many lifetimes ago, when we were all young. Look inside . . . sewn within the lining, our crude syllabary and a comparison dictionary. All made by referring to the antique letterbugs. Some of those bugs still survive. You must look for them—borrow them—learn your own words, add what you can to our knowledge."

"Why us?" Jebrassy asked.

"Better to ask why *you*, young warrior," Grayne said. "I would have passed this all on to Tiadba. That was my plan—until she chose to be adventurous. For a time, angry with her, I thought I would die with our box locked, taking my revenge against a world that made no more lovely and *sensible* sisters. But I have my instructions."

Tall Ones? Jebrassy held his tongue on this question, but still blurted, "You guide the marches. You arrange for equipment, you send them . . ." He could not untangle this knot.

"True. I have been used, but have always hoped—in my defense— that someday, individuals at least would return, and tell me of what lies

beyond the border of the real. None has. How many have I condemned?" She wiped a tear, then straightened and assumed her sama
mien. "Here is our secret—what the sisterhood discovered. Lassidin
and I listed the most promising Tiers and levels in the syllabary. The
false shelves in all the inhabited levels are locked and useless. Only in the
deserted levels do they sometimes free a book. Look to those shelves.
They are not always the same. Understand why, and how, and you will
learn what we learned.

"Now . . . there's very little time, young breeds," Grayne said. "I believe the Bleak Warden will soon pay me a visit. But before that happens, I must arrange this final march."

Jebrassy looked down, excited, confused—and frightened.

"Your first challenge is to learn what you can—so very little, but it
might save your lives. Then—you will be taken into the flood channels,
to begin your training."

CHAPTER 30

All the water of the Tiers flowed through this conduit, which vanished
in low mists beyond where Jebrassy stood, at the edge of the outer
meadow. The water made a dismal, sleepy sound as it dropped along its
sluice. It was clear and smelled wet and a little sad. He measured with
his arms and fingers the distance between the top edge of the sluice and
the dirt that surrounded it—that same pebbled, granular, brown-gray
soil found everywhere in the Tiers. He was still trying to understand
everything at once—and it made his head hurt.

Farther back, closer to the bridge, the conduit had been higher. Perhaps the water didn't reach the far wall, but vanished into the ground,
absorbed as if by a rag. Somehow, the ground, granular and rough,
sucked it down, spread it out, purified it.

*Whatever pulls the water, pulls me. And does the ground tug the water in
and out the same way it tugs me? I don't know anything about where I live.*

Confused, frustrated, he felt like striking out—always his first im-
pulse when he confronted his abysmal ignorance.

He stood and turned at the sound of footsteps. At first he couldn't see who it was over a rise in the meadow—but then he made out Khren's round, shock-furred head. Beside Khren paced three young breeds, all wide-eyed with anticipation.

Tiadba had said he needed to find four helpers, and that she would meet them all at the spiral stair core that rose through the inward end of the first isle Tiers. They were going to visit an abandoned level high in the Tiers. They might spend all day searching just a few of the halls that radiated from the stair core—a very small part of the abandoned levels—and with the lights dimmed, a few extra pairs of hands and bright, young eyes would certainly be useful. Still, Jebrassy felt uneasy that they would be sharing their rare time together with others—even uneasy about Khren, who had been with him on so many adventures.

The young males ran down to the straight road and clustered around him, touching fingers and giving sharp whistles of greeting.

"Shewel, Nico, Mash—this is Jebrassy," Khren said. "A very unwise and devious breed." They were impressed; Khren had obviously been filling their heads with nonsense.

"You're a warrior," said Shewel, the tallest, a gangly young male with wide-spaced eyes and reddish scalp fur.

"Not much time for fighting now," Jebrassy said.

"He has a glow to fill his empty hours," Khren said, and Jebrassy shot him a look. Khren danced aside, as if he had thrown a rock.

The young breeds were breathless. "What are we looking for?" Nico asked. He was pale, his hair and fur silver, his eyes light blue—handsome enough, but with a high, piping voice. "Is there food buried out here? Strange things the wardens hide?"

"Nothing like that," Jebrassy said. "We're going to search an empty level in the Tiers."

"Looking for dream-ghosts?" Mash asked. He was a strong, square-headed youngster—the youngest, Jebrassy guessed, but also the largest. Breeds sometimes told their young a tweenlight tale that the most beautiful dreams broke free when one awoke and flew off to hide in the deserted levels, where they might be gathered in baskets and brought back to sweeten future nights. Bad dreams—obviously, those should be avoided. "Bright or dark?" Mash persisted, defensive, as the others scoffed. He circled the group as if embarrassed to join them.

"No dreams. We're going to explore the shelves and look for books. Try to pull them out. Real books we might be able to read."

"No!" the group chorused, disappointed. They knew all the books were false. "That's stupid—a waste."

"A large bag of sweet chafe and tropps to anyone who finds a real book," Jebrassy said. "And whether we find any or not, we share three bags when we get back, so everybody goes home full. But none to slackers."

That motivated them up to a point, and they fell in line behind Khren and Jebrassy as they crossed the mid-line bridge to the first isle.

The lower tier levels were still populated, so they entered off the inward esplanade, keeping clear of the small groups of occupants around the lifts, and ascended the winding stairs through one of many ventilation cores—the steps gritty with disuse.

The group waited at the tenth level, where Tiadba had instructed them to gather. All the levels above the tenth on this end of the bloc had been abandoned in living memory, after three intrusions in a single wake—a fluke, perhaps, but enough to scare off all families and even young singles. None of the niches showed signs of having been lived in recently—all were filled with broken furniture, debris, and frass deposited by rogue letterbugs and pedes.

As Jebrassy paced, he glanced down the halls radiating off the stair core. Two lost letterbugs flitted about in the draft that rose here—too few, too widely scattered and disorganized to form interesting words, forlorn remnants of more cheerful wakes, when umber-borns had laid them out on shake cloths and played their learning games.

The young breeds, bored, played a few rounds of arm-off, then shook out their wrists and ran down a hall to practice tugging, so they said, though none of the halls on this level had shelves, much less spinebacks. "Don't go far," Khren called out, well aware how short the attention span of a young breed could be. "She's late," he observed to Jebrassy, his voice low and nervous. "They say intrusions never strike twice in the same place . . . but I'm not so sure."

The two friends split a wad of bitter chafe and thoughtfully chewed the fibers, until the silence seemed to overwhelm them. They could no longer hear even the scrabbling and whickering of the three youngsters. The letterbugs had vanished as well.

"They're wandering too far," Khren said. He squatted, refusing to accompany Jebrassy in his back-and-forth around the stair core. "I should go find them." But he did not get up. Khren much preferred contemplation to actual movement, even when he was anxious.

"They're fine," Jebrassy said. "A shout will fetch them. Patience."

"How reliable is your glow?" Khren asked.

Jebrassy was about to answer, but they heard soft steps echo and Tiadba appeared, stepping quickly through the balustrade. She wore the same pants and shift tied at the waist that she had worn at the Di-urns, and she looked tired. "Sorry I'm late," she said. "Gray wardens. I had to go out and around on the first level so they wouldn't follow. Why would anyone come *here*, after all?" She peered accusingly at Khren.

"I didn't say anything," he responded, spinning two fingers resent-fully.

"Of course not," Tiadba said. "Did you find helpers?"

"Khren recruited three," Jebrassy said. "They're green sticks but lively. They're already out hunting."

Khren glanced at Jebrassy, still stung, and excused himself to go join them.

"He's an honest breed," Jebrassy said when he was out of hearing. "Leaders have to take care with their words."

Tiadba sniffed. "Grayne tells me the best hunting is above the fifti-eth. Those levels have been abandoned for hundreds of generations. For some reason, that loosens the spinebacks even more—so she says. She says—"

"How does she know so much?" Jebrassy asked. "Who talks to her? Tall Ones?"

"*Breeds* talk to her," Tiadba said. "She's been a sama for a long time. Breeds come to the market from all the Tiers to consult with her. She's as close to a real teacher as we have. But I was going to tell you—"

A racketing echoed down a long hall, preceding the return of Khren and the three youngsters. More introductions went around, and Tiadba softened the critical tone she had used earlier. The young breeds weren't shy around a female; if anything, they ramped up their raucous sport-ing, and it seemed they might explode any moment. Only Nico ap-peared willing to maintain a kind of philosophic dignity.

"We'll race! Fifty—that's near the top," Shewel called out as he started up the spiral stairs. His voice echoed back. "We could climb out on the roof!" The others followed close behind, but Mash trailed—slower and a little abashed.

"What do we need books for?" he asked. "Even if they're real, they'd only tell us about the times before there were breeds. Who cares?"

"It's a game," Tiadba said. "That's all. You can read, can't you?"

"I can riddle any letterbug challenge, as long as it's fair," Mash said. "And I can read anything a teacher puts in front of me. I'm big, but I'm not dim."

———

The fiftieth level had a desolate, muggy smell that sent shivers down to Jebrassy's fingers. Just a few levels below the roof of this bloc, the stair core had expanded to almost three times its diameter at the ground floor, making the risers shorter, the steps wider, and perversely increasing the distance they had to climb. He stumbled several times. None of the other stair cores were like this, which increased the feeling of strangeness—an inappropriate place for breeds.

The youngsters did not seem to notice. They had already radiated off, drawing marks in the grit before each hallway they investigated. There were over twelve halls stretching away from the core at this level, and hundreds of niches—all empty. Not even the rustle and flap of lost letterbugs broke the ancient hush.

Nothing alive seemed to want to be here.

The three youngsters quickly filled that silence, counting out how many spinebacks they had fruitlessly tugged. Their voices echoed and grew faint the farther they ran, until they could barely be heard at all.

"I'll leave you two and join them," Khren said. "Three's an awkward number, don't you think?"

Jebrassy was about to protest, but Tiadba thanked Khren and off he went, with some haste. He did not like being around Tiadba, obviously, which did not puzzle Jebrassy—she had not gone out of her way to make friends.

Tiadba took this opportunity to brush his shoulders with her hands. "Did you see?"

"See what?"

"I saw it just before Khren spoke. I wonder if they'll even notice."

"Notice what?"

Tiadba pushed him to the angle of an unexplored hall, one the youngsters had not marked. Here, six shelves rose on each side, each stretching ten arm lengths, filling the spaces between niche doorways, outward into the gloom—to the very end of the hall. False spinebacks marched off in solemn relief as far as they could see. "Wait. *Look.*"

He wasn't paying attention. Guilty, he leaned forward and forced himself to concentrate on the titles, frowning as he walked along the middle row of spinebacks. "What am I looking for?" he asked, trying to keep his voice level, his tone humble.

And then he saw it. The titles changed—the odd letters seemed to crawl, rearrange, and fix themselves again, as innocent and permanent as he had always assumed they were. The sight did more than startle him. He couldn't stop himself—he stumbled back and bumped against the shelves on the opposite wall. Then he looked toward Tiadba, ears hot with surprise. Such impermanence in a timeless feature like the false shelves was almost as frightening as an intrusion.

Tiadba did not laugh at him. "Is that what Grayne was talking about?" she asked, awestruck. "Here, everything changes, I mean—because nobody's watching?"

"We're watching. Why change it in front of us?"

"I . . . do . . . not . . . know," Tiadba said, but she reached out and tugged at a false book. Of course, it refused to budge. "Grayne was being too sly. This is a puzzle. We have to riddle it to be worthy."

"I'm clueless, but that's always been obvious," Jebrassy said, ears still warm. "I don't like it here."

"Maybe these shelves are showing us what happens everywhere, when the breeds sleep, and we're too ignorant, too unobservant—or we sleep too soundly—to notice or even care. We could learn these old symbols. We could write them down on shake cloths and then compare them after a few sleeps—"

Jebrassy suddenly caught on. Momentarily forgetting his fear, he returned to the shelf and fingered the spines, but did not tug—presuming he had not earned that privilege, not yet. "The books that *could* come loose, that can be pulled out, are always the same," he said. "But they move around. The titles move. Is that the secret?"

Tiadba smiled and reached out to pull on a few more spines. No luck. Then she whistled with excitement and raced down the hall.

"Maybe they're like letterbugs," Jebrassy said, moving toward her. "Maybe the books on the shelves actually *breed*. Maybe the titles make new titles—maybe they make new books."

"I don't see how it helps to know that," she called back.

"How *could* we know?" Jebrassy murmured, his shock of discovery dissipating as quickly as it arrived. "We can't read them . . . we don't know which ones to pull . . . they shift around or multiply each sleep when nobody's looking . . . and that means, since the shelves never grow, some titles vanish . . . *Frass*," he swore. "It's a *dice game*."

"And the dice are loaded!" Tiadba said. "We can't win. We'll never find a book. But Grayne's sisterhood found a few anyway." Her face lit up. "Isn't that the challenge? Isn't it wonderful?"

Jebrassy peered after her. "Well, that can't be all there is to it," he said. "We're missing something important."

"Call your friend and the young breeds," Tiadba said. "Maybe they'll help us—maybe they'll find their own books."

Jebrassy looked across the core at the other hallways, radiating to the outer Tiers, thousands of shelves . . . he couldn't begin to think how many titles. "This is going to take *forever*."

"What's that mean?" Tiadba asked.

Neither of them had ever heard that word before—it was not part of the breed tongue.

TEN ZEROS

Before crossing Forty-fifth Street, in front of a motion picture theater, Whitlow looked both left and right—after so many years in London and Paris, he still could not decide which direction horse-drawn or gasoline-powered vehicles might descend upon him.

Whitlow lacked any sense of general danger, actually had less sense than the people he hunted. Minus the charm of the Chalk Princess, he would likely have died a thousand years ago, in the last Gape of burning Cordoba.

There were no items of interest to be found in any of the area hock-shops. He hadn't expected any—forces were obviously working in opposition, building toward a confrontation.

The theater marquee indicated that a film called *The Book of Dreams* was being screened. That brought out a broad smile, unveiling strong thick teeth, all alike and the color of old ivory.

He wore his best suit, a little tatty after fifty years but well-mended. Invisible reweaving, indeed. He had administered a biweekly sponge-scrub in his studio flat in Belltown, greased his thinning black hair, trimmed and waxed his narrow mustache, and slipped on wool socks and high-laced black boots he'd had made in Italy to fit his deformed toes.

He then donned a new fedora.

It had been good to see Max Glaucous again, his young protégé, after so many decades—more than a century, really. As time wound down, the past seemed to bunch up, forming humps and valleys, difficult to judge distance or terrain . . . but no matter. Glaucous had always been a productive hunter, though by Whitlow's standards a little brusque and obvious.

Whitlow himself had been in Seattle for over a month, having sensed a confluence, a drawing together of significant world-lines—well, of course, having been accorded the *grace* of some of the Moth's vast well of knowledge. For one of the Moth's talents lay in knowing when others were approaching points of desperate choice; and in particular, points of collision with the Chalk Princess or her employees: a specialty whose importance was not to be casually dismissed, nor discussed with the likes of Glaucous.

Whitlow knew better than to come anywhere near Glaucous while he was collecting—knew even the danger of announcing his presence in Glaucous's city. But their Livid Mistress expected her due, and Seattle was now home to at least two and possibly three targets.

The third target not only elusive, but problematic. Some in the profession doubted that one of this type would respond to any inducements, and yet might be more powerful than either of the others, or all of them combined.

The bad shepherd.

For decades, Whitlow had maintained a remote and watchful presence in cities around the world, without drawing attention from other hunters, and often enough without poaching their prey. For the Chalk Princess had, months after the Great War, set him a particular task: to find the one shifter who *did not* dream of that Citie over which she maintained, some said, eternal watch—in another existence. It was his custom to keep a cadre of irregulars on a payroll of money or drugs or both; a select few who lived their lives like insects under rocks, shy, watchful creatures with nothing to lose but their own brief, painful stretches of time. Fifty or so in most cities sufficed, randomly positioned. Shifters seemed to always come into loose contact with such unrooted beings, as if their own world-lines—so tightly controlled—were attracted to briefer and more ragged threads.

Might even merge with them—under some circumstances.

Whitlow had seen that happen 634 years ago, in Grenada. Had conditions worked out, had he—masquerading as a Jewish dealer in antiquities—managed then to capture his chosen prey, there would have been no need for all these subsequent centuries.

The mummer called Sepulcher was one of his, and had alerted him to the existence of a Shifter named Jack, whereabouts otherwise uncertain. That was Glaucous's prey.

And now, another scout was telling tales. Six blocks east, the thin, angular woman named Florinda stood in the shadow of an awning over the entrance to a small bookstore. She was speaking with a plump older woman with white hair and a round, finely wrinkled smoker's face. Florinda sensed Whitlow's approach and craned her head until her neck corded like rope. Her eyes opened wide, startled, expectant.

As Whitlow and Florinda spoke, the white-haired old woman mumbled and stared blankly at the street.

Afterward, Whitlow paid Florinda in her most desired coin.

And that night, as she lay beneath a freeway overpass, drifting in and out of drugged sleep—rain pattering on her blue tarp, and the first few, distant flashes of lightning picking out her sweet, cooling, smoothing face—she slipped free of all this world's lines and binding threads.

In his tiny studio apartment, Whitlow pushed back his head, closed his eyes, and smiled as if at a beautiful passage of music, waiting for the storm to gather strength and take a shape—a familiar, feminine shape.

Only days until the end.

And always the unanswered question: *Why do our giants bother with such tiny grains? We swirl all pointless and ignorant in the great wet surge of worlds.*

Why care at all?

CHAPTER 32

Queen Anne

Jack sat in the dark at the small kitchen table, warm cup of tea in hand, but tea this early morning provided no comfort. Burke was late; maybe he had hooked up with his waitstaff friends and gone clubbing.

Except for a heavy rain and flashes of lightning to the south, quiet.

He looked at the clock on the stove. Two A.M.

Burke kept a phone under a pillow behind the couch. He often slept through the day but was superstitious about turning off the ringer; hence, the pillow.

Jack fingered the piece of newsprint. The 206 prefix would be a local call. No additional charges on Burke's precious phone. The worst that could happen, he might connect with a lonely crank and they would compare the dismal weather and their boring nightmares. That in itself might not be a bad thing—a sympathetic ear.

He reached under the couch to remove the pillow and retrieve the phone. The answering machine mounted beside the cradle blinked red: forty old messages and two new ones. Burke was superstitious about erasing old messages. The first new message was from someone named Kylie at the Herb Farm.

The second was from Ellen.

"This is for Jack. My apologies. That was a bad start. I thought it would be fun to talk things over with the girls. Your exit was impressive. Could you do it again—on cue?" She sighed. "I found the newspaper, Jack. This must be a difficult time for you. Don't be rash. Please. Call me immediately. Whatever you do, do not—"

The machine beeped, its memory full. He touched the box in his pocket. Three numbers to choose from. Harborview, the classified ad— or Ellen. More out of embarrassment than anger, he did not want to speak to Ellen now. He stared at the western corner of the living room. Two walls meet the ceiling. Three lines make a corner. Push the corner out like a rope, to infinity . . . twist all the lines together . . . much stronger.

Which path, which consequence?

Now you're just being irrational. Make up your mind.

He jerked as if someone had puffed into his ear.

Get it over with. There's work to do, and either you're going to help or you're not. Just do something.

He picked up the phone and dialed the first number that came to his fingers.

Naturally enough, it was the number in the ad—and he was calling a complete stranger at two in the morning. Somehow it felt right—a *sweet pathway.* All would be well.

It was picked up at the other end before the first ring had finished. "City desk," a husky voice said. "Journal of Oneiric Fancies."

"Is this the number to call . . . about dreams?"

"Does it sound like it is?"

"I have the wrong number—I'm sorry."

"Explain yourself. It's still early."

"I need to know about the Kalpa," he said. He sucked in his breath and masked the mouthpiece with his hand, startled by that word—that place.

"Name and address, please." The voice was raspy, confident—not a bit sleepy.

"Beg pardon?"

"You asked about the Kalpa," the voice said.

"I don't even know what that is."

"Are there lapses? Lost moments?"

"I think so."

"How often do your dreams occur, where and when—petty details."

"I've seen a doctor—"

"No doctors. I need details. My pen is poised."

"Is this some sort of a business? Who are you?"

"My name is Maxwell Glaucous. My partner is Penelope Katesbury. We answer calls and sometimes we answer questions. Time is short. Now . . . your name and call number, please."

"My name is Jack. My phone number—"

"I have that. A *call number* is what I am after. You have been issued a call number, have you not?"

"I don't think so. I don't know."

"There *is* such a number, you *have* such a number," the voice said with certainty. "Go find it, then call again, I suggest sooner rather than later. If someone else should learn about your lapses, it might not go well for you. We can help, however."

"Do you know what's wrong with me? Is it serious?"

"Certainly it's *serious.* But there's nothing wrong. It's a marvel. You are blessed. Find your number and call us back."

"Where would I look?"

"You have hosted a visitor. Look in his effects—whatever he's left behind." Glaucous coughed and hung up.

Jack sat for a moment, face red, both angry and curious—then walked on quivering legs to his small bedroom and pulled back the trunk.

The folio was gone. He stared in astonishment, then ransacked the room, looking under the bed, pulling back the sheets, the mattress, returning to the trunk. Nothing.

He felt in the shadows behind the trunk. His fingers swept out a small hexagonal piece of paper. He picked it up. The hexagon had been intricately folded, like origami or one of those mathematical puzzles kids learned how to make in school. It was clever, so tight he could not pry it open far enough to peer in. No loose bits. As far as he could tell, all the corners and edges met inside.

You'd have to have very clever fingers indeed to fold a piece of paper that way.

"Stop it!" Jack shouted to the room's still air. He squeezed the folded paper between his fingers from two opposite sides, then from another angle—trying all combinations to get it to pop open, to flower.

Nothing. Then, tentatively:

They want a call number. The catalog number of your special volume. Whatever you do, don't give that to them, under any circumstance.

"Why not?"

No answer.

"To hell with you." He felt a growing pressure in the air, fogging his thoughts.

Jack looked up. Someone was climbing the stairs. Footsteps outside—heavy thumps. He hoped it was Burke—someone to talk to. So much had happened today. The pressure increased. His head began to hurt. Anything to make it stop. The rain and wind blew harder.

The thumps slowed to the pace of an older person—a cautious person—not Burke, who was quick and athletic. Jack suddenly wanted to be anywhere but where he was. Then the sensation passed, painted over by another wave of pervasive sweetness. All would be well . . .

Across the curtains in the living room window, something big cast a shadow. The big shadow passed and a smaller shadow replaced it: short, broad, like a gnome.

A heavy fist slammed on the door, rattling the frame and the wall and shivering the curtains.

"It's Glaucous, dear boy," cried a rough voice—the same voice that had answered the phone. "I've brought my lady to meet you. Let's find that number, shall we?" The fist slammed again and the voice added in an amused undertone, "Easy, dear."

CHAPTER 33

The Green Warehouse

Ginny paced in front of the thick steel door. She laid her ear flat against the cold, thick-painted metal, listening to voices on the other side. Murmurs . . . rising and falling pitches, several women speaking with Bidewell.

She made out only a few phrases. " . . . all here. Gathered . . ." Then, Bidewell, "The girl doesn't have it with her . . ." And another, deeper female voice, "Pawnshops, the usual . . ."

Ginny drew her brows together, then twisted her neck to look up. A thin blue-gray light seeped from the skylight into her makeshift living quarters, pressed between stacks of crates and cardboard boxes, all filled with books. Big drops of rain blundered with dull *tunks* against the wired glass in the high arched panes. A storm was gathering. She could feel the electricity, the moisture in the air. Two bolts of lightning struck nearby, flashing violet. An instant later thunderclaps shuddered the old warehouse and echoed from far skyscrapers.

She appraised the rumpled bedding on her cot, the chipped antique bureau pulled into place at the cot's foot. This part of the warehouse was large, dusty, drafty.

Once, she had enjoyed rain, even thunderstorms; not now. But the storm wasn't hunting her—not this time. The warehouse was protecting her.

No, this storm was after someone like her, someone else who had read an ad or seen a billboard alongside a highway and was about to make the mistake of his or her life—and Ginny thought she knew whom: the young man on the bicycle at the Busker Jam. She wanted desperately to warn him, find out what he knew. There wasn't much time left for him, for her, for anyone.

The storm was here.

All of us—cut loose and bumping into the end.

That image made her suck in her breath with a sad hiccup.

For a few moments she paced before the door, biting her thumbnail. All her nails had been chewed to the quick. Her mother had once told Virginia she would have pretty hands, if only she would stop chewing on them. Quickly bored with chewing, she twisted a strand of hair until it draped in an elongated ringlet over her nose.

Enough.

She lifted her fist to the huge sliding door. Before she could strike the first blow, the door groaned, then pulled aside wide enough for Bidewell to shove through a scrawny arm. With an emphatic grunt, he heaved the door back on its track until it bumped against a rubber stop. All the while, he carried on his former conversation. "We shall use the century rooms, I think. I've kept them empty and ready. If you're sure you can find them all."

In Bidewell's private library, in the rear half of the warehouse, three women sat in high-backed reading chairs. White lightning flashed through a tall window covered with steel bars, carving brilliance on the ceiling-high shelves.

"We'll find them," one woman answered.

All the women were older than Ginny by three or more decades. One had short brown hair and green eyes and wore a long green coat and brown skirt; she had answered Bidewell. Ginny turned to examine the second woman, with long red hair and a pretty, round face. Though her gray eyes seemed confident, she picked at a brass button on her denim jacket and smoothed her cut velvet dress.

Ginny's heels scuffed on the old wooden floor as she faced the third woman. This one, dressed all in purple, a rich green scarf draped over her shoulders, was stout and older than all but Bidewell, and her eyes were bold and black. Ginny did not like the way this woman assessed her: unrolled, weighed, measured, ready to snip off a length.

She was not sure she liked *any* of them.

Bidewell smiled, revealing strong teeth like mottled bone tiles. "Would you please join our group, Miss Virginia Carol?" he asked. "A little premature, perhaps. Dr. Sangloss is not yet here."

Ginny remembered the doctor who treated her at the clinic, who told her about Bidewell and the green warehouse. Nothing surprised her now.

The pawnshop—her stone.

The women regarded her with wary curiosity, awaiting her reaction. *I might bite. Who are they?*

Another rumble of thunder.

The woman with the green coat got to her feet and extended her hand. "My name is Ellen," she said. Ginny held back, but the woman advanced. Given no polite option, Ginny relented and shook with her.

Ellen then introduced the redhead, whose name was Agazutta.

The stout woman with the appraising look was Farrah. She said, "The storm is just getting started, Virginia. This time, it's not after you—not yet."

"I know that," Ginny said.

The stout woman continued. "We have an hour at most. We should have made our move sooner."

"I've been slow, it's true," Bidewell confessed. "A little tired of late. Forgive me. We need you, Virginia, because none of us is a fate-shifter."

"What's a fate-shifter?" Ginny asked, and then it dawned on her. Her mouth opened. Her eyes narrowed. Suddenly, she was more than suspicious—she was frightened. She had never told *anyone*, for fear of losing that which she wasn't even sure she had—and now others knew. That either made it real, a confirmation of years of frightened dreams and desperate hopes, or a shared delusion.

A roomful of crazies, just like her.

Introductions over, Ellen held up a plastic bag and pulled out a crumpled tabloid, the *Seattle Weekly*. "I found this in my recycling bin," she explained, and opened the paper on the wooden table to the classifieds. A small section had been torn out, about the size of one or two personals. "Virginia might know what it means."

Ginny turned away, face red.

"No need to be frightened or ashamed," Bidewell said.

"Of course not. Where *is* Miriam?" Agazutta asked, looking to the wooden door at the other end of the room.

Farrah continued to stare at Ginny, patient, implacable. Measuring. "The girl knows," she said softly. "She's been there—and escaped."

Ginny glared at her, then the others, helpless, defiant, like a deer surrounded by tigers. As if on cue, Minimus leaped onto the table and sat by the paper. He lifted a white paw and scratched madly at the tabloid, shredding it.

"There is the question these hunters always ask as they lure their young prey into a trap," Bidewell said. "Someone is about to answer."

"A young man named Jack," Ellen said. "Another like you, Virginia. A fate-shifter."

"'Do you dream of a city at the end of time?'" Ginny whispered.

"We know," Farrah said. "Our time's shorter than we thought. What can we do?"

The wooden door at the far end of the library opened and Miriam Sangloss entered. "Finally," Agazutta said.

"Apologies." Beneath a dripping brown slicker, Sangloss wore a short white lab coat, blue blouse, and jeans. Under her left arm she carried a black leatherette folio. "Sorry I'm late." She removed her slicker and looked around the room, sensing the tension, then grimaced and added, in an aside to Ginny, "Glad to know *some* people take my advice."

Bidewell cleared a space on the table, pushing the shredded tabloid into a wastebasket.

Sangloss laid down the folio and untied it. "I'm now a burglar," she said, and explained how she had just ransacked a young man's apartment in the Queen Anne neighborhood. "I got the address from his clinic record. I found this, but couldn't find his sum-runner. He must have it with him."

Again, Ginny blinked in surprise.

"They've collected him and his stone," the redhead, Agazutta, said, and slapped her hand on the top of a chair.

"Perhaps not yet," Miriam said. "But soon. He's a very confused young man."

"No more confused than the rest of us," Farrah said.

The rain hissed on the roof. Minimus looked up, pupils round and deep.

Bidewell turned to Ginny. "You should not be afraid of us, Miss Carol. We preserve and protect. The ones on the other end of that ad . . ." He shook his head. "They're the monsters."

"Now that *that's* clear," Miriam said, "let me show you what I found in Jack's apartment." She opened the folio and laid a short stack of sketched pages before Ginny. The topmost had been executed in water-color, crayon, and dark pencil, with daubs and sweeps of pastel color. "Anything look familiar?"

Against her will, Ginny angled her head and looked down at the first drawing. *Tiadba.* The word—a name—just popped into her head. Re-membering was difficult. *My visitor . . . Tiadba has seen these. They look like ships surging into a heavy sea. They must be huge, all three of them . . . whatever they are. And now she's sorry she ever left their protection.*

"That's a yes?" Miriam asked, eyes bright. She flipped to the next sheet.

Ginny covered her mouth and looked away.

What had been sketched there, with crude skill and determination, was the last thing she would ever hope to see. A huge head rising on a weird scaffold over a rolling black land—tiny, fleeing figures giving it perspective. The head was big as a mountain, its one round, dead eye fixed on a distant point, stabbing a sharp gray beam through smoke and fog. A moan seized in her throat and turned into a fit of coughing.

The Witness.

"Poor child," said Farrah. "Get her some water, Conan."

"I'm sorry," Miriam said. "It does look grim, doesn't it? I wish we could put all the pieces together. We've never actually seen these things."

"Neither have I," Ginny said. "Not personally . . . I mean."

"In dreams," Bidewell said. "Have you met the young man who drew these?"

Ginny shook her head. "Is he the one they're collecting?"

"Let's hope not," Miriam said. "Ladies . . ."

They all stood.

"We need you to come with us," Ellen told Ginny. "Conan will stay here, as always."

"I have no choice," Bidewell said.

"Where?" Ginny asked, glancing between them.

"We'll follow the storm," Miriam said. "Track the lightning. It's going to get worse, and nobody knows what this young man will do. If he's as talented as you, he might just survive until morning. Oh, and one more thing." The doctor reached into her lab coat pocket and pulled out a package wrapped in brown paper. "I found this in a shop near the clinic. Paid quite a lot to convince the pawnbroker to part with it."

CHAPTER 34

Jack's thoughts fluttered like a bird in a net. Less than five minutes had passed since he'd made the call. He could climb off the balcony, swing to the porch below . . . run off down the alley. But a sugary warmth stopped him.

On the other side of the door: friends, thick and sweet as treacle. No need to flee, no need to fear. His feet would not move. Every path equal. Every outcome a good one.

"We are here!" Glaucous cried. "You called, and we are here to give you the answers you need." Then, almost inaudibly, "I'm afraid I've stunned him. You may force entry, my dear."

Even after the third heavy bang on the door—as if a concrete block were about to shiver the poor wood to splinters—Jack could feel excellent conclusions everywhere.

He recovered enough to step back. The fourth slam bent the door like a piece of cardboard and blew it from its hinges, twirling the jamb's jagged splinter on a bent dead bolt. Wind blew into the living room. Somewhere, Jack's rats squeaked. Despite the noise, the rush of wind, and the drops of rain, Jack did not feel afraid; his feet might as well have been glued to the thin carpet.

A short, taut, bulky man in gray tweed entered and removed his flat cap with thick, ruddy fingers. His face was flat and pink as a doll's, a hideous doll—and his eyes, small and efficient, swept the apartment and Jack with a minimum of motion. His instant smile was toothy and broad, like a Toby mug. He radiated sincerity and human kindness. "Good evening," he insisted. His presence commanded respect—demanded cheer.

"Hello," Jack said.

Through the frame of the broken door he saw a shadow loom, a heavy arm draw back, and at the end of the arm, an impossible hand—the hand of a comic book hero or villain, square-knuckled, fingers flexing with power and pain. The shadow drew into the light: a woman, very large. She rose up forever. Her face was the white of packed ice or bone china. Raindrops fell along the curves and dips of her whiteness, down to the tip of her blunt, large nose, where nostrils opened like black manholes. Her eyes opened to central, cataract blankness. A quick smile on her thick, greenish lips, glittering with moisture, revealed small, precisely socketed teeth. A scut of hair splayed out beneath her flat, ludicrous hat like dead gray moss.

The rats shrieked like terrified children. Both Glaucous and his companion had to be imaginary, Jack was certain. They had to be symptoms of the final and fatal dropping of all his marbles.

"Shall we come in?" Glaucous asked, though he was already through the opening.

Jack used all his will to back off another step. He could almost hear the awful sweet glue pulling up beneath his soles.

The huge woman stooped to pass through.

"This is my partner," Glaucous said. "Her name is Penelope."

Jack sucked in his breath and half twisted, but the gnome's sorrowful disappointment held him. Things seemed to fall into place; gusts of air, flits of dust, turns of tiny events conspired to hold him steady. That was interesting. That interested Jack no end.

Glaucous turned to say something more to his partner.

Jack unexpectedly broke loose. Momentarily free of the glue, nothing could have prepared him for the dread the pair exhaled, like the halves of a hideous bellows; they wheezed out terror. Without a thought, he dashed between world-lines, intruding on other selves—an unnoticed melding of ghost-soul upon ghost.

Yet something reached through and *snagged* him.

Glaucous pulled the adjacent world-lines in *toward* his own—changed circumstance directly rather than fleeing it. Jack had never heard of such a thing—but then, he was young. He focused on the man's power, his skill, trying to feel his way through to any possibility of shaking loose again. Glaucous was strong, but Jack was stronger at exploring all the available paths, despite the spreading treacle. He would not be held, even by these two; *he would not be pinned.*

Glaucous lowered his gaze. "You want to escape, but all ways seem good. Which way to turn? I am a happy fellow. All ways seem sweet to me—and thus, to *you.*" He flicked a round shoulder at his companion. "Penelope, he is not convinced. He wishes to leave us. Convince him."

The large woman tilted her head back on her short neck and

shrugged open her long brown raincoat, let it slide off. Her broad bare shoulders shone moist and dimpled like sweating dough.

Jack could not look away.

Beneath the coat she wore no clothes, yet she was not naked. Dark masses covered her lumpish modesty. Her body was swathed in crawling clots of wasps—yellow jackets, thousands of them breaking and rippling in slow waves across her flaccid flesh, draped in buzzing shreds around knees and ankles, a living gown.

The one real horror of Jack's existence, the one fate he could not elude: a swarm of angry, stinging insects. He had learned painfully that insect colonies and hives drew their own snarled road maps of fate, thousands of individual world-lines tangled like overcooked spaghetti, knots of furious determination. Wasps, bees, even ants—could fan out and block his decisions, mire his movement from strand to strand among the world's infinite fates.

Wasps had helped teach him the limits of his talent, and had also sensitized him to their venom: one more sting would be enough.

They know what I am!

The wasps rose like black mist, evaporating from the woman's body, zipping around the room. Revealed, Penelope was a stack of lumps, rolling heaves set upon legs like trees. She was not shy; her vacant smile did not change as wasps filled the apartment.

There was no way he could escape all the swooping, darting insects.

"Penelope, dear, let us do what we do best," said Glaucous. "Let us help this poor young man."

For a creature of her size, Penelope was swift, but Glaucous was even swifter. The room filled with grabbing hands and buzzing wings, small, hard, striped abdomens thrusting long stingers, faceted black eyes searching and hating until insects and humans seemed to become one.

A noise like giant cards being shuffled, slapping, slamming, *snapping* into place.

Jack *moved*.

Before Glaucous could grab him with his outsized hands, Jack came unstuck from the treacle and dread and jumped across hundreds, thousands, of fates, whole cords of fates at once, the greatest effort he had ever made, greater by far than the effort in Ellen's house—just to escape those awful stingers.

Glaucous stared down at the young man lying limp on the floor, and a fissure of doubt appeared in his squat, craggy features. He remembered how wretched and disheveled the old crookback's dying birds had looked as he tossed them into the road one by one for the rats to gnaw.

"Has he fled?" Glaucous asked, bending over the body.

"He's right there," Penelope observed, waving a huge hand on which wasps still crawled.

Glaucous regarded Jack doubtfully. Jack's eyes opened wide, filled with empty terror.

Glaucous reached down and felt the boy's pockets. In the light jacket—a piece of folded paper. He reached in. A shock tingled up his arm and made his teeth clack. As his hand withdrew, the paper came with it.

No need for Whitlow to confirm they had the correct prey. But he did not dare remove the box.

Stone and quarry must be delivered together.

CHAPTER 35

The first far strand Jack reached shocked him nearly senseless. Seattle was being rocked by an enormous earthquake. He moved off that path with hardly time to feel the uplifting slam and careened through a flash-blur kaleidoscope of alternatives until the colors dulled and the flickering slowed and he hammered up against something he had never experienced—not that he had experienced *any* of this before: a barricade or glassy membrane. For an instant he could almost see through it—but something pulled him back, protecting—restraining.

What lay beyond that membrane was worse than where he was, and where he was . . .

His flight stopped. He was stunned—he needed time to recover. No world-line had ever been like this.

It felt *dead*. At the first breath, soot and ashes seemed to fill his nose and lungs. The apartment building he and Burke had once called home had not changed in size and shape, but all vitality had been sucked from its walls and timbers. A sick unsure light fell through the broken window. Paint dropped in slow flakes from cracked wallboard. The moisture in the air did not refresh his parched throat; it seemed to burn like a mist of acid. Off balance, he kicked out one leg—and stepped on a carpet of steel syringes, hundreds scattered over the floor.

Something moved in the corner of his eye and he spun about, crunching needles—this Jack wore thick-soled boots. He saw no one, nothing alive. The rooms were empty, silent but for the patter of falling flakes of paint. He lifted his bare forearms and held them close, unbelieving—flesh pricked by needle tracks, scabbed over, painful.

Wherever he was, he was sure he had eluded Glaucous and his giant, doughy partner. But that did not encourage him. He had had a knack lately of going too far afield, of shifting not just his immediate fate, but the *quality* of his intended world.

He had, for example, fled from Ellen—and ended up on the line where he felt compelled to dial the phone number in the newspaper ad, without sensing the downside. Not a good plan, not a good circumstance.

And now his fate had just turned much worse.

One requirement of his crazy ability—or symptom of his neurotic imaginings of power and control—had always been the conviction that he *could tell* when things were going to get worse, before they did. Without that precognition, his jumps would be random—of no value at all. Yet now he could detect nothing worse than where he already was— except what lay in wait behind the hard, translucent barricade: corruption itself, a festering discontent mixed with . . . what?

Emptiness?

"Anybody home?" he called, his voice a croak. "Burke?"

Small things scuttled in what had once been his bedroom. His rats? He crossed gingerly over the warped floor, scuffing through a tinkling scatter, crunching and breaking needles with a sound like falling icicles.

Peered around the corner.

In the small room squatted the trunk that had been with him since the death of his father. The trunk where he kept his most valued possessions. Behind which he had found the folio.

He touched his torn pocket. The box—still there.

Checking the solidity of the floor with a tapping boot, applying half his weight, then full pressure, he crossed the bedroom. The trunk's boards had warped. He lifted the lid. The trunk was empty except for a gray, slushy film.

He let the lid fall and backed out of the room. On the back porch, Jack pushed open the sliding door—broken glass lined the frame—and stepped out. Across the street, all the buildings had collapsed into piles of gray and brown rubble from which beams and boards pointed up like dead fingers. Muddy water streamed down the gutters and over the cracked and heaved asphalt, pooling and swirling in the dips as if there had been a heavy rain and the drains were clogged.

A dead-end place in a dead-end time. No hope as far as he could see, no life . . . and for how long? How long had this world been dead? Hours?

Years?

By the looks, the smell, it had never been truly alive.

Wherever and whatever it touches, it takes hold. You've seen it before. You will see it again . . .

Everywhere he stepped, in every room, needles had been carelessly cast aside. He pulled up the sleeve of the filthy jacket and stared again at the puncture marks. A fresh one oozed a serum-yellow drop. Jack could feel the drugs cloud his mind. He fought the lethargy, the hateful, bitter satisfaction of having just scored—and listened to the noises outside: wind, rain, water, the underlying rasp of falling dust and debris. The very air smelled sour as old vomit. How could anything live here? He needed to find a way down the stairs, away from this comatose neighborhood, across the city—maybe this was just a local phenomenon, an unfortunate slum.

But he knew the blight wasn't local. It was *everywhere*. He had landed in an awful trap. He had managed to jump to a perverse line of least opportunity, surrounded by an infinity of purgatories—all of them bordering on hell. All adjacent paths were dark—a fecund void smeared across any jumpable distance, tainting vast bundles of world-lines, a metaphysical disease that could not be measured except in billions, trillions, of corroded, corrupted lives.

The joy of matter is gone.

Then, out of the corner of his eye, something moved—and when he jerked around to look, this time, it was still there.

CHAPTER 36

Penelope slung the limp, heavy sack over her bare shoulder, then stooped to grab her coat. Huge and still naked, she tugged coat and sack through the door with several hard, bruising bumps, then humped the sack into a better carrying position and hauled it down the steps, dropping it near the yawning rear doors of the old van.

Rain fell in sheets. Lightning flashed like the blink of a huge eyelid.

Glaucous stood in the empty apartment, chin in scarred hand, thinking over the folded piece of paper pinched lightly between his fingers like a captured butterfly. Best not to meddle, though he had long been curious about how such things were folded and what they actually contained. He slipped it into his coat pocket. Something key was missing. Yes, they had the call number, they had their boy. They even had the box; but not the final part his employer was willing to pay for, in money and dispensation. Despite the wasps, the boy had made his leap, leaving behind a dangerous vacancy. Delivering other than a complete subject could be painful—even fatal.

Glaucous leaned over the walkway's iron railing. "Penelope!" he shouted into the rain. "We've bagged a shill. He's gone."

"Here he is—he's *here*!" his partner wailed.

"We can't take any chances. We'll have to stay and hope the boy returns—or cut him loose."

Penelope let out a hollow curse. Then, like a little girl about to cry, "Why didn't you tell me *before* I carried him all this way?"

A balding man with a mustache, in his mid-thirties and tired, was climbing the stairs, raincoat flapping over his white kitchen work coat. He paused at the top and tracked the busted-in door, then turned at the sound of that infantile voice rising through the rain—and caught sight of Glaucous. Slower, more cautious, he tried to sidle around the strong-looking gnome.

"Begging your pardon," Glaucous said, leaning in toward the rail.

"What the hell is this?" the man asked.

Glaucous pitched him a bizarre smile, then slipped aside and glided down the stairs, feet a blur, using his thick hands as runners. "Sorry!" he called.

Jack's roommate poked his head through the broken door. Wasps filled the apartment. Swearing, he swatted about his face.

Glaucous joined Penelope. "No matter about the boy—I'll snag him. Let's move on."

She had propped the loose, bagged form against a retaining wall, dripping and still. Face expressionless, she drew up her coat and covered her massive nakedness.

Jack Rohmer had fled so far that at first Glaucous could not even smell his spoor. Glaucous was certain that Jack would rejoin their path soon, in sheer desperation. There were now so many moribund pathways, so many diseased lines that led nowhere.

Oh yes, he, Glaucous would fling his sweet net across the black shimmer of broken fates, and with another deft snap, Jack would fly straight back, frightened out of his wits. All would be well.

The roommate shouted threats from the third floor.

Glaucous waved his hand at the bag. "Lift. Carry. Bring him along, my dear."

CHAPTER 37

The apartment's other occupant took color and texture from the needle-littered floor, the scabbed walls and caved ceiling. It made a sound like hard snow falling on a black evening—never ending, never changing. This was its only voice. It had been waiting, trapped in this room, *forever*, and now it complained to anyone who could listen. Jack had simply not noticed it until now. Looking at it, he was paralyzed.

The occupant took the initiative and moved—without moving. It changed position, Jack was sure of that—but not convinced he *could* be sure. As he turned to track the flaw, the blur, where it now stood between him and the door, he saw that it had been *there* all the time, and nowhere else. He had been mistaken.

He was noticing it again for the first time.

Jack's eyelids twitched and tried to close. Drugged sleep wanted to drape him like funeral laundry. He needed to stop *seeing*, get away from the impossible thing between him and the door. His mind was not able to process and remember. His engines of memory were shutting down. Soon he would be stuck here just like the other. He would protect himself in the only way left to inhabitants of this purgatory: by gathering up floor, wall, and ceiling, and hiding *in plain sight*.

"I don't want to make trouble," Jack said, shivering. "I just want to get out of here."

The sound of hard snow resolved into a grainy, steady weeping—tears of frozen grief—the saddest sound he had ever heard. The other dropped its camouflage, became more solid and human—two arms, a lump for a head, a trunk divided at its base into two legs.

"Where will you go?" it seemed to ask. "Take me with you."

"I don't know how." Jack could just make out a face with a hole for a mouth and two sunken green pits for eyes.

"Take me outside."

"You can't leave?" Jack asked, feeling sick.

"No," it hissed. It came closer—had always stood right beside Jack, would never leave him, limb stretched as if to place a hand on his shoulder—but there was no hand.

Not yet.

The trap was closing.

Jack could not jump. No paths, no freedom, nothing but pestilent strands of not-color, not-darkness, each ending in a pulsing, tumorous knot, ready to spread and consume everything.

The fabric here is rotting. Strands have come loose. Their ends double up and stick to make loops. That's where I am. I'm in a looped world.

Jack leaned back to scream.

The scream trickled out, no more than the squeal of a small, dying animal, no louder than the crying of his rats.

"Stay . . . I've left some food for you," the shape said.

Jack suddenly recognized the blurred face.

This was Burke. His roommate.

A hook snagged Jack's spine and jerked him back with a jolt of unbelievable pain. Before he had time to think about death and speech without voices—about the formless paw on his shoulder, welcoming him to an unchanging forever—he was yanked with considerable force and even more pain.

He tried again to scream—really gave it all he had. The strangled noise dopplered across a thousand gray, dead-end paths—and *slam*, he was jerked hard in another direction, through thousands more lines— the fragments of light that reached his eyes growing brighter and warmer, then darker and colder—and again he was snagged, tugged back—in no time at all. Someone wanted to reel him in and Jack knew who it was—could feel that same sickly sweet, oh so reassuring touch, like the finger of a fly fisherman on a whipped-out filament.

Jack Rohmer was being pulled from rivers of misery by a master fisher of men.

CHAPTER 38

West Seattle

Glaucous drove south in the slow lane, then turned onto the West Seattle Bridge. He blew a piercing trill through his lips, guided by no particular tune. Every now and then he would wince, jerk back his head, and grimace as if clenching something between yellow teeth. "Got you," he muttered, and wiped his hand across his brow.

Penelope lay against the window, tiny eyes languorous. A lone wasp crawled from her collar and wobbled along a thick fold on her neck. The rain droned on the van's roof and the wipers swiped. At this hour of the morning the old elevated road was almost deserted. Dawn staked a feeble claim to the east, a vague lightness in the wet gloom.

In the back of the van the sack stirred.

"Ah," Glaucous said. "Is it no longer a husk, a shill?"

Penelope brushed a wasp from her nose and cracked it under her thumb. Glaucous admired her strength and her steadfastness—but not her personality. She felt no affection for anything, really. His fourth partner, Penelope had stuck with him the longest—over sixty years. In return, she had not aged, but had grown large and unattractive. Others had withered and shrunk. Once, for a time, he had carried his second partner in his pocket. Over a few days, his third had simply faded as if left out in the sun—and then, one morning, had vanished. As far as he knew, she was still dwelling in their old house—not that anyone would ever see her, and not that it mattered.

Penelope's eyes opened. "*It's* back, I think."

He turned judging eyes on her. "How can we be certain?"

"It's crying," Penelope said.

———

The canvas sucked up against Jack's mouth. His own harsh breath clung to his face with a stale, comforting certainty. He might suffocate. He might die. Anything would be better than where he had been—the shoddy lands, where rot and despair ruled.

And Jack *was* crying, quietly and steadily. Having been jerked from purgatory, having come so near to hell, his tears had nothing to do with bravery or fear, but with grief greater than anything he had ever experienced.

The joy of matter is gone.

And when he reluctantly remembered that which he had nearly broken through—a barrier like a scab over an open wound—

"He smells like burning," Penelope said.

"Leave him be," Glaucous said, but a worried cast came into his eyes. He glanced out the window at the rain, the lightning. The air seemed more turgid, gray light pulsing under the storm in broad, thick waves. Or was that the blood pumping through his chunky, hard heart?

Glaucous blew out his worries. "We shall give him a fine scrubbing. Hell hath no worse smell."

"Not hell," Penelope said.

Jack listened from the sack. He *did* smell—and the smell was foul. Holding his nose did not help, so he tried his best to ignore it.

With a tremendous effort, gathering all his courage, he dipped a toe back into the currents of fate. All near situations were tense, tight-packed. Under those circumstances, even the strongest world-lines tended to weave in and out. He was traveling in a truck or van. Nothing in the way of accidents, blowouts, mishaps of any useful sort, presented themselves. He was too far down a strongly developed line. All available alternatives kept him *here*, but perhaps not in a sack so secure, so lacking in rips and seams . . .

"Don't even try it, my fine stinkpot," Glaucous advised from the driver's seat, and again, that voice—like a mother soothing an upset child—bathed Jack in cloying sweetness. All would be well . . . He was too exhausted to fight. He almost welcomed it—the sugary sense of rightness fermented into a spiritual liquor, dulling all hope, all pain. "We'll be home soon," Glaucous said. "You'll like it there."

"Will he?" Penelope asked. Her seat creaked miserably as she arranged her bulk. "*I* don't."

"We will wash away that taint, before something else smells it. Something premature and perhaps too eager." Glaucous made a chitinous cluck-clicking behind his mouth, sharp and loud. Jack could not see how he did it.

Like claws snapping.

PART TWO

BROKEN LOGOS

FOURTEEN ZEROS

CHAPTER 39

The First Bion

His feet planted firmly on a disc of cold, hard light, Ghentun flew up between the glowing silver conduits, through lustrous canyons, between dazzling miles-high walls, to the highest levels of the First Bion—the urbs of the Great Eidolons.

Once—if the myths could be believed—humans had thought the universe might last no more than a few tens of billions of years. No one in the Brightness—the warm, brilliant womb of the last trillion centuries—could have guessed how long history would drag on, how often its cruel patterns would repeat: wars that filled tens of billions and even trillions of years, eating away at the lives of quadrillions of thinking beings—consuming countless heavens in the idiotic flames of countless hells.

The inevitable rise to immaterial godhood of billions of civilizations had been followed by the equally inevitable collapse back to individuated bodies in benighted ignorance of what had been lost . . . A cyclical rise and fall, like a beating heart torn by endless and merciless time.

Nor could any who lived during the primordial billennia have guessed how decayed and fragmented the aging cosmos would become, its parts requiring redesign, supplanting, replacement—and now, how the lost shards of times past would break loose, drift, and bump up against the present.

As for the late Trillennium, in the shadow of the Chaos: broad legends described the age of the Mass Wars. Bosonic Ashurs had returned from their mastery of the dark light-years, seeking ascendance over all . . . and were subdued by the mesonic Kanjurs, who in turn were defeated by the Devas—patterned from integral quarks. Devas were then forced to give way to the noötics. Noötic matter was hardly matter at all—more like a binding compact between space, fate, and two out of seven aspects of time.

The noötics—calling themselves Eidolons—gathered survivors from the last artificial galaxies and forced nearly all to convert. The last remnants of old matter were preserved and transported to a number of reliquaries with the longest continuous histories—including Earth.

Only the servants of old Earth—Menders and Shapers mostly—were given dispensation to remain primordial. Many converted anyway. For a time even Ghentun had succumbed—before being recruited as Keeper. Noötic matter guaranteed safer and more cooperative environments, more efficient thought-patterns, and more diverse and minutely controlled utilities. In noötics, each particle was preprogrammed with a variety of behaviors, which could be integrated into unparalleled servitude.

The complete mental control of one's noötic self led most such intelligences, over the last ages of the Trillennium, into eccentricities without number—but guaranteed their dominance.

For Ghentun, the legends of the Mass Wars still contained one great lesson. In the society of would-be-gods, a humble man is always polite.

———

The photon disc passed swiftly through alternating regions of mass and light, solid dwellings and roads along which solid citizens moved, yet when that motion tired them, the citizens lifted like whirlwinds to whisk off to more ethereal paths—wit-courts pulsing with the arts and challenges of ten trillion years of history.

The disc flew over ribbon boroughs populated by former Devas, who now refused any but a narrow band of extreme technologies. They insisted that their boroughs be stacked like spools, slowly unwinding ribbons of renewal and locality, each half a mile wide and festooned with pop-up dwellings, experience galleries, and regeneration farms. Crowds of images—projections of the boroughs' citizens—took shape around Ghentun, exhibiting vague curiosity—but seeing only a lone and lesser Mender, they flattened and faded like cast-aside portraits.

Sometimes, Ghentun felt that the more advanced urbs in the Kalpa were no less strange than the Chaos outside—until he saw the Chaos again. The high urbs and ribbon boroughs were positively cozy and familiar by comparison.

Even here it's difficult to misplace your wit—your soul—but out there, beyond the border of the real . . .

The photon disc wove expertly, dancing a pretty path for its own amusement, it seemed, then slowed and communicated across the last miles with the Astyanax's security detail, swarms of machines little different except in size—and deadly power—from the wardens in the Tiers.

On the highest level of the Kalpa, surrounding the roots of the Broken Tower, urbs like tremendous jellyfish rose from mountainous foundations, capped by a diffuse blue glow that spread across the ceil. They slowly undulated vertical fins six to eight miles high, glowing purple, green, and red. Looked at more closely, the fins resolved into stacked horizontal dwellings, always shifting with respect to those above and below, never repeating the same perspective.

Each housed millions of Eidolons.

Even here, in the last city . . .

Boredom, boredom, repetitions of endless amusement, followed by sad forgetting, then fresh delight . . .

A tiny bright image appeared among the swarms of sentinels as the disc approached the reception platform—a sphere sporting an equatorial belt of emerald light, the scepter that announced the presence and privileges of the Astyanax of the Kalpa.

The sentinels verified Ghentun and parted to give way.

Ghentun stepped onto the platform and the disc vanished with a small pop, liberating a blue glow that spread across the floor, leaving behind red and gold polygons—ritual displays as old as the office of the Astyanax himself.

The polygons spread to mark the Keeper's path.

The path led to a simple door. Through that door, he knew, lay the Astyanax's most private dwellings and offices. For the first time, this Keeper of the Tiers was being allowed a meeting with the last City Prince in his innermost sanctum.

CHAPTER **40**

The Tiers

The young breeds returned from their expedition clutching only three books—and Tiadba had found all of them.

Khren and the others had split off after a few hours and moved on to other amusements.

Jebrassy accompanied Tiadba to her niche, where she laid out the shake cloths and Grayne's cape on a table, then arranged three jars packed with borrowed letterbugs.

He stood back, awed by these proceedings—he had never thought letterbugs would be of much use, had once felt contempt for those who raised and traded them. And now—to use them to read an actual book, in an ancient alphabet—he was not superstitious, but the room already seemed too full of the ghostly past.

Beyond the balcony, the first orange light of a new wake spread across the ceil.

Tiadba looked down on the jars and the books with pride. "My crèche mates have always wanted to know what their old bugs have to say." Her face gleamed as she glanced over her shoulder at Jebrassy, in the shadows.

"How long will this take?" he asked.

"We have less than ten wakes until the march. If we don't sleep . . ." She touched the fine fur on her nose, then gave him a taunting, humming whistle. "Frightened, warrior?"

"You better believe it," he said. "You should be, too."

"We've seen and done so much together. We've found our books."

"You've found *your* books," Jebrassy corrected.

"We're going to be trained for a march. What more could we want—what could possibly frighten us now?"

Tiadba pinned up the shake cloth, already marked with the common symbols and the words most often spelled out by younger letterbugs. Their task would be to make notes of the words that the old bugs formed from their unfamiliar letters; compare them to the new—find similarities; then transliterate.

Perhaps then they could puzzle through the books, like Grayne and her sisterhood before them.

"The books won't let us know what's out there now, more's the pity," Tiadba said. "Your visitor said last sleep . . ."

"What else did *my visitor* say?" Jebrassy asked, face wrapped in a scowl. "Did you make love with him?"

"One question at a time," Tiadba said, touching both her ears. Jebrassy liked that elevated, tutorial gesture least of all among this glow's mannerisms. The trouble was, her other gestures and touches he *did* like . . . too much.

There was no going back, with or without visitors, with or without a book.

"He said very little," Tiadba remembered. "He wasn't cheerful. There seemed to be trouble in his world. He was facing a challenge. And no, we did *not* make love. We're much too disoriented when we stray. What he said was, the book talks about a journey far outside the Kalpa, toward the *stars,* whatever that means."

"I'm getting tired of being *taken*," Jebrassy said, using the word for a squatter's habitation of someone else's niche. "And even more tired of being ignorant." He hitched up his short curtus before squatting on a stool next to the table. "So, down the chute with it. Spread the bugs."

Tiadba handed him a soft gray stick to be used on the finely woven shake cloth, then opened the first jar and tipped it out. The bugs— long and shiny black, with five legs on each side and brilliant blue eyes, dropped out and chittered, none the worse for being tightly packed, but eager to spread out, team up, and resume their endless wordplay.

In the two adjacent jars, letterbugs had been arranged in bundles, heads up beneath the pierced lid, twitching short feelers. She dumped them out as well. The more bugs, the longer the words.

Tiadba took up her stick and sat beside Jebrassy. As the old bugs pushed together in parallel rows, he was already recording the simplest combinations.

Tiadba reverentially opened the first book.

———

Two wakes of hard, weary work passed before she would allow them to make any guesses about the text. Jebrassy already knew the name *Sangmer* was there—he turned out to be more skilled than Tiadba at transliterating from the old alphabet. But it soon became apparent the book was not just *about* Sangmer, it had been written *by* him—a new concept for both.

"What would it be like to actually *write* about one's adventures?" Tiadba wondered as they shook out an edge of their cloths, where their transliterations and thus their translations had been proved wrong. Gray stick dust fell in a fine cloud to the floor.

"First, you have to *have* adventures," Jebrassy observed dryly. "Ancient breeds are too humble to presume." He lay back with a yawn and a half stretch, inviting seduction.

"Nonsense," Tiadba said. "I'm a breed, and I'm not humble. Neither are you."

"No," Jebrassy admitted. "But I'd be embarrassed to write my life from start to finish. It wouldn't be interesting—not yet. It wouldn't be proper."

"Presumably you'd only write the good parts," Tiadba mused. "Otherwise, your readers . . . did I just make up a word?" She looked pleased. "Your *readers* would find they had better things to do. Like . . ."

She lay down beside him, and Jebrassy was gratified to learn he still could distract her from their work—however briefly.

———

Before the ceil brightened with the fourth wake, they could make out with some clarity the book's opening paragraphs.

Not quite knowing how to use a book, they had tried starting from both ends, and then, confused, thumbed through to the middle. Gradually they realized that this book was unlike the stories breeds told their children, which always began in the middle, at a perilous moment, and only after more adventures returned to the beginning, to explain what those adventures meant. Breed tales had a puzzlelike quality.

This book actually began at the beginning—opening the cover from the right—continued through to the middle, and then concluded at the end, near the left. Once transliterated, the language was not very different, which struck Jebrassy as odd—so much time had passed. "This is supposed to be old. Why do we all tongue with so many of the same words?"

"If it was too strange, we couldn't read it," Tiadba said. "And somebody wants us to read. Or, maybe we've been held back," she said. "We're not *natural*." Here, she used a word that usually described a young one's easy introduction into a sponsoring group. "Let's read out loud what we've got so far. It's not that hard, actually."

After a while another doubt struck Jebrassy. "Sangmer's not a breed," he said as they fed the bugs from a small bag of dried cutsloop and pars. The bugs sang softly as they chewed. The older bugs apparently did not like pars, for they separated the dried grains and nudged them over the edge of the table.

"So?" Tiadba said. "Maybe he was a Tall One."

"Some of these new words are strange. I can barely sound them. What's this one?"

"I think it's a number. A very big number."

"And what's a 'light-year'?"

"Just read . . . We'll figure it out as we go. Read," she ordered, flicking his small ear with her finger.

Jebrassy began again in earnest. Tiadba took up when he faltered, and together they read the preamble—the introductory pages—and assumed, like innocents new from the crèche, that what they read was true, though so much of it was beyond their understanding . . . mere sounds rising from the pages, but sounds that conveyed a creepy, compelling sort of sense, as if they shared something innately with the author and the people he described.

We traversed a ruined course between broken galaxies in a demented ship—died, revived, and wished to die again—and came home along an even harder track, carrying Earth's salvation—and when we returned, we found ourselves splintered by our triumph, celebrated in our madness, surrounded and adored by those we had once hated as mortal enemies.

Through this, I achieved power and a small measure of freedom—and then gave it all up for love, and lost that as well. So much for my voyage to the Realm of the Shen, who claimed no human descent, nor any gens relation with the five hundred galaxies.

I tell this now to arouse enthusiasm in a Kalpa that cares little for what lies outside its walls, seeking a second dispensation—permission, if not a commission, to make one last journey, far shorter, far more dangerous, from which little doubt none of us will return.

Jebrassy sucked in his breath. "This is not going to be a happy story," he said.

"I think you're right," Tiadba said.

Jebrassy gently pushed aside a letterbug that had crawled up on the book, and together, fingers intertwined, they turned to the next page.

They found what followed tougher going, especially as the bugs tired of being rearranged and neglected to form useful rows.

Eventually, Jebrassy closed his eyes and napped. Checking to make sure he was asleep, Tiadba jumped ahead through a finger's width of pages. She thought she could *feel* the book—its connections, its shape—and that left to her own devices, she would instinctively open to pages that could *almost* answer her questions.

My wife, condensed out of lost principles—

Bright nimbus, eternal shadow—

Ishanaxade—the most willful, intelligent, and powerful female I have ever known—ever reconciled, even made flesh. In our life, she sought perfection through conflict, honing through strife, correction through victory and defeat—Gens Simia's greatest contribution to the human triumph of the Trillennium, so she claimed, with a strange knowledge I dared not dispute.

And like all Devas, she linked herself to Gens Simia. Even the daughter of a Great Eidolon, unique of her kind, clung to the families of a past—however manufactured they might be, certainly in her case.

My parentals, equally irrationally—and like all Menders—claimed descent from Gens Avia, a heritage reaching far back into the Brightness, associations none now understands—but what threads remain are cherished.

In the middle of our wedding, my parentals insisted on collecting the traditional fee for the legendary devouring and swallowing once carried out against us by Gens Simia: the Consumption. Perversely, Ishanaxade reveled in this myth. She paid the fee with enthusiasm, and I soon learned why; when she asserted this dominance in our marital chamber.

This became the cause of our first dispute as bound partners, a foolish argument over the Feast of Parts and Nests. In the midst of all those archaic, ritual distractions, I submitted—and endured, keeping my silence as she nibbled at my "drumstick" and my "wing," and then began on my "thigh." I had to subdue all my natural responses to maintain dignity.

When she looked up at me, lips rouged in blood, and while my tissues swiftly regrew, she declared we had a perfect balance—that she would always consume, and I would always provide, and survive to collect my paltry fee.

I think she meant this in jest. However, I soon found it wearisome.

Tiadba underlined the last few words with her finger, unsure what any of it meant. She felt an angry unease at things she could not understand. "Did she actually *eat* him?" she whispered, aghast. She wasn't sure she wanted Jebrassy to read these parts, and thought about tearing out the page—even gave it a tug, but it was too tough.

Still, something in her stirred. The measured layout of unfamiliar words sank deep, brought up memories she didn't think she had personally lived to acquire.

Half asleep, before turning another page, she glanced at Jebrassy— so peaceful, lying beside her—and thought of partners, pairs, lovers— across all the incomprehensible words of time.

CHAPTER 41

The Astyanax met Ghentun standing before a transparent rack of glittering noötic instruments, which he was applying meticulously—without touch—to a simulacrum. The subject bore a faint resemblance to one of the ancient breeds, though larger, blockier, less graceful, and with less fur.

All around them the chamber shifted at the whims of the Great Eidolon. Several times Ghentun had to move to avoid being burned,

frozen, or simply crushed. Out of respect, he had set his cloak to minimum, but now he surreptitiously strengthened its protection.

And this was the Astyanax trying to be polite.

"I wonder," he began, rotating the simulacrum. "Is this what our terrestrial ancestors once *really* looked like? Not as pretty as your ancient
breeds, to be sure . . . but somehow, in its awkwardness, its crudity, more
convincing."

"Quite convincing," Ghentun said. "But we'll never know. Those
records are long since lost."

"Fun to speculate," the Astyanax mused. "If you don't mind a little
competition."

The simulacrum blinked at them both with obvious astonishment.

"Do you think if I confirmed its shape and set it loose in the Tiers,
that it would *dream*, Keeper?" the Astyanax asked. "Would it behave as
our ancestors once did, shedding their discarded world-lines, their un-
traveled fates, each time they sleep?"

Eidolons rarely mentioned fates. Their makeup precluded variation
along the fifth dimension—all fates were automatically optimized into a
single path. That inflexibility made them peculiarly vulnerable to the
Chaos.

Ghentun walked around the simulacrum. "It's a possibility," he said.

"If we could ever trace back along the combined chord of this creature and its gens," the Astyanax continued, "linking up such a sensitive *animal*, made of primordial matter, with its closest ancestors,
however far back . . . could it actually *testify* to those lost times? We
would have to assume that its world-line would link and match with
similar world-lines, retrocausally—like the mating of primitive ge-
netic strands."

"The experiment has been tried. It's always failed," Ghentun said,
unsure what the City Prince knew, what the Great Eidolons had told
one another across half an eternity of subterfuge.

"Yet that is precisely what you seek—confirmation of something in
the remote past. The final destruction, am I right?"

"You are never wrong," Ghentun said.

The Astyanax froze the simulacrum and then dissolved it. The primordial mass dropped into a glistening lump on the platform. "Idle
play," he said. "Have you spoken recently to the Librarian?"

"I made a visit to the Broken Tower seventy-five years ago," Ghentun said. "A meeting was scheduled to discuss the Tiers, but I have not yet been summoned." He knew better than to try to hide obvious truths.

"You reported a change in the Tiers to the angelins in the Broken Tower, Keeper. I assumed *someone* would let me know eventually. The Librarian and I, after all, have long co-ventured in this study."

"It is not my place to carry messages between Great Eidolons." Ghentun knew he was being provoked. He expected little more from an Eidolon—compared to the City Prince, he was less than a pede crossing a dusty road.

"I've heard the Librarian is still working on his radical solution to our difficulties," the Astyanax said.

"Many rumors descend from the Broken Tower," Ghentun said. "I'm not informed enough to know what to believe."

The Astyanax surveyed him. Little could be hidden—a Great Eidolon could map a Mender in seconds. "Menders and Shapers have been engaged for half a million years at least with the current variety of ancient breeds."

"Nothing our Shaper does would surprise me. She so rarely does what I ask."

The Astyanax showed a glim of humor. The backscatter made Ghentun's cloak fluoresce. "Sometimes I feel this city will never be controlled. I would almost welcome a chance to see how the Typhon could manage it."

Despite himself, Ghentun shivered.

The Astyanax observed with approval. "You are obviously in no mood to betray the Kalpa, Keeper. Nor would you betray your Librarian. No secrets here, Mender—only your ignorance of the past, of what actually happened between the Librarian and the City Princes. Still, I would like a discreet and open copy of your report on the Tiers—the report you will deliver to the Librarian when he summons you."

"Of course," Ghentun said.

The Astyanax made no sign of dismissal. Something changed in the air of the chamber. The angelins shivered and blurred, on high alert—and with a jerk of surprise, Ghentun realized he was now facing the City Prince's primary self, directly controlling this epitome—which looked as if it were barely up to the task. The glow stung Ghentun's eyes. But the tone-color of the epitome's words, directly from the core of the City Prince, became less provocative, almost casual.

The angelins now gave Ghentun full focus, a kind of astonished warning that this intimacy was unprecedented. Theirs had become a meeting of presumed equals, and the angelins found this almost unbearable.

"I remember him most vividly as the Deva, Polybiblios," the City Prince said. "A tiny thing when he first came here, compared to what he is now. He has brought so much trouble, along with the grace of *survival*.

"I've supported—tried to control—supported again, the Librarian, tried to understand his plans, the way he thinks—all of him. I've failed. There is inequality even among the Great Eidolons, and I have become the inferior—no doubt about that. But the Librarian would long ago have destroyed what we have left of time, if not for the efforts of the City Princes. The Kalpa has survived an extra few hundreds of millions of years—much of a sameness, to be sure, an elderly repose after reckless youth and endless maturity."

A simple visual appeared between them—three pieces of a twisted puzzle. They came together, making a deeply patterned ball smaller than Ghentun's clenched hand.

"I'm giving you a memory, Keeper. A message to convey, if you will. It will rise again when the time is right—when there is no time. Until then, it will sink deep, out of sight."

Ghentun felt his attention flick left, then right. The puzzle . . . swooping bands interlaced around a cross, the whole spinning and whirling at the center of . . . nothing . . .

The nothing drew him, and for an indefinite moment fixed his thoughts. Ghentun listened to the Astyanax's voice, rich and compelling. Even as the story was told, and slipped down and away from consciousness, Ghentun asked, trembling at his boldness, "Why did you send her away?"

The answer remained in his immediate memory though all else faded:

"I doubt you can understand the humility of an Eidolon, Mender. But in all my extensions I have tried to exercise humility. I saw a grave danger to the Kalpa. Had all the parts of the Babel been brought together, they would have triggered the end of the Kalpa—and everything else. Their completion and unity would have beguiled the last great forces of our cosmos into *starting over*: Brahma, the moving still-ness within, who will awaken; Mnemosyne, the reconciler, who walked among us for a time, but who must return to her true nature; and Shiva, who will dance in joyous destruction. Do you understand what a Babel is, Keeper?"

The Astyanax touched his cloak, and Ghentun saw homunculi—servants of the Babel—climbing spiral staircases from balcony to balcony, arrayed along a wall that stretched up, down, to left and right—seemingly forever. The balconies provided access to bookshelves bearing prodigious numbers of ancient bound volumes. Farther along, other staircases rose to impossible heights and descended to limitless depths.

One by one the homunculi pulled volumes from the shelves, examined them, frowned, and replaced them. And moved on, book after book, shelf after shelf, level after level.

A reverse swing of his point of view revealed, across a narrow gulf, another unbounded wall supporting an equal number of books, on an equal number of shelves. The two apparently infinite walls of shelves seemed to meet and vanish in a vertical curve. Ghentun grudgingly admitted the curve was a nice touch, signifying a distortion of space—and an eternity of search.

Strings of symbolic data beyond counting—certainly for a Mender. And probably even for the Librarian himself. Every history, every tale, every sequence, every theory right and wrong, lost in vast mazes of churning, indecipherable text . . .

"Nothing will be beyond the scope of the Babel, combined and completed. All is there—all possibilities, all nonsense, all pride, all defeat. Truly it will be the greatest thing ever created. And the most dangerous."

A question seemed to flame into Ghentun's mind, even though—perhaps because—it was unanswerable:

And which would be more important to a universe—the random nonsense, or the things we think we can read and comprehend?

"I know nothing of this," he said, eyes lidded, yet he was terrified to his very center. The Babel would be so much larger than any universe . . .

"No need. Recognize only that you haven't finished your work," the City Prince told him. "And finish it you will. Within a very few wakes, the Chaos will break through all our defenses. I acknowledge defeat.

There is no choice, no reason to delay. I have transferred the city keys to the angelins in the Broken Tower, and my authority goes with them.

"I am aware that you have long hoped to follow your ancient breeds outside the border of the real. Go now, Mender. There are no longer city rules to stop you. Do what you must to get your breeds to Nataraja—if it still exists. What matter of a few wakes and sleeps? The Librarian's plans will proceed.

"We will not meet again—in this creation."

The Astyanax turned gray as old stone and his presence passed to another location.

The extraordinary meeting was over.

An angelin escorted the silent Ghentun back to the platform and a waiting photon disc.

He had been charting the intrusions long enough now to understand much of what the Astyanax had said or implied. The reality generators were weakening to such an extent that they could no longer protect any of the bions.

Ghentun knew he had to act. He had to put a humane end to this experiment—make one last attempt to fulfill the task he had been given, ages before; whatever the Eidolons wished, and however they debated the nature of the end of time.

The Keeper was only vaguely aware that he might be the last weapon in the City Prince's arsenal.

CHAPTER 42

The Tiers

For the sake of Grayne, the Shaper joined Ghentun and did what she almost never did—she left the crèche.

They came invisibly upon the old breed in her niche and stood over her while she slept. The Shaper was obviously pleased that Grayne was still capable of dreaming, despite all interference. These breeds were strong with dream. She knelt and applied broad, smooth fingers to Grayne's forehead, then said, "Tell us who will be best for this last march, and who will be best for a journey to the Broken Tower."

Grayne did not need to speak to answer.

The Shaper released her, and Ghentun stepped forward. "Her chosen pair seem smart. She's always been a good judge."

"A breeding pair?"

"They haven't discovered that yet."

"Would it be wise to separate a breeding pair?" Ghentun asked rhetorically. The Shaper did not bother to acknowledge there was a question. It was not her place to render such opinions, and never would be, thank the city. She merely shaped—she did not ponder overmuch.

"They've searched the deserted Tiers for their books, as always," the Shaper said. "She steered them toward those shelves that tend to repeat the tales of Sangmer and Ishanaxade. Separated lovers . . ."

"Can you tell what she's dreaming?" Ghentun asked.

"Oh, I've known that for an age," the Shaper said. "All the trainers share the same dream, since the first batch. She's dreaming she's part of a group of ancient females—in the Brightness, apparently. Details obscure, of course, but they seem to seek out talented youngsters, just as she and her sisters have done." The Shaper touched Grayne again and murmured, "Pity to lose her, after so many challenges. A favorite."

Grayne twitched. Her face betrayed a secret anxiety, not in the least connected with their presence.

Ghentun closed his eyes. "Then I know her," he said.

The Shaper could not suppress *all* curiosity. He looked back at Ghentun. "How? Are you dreaming as well, Keeper?"

"Retrieve the trainer's books."

The Shaper paused, looking down on the old breed. Then she reached for the trunk, opened the finger-lock latch, and removed all the books—five of them. They stacked easily in the Shaper's many arms. "Let's not wake her," the Shaper said. "Such a loss would be exquisitely painful to her. Not that I'm sentimental."

They backed out of the sama's niche. A Bleak Warden entered, slow and silent. It settled to spread its folds over Grayne, and with a slight stir, before she could open her eyes, she was no more.

A mercy, considering what was soon to come.

"Bring me the male," Ghentun said.

"And the female?"

"She will march. Pick others—friends, if they have any. Complete the sama's travel group however you can, and speed their training."

CHAPTER 43

The sound began low and heavy—a bass hum that vibrated the walls of Tiadba's niche. Jebrassy opened his eyes and twitched an arm, knocking one of the precious books off the sleeping pad. The last thing he remembered before falling asleep was Tiadba's soft, steady breath—sweet and soothing. But the bed next to him was empty.

He sat upright, listening, and thought that the thumping might come from Tiadba moving around.

Where was she?

But the sound was much too loud. It felt as if the Tiers themselves were shivering apart.

He pulled on his curtus and stumbled over the scattered bedclothes to the door, which had opened halfway and seemed to have stuck. Somehow, that frightened him more than the sound, which grew even louder.

The shaking made it difficult to stay on his feet.

Over the deep rumble came another sound, no less frightening but higher-pitched—wailing and shrieking, like creatures in horrible pain.

He squeezed through the opening and fell to his knees in the corridor. His hand nearly touched a deep, greasy blackness spreading along the floor of the hall like a hole cut into the substance of the Tiers—and growing. His eyes tried to focus on what had fallen into the hole—a fleeting impression of blurs that might have been two or more breeds, trying to swim against the blackness—and then something grabbed his shoulder and whirled him around.

A huge warden nearly filled the hallway, its wings folded, strong, hard arms extended, one clutching Jebrassy, the other throwing a net, a thick cross-weave of glowing fibers that sucked itself in over the blackness and seemed, for the moment, to hold it back.

The warden pulled him away. "You are going," it said, in a voice both passionless and irrefutable. Jebrassy was lifted from the floor and dangled like a doll. He swung his head just in time to see Tiadba squeeze past the warden's gray carapace into the half-open door of the niche.

The shriek and the roar grew, and to it Jebrassy now added his own shouts of pain—and a question: *"Why?"*

Then Tiadba was back in the hall. She had retrieved a bag—their books. Turning her back to the warden, cringing, she allowed herself to be grasped and lifted. They both stared straight into the roiling dark that filled the opposite end of the corridor—

The roar, the wailing—

The net holding back the blackness had dissolved. The blackness advanced, offering at the crest of its dark wave three, four, five breeds— Jebrassy could not count them all—bobbing and twisting in ways nothing could twist, terrified, turning inside out and then skin side outward again, while still horribly alive, arms and legs moving with impossible speed—heads spinning like tops.

The heads began to grow, the blurred eyes to expand, as if they would explode—

Tiadba added her screams to theirs.

And Jebrassy *knew*. He had seen this before, smaller, more concentrated. They were on the leading edge of an intrusion—like the one that had sucked away his mer and per.

With a jerk, the warden retreated down the corridor, bumping and scraping the walls. Behind them the hallway squeezed itself into a wall and golden wardens gathered around the stair core to throw nets everywhere—

Their own warden spun them, pulled them inboard to avoid banging them against whatever chamber or new branch of hall they had entered, smooth and silvery—a hall or pipe he had never seen before.

A lift! Like the one in the Diurns.

Jebrassy tried to reach for Tiadba but could not quite brush her with his fingers. She was alive, he could see that—she clutched the bag of books tightly to her chest—but she squeezed her eyes shut and bowed her head as if in submission.

The journey along the shining pipe took almost no time, the air rushing by so quickly that despite the shield of the warden's body, Jebrassy's clothes were nearly torn from him. He felt his exposed skin grow warm—and then they flew from an opening in a far wall. The warden spread its wings and they rose in a gliding curve over the third isle. Jebrassy managed to open his eyes long enough to see how high they were—and was instantly sick.

He could not see Tiadba now—except for a foot thrust out from under the second wing—but with his stomach empty, a kind of fated calm came over him.

The first and second isles had been carved open, exposing dozens of levels. He looked with odd dispassion over broken and scalloped walls, whirlpools of retreating darkness—falling breeds.

The air smelled rotten and burned at once. Half the ceil was gone, exposing something he had never seen before—the city *above* his sky, bits and pieces of unknown architecture, spirals and silvery arcs, walls and walkways, moving in an intricate dance of remediation, trying to reassemble and re-create safe havens for other citizens—

Citizens above the Tiers, also suffering—perhaps dying—

The warden lifted them over a cloud of dissolving darkness, but not without exposing them to a stench so great Jebrassy wanted to be sick again, but could not—

He heard Tiadba weeping. The warden's wings and arms re-arranged for swifter flight, allowing them to look into each other's eyes across the short distance, and in her expression there was something outside Jebrassy's understanding, outside his range of sympathy—

Tears streamed from her cheeks and blew off behind. But behind the tears, she was laughing—weeping and laughing at once with terror and with glee.

And then they were struck—something ugly and resentful reached out and pierced the warden, turning it black and crusted—then just *touched* Jebrassy—and his body filled with a violation unlike anything he had ever known before, and pain—pain so deep he could not give it voice.

TEN ZEROS

CHAPTER 44

Puget Sound

The storm began at sea as a tight, dark streak of cloud, like the smear of a giant brush loaded with gray mud. In the early morning hours, it spread quickly over the Olympic Peninsula, sucking in all the dark clouds, tightening and directing its spiral of winds, accumulating and controlling the charges behind the jagged lightning—then flowed across Puget Sound, where it formed the shadowy suggestion of an impossible giant—a female giant.

The shadow blew inland, then south, and swung back. It could not seem to find what it wanted, and so it lashed its wings against the city. Most frightening was not the continuous deluge of rain, but the lightning, which struck in clusters, in a rainbow of colors, and with a pummel of explosive reports, like the pounding of huge fists on a cathedral organ.

Heads turned and eyes averted, the citizens watched in mounting fear as the flashes grew more intense and more frequent. Not content with leaping from sky to ground, the lightning began to arc sideways, lancing between skyscrapers, blowing out windows, and crawling along the exterior lines of beams and girders, wrapping the towers in a lace of frustrated electricity—only to erupt again near ground level, stabbing through the tight-packed buildings like sabers through cheese.

Sirens howled. Fire trucks and police vehicles added to the keening cacophony as far north as Lake Union. The storm compacted and gathered purpose. From above, it now formed a fat arrow paralleling the I-90 bridge, broad fletches over Lake Washington, powerful head probing: dumping, flooding, flashing.

It had found what it was looking for.

It followed an old white van.

CHAPTER 45

Wallingford

Uh-oh.

Something unlikely this way comes.

It took Daniel less than a minute to decide that the storm might be a hunter—but it was not after *him*. It raged south of his neighborhood, south of downtown.

As the rain began, then the lightning, he turned away from the morning drivers and their cars, working their way west along Forty-fifth to the freeway. He was done with street corners and begging. This morning, he was no longer just one of a thousand gray men and women standing on the littered curbs of a thousand on-ramps. That life was over. A new one had begun.

Above all, he was a survivor.

He looked south to follow the storm's progress. Not even the flash of lightning and horizontal twists of clouds could break his new sense of physical joy.

For two hours now he had been enjoying freedom from the snake in his gut. What was left of Fred was no longer capable of putting up much resistance. This body was young, relatively healthy—though not in the best of shape.

Back in the house, Mary was still asleep—and Charles Granger lay dead on the couch, covered with a blanket, pitiful and spent. At least that was not his fault, Daniel thought. The broken-down pile of meat had simply given up.

Healthy again, Daniel had a fierce, unreasonable pride in his strength, his abilities. As well, he had no doubt now that there were others like him in the city—and they were about to be collected.

To himself, he cheerfully sang, *"Dirus irae."*

He did not want to be caught in the open when the storm found what it was looking for. Even a few miles away the side effects would be unpleasant.

And he needed to retrieve his boxes, hidden behind the fireplace in the abandoned house.

CHAPTER **46**

West Seattle

The van shuddered as it left the West Seattle Bridge. Squat and low in the driver's seat, pale with tension, Glaucous swerved around a car stalled in the left lane—corrected the van as it rose on one set of wheels, jerked it back on a straighter course, then took the time to wipe sweat from his eyes with scarred knuckles.

In the back, tied up in a heavy canvas sack, Jack Rohmer had worked his arm through the drawstring and waved his fist as he rolled back and forth over the cold metal floor.

Glaucous had stopped his trills and whistles of birdsong. Now he was selling things, long ago. "Costards, pippins, starberries, currants!" he called, in the full glory and joy of the old times. Penelope discharged a sharp grunt as lightning blasted a passing utility pole. A transformer sparked and tumbled over their windshield, bounced along behind them.

All the while, Glaucous was muttering words with no apparent sense or connection to their journey or their peril: "Shoestrings and jute! Oakum and fiber! Paper and rags, any old iron! Scallions! Onions! Leeks! Bones and *FAT*!" (This as lightning struck again) and "Plasters and pastes! Plasters for all, plasters and poultice, what ails will draw!"

A stench filled Jack's nose, rank and oppressive, not just the sweat and confinement of the bag, but a taint from his recent jaunt. He had jumped too far, crossed into a diseased knot of world-strands, dissolving, looping—stinking of something awful.

He knew that the van was being followed, that his reek was being tracked . . .

Glaucous seemed to share the same opinion. In between his pointless calls—he was now working his way through "Bluing! Blue stuffs! Indigo!"—he paused and leaned toward his partner, as if to speak in confidence, then, shaking his head, pulled back and wrenched his spine straight, his shoulders as square as they could be, incredulous he would even think of giving voice to such thoughts, whatever they might have been.

He could not afford doubts—not now.

Penelope had broken the armrest from the van's door and held it out, squeezing the plastic and steel like a banana. Her eyes almost popped from their fat-draped orbits.

Speckles of weird light danced on their faces.

Glaucous clapped a hand over his mouth and nose and stared above his thumb, eyes wide.

"What *is* that?" Penelope shrieked, her vocal register that of a frightened kindergartener.

"It is *magnificence*!" Glaucous shouted. "It is power and promise, a plight, a troth!" His words belied his expression; brows low, piggish eyes receding into his skull.

Jack now had his arm out of the sack up to the shoulder and was squirming to push his head through.

"What are you *saying*?" Penelope squealed.

"Something is hunting us! Too eager, waiting too long!"

"Hunting *what*? You promised we would be safe!"

"*I* will be safe." Glaucous gave her a guilty glance, then wheeled the van onto an off-ramp and said, with grim curiosity, sunken eyes on the rearview mirror, "I turn up this road—bolts like giant feet, stamping feet, they follow and turn *with* me! I have not seen this before, believe that, dear queen of buzz and hum—not before, not ever. We have not called for a delivery, yet I sense something other than a Gape. The Chalk Princess is anxious. More than we bargained for. A large bite, this youngster—more than we can chew!"

Jack was beyond fear. The cloying treacle and liquor of Glaucous's talent had pinched to sour vinegar, stinging in his nostrils and brain, opening up choked glimpses of branching, looping world-lines—none of them good, all of them in fact awful.

What was happening had never happened before, not in Jack's experience, nor in the experience of any ancestor who had ever contributed to the sum of the genes ratcheting in his flesh and blood—even as far back as the primordial slime.

CHAPTER 47

Wallingford

Daniel drew up Fred's gray wool jacket and walked west, shoulders hunched, feeling the storm gather its power.

A sharp jerk of sense had reversed his arrogance and pleasure at his new body. The storm wasn't after him—but it would work quite well as a distraction. He had been too preoccupied to pay close attention—stupid, stupid!

There was almost certainly another target nearby—another fate-shifter. Maybe more than one. But someone in the employ of the thing that hunted them could still set his sights on Daniel. He would be special. *I no longer dream of the city. I don't know why—I just don't.*

A bad shepherd—isn't that what they call me?

Lightning whited the facades on his right. Just blocks from the turn to his home, as he walked beside the big lamp shop, all the chandeliers, switched on for the morning trade, suddenly went dark.

The air *hissed.*

Daniel had to drag his new body by main force toward the abandoned house. Fear was bringing Fred back, unpleasantly strong, and Fred most certainly did not want to go. Daniel could not jaunt again, even had he the strength, the concentration. The corrosion would be everywhere. Nothing but hideous, gray looped worlds bunched up between this dissolving segment of history and whatever lay at the end: tumbled lengths of fate, frayed out, soaked and sour-smoky with decay.

Another voice—not his own, not Fred's. Fred was already being pushed back like a slug under a stone.

Why bother, Mr. Iremonk?

Lightning flew down the street, sizzling, blinding, and struck a fire hydrant. The blast nearly knocked him off his feet and shattered all the glass in the lamp shop windows.

He stumbled on, whining like a kicked dog.

You have an appointment, long delayed.

People on the sidewalks were screaming, running.

He whirled around. An old woman in tight pedal-pushers held an inverted black umbrella in one hand and dragged a terrier along behind her, on its side, legs kicking. Each time the dog got to its feet, she jerked the leash so hard it fell over again. Big splats of rain—drops the size of baseballs, mixed with sharp chips of ice—hurled from the churning sky.

Just a few miles from the center of the storm.

The sweep of her robe, merely that. Nothing compared to the Gape. Remember, Daniel? Poor bastards, all of you. But especially you.

Half a block behind him, Daniel saw a small man with oily, slick black hair. Daniel turned left. Across the street waited another—slender, dressed in old black clothes shiny with water and age—and a block east, a third, clutching a dripping, battered bowler hat in one white hand. All were smiling, enjoying the storm—ignoring the rain and the ice.

Where is the net's fourth corner, Daniel?

Trying to run backward, he almost fell, so he swiveled, arms windmilling, and lit out—gave it all he had. He wouldn't look back.

Had to reach the house.

Had to.

CHAPTER 48

West Seattle

The storm had a dead, hollow voice. It had never known hunger, care, passion, or any growl of hormonal surge; its voice had never vented from flesh or form.

The storm was a thousand spins and drafts of wind and water, filled with restless veins of flash and charge, and all it knew—all it could possibly know—was that it had been set free, liberated from probability, and that it had a power no storm had ever before possessed.

It could gather, it could kill—*with malice.*

One wet black swirl had almost caught up with the white van.

"My dear, it is our quarry, our cargo!" Glaucous shouted over the roar. He jerked his thumb toward the back. "He trails a *spoor* . . ."

"Of *thread?*" Penelope shrilled.

"Spoor, not spool! He exudes, he *stinks* of the bad places, not hell— though he must have come very close, dipped an ankle or a knee . . . *Violet*! Indigo! Blue! Red! Red bolts and orange! All for madam's delight!"

Jack needed all his strength. He pressed his feet against the doors at the rear of the van, clutched the sack around him, rolled, grunted—

The light from the windshield darkened. Glaucous and Penelope screeched like terrified parrots.

Jack peered out of the hole he had pushed through the cinch, between the silhouettes of the massive, cowering woman and the driver— through the van's windshield. There, he saw something inexplicable. The vision refused to be cataloged or stored away, even in short-term memory.

A seam, a gap, a failure.

A face. Extraordinary beauty—and rage.

Jack immediately forgot what he saw.

Glaucous looked to his terrified partner. In one bright flash he saw the intensity of Penelope's fear and knew that she knew. A fatal mistake had been made. However long their relationship—whatever her strength and talent—she would have to be the one. Not for the first time, Glaucous would sacrifice a valued partner.

The storm could not wait. It struck with all its pent-up force, spending all its power, everything hidden within, at once.

A black wall of cloud plummeted.

The windshield shattered.

Darkness hammered.

The van flipped and skidded along its side, rolling Jack with a bone-bruising thump onto the ribbed panel. Through the sack, the skin of his back burned as friction heated the metal. Jack rolled and kicked and pushed his head and one arm through the cinch.

The van ricocheted off a jersey barrier and flipped again. Suspended in space, Jack drew up his knees, rounded into a ball—all he could do to avoid breaking an arm, a leg, his neck.

From the front seats came twin explosions of breath as belts jerked tight.

The van slammed down on its roof.

CHAPTER **49**

Wallingford

As Daniel ran up the steps of the house, he observed the fourth corner of the net. A small piebald man stood on the porch of the bungalow. Rain fell in such volume, Daniel could barely make out the house, much less the figure waiting for him there—paleness within shadow, shrunken, like a hideous dwarf.

Daniel was soaked. The tall grass in the yard lay flat, submissive. Pieces of ice bounced on the sidewalk and the roof, struck his head and shoulders. Blood trickled down his forehead, diluted by rain. Not a good performance for a man used to walking between raindrops. Lightning played to the south, where he supposed the real search was under way—where the main target was being harried.

Assume nothing. Perhaps it is you, *after all.*

He instinctively reached ahead with his feelers. All paths were distorted, tangled. More alarming, he saw an echo float by—a half-seen rebound of Charles Granger, slouching backward toward the freeway, oblivious—

And then, another—Fred. *Himself,* bouncing back from just a few minutes in the future. Their broken piece of history was rapidly approaching an impenetrable wall—and he had no idea what would happen then.

The piebald dwarf on the porch advanced—and changed. This was no mere solid figure. Daniel had seen such before, in the bad place—forms and figures that defied dimension. Descending the steps, the dwarf grew as if reflected in a curved mirror. The closer it came, the larger it would be—and the more powerful. By the time the figure reached him it would loom high enough to brush the black, swirling clouds.

Daniel looked back and saw the other men in their antiquated suits, cringing at the rain and the ice—human and solid after all, capable of pain. The grass steamed. The air cooled, turned thick as gelatin. All darkened.

He felt heavier—tried desperately to reason, to be smarter than the poor bastards around him. Echoes from the Terminus at the end of this world-line would temporarily increase the local mass quotient. Time would begin to slow. At the Terminus, for most observers, it would stop or echo them back a few days, a few hours, where they would live those brief segments over and over, hapless as robots repeating a programmed loop.

Slices of history were now floating like chunks of meat in a half-digested stew—nothing left of the future, he surmised, but the wall, and around that, a thinned-out, dimensionless vacancy in which nothing could think, nothing could live.

He had worked this out some time and many fates ago—back when he had been Daniel Patrick Iremonk through and through, calculating what it would be like for his time to come, this way or that, to its inevitably mixed and messy conclusion.

The huge piebald figure reached down and brushed at Fred's—at Daniel's short brown hair, stroked his high forehead, still bleeding.

The Moth.

He held still—just for the moment.

It told him: *Sum-runner. Fetch it.*

The others had managed to form a triangle in the yard—no escape. "Do what the Moth says," instructed the closest, a lithe old man with an experienced face and one distorted foot, standing by the concrete steps cutting up through the overgrown yard.

"Of course," Daniel said, and tried to walk around the dimensionless figure, to obey, to comply—the only choice he had, really. The rain pounded, streamed, drops curling in the air—hitting from all directions—no straight lines down, so many fundamental rules changing—

Never figure it out.

The Moth blocked him with a massive finger. In warning, it reached back, its hand diminishing to a point, and brushed the house. The house bleached, turned white, its outlines crumbling to calcined powder. Little more than a polite admonition. If Daniel did what they asked, they might let him go, they might not kill or transform him. A pang of disappointment—who could possibly be more important? Who could jaunt as far, calculate, and understand the shape of the end of the world? He was the best. Maybe they knew. They could make him one of their own. A slave. That was likely what they were planning.

How gratifying. No thanks.

Two more translucent echoes vibrated past—one of Granger, the other of Fred. The Moth itself seemed to spread, sending ghosts of its unlikely self backward. It was using far too much energy—it would push more rapidly up against the Terminus than anything else near the house.

The house reacquired some of its color, but still seemed about to collapse. Even at his highest fever of perception, Daniel had never actually been able to see the multiverse in all its near-infinite variety—until now. *You always learn more when something breaks—when it begins to die.*

He had only one chance—to push past what they called the Moth, to retrieve his stone, and hang onto it with all his strength. Daniel lowered his head and squeezed under the Moth's distorted legs, through its diminished substance. The piebald giant flickered and whined. Daniel could feel it fading. All illusion now—edges undone, strength gone—losing connection with the source of its power, the Mistress of all the corrupted world-lines that surrounded them.

The three figures in black became agitated, then dismayed, yet the storm was growing weaker and the air was warming. A retreat was under way—the Moth was getting out while the getting was good. The human servants of their Livid Mistress were being discarded, left behind.

Apparently, this was not what they had expected.

Daniel stood on the porch, dripping pools around his feet. He slammed against the front door. Wood-rot did half the job, and a crowd of him suddenly flew into the living room, surrounded by puffing dust from a hundred variations of shattered door—motes of dead and dying futures that had once been only seconds away.

Amazed, he realized he could still move.

Dimensions are never exactly perpendicular—never precisely straight—less so now than ever. He turned sideways, screamed as disappointed futurity raised blisters on his face and hands.

A crowd of Freds arrived at the fireplace, reached out for the one loose brick—it became hot with the radiated heat of so many hands—and the boxes they all knew were hidden behind that brick.

The echoes vanished in a wink.

He had seen it before. World-lines swaying and attempting to reconnect, invisible to all others—forcing time to a crawl, reducing the light outside to a mist of shadows.

They had struck Terminus—and then rebounded.

Everything had been reset, pushing them back a few hours—a few days at most—everything in the city, the world, this segment of the multiverse, bouncing off the cauterized five-dimensional scab that now capped the end of all cords.

On the occasion of the next impact—in a few hours, a few days, no more, he was sure—the bounce would be shorter, and shorter still after that, until finally they would simply freeze in place, pressed flat: no time, no space.

No hope.

Daniel pushed through the thick air to the doorway. Kicked aside dust and debris, stood on the sagging porch. The others—the strong, emaciated men in their soaked black suits—were trying to flee.

All but one.

Now he remembered a name. *Whitlow.*

The memory returned like a sliver of ice shoved into his brain. A memory of compromise, betrayal—the betrayal of an entire world.

The bad shepherd.

Daniel's lungs emptied in self-loathing.

Whitlow stood on the porch, smiling and unafraid. He had not changed—always the same slender, confident, dignified old man across all of Daniel's world-lines.

Always the clubbed foot.

Whitlow's gaze seemed to briefly caress what Daniel held in his hands. The man with the club foot smiled, showing even, ivory-colored teeth. "What's your name now, young traveler?" he taunted. "Why so eager? Where can any of us flee, but into Her arms?"

Whitlow casually brushed past Daniel, into the house.

And Daniel turned to join him.

CHAPTER 50

West Seattle

The van's rear doors flung wide. Jack rolled onto the asphalt and tumbled for a dozen yards before slamming into a concrete curb. His exposed hand dipped into a gutter. Water rushed black and silver over his clutching fingers. Dazed, he tore through the abraded sack, spread holes for his other arm, then his torso, kicked his legs through, rose on hands and knees, peeled off the rags . . .

Stood, head spinning.

For a moment, he wondered if he was losing his sight, or even if he'd died—everything around the accident had skewed, ripped, and was slowly reassembling, like a tossed puzzle reversed in time.

He looked up and saw the lightning bolts turn upon themselves and spiral up into a spinning funnel, spitting and hissing like snakes. Rising in the middle of the funnel, he saw a writhing, lumpish form, nearly all middle, with tiny, wriggling arms and legs—falling free, diminishing, flailing, only to be grabbed again by the lightning and lifted higher . . . all the while crying out, a girlish shriek audible even above the roar.

Power lines torn loose from their poles tried to follow, curling and snapping and then straining straight as drawn wire. They broke loose and shot up, then went limp—and fell back like lost pieces of string.

The funnel closed. A deluge like the upending of a huge bucket flattened Jack where he lay, pressing his head onto the asphalt until he feared he would drown.

All stopped.

Everything became unnaturally still. Any motion was difficult—painful.

He blinked muddy rain from his eyes.

The downpour, the lightning, all of the weirdness—over. For a moment—deep quiet. Nothing but a soft hiss of rising steam and a light, ominous crackle like crushed cellophane.

The van had wrecked in a residential neighborhood. Old houses, square and neat, ascended a low hill below a water tower. The houses had blackened—not burned, but converted to a dark, glassy substance, like obsidian. The water tower sprayed liquid from all its seams. Knee-high shining black spikes filled the roadway. As Jack stood by the curb, more spikes shot up, shoving aside his feet, kicking the van around and piercing two of its tires.

The air sparkled with an absence of color, absence of sense. It smelled burned, as did Jack—burnt by a cold, timeless fire.

Inside the van, Glaucous was gasping for air between harsh, guttural yells. The yells became an awful, continuous screech.

Then—nothing.

Everything that Jack looked at hurt his eyes, his brain. The muscles in his neck twisted, fighting over which direction they would or would not turn. He flung up his arm.

Against his better judgment, he looked again.

The not-colors had been filled in like gaps in a coloring book, but the burnt smell remained. The water tower gurgled and spewed its last few thousand gallons. The spikes melted into the asphalt.

Rainwater cascaded from overflowing gutters.

The houses had returned to a kind of normality.

Shaking out a bruised shoulder and favoring a wrenched ankle, he lurched toward the van. He knelt by the shattered windshield. Wet and unable to fly, the last of Penelope's wasps crawled along the crazed edge of glass, twitching and buzzing. Each cast flickering duplicates that peeled away, then returned to merge again.

He looked at his hands—the same stuttering shadows. Something huge had just happened. Time was vibrating like a plucked string.

Jack peered into the van. The driver's seat was empty.

Both seats were empty.

Nobody left to save.

CHAPTER 51

Ellen drove Miriam's old Toyota. Agazutta rode shotgun. Farrah sat in the back with Ginny, who watched a necklace of amber beads swinging from the car's rearview mirror. They turned up one wet street and down another, searching for someone—someone young and male, Ginny gathered from spare snippets of their talk.

Even now, water slopped along the gutters and spilled from overpasses and off-ramps, slowing their progress.

Things had once again crossed the line from puzzling to inexpressibly weird. She was surrounded by spooky, middle-aged women. They were all so *curious*, but however much they seemed to care, however much they seemed to have a plan, they were just as reluctant as Bidewell to answer big questions. Too many *wait and see* moments. She felt tied to their destinies in a way that made her suffer like a caged animal.

The storm had been hunting. That's what the women had argued about before taking the West Seattle Bridge. Storms didn't do that, of course.

Agazutta looked over her shoulder. "What do you feel?" she asked Ginny.

Ginny shook her head. There was nothing ahead but a frightening solidity—a flat, looming blankness. "You tell me. I'm just riding along."

Ellen said, "The storm might not be the only unusual event today. You might be able to help us save someone else, someone as important as you. So please, Virginia—tell us what you feel."

"We're like a log that's fallen out of the fireplace," Ginny said, then dropped as low in the seat as she could, miserable and scared.

Farrah rubbed her nose. "It *does* smell burned."

"Are you *really* witches?" Ginny blurted.

Agazutta snorted. "That's a joke, dear. If we had any *real* powers, do you think we'd have allowed this to happen?"

Ellen said, "If anyone has magical powers, it's probably you, or Bidewell. Not that we've seen much evidence of it lately."

"Those books," Farrah said.

"Fabricated," Agazutta said.

"They're old," Farrah countered.

Ellen made a sound between a tosh and a splutter. "We have to trust him. We don't have a choice. And we have to trust Ginny."

"She's sullen," Farrah said.

"So were you, in the beginning," Agazutta said.

"Hell, I'm *still* sullen," Farrah said.

"Are you a lesbian?" Ginny blurted.

A brief but chilly silence followed. "There seems to be a fundamental misunderstanding," Farrah said. "Someone explain to the girl."

"Fundamentally, it doesn't matter," Ellen Crowe said. "Except for me—"

"Except for *her*," Agazutta emphasized with some resentment.

" . . . this group is sworn to celibacy," Ellen finished.

"Which explains why we drink so much and read steamy novels," Farrah said.

"Why aren't *you* celibate?" Ginny asked Ellen, craning her head forward.

"It has nothing to do with magic, but a lot to do with fishing," Agazutta said. "You're not the bait, my dear. *Ellen* is the bait."

"No one believes me when I say it's all—" Ellen began, but Agazutta interrupted.

"Is that him?" she asked.

Ellen peered through the windshield at a skinny young man walking with slumped shoulders and drenched hair over uneven sidewalk. The Toyota slowed. Despite herself, Ginny sat up. The young man was unaware of their presence—or working hard to ignore them.

"Such a bedraggled puppy," Agazutta said.

From behind he looked like the one Ginny had seen riding a bike through the Busker Jam. As soon as she could see his face, she cried out, "Stop!"

Ellen braked the car with a short squeal. This caught his attention and he looked sharp left, then broke into a run.

"You scared him," Agazutta said.

"Well, *excuse* me—"

"He's getting away!" Farrah cried. "We'll lose him. He'll jump!"

They all seemed to know what that meant. Agazutta was glancing up and around as if expecting a 747 to fall from the sky, or a tree to march out in front of them.

"He can't," Ginny said.

"Can't what?" Ellen asked.

"He can't *escape*," Ginny said, recognizing something in the young man's posture, in his sad response to their presence. "He's run out of places to go."

The car caught up and Ginny rolled down her window. "Wait!" she called.

The young man glanced left again. A raised block of sidewalk caught his toe. With a startled *yawp*, he fell on his hands and knees. Ginny banged on the door with her fists. "Let me out! Let me help him!"

Ellen stopped the car.

"Child safety lock," Farrah reminded her, and she *hmmed* and pushed the release button. The door swung wide and Ginny spilled out. She straightened, held her head high, and approached the young man slowly, as if he were a wounded leopard. He rose to a squat and glared at her. Something about his outline wavered for just a moment—he fogged and shivered.

"Please don't," she said. "Please stay."

His outline firmed, and he faced her with fingers and arms flexed. "Why?"

"We've met before," Ginny said.

Jack glared at her.

"The storm was chasing you, wasn't it?" Ginny asked.

"I don't know," Jack said.

"We can't escape," she said. "There's a warm place and friends— I think they're friends—not far. Come with us."

"Your car is full," Jack observed. "Unless you want me to ride in the trunk."

Farrah opened her door and thumped her hand on the roof. "Squeeze in. You're skinny."

"Get out of the wet, Jack," Ellen said. She waved with a reassuring smile.

Jack stood and peered through the windshield. He pushed aside his wet hair. "Now you're scaring the hell out of me."

"I met most of them today," Ginny said.

"Who are *you* supposed to be?" Jack asked.

"I don't know," Ginny said. "Not anymore."

CHAPTER 52

The Green Warehouse

Jack stood behind the warehouse gate, staring at the gray ghost of First Avenue South and shivering in the ashen chill that oozed through the chain-link fence. Ellen had parked the car and the women had gone up the ramp into the warehouse, leaving him to stand by the fence. He told them he needed a moment to adjust.

Ginny had returned to watch from the door.

In just a few hours, in what passed for personal time, the city outside the green warehouse had turned into a flickering forest of shadows. Clouds roiled too quickly, colliding and shooting up to vanish in the gray sky.

On the way back from West Seattle—theirs was the only car on the road—they had witnessed people walking, echoing back, starting over, half aware. Some seemed to catch on to their awful dilemma, enough to be frightened.

More frightening still, most couldn't tell the difference.

Somehow, the stones in their boxes, and now the warehouse, smoothed things and protected them all—once they had ricocheted off Terminus. That was what Ellen had called it in the car—Terminus. The end, yet not exactly; more like a ball slowly bouncing and rolling to a stop.

The sadness Jack felt was almost beyond bearing. Out there, so many confused, lost people, trying to reclaim their lives in a stuttering time that kept drawing them back, that would ultimately—when the ball stopped bouncing—press them down . . . Ignorant and immobile, like so many flies stuck in tar.

It had happened so suddenly—but not without warning.

Ginny finally could wait no longer. She walked down the ramp and stood beside Jack, arms wrapped around her shoulders. She was younger than him, maybe eighteen, but the look in her eyes told him she was no mere girl. They hadn't spoken two words since the end of their fitful, gray journey back to the warehouse.

"How did the storm find you?" she asked.

Jack shrugged, embarrassed. "I called a phone number," he said. "A man and a woman bagged me. After that—I'm still trying to figure it out."

"It was the Gape," Ginny said.

"Gate?"

"Gape. It's what happens when you meet the Queen in White."

"Who the hell is that? Another old woman?"

"I don't know. Just one of her names. Let's go back in. It's warmer, and you should talk with Bidewell."

———

The air in the green warehouse was sweet with the smell of dry wood and old paper. Jack looked around the high walls, unpainted slats lathed over studs, thick beams carved from the hearts of grand old cedars. High windows and skylights cast a gray, filtered light. Stacks of crates and cardboard boxes rose everywhere. Ginny followed him like a little sister as he explored. He didn't like that at first.

He stepped up to the broad metal door and tapped it with his knuckles. On the other side, the book group women were talking with an older man. He couldn't make out what they were saying. He glanced at Ginny. Her eyes glistened with a quick shyness, like a yearling deciding whether to bolt. "What's on the other side?" he asked.

"That's where Mr. Bidewell keeps his office and his library."

"More books?"

"Lots. Old ones, new ones. He has crates of them shipped from all over the world. Some are impossible. I don't know where he finds them. I was—am—helping catalog them. The ones who kidnapped you . . . what were they like?"

"The man called himself Glaucous. There was a big woman—huge. I think her name was Penelope."

"Another pair came for me back in Baltimore. I got away, but they followed me here. Dr. Sangloss sent me to Bidewell as soon as I arrived."

"You're lucky. These two used wasps."

Ginny's eye narrowed. "Wasps?"

"Yellow jackets." He waved one hand, fluttered his fingers. "They buzzed after me when she opened her coat."

"Oh, my God."

"What about yours?"

"A man with a silver coin. A skinny woman who started fires with her fingers."

"I've always known things were odd," Jack said, "but not like *this*. Not as weird as my dreams."

"What do you remember about your dreams?"

"Not much," Jack said. "Do you dream, too?"

She nodded. "All fate-shifters dream. That's what Mr. Bidewell told me."

Jack sucked on his teeth and tried to look calm. "Fate-shifters?"

"You and me. We shift when the odds aren't in our favor." She drew her hand across the level of her shoulders. "Sideways. You know that, don't you?"

"I didn't know it had a name," Jack said.

"But it doesn't make our lives easy," Ginny said. "I still make mistakes. Sometimes I think . . ." Again the furtive look.

Jack began pacing the perimeter of the warehouse. Ginny followed, uninvited. "Why wasps?" she asked.

"There's no way out of a room full of wasps. The odds are against you everywhere." He did not feel like describing the world-line he had been forced onto, or how that might have distracted the storm—the Gape. "What are they talking about? Us?"

"I don't know," she said.

They completed a circuit to where Ginny had made her little square among the boxes, and she lifted the curtain she had hung for privacy, inviting him in. Jack sat on a small crate, reluctant to take the single wooden chair—more reluctant to sit on the bed. He crossed one leg. "I'm a busker," he said.

"I saw you at the Busker Jam," Ginny said.

"Funny I didn't see you."

"You were mad at something, I guess."

"What do you do?"

"I get in trouble, then I run away." Ginny sat on another box. The corner puffed dust and sagged and she got up, brushed her jeans, and sat in the chair.

"Run away from where?"

"Where *to* is all that matters." She shrugged. "We've met before. I'm sure of it. Not just at the jam. Don't you remember?"

Jack shivered again, and not just with the cold. He was letting it all down and he didn't want to, not in this place and not in front of this girl.

They looked up in wonder and fear at the high small windows. Darkness had fallen. Day might never come again. Two stars shone through the glass panes. Jack tried to imagine time stopping, freezing, then bouncing back—whatever it was doing—all the way out to those stars.

He couldn't.

He got up, lifted the curtain, and returned to the back of the warehouse.

Ginny followed again.

Jack pounded on the sliding steel door. The voices behind the door droned on as if nothing had happened.

"They'll let us in when they're ready," Ginny said. "A busker is a street entertainer, right?"

"Yeah," Jack said.

"Why would a thunderstorm be interested in a juggler?" She covered her mouth.

Jack looked at her, bewildered. The way she laughed—fey, dauntless—gave her a radiant, awkward bravery that shamed him. "Who is Bidewell?" he asked.

"His full name is Conan Arthur Bidewell. I think he's been here for a long time."

"He's, like, the Great and Powerful Wizard?"

"He seems to think so. He's spent his whole life collecting books," Ginny said. "There are rooms here that haven't been visited by a human being in over a hundred years. So he says. I think he wants to put us in them and see what happens."

"You believe him?"

"I don't think he's lying," Ginny said.

The sliding door rumbled opened. Miriam poked her head out. "You can come in now. Jeremy—"

"Jack," he said.

"Jack . . . time for you to meet Mr. Bidewell."

Ginny walked beside him.

"How can you just accept all this?" Jack asked.

"I've had my moments," Ginny said. "I always come back. It's safe here, for now—the safest place in the whole city, maybe the whole world. Out there . . ."

No need to say more about the streets, the city, the sky.

———

The old man—Bidewell, Jack assumed—stood beside a long wooden table on which someone had positioned a short stack of medium-sized hardcover books. He wore a dark brown suit covered with patches and mended holes.

Miriam joined the other women, and they all sat around a wood-burning iron stove whose square mica eye glowed a friendly orange. Agazutta took the single overstuffed chair, lounging like a spoiled movie star.

Jack and Ginny stood at opposite ends of the table like students awaiting an exam.

Bidewell studied Jack, then pulled two books from the stack and let them fall open to their middles. He pushed one across the table toward Ginny and the other toward Jack. Both looked down. The pages were incomprehensible; no words, no paragraphs, just random lines of letters and numbers. Jack looked away and closed his book with a sharp crack.

Ginny left hers open. Bidewell had given her *The Gargoyles of Oxford* by Professor J. G. Goyle. She recognized the binding, but could no longer read any of the text, and the pictures seemed muddy and vague.

A third book, the name on its spine also scrambled, was passed among the women.

"You may have noticed the effects of what you experienced outside, what some call the Gape," Bidewell said as this book was carried back to the table by Agazutta. "Actually, two events have concurred: the Gape, and Terminus. The Gape cuts us off from our past. Terminus cuts us off from any future, and so, by and large, we are cut off from both causality and eventuality, the two pulsing waves of time. The results are obvious, outside. In here, my library is a ruin, but it still offers some protection."

"*All* the books are ruined?" Miriam asked, incredulous. "I mean, you *do* collect curiosities."

"As many as I've examined, including those with which I'm quite familiar," Bidewell said. "Outside these walls, every book in our region—perhaps every region we could ever hope to access—has also been scrambled. I've not seen this before, not on such a scale."

Jack set his face in a vacant expression—waiting.

"Virginia, you have regained possession of your odd little stone. Now there are two," Bidewell said. "Jack, Ginny, could you remove your stones from their boxes . . . ?"

Jack puzzled open his box. The stone lay inside, twisted and black, shining with a single deep red gleam.

Ginny lifted hers. "Both present and accounted for," she said, trying to be cheerful.

"Given their shapes and the way they appear to nest together—but no, we will *not* attempt that, please keep them separate—I suspect that a third exists, and perhaps more. None of us knows where they might be. None of our sentinels and outriders has reported a third individual with your abilities. But for now, we can't worry about that. What is outside this warehouse for the time being is beyond our control."

Agazutta sniffed.

Bidewell nodded. "If they are what I think they are, then they have nearly completed their long journey—they have *summed*. Bring them to the center of the table, please, and give them a slow wave over this volume. I've chosen a particularly valuable book, one I've kept in reserve for some time—but which is presently unreadable. Children . . ."

Jack stood beside Bidewell, following Ginny's lead. Bidewell opened the book to the middle. Both held out their stones. The women crowded the opposite side of the table to see.

Jack and Ginny held the stones over the pages.

At first the text remained scrambled. Then, as if caught in a glowing light of reason, the words began to return—a few, then sentences, phrases, entire paragraphs.

No letters moved, nothing visibly rearranged, but the book under the two stones slowly became readable.

Jack couldn't help glancing at the first paragraphs to become clear—reading upside down, a trick he had learned years ago.

> Language is as fundamental as energy. To be observed, the universe must be reduced—encoded. An unobserved universe is a messy place. Language becomes the DNA of the cosmos.

He looked up. Ginny had been reading as well.

"I am humbled by the power you children possess," Bidewell said reverently. "I've waited centuries to observe this effect. It confirms so much that has been, until now, mere philosophy."

"What *are* the stones?" Ginny asked, her hand and the stone trembling. "I've had mine as long as I can remember. My parents had it before me. I've never been away from it for very long. But I have no idea what it is."

"Jack?" Bidewell inquired, watching him closely, but with a confident air.

"My mother called it a sometime stone. Sometimes it's here, sometimes it's not. Once, she called it a library stone."

"Curious. *Library* stone. As if she might have known."

"Known what?" Jack asked.

"For now, these are still just partial shells—journey finished, full and strong, but immature. Even so . . . as you can see, they have remarkable powers." Bidewell gripped both their extended hands and pulled them slowly apart. The text below remained comprehensible. In fact, the patch of legibility continued to grow. "There have been many such over the ages. Some failed and became lumps of useless rock. Some were captured—along with their guardians—and we assume those were sequestered or destroyed. In the names given to them, I suspect, we have clues as to their ultimate nature and function. You may put them away for now."

"If something has scrambled all order—how can we think or see?" Miriam asked. "Why isn't our flesh scrambled?" Her voice rose. "Everything should just fall apart!"

Her disturbing observation was met with grim silence.

Bidewell flipped the book's restored pages one by one. The old man actually had tears in his eyes—tears of relief and awe. "We are just beginning to see how deep the mystery is. For better or worse, all time, everywhere, is now subjective. All fates are local." He lifted his gaze to a large electric clock mounted over the sliding steel door. The hands were bent and jammed as if invisible fingers had reached inside and twisted them—and the second hand lay at the bottom of the glass. "No timepiece will tick out our remaining seconds. If we end flattened and frozen against Terminus—we are lost. Even these stones will be useless. But we cannot rush the tasks that remain for us. First, we must get to know each other." Bidewell pulled a folding chair forward, gripped its seat, and smiled at Jack.

Jack sat, eyes sharp.

"Just for this occasion," Bidewell said, "I have laid in a small feast. Ginny knows where cans of soup and the makings for sandwiches are stored. Ellen, will you begin?"

They sat down to pastrami on rye and tomato soup warmed on the stove. Farrah produced a bottle of red wine and a corkscrew from her capacious handbag. "Wonder what Terminus does to wine?" she asked. She poured a small amount of the dark ruby liquid into a tumbler, sipped it, and lifted an eyebrow in approval, then poured around. "It's hard to spoil a cheap merlot."

Ellen lifted her glass and swirled its contents. "The four of us really did start out as a book group," she said. "We still get together twice a month to eat and drink and discuss literature."

"We're well-off," Farrah said. "Leisure becomes an attractive nuisance."

Ellen resumed. "Anyway, *ladies,* after Agazutta's father passed away, she cleaned out his house. The house had been in the family for over a hundred years. In the attic, she saw an old, dusty box pushed far back

into a corner. Inside, she found an unusual book. It had probably been
there since before her grandfather's time."

Bidewell rubbed his hands, then leaned against the edge of the table.
For all his apparent age, he seemed flexible—not spry, but flexible. And
tough.

Agazutta seemed bored by this recounting. "Blame it all on me," she
said.

"Agazutta brought it to our group. After a bottle of pinot gris and a
fine melon salad with pine nuts and prosciutto, we all agreed the book
might be rare—though it was not in English, nor in any language we
knew. It seemed to be part of a set. So we thought it would be fun to take
it to a dealer in such things—a man I know, John Christopher Brown."

"They dated in college," Farrah broadcast to the room.

"We did," Ellen confirmed, with a short stare. "Can I tell this my
way?"

Farrah smiled sweetly.

Jack hunched down in the folding chair.

"Mr. Brown owns an antiquarian bookstore on Stone Way. He seems
to know everything about books and a little bit about everyone involved
in books—old books, odd books. He knew of a local buyer interested in
just this sort of item."

Bidewell listened as attentively as a child.

"Our dear Conan," Ellen said.

"Ah," Bidewell said. "I am drawn into the picture."

"You drew *us* in. At any rate, you bought our book. At first, Mr.
Brown kept you anonymous, but passed along a portion of the sum
Conan paid—a suspiciously large sum, enough to make us happy to
continue to search through our attics, our basements, even the walls of
our houses."

"Farrah found another," Agazutta said.

"In my basement, in a shoe box. I had never seen it before. Really—
it might have just popped up like a coat hanger in a closet. It wasn't
old—from the 1950s—a paperback, in fact." She added, eyebrow raised,
"With a lurid cover."

"A lurid cover—and every single word misspelled, except on one
page," Agazutta said, "which it turned out was transliterated Hebrew.
Mr. Brown sold that book for an even larger sum."

"Remarkable ladies," Bidewell said, "to have located two such curious volumes in their immediate environs. They obviously had a knack. I gave Mr. Brown permission to refer the ladies to me. Such finds do not arrive entirely by chance."

"How *do* they arrive?" Ginny asked.

"Not to be known—" Bidewell began, and without skipping a beat, the entire group—except for Jack—echoed:

"Not to be known, surely, not to be known!"

Bidewell bore up with patient good humor. "The paperback was intriguing—yet merely a symptom. However, what the lovely Witches of Eastlake had happened upon, with their first discovery, was the thirteenth volume of a remarkable and elusive encyclopedia."

"Here we go," Agazutta said.

"One set had apparently been printed in Shanghai in the 1920s, to the specifications of an Argentinian named Borges. There are no records of Señor Borges except his nameplate in the index volume, and his signature on page 412 of volume one. And so our ladies had made one of the most magnificent finds of this century—a volume of the lost *Encyclopedia Pseudogeographica*. Only one other volume is known, incunabular, recovered in Toledo in 1432 and currently held in the British Library under lock and key—with excellent reason, I might add."

"It's a good thing we couldn't read it," Farrah said, stretching like a cat. Which reminded Ginny—she had not seen Minimus or any of the other cats for some hours. They likely had found hiding places until events and new guests settled. "We might have gone mad."

"Madder than we are," Agazutta added.

"But who would know?" Ellen muttered.

Bidewell's laugh was light and rich, like a perfectly baked cookie. Despite himself, despite everything Jack had experienced, he was beginning to like the old man.

"Suffice it to say," said Ellen, "we all found Mr. Bidewell handsome, fascinating—"

"And wealthy!" said Agazutta.

Bidewell peered around the room with satisfaction bordering on smugness, as if, at long last, he had assembled a long-desired family.

"The rest is history," Ellen said.

"Pied history," Farrah said with a small, half-concealed yawn.

"Which means?" Ginny asked.

"History comes in two colors. Everyone else lives one color,"

Agazutta explained. "After meeting Mr. Bidewell, we now live the other."

"What does any of this have to do with me? Or with her?" Jack asked, nodding at Ginny.

"I should rekindle our fire. It's getting cold," Bidewell said, pushing away from the desk. "Jack, there are logs and old newspapers in the hopper. We shall pour another glass and toast lost memory. *Temps perdu,* quite literally. For that is the talent we shall speak of soon—order, chance, times lost, and the recovery of objects that never were, yet ever shall be."

Jack picked pages of newspaper from the curved hopper.

The pages were blank.

CHAPTER 53

Wallingford

Grayness and dusty sweeps of shadow, a glazed, darkling sky, clouds jerking by in spasms like dying animals flopping and kicking across the heavens—

The rough abandoned house at the center of so many of Daniel's lives, desolate beyond description—

Freezing isolation made worse by the fact that he was not alone— that he had Whitlow to contend with.

Whitlow had entered the old house, passing Daniel on the porch, and now faced him with a wry, twitching smile across the short distance between two old chairs on the water-stained and warped floor—where he and Daniel had seated themselves, nowhere else to go, just as clocks everywhere had stopped humming, whirring, ticking.

"Let's discuss your future, young fate-shifter." Whitlow's words blurred across the short distance between them, followed by a dozen variations as all the remaining, cut-up strands of fate tried to sum. "Let's discuss what is to come, now that you have a strong new body . . . before your memories fade again, always a problem for your kind . . ."

Whitlow had repeated these words so often, Daniel had lost count. There could be no finer punishment for all his sins than this—and yet, he could not just throw aside the stone and end it all.

He knew the stones in the boxes offered a circle of protection—and did not want to experience what it would feel like if he, like Whitlow, fell just on the edge of or outside that circle.

I've survived worse—the worst, I think. But my memories are vaguer than the murk outside. If I could only think clearly!

If I could make a move—any move—

He still had hope.

And so he gripped the boxes. At least there would be no hunger, no real pain. He could sit without moving, going through each train of thought in smeared iterations, the changes so slight no outside observer could ever know the difference—

For now, Whitlow had been stymied—perhaps even defeated—by Terminus. The marionette across from Daniel labored as if strung from the hands of a broken clock. "Let's discuss . . . what our Livid Mistress will have in store . . . for such a fine young betrayer of worlds . . ."

Daniel leaned back and held the boxes at arm's length behind him, removing their circle a few feet from Whitlow. The seated marionette slowed and fell silent, until Daniel's arm tingled and he folded it back.

The others—Whitlow's partners, lost out in the vibrating murk— would never arrive to help their boss. As for the Moth—whatever that was or had been, no sign from that quarter, either.

With a suck of breath and a cough, Daniel realized that any certainty, even doom, would be better than this staggered eternity.

Still, his feelers—blunted, singed, traumatized—were sensitive enough that he knew this was not all there was. A refuge existed somewhere. Had Whitlow not found him, he might have made his way to that refuge just in time to elude all this.

Caught—something less than frozen—facing a nemesis something less than toothless . . .

Fully capable of boring Daniel to screaming insanity with his threats and schemes, like thin acid dripping on acres of exposed skin.

". . . before the memories of your past exploits fade and get eaten away by a fresh and resentful new mind. The Chalk Princess has such hopes . . ."

———

Something changed.

Daniel felt a thrill in his spine, an unmistakable difference in the room's atmosphere. Though how he could recognize or even detect this in his present state was not clear. But here it was. A loosening. Something powerful jerking at the damaged strands, shaking them out, squeezing a few last hours of usable chronology that something might be done.

Would be done.

A knock on the door stabbed sharp and painful through Daniel's ears. He forced himself to stand—amazed that he *could* stand.

Whitlow's eyes followed and his white face twitched, like a corpse jolted by an electric charge—but that was all he could do.

Daniel crossed the damp boards and opened the door. A crash and roar buffeted him—ice calving from glaciers, mountains slamming against mountains, giant knives ripping up the sky.

Worlds—histories colliding.

Just outside the door a bulky shadow cringed, then separated itself from the confusion and squeezed inside by main force of will.

"A little help," said a squat, powerful man, hands outstretched, thick fingers grasping. His gray suit dripped water. "The Queen in White has abandoned us. Pardon me if I say it—I seem to have what you need. And pardon me again if I ask—what in hell *are* you?"

CHAPTER 54

The Green Warehouse

The book group ladies retired to a far corner with a few cots and blankets and pillows that Bidewell pulled from an old brass-bound wooden chest. Their lanterns cast long, dancing shadows on the warehouse's walls and ceiling.

Before he retired to his own quarters, Bidewell pulled down a volume from an otherwise bare shelf. The volume bore on the base of its spine the number—or the year—1298. In view of Jack and Ginny, he winked, put the book under his arm, and bade them good night.

Then he slid shut the steel door.

The warehouse became still.

Ginny gave Jack an uneasy glance and retreated into her space.

The ladies and Ginny had helped Jack clear another space a few yards away and provided him with another cot and blankets. Everyone in their little squares, insulated, protected. Waiting.

He sat on the edge of his cot and let his shoulders slump with exhaustion.

Ginny's cot creaked on the opposite side of the stack of boxes and crates. They seemed far enough from the others—if they spoke softly, no one else would hear. "Is it time for stories?" she whispered.

"Sure," he said. "You first."

She walked around the crates, pulling along a chair, and sat, knees together, booted feet askew.

"I'm eighteen," she said. "How old are you?"

"Twenty-four."

"People say I'm lucky, but bad things keep happening."

"Maybe they'd be worse if you weren't lucky."

"I answered the ad, just like you. I called the phone number."

"Jesus," Jack said.

"Some of it's hard to remember," she began. "I came from Minneapolis. I was living in a house full of musicians, musical types—they all played instruments, deejayed raves. We chipped in and did odd jobs. They said I brought them luck because we kept getting better gigs, play dates, black sick jams."

"That's good?" Jack asked.

She nodded. "I loved it. We were free and we ate total shack and I felt . . ." She glanced at Jack.

"You've lost me," he said. "But keep going. I'll catch up."

"One day . . . I knew my friends were forgetting about me. I thought it was the drugs." Her voice and face hardened. "We would hang out in old houses, talk about music, movies and TV, stuff that passed the time. Every week or so they acted just like I was new. They didn't remember anything about me. Sometimes it hurt so much I would go off by myself, but I didn't like being alone. I asked, what would happen if *I* stopped remembering who I was? I did a lot of drawing."

Jack winced, her voice had become so flinty.

"They were snuffing up X—Ecstasy. I tried it a few times—they all thought if you didn't do X, you were a hard case, unable to form true friendships. It made me so happy and loving. I would give anybody everything I had, all the loving little twinkles in my little brain just lining up like pinball hits. Anybody could walk in and I'd feel that love-juice flooding me, I was so *grateful* . . . I couldn't hand out my goodies fast enough. And it didn't matter. They still forgot me."

"Wow," Jack said.

Ginny watched his expression warily. "Yeah. All the time I was with them, I didn't jump the lines—I didn't fate-shift. I thought that was over. I thought I had a home. But I was still having the dreams. I'd draw—that was fine, everybody liked weird art. Everything creepy, everything about death, is fine, dying is the ultimate giving. Eternal giggles. And then, everyone would forget. They'd think I was new. They'd tell me their stories all over again."

Jack sat quiet, letting her get it out.

"I would have died," she murmured. "But then this . . . person came to me, the one who did most of the really strange drawings—when I was gone, blanking out. She's part of my dreams, too—I think. One day she left a note. It was in little block letters—like it was written by a child: 'Put your skin back on. Get out. We have work to do.' And I knew just what she meant. This wasn't love or even friendship, what we were doing in that house, it was turning oneself into a snail between a boot and a sidewalk. I had no defenses left, just raw nerves. So I quit the house and I quit the X and all my friends, and after a few days I was sitting under a bridge, out of the snow, when I read an ad from a newspaper I was using to stay warm." She drew quotes. " 'Do you dream of a city at the end of time?' And a phone number."

Jack winced again.

"I still had some charge on my cell, so I called the number, mostly just to have something to do. Another bad decision, right?"

Jack lifted one corner of his lips.

"That's what I do. I run away from good decisions, toward bad decisions. This was the worst, I think. A man came to the bridge and picked me up. He looked young, Asian—in his thirties, tall and skinny but fit, with deep black eyes. He drove an old gray Mercedes. There was someone in the backseat—a woman. She wore a veil and never said a word. She smelled like smoke. We left the city behind. Off the highway, the man and I got out and had lunch at a diner, but the woman never left the backseat. She wasn't dead—I could hear her breathing.

"After we ate, back on the highway, she started a fire. The guy had a fire extinguisher under his seat. He pulled over and opened her door and yelled and sprayed foam all over. She whimpered but never said a word."

Jack's fingers knotted in his lap.

"I thought he looked young, but his tiny black eyes were old. Mostly, he was friendly. The front seat was so comfortable—heated, soft but firm. He did tricks with his silver dollar—one-handed, the other hand on the wheel, pretty clever. The coin did everything he wanted it to— like it was alive and he was its master.

"He remembered my story—what I told him as we drove. We might go on forever, tricks and stories and the long, straight road. I was so out of it, so accepting—still just a little fool, I guess.

"We finally came to a big house out in the woods near St. Paul. There were piles of lumber and stuff all around, but I didn't see any workmen. The guy told me they had found an old vault under the house with thick walls where things could get really quiet. They put me down in the vault and I slept for a couple of days. It *was* quiet. I got better, stopped gritting my teeth and biting the insides of my cheeks. I felt so lucky, and thought maybe I was learning how to feel gratitude, real love. He would visit every day, bring me food and clothes, and I knew from the beginning he wasn't interested in sex—he respected me. I thought this was a good place. He was good to me. My dreams stopped."

Ginny had started shaking, little tremors at first, but now her teeth were chattering. Jack reached out to touch her arm, but she pulled it away.

"The last time he visited, he told me we were going to take a walk. We climbed the stairs out of the basement, and the wind was whistling outside. It was cold—below freezing. The air smelled like snow. I noticed that they hadn't put in carpet or wood floors—just plywood. It was really just an old abandoned house that had never been finished. He said we were going to meet the Queen."

Jack pulled his hands apart so he wouldn't bruise his fingers.

"He said the Queen paid him to find special people. Somehow, I saw that the guy's clothes were actually pretty shabby. She couldn't be paying him much. And now his skin looked old. I thought maybe I'd found myself a *real* vampire—a poor one." Ginny's voice dropped below a whisper. Jack could barely hear her.

The warehouse creaked. Yards off, a cat meowed. The meow echoed around the rafters as if there were dozens of cats.

"He was as afraid of the woods as I was. I knew the Queen wasn't the woman who started fires, because we passed the car when we walked into the trees—just parked there, on the dirt driveway. Smoke was drifting out of an open rear window. The woman was inside. I saw her veil move. She was looking right at me but I couldn't see her eyes."

"You didn't run?"

"I couldn't. I couldn't even think about jumping the lines because I knew the woman in the car would set fires everywhere, and she wouldn't even need to leave the backseat. I could almost *see* her doing it—hundreds of little blazes dropping from the air. She'd burn the woods, the house, any path I tried to take, anywhere I tried to go."

"Using fires—like wasps."

Ginny glanced left for a second, chin down, defiant, working hard to get it all out. "I wonder how many of them are out there, hunting us?"

Jack cocked his head. "No idea."

"We walked between the trees for five or ten minutes. I thought we were walking in a big circle—we kept passing a black lake covered with green duckweed. Everything was getting dark. There was a storm coming in, low black clouds—lightning."

"Sideways lightning?"

Ginny nodded. "Then he said something about a moth. Maybe it was *the* Moth. 'The Moth is coming to introduce you.' The trees—I noticed that their branches grew down into the dirt. The leaves moved, independently. But they weren't really moving, they were just changing—getting bigger or smaller, shifting left or right, but without moving—because the trees were black and *solid*, like stiff tar. I thought, maybe each time a tree seemed to move, it was becoming a different tree—I don't know how to describe what was wrong with them. The guy with the coin seemed as scared as I was. He said, 'The Queen in White expects perfection. That's part of her charm.' I asked him how old he was, how old the Queen was, and he said, 'What an odd question.'

"I think I saw another man—but it wasn't a man. It stretched up and out until I could see right through it—right through him. We came to the center of the woods. I knew it was the center, but we had never left the circle. Maybe the path was a kind of spiral, but special—curving inward, but not in space. There was like a big lake of frozen jade-green water—all carved up, gouged out. I couldn't see the sky over the lake—it just wasn't there."

Jack didn't want to hear any more. He shifted a few inches to his right, as if she were a package about to explode.

"The clouds dropped and cut off the trees. Leaves fell like little flat rocks, ice cold. They stung when they hit my head and my arms. The light became gray and icy. The shadows had edges sharp as knives—if you walked over one, it could cut you. Everything smelled like lemons and burning gravy and gasoline—I hope I never smell anything like that again.

"'Don't say a word,' the thin man told me. He pocketed his coin, held out his hand, wiggled his long fingers. I couldn't help it—I showed him the stone, still in its box. He reached out as if to take it, but instead he backed away and said, 'Don't move. Don't look. I'm sorry.'

"He started running. He left the circle we were on, and I heard him crashing through branches. I guessed that the circle was a trap—I had been hypnotized by the spiral. I couldn't lift my feet."

Jack covered his mouth.

"The same clouds . . . in the sky . . . like the ones that flew in over the city to get you," Ginny said. "The man wanted to deliver me to something that didn't belong here, something angry, sad. Disappointed. I stood between the trees. The leaves were spinning around the Queen or whatever it was in the center . . . I couldn't see her. But she was tying up everything into one big knot. Her knot was the center of the spiral. I didn't believe it, but I understood it—everything that *could* happen was *going* to happen, and all of it would happen to *me*, and some of it would even be stuff that couldn't happen.

"I was about to see *everything,* all at once. I turned around—completely around—and the trees spun by, but only halfway, and I saw the man in the trees—he lowered his hands and his eyes were like snowballs in his head. I turned around again, completely around, knowing that I would not see the Queen again until I had spun twice. Does that make sense?"

Jack closed his eyes and realized he could see the sense that it did make. "In that place, you have to turn twice to rotate a full circle," he said.

"I thought you'd understand."

"It's got a different logic, like the jumps we make. Did you see her?" Jack asked.

"I don't call it seeing. But yes, I suppose I did. She was at the center of the jade lake. She wasn't dressed in white, she didn't wear anything. At first I didn't know why the man called her the Queen in White. Maybe he saw her differently, or knew something else about her. She was very tall. If I came from somewhere else, saw with different eyes, I suppose she might have been beautiful. She had limbs or arms or things coming out of her that I didn't recognize, but they looked right—they fit. Even so, I knew that if I came near her, she would suck my eyes right out of my head. I felt like a piece of bloody ice. She just stood at the center of her knot, watching, infinitely curious, curious like a hunger, curious like fear—she wanted to know everything about me. And so *angry*, so disappointed. I wanted to tell her what she needed to know, just to end her disappointment, her rage—but I couldn't explain it in words. Instead, what I had to give her would shoot up out of my skin, all the places I had been and things I had done or would do—past and future, all my selves, just a big, chewed-up mess flowing into her knot. She'd end up wearing me like a dress or a scarf. I didn't think I was going to die—but I knew that what was about to happen would be worse than dying."

Jack sat stiff on the cot, hands trembling under his thighs. "Umhmm," he murmured.

She smiled. "But I'm here, right? So relax."

"That's not easy," he said with a nervous grin.

"Well, deal. I had been holding something back—didn't even know it, lucky for me, because I might have told her. Maybe *you* know what I'm talking about."

"Maybe."

"Tell me what I did." Ginny looked straight at him.

Jack made a circular scissors motion with his fingers.

"Yeah. When I was finished—and it took just an instant—I was flat on my face, covered with leaves. Trees had fallen all around and water was everywhere—steaming but cold. Duckweed hung on all the trees. The lake had flung itself up out of the hollow, and I didn't see the man again—I don't know where he went. The whole forest was flattened."

"What about your stone?"

"I dropped it, but then I found it," Ginny said, nodding. "It was right near the path, still in its box. I picked it up and walked back between the trees. Near the house, I saw that the car was gone. I was alone. You must have done the same thing, Jack. So tell me what I did that made them go away."

He still couldn't answer.

"Can we *slice* world-lines?" she asked. "Not just jump between them, but cut them into pieces, *kill* them?"

He shook his head. "It's something to do with the stones summing up. They're part of us. We can't lose them unless we die."

"I knew that when I pawned the box. It always comes back to me. Did *you* cut things loose? In the storm."

"I don't remember. I don't think I had time."

"Hold my hand," Ginny said, and held it out.

He didn't hesitate. Her fingers were hot and her skin seemed to glow a faint cherry-red like the iron stove in the next room. "You're burning up," Jack said, but did not let go.

"Sometimes I do that. It'll pass," Ginny said. "I survived, didn't I?"

"You sure did."

"I know why they want to catch us," she said. "Whoever they are."

"Whatever they are," Jack added.

"They're afraid of us."

He squeezed her fingers and the heat subsided. "Makes you wonder about Bidewell. What are we getting ourselves into?"

"Bidewell's not afraid, not of us," Ginny said. "That's why I came here. No knots, no fear—just quiet and lots of books. The books *are* like insulation. I still feel safe here. My stone is safe, too—for now."

Jack let out a low whistle. "Okay," he said.

"You're not convinced."

"It's quiet—that's okay. But I'd like for everything just to get back to normal."

"Was it ever normal—for you?" Ginny asked.

"Before my mother died," he said. "Well, maybe not normal—but fun. Nice."

"You loved her?"

"Of course. Together, she and my father were . . . wherever we ended up, we had a home, even if it was just for a day."

Ginny looked around the warehouse. "This feels more like home than anyplace I've ever been. What about you? What's your story?"

"My mother was a dancer. My father wanted to be a comedian and a magician. My mother died, then my father. I wasn't much more than a kid. They didn't leave me much—just a trunk, some tricks and some books on magic—and the stone. I didn't starve—I had learned how to play guitar and juggle, do card tricks, that sort of thing. I fell in with a tough crowd for a while, like you, got out of it . . . learned the streets, started busking. Managed not to get killed. Two years ago I moved in with a guy named Burke. He works as a sous chef in a restaurant. We don't see much of each other."

"Lovers?" Ginny asked.

Jack smiled. "No," he said. "Burke's as straight as they come. He just doesn't like living alone."

"You've met those women before?"

"I know Ellen pretty well," Jack said. "I met the others a few days ago."

"Did you do those sketches that Miriam found . . . in your apartment?"

"I'm a lousy artist. The other one did them. My guest."

"Where's he from, do you think?"

"'The city at the end of time,' of course," Jack said, trying for sarcasm, but his voice cracked.

"Mine, too," Ginny said. "But the last time I dreamed about her, she's not there. She's outside, lost somewhere awful."

"The Chaos," Jack said.

She looked down at the floor. "I don't want to talk about it."

"All right," he said.

"Jack, do *they* have stones like ours?"

He shook his head. "I don't think so."

"Maybe we're supposed to bring them."

"I don't see how. They're there—we're here." He pushed back, then looked down at a large cardboard box labeled VALDOLID, 1898. "What kind of books does Bidewell collect?"

"All sorts," Ginny said.

Jack pulled up the interleaved flaps and lifted out a dusty volume. The book's hinges had cracked and the leather left powder on his fingers. The gold-embossed words on the spine still did not mean anything. He looked up. "Gobbledygook Press," he said. "I guess the stones aren't finished."

"A lot of his books were like that before. Bidewell seems to know the difference."

"Makes as much sense as everything else." Jack was about to put the book down, but something tugged in his arm—the faintest pull on a hidden nerve—and he turned to a middle page. There, surrounded by more nonsense, a paragraph poked up that he could (just barely) read:

> Then Jerem enterd the House and therei found a book all meaning-less bu for these words:
>   Hast thou the old rock, Jeremy? In your pocket, wihyou?

Ginny watched him closely as his face flushed, as if he had been prancing around naked. Tongue poking the inside of his cheek, Jack slowly flipped through more of the book. Nothing else made sense.

"What is it?" she asked.

He showed her the page. She read the lines and her jaw fell like a child seeing a ghost. "All the books are different," she said. "I'm not in any of them."

"Have you looked?" Jack asked.

She shook her head. "There wasn't time."

FOURTEEN ZEROS

Tenebros Flood Channel

Pahtun had grown accustomed to living in the perpetual tweenlight of the outer reaches of the old flood channels. He seldom went up into the Kalpa and was content performing his duties on the wide flats, away from the wakelight glow over the Tiers—he called them by their old name, the rookery.

Pahtun had been training marchers for longer than there had been breeds. A lofty, slender man with an experienced brown face, he strode along the channel floor, eyes silver-gray with caution. He knew the city was dying. It had been dying by degrees since before he had been made. Now, it was likely to finish its dying quickly.

Wakelight grew fitfully over the distant ceil. Red rings pulsed and flickered around the cracked and battered patches left by the intrusion that had blown through the lower levels of the first bion, directly over his head, and nearly claimed them all.

He finished his walk of twenty miles from the camp up the Tenebros channel, to the rendezvous between the first and second isles, and waited for the brown wardens to descend with their half-conscious burdens.

This time there were only nine rather than the usual twenty. "Great destruction," the lead warden explained. "Many lost. These may be the last."

The young breeds crawled into the shade of the low channel trees, moaning softly. Pahtun examined them one by one as the wardens flew away. He lifted their heads, using his flower-finger to sense their vital levels, and found them fit—the wardens never delivered injured or incapable breeds.

As they recovered, he helped them to their feet, soothing with low crèche songs. His three cohorts had walked across the channels to the sandy stretch by then. More obviously jaded, with much less time on the job, these younger Menders still attended to the recruits with patience and skill. They soon had them walking in a single column toward the dark outer wall and the training camp that had waited there for as long as there had been Tiers or marchers—too long to contemplate, as far as Pahtun was concerned.

Six males and three females. He watched the dazed breeds and, as always, both envied and pitied them—they were few, they were small, they were confused. He wondered what they would see on their journey.

Only young breeds were ever sent on the marches—grown of primordial mass, cultured in the Tiers, and afforded the best instincts, some of which would truly awaken only in the Chaos. Personally, this version of Pahtun had never ventured beyond the middle lands. If these nine made up the last march to be delivered to his expert care, he might never learn the whole truth about the Chaos and the Typhon.

He showed the breeds to their tents and made sure they were comfortable. Soon, they were sound asleep.

The cohorts made their own camp nearby, away from the breeds and away from Pahtun's solitary tent. They held the trainer in some awe—but considered him old and peculiar. After all, what was the point of all of this?

Perhaps there was no point. None of the other Pahtuns, sent into the Chaos in violation of the rulings of the Astyanax, had ever reported their discoveries. And none of the marchers he'd trained had ever returned.

CHAPTER 56

The Broken Tower

As requested, a living breed, crèche-born of primordial matter, for whatever purpose the Librarian might devise.

Ghentun stood on one side of the high, empty chamber, a dozen yards from the nearest soaring window, surrounded by a slow, enveloping shimmer. At his waist floated the young male, curled in anesthetic oblivion, injured but already healing—treated and protected by Ghentun's cloak.

The Keeper of the Tiers could only feel numb. He could not conceive of any action that would make any difference now.

Delay, decadence, conspiracies beyond counting or comprehension—the inevitable sapping of the city's vitality in the face of millions of years of warding off the unthinkable—had brought the end closer than even he had imagined.

Upon arrival, Ghentun had circled the chamber to look down through the high windows at the Kalpa's three remaining bions. The intrusion had severely damaged the lowest levels of the first bion, whose foundations enveloped the Tiers and from whose rounded crown rose the Broken Tower. It also wreaked tremendous destruction on the southern and the tertian bions. Both sent up dismal, spiraling plumes of silvery smoke to the limits of the inner pressure barrier.

Outside the border of the real, the monstrosities drew closer, as if warming themselves on the Kalpa's fires of destruction. The Witness's eternally spinning beam had accelerated, and its huge mountain of solidified flesh—once human, now ageless and beyond pity—pushed in toward the Defenders, anticipating another sacrifice.

The Tiers had always attracted the strongest, most destructive intrusions. Now Ghentun wondered if one reason for this attention was floating beside him. He comprehended that since the creation of the Tiers, the Typhon had been probing the city as if with special knowledge—if such a thing could know or make plans.

He looked to the east, away from the Witness, for the last party of marchers, hoping they might leave before the final collapse, before the Typhon's triumph.

The Librarian had dallied for millions of years. Mind beyond measure—how could Ghentun criticize or even understand? But there had never been a plan that he could discern—certainly not one that could be explained to a Mender or a breed. He was really no better than his charges, no better than this brash, crèche-born youngster, who had persisted despite all the deceptions and intellectual barricades set in his path.

Like Menders—like Ghentun—breeds understood shame, as if their primordial stuff preserved a heritage of that ancient emotion lost to the Great Eidolons.

An angelin approached, appearing at first as a tiny speck silvering outward from the center of the chamber, then suddenly nearby—a few feet away. As before, it was female in form, pale blue, and no taller than Ghentun's knee—but this time it seemed to prefer the appearance of walking rather than drifting about or flying.

It might be the same angelin he had spoken with before—and it might not. Identity was of little importance to this class of servants.

Ghentun nudged the breed. Jebrassy raised his head and blinked, looked around, but remained curled, as if savoring a few last moments of warmth and sanity.

"All honor to the Librarian," the angelin sang, its voice like trickling water. "Is the experiment concluded?"

"Yes," Ghentun replied.

"You've brought the requested specimen from the Tiers?"

"I have. Does the Librarian request my presence?" Ghentun asked doubtfully.

"You will accompany the young breed."

Jebrassy pushed out his legs and slowly dropped to the bottom of the cloak, where he stood on his own, beneath the gaze of the Tall One. He turned to stare in awe at the blue form a few feet beyond, radiating deep cold despite the cloak's protection.

Jebrassy had moved well beyond confusion or fear. Anything could happen. He almost hoped it would—all of it, just to get it over with.

Then he thought of Tiadba. He shuddered at the realization that he had just emerged from a dark sleep. But for how long? Where was she? Had she been sucked into the intrusion? Was she even alive?

Jebrassy growled and shoved his hands against the shimmer.

A small voice spoke in his ear like the high chirrup of a letterbug. "Don't do that. It's cold out here, and the Librarian wishes you comfort and health. Both of you will follow this silly blue form. It is my pleasure to escort you to the most wonderful place in all the Kalpa. Possibly the most wonderful place left to humans in all the cosmos."

Jebrassy looked up at the Tall One, then back to the small blue figure, puzzled—they thought they were *all* humans, despite appearances, was that the secret? He began to move his feet in a shuffle and discovered that the shimmer followed him—and so walked at a normal pace, keeping up with the naked blue image. Ghentun stayed beside him.

Not even the sweep of a knife-edged beam of gray light across the smooth roof of the chamber—like a threat of instant blindness—slowed their progress, though it made Jebrassy cringe.

When they came to the center—a walk of what seemed only minutes—he looked back and studied the far curved rank of high windows and suddenly understood where they were—remembering the stories in the books.

"We're in Malregard, aren't we?" he asked Ghentun.

"Some once called it that," Ghentun said. "We're both of us far above our neighborhoods and rank, young breed. In the region of the Great Eidolons. They neither think nor act as we do."

"But we're *all* humans," Jebrassy said.

The Keeper touched his nose with amusement—a breed gesture.

"Watch your step," the angelin warned. "You should close your eyes. We're vectoring to the top of the tower—what's left of it, of course."

"What broke the tower?" Jebrassy asked.

Ghentun made a small, ambiguous sound. "You needn't concern yourself with the past. There's far too much of it. You should only look ahead. For once, the future is scaled to fit you."

Jebrassy did not know whether to be insulted.

Silvery curves danced around them, as if they were moving, yet he saw no change. And then—they stood beneath a terrible sky, filled with hoops of flame and spinning worlds. Something looked down upon them, impossible to actually see or measure—and Jebrassy thrust his clenched fists to his eyes.

He thought he was falling—that he was back with Tiadba flying over the Tiers, and the warden had let him go—

Voices sounded all around, saying nothing he could understand, and a deep booming buffeted his body.

Jebrassy could not stand the thought of falling without seeing where he was going to hit. He had to know. He lowered his arms, but for a moment his eyes refused to open. He had seen too much already—something bright and multicolored, and from it great sweeps of silver rising high into an arched grayness, grasping and moving brilliant red shapes, like farmers using tongs to swing bales of chafe . . .

Above—below—he couldn't tell which—thousands of white figures were arrayed in positions of restful waiting, hands clasped behind their backs. Each had two arms, two legs, and a round white head. They had no faces, no features, nothing but smooth whiteness.

He wasn't falling. He was floating—upside down, it seemed—over an immense tangle of causeways, along which the many white figures stood in rows or moved about in astonishingly different ways. Some of the figures walked, many drifted close to the roads, a few zipped up and over the whole expanse with dizzying speed, swooping soundlessly and shedding more of those beautiful silvery curves. Still others simply vanished, and the rest, tens of thousands—in long rows that stretched off into obscurity—awaited instructions, like an enormous army of blanks.

The angelin came into view and gave Jebrassy a nudge. Even through the shimmer its touch nearly iced his toes, but he came right again with a slow rotation to face the rainbow brilliance and the tongs that reached up and out, grasping flame-colored luminosities and pulling them down.

"The Keeper has delivered a breed," the angelin announced, its voice so sweet it made Jebrassy's ears hurt. And then, another message—not from the Tall One nor from the blue form, and not so much a voice as a beam of words half seen in the shimmer that protected him.

Let the primordial find a place where he can heal. We will meet when he is whole again and calmer. I would not wish to dismay him. He is, after all, the most important citizen in the Kalpa.

Jebrassy looked up at the Tall One who stood by his side.

"So be it," Ghentun said. "After five hundred thousand years, I have fulfilled my duty to the Eidolons."

CHAPTER 57

Tiadba stood on the outskirts of the training camp, along the broad, flat outer reach of the channel, lost in melancholy. She could barely make out the distant shapes of the three tablelike isles where she had spent her entire life. Blocs were stacked high on each table like jumbled cards, softened and shaded by the mist that puffed from the channel floor.

As the light over the blocs dimmed, drawing those far Tiers into sleep, she turned toward the overarched blackness beyond which lay— so they had been told—the outer works of the Kalpa and the reality generators that protected them from the Chaos. Her body felt like a coiled whip about to be snapped. She was ready. Time was flowing too quickly—not quickly enough.

They were being trained. The march was on . . .

Just when she thought she might be able to go on without Jebrassy, might be able to stop obsessing over the paths they would never follow together . . . she remembered the last sight of her young breed male, dangling from the grip of the brown warden, and grief flooded back.

There had been an awful noise, breath-snatching flight, painted swirls of darkness—a terrifying, inchoate presence. Tiadba had withstood all of that. The wardens had dropped nine breeds in the flood channel—so she assumed. She remembered nothing of those early moments. She did remember that they had crossed a wide plain under a darker portion of the ceil, featureless but for drifts of rock-dust. The short channel trees that clumped in the old mud had soon given way to an immense flatness, vanishing into shadow on each side. They were all close to panic, terror replacing bravado even as they neared the end of this first stage of their journey and saw the huge arches that marked the outer channel bounds.

Perhaps Jebrassy had been protected and survived as well; perhaps he was lost somewhere nearby and would wander into the camp at any moment. But she wondered how she could still believe. She doubted he was still in the Tiers. Either way, he was not with her and she longed for him.

The breeds rescued from the intrusion were not entirely the mix Grayne had been planning. Denbord, Macht, Perf, and Tiadba were the only members of Grayne's group that had made it to the channel.

Nico, Shewel, and Khren had helped Tiadba and Jebrassy search for loose books in the upper Tiers—though they had found none of their own. Mash—the fourth searcher in the upper Tiers—was sucked up in the intrusion, so Pahtun said. Tiadba had liked Mash. Others in Grayne's group also vanished, and so the substitutes had become necessary—willing or no.

The two other females—Herza and Frinna—were unknown to her, kept to themselves, and said little to anyone.

Khren, the strongest, had known Jebrassy most of his life. He had trained to be a pede-runner and repairer of meadow carts—when not fighting alongside Jebrassy in the little wars.

"I'd have never joined a march, and they'd have never picked me—so it's even," Khren said in camp. "Going out there might be better than kicking pedes and mounting wheels—or it might not. They just better not get too swift with me, that's all I'm saying."

"They" were the five Tall Ones who had guided them along the channel to this camp, and in particular the trainer, an experienced-looking Mender named Pahtun. They were all learning more about Tall Ones than they had ever imagined possible. Tall Ones were divided into two types, it seemed: Shapers and Menders. Shapers were rare and never seen. All the escorts were Menders.

Esolonico—Nico for short—and Shewel were shop-breeds, loaders and stackers learning to run market stalls; common types, though Nico fancied himself an expert on hidden wisdom. Tiadba doubted Grayne would have agreed.

Denbord had been senior to her in Grayne's group, but seemed unsure about that now, since she carried the book bag, and Grayne had not sent him on his own search. He was a slender, thoughtful type, just the opposite of Jebrassy.

Their small camp had rudimentary facilities—six tents of translucent fabric open at both ends, and inside, flat sleeping pads. One remained empty—two males each filled three tents, and Tiadba had a tent to herself.

Frinna and Herza were pale, quiet types from the lower Tiers on the second isle—what Tiadba's mer and per would have called cart-glows, or worse, dims. Tiadba herself felt no discomfort at their stolid quiet, yet she was certain—again—that Grayne would never have picked them.

None of them had dreams or visitors.

A few dozen yards beyond the tents stood a large round hut, silvery and hard, in which the trainers kept the tools and armor the marchers would use on their journey. Few provisions had been made for comfort or privacy, though fresh produce was delivered daily from the meadows.

"Enjoy it while you can," Pahtun remarked. "Out there, no more eating or drinking. You certainly can't live off the land. Your armor will nourish you."

Twelve wakes and twelve sleeps passed mostly in vigorous exercise—for stamina and strength—and walking around the dust-drifted channel floor, barely better than sulking in their tents or fidgeting and scrapping.

———

Pahtun seemed older than the other four. Khren thought Tall Ones could look as old as they wished; didn't they all live forever? Nico doubted that. Since none of the breeds felt brave enough to ask, Tiadba assumed that Pahtun was the oldest because he moved with deliberation, spoke clearly, and used breed terms all could understand, as if he had dealt with their kind many times before.

Despite the late and forcible recruiting, only three voiced any inclination to leave. One came from Grayne's group: Perf, a gangling, clumsy breed in middle youth who was miserable away from his niche and let everyone know it.

During one sleep, Herza and Frinna tried to sneak off but were retrieved. They did not try again.

After that, Perf didn't even try.

CHAPTER 58

The Broken Tower

A warm shadow drifted over Jebrassy as he lay in the small room, so very like his sponsors' niche in the Tiers. He felt as if he were being weighed and measured—in ways he could not understand, but deep and fundamental.

The exam was painless but he did not like it. "What's happening?" he asked.

No answer. Instead, the measurement seemed to change focus, moving up and out, and found *him*. His thinking self.

"What are you doing?"

The warm shadow expressed satisfaction. Then a voice sounded, so pleasant and familiar he was sure he'd heard it before—but couldn't remember who it might be.

"Do you know what's happened to you?"

"I've been brought to the Broken Tower."

"Do you know why?"

"We're too stupid and weak to be told such things."

The voice became more immediate. "On the contrary, you've done well. You're probably the strongest creatures in the Kalpa. Certainly the most important, now that my work is almost done."

"You're the Librarian?"

"Part of him—a part that has managed to keep some level of sanity over this half of eternity. Do you know about Eidolons?"

"No."

"Well, no matter. The Librarian has become a Great Eidolon, which means he can no longer understand what it means to be small and insignificant. So he sets apart a few of his many selves, called 'epitomes,' and they fulfill that function. You're talking to one now."

"You're not cold, like those blue things."

"I am closer to the core of the Librarian. What you tell and show me, the Librarian knows immediately."

"I'd like to see you."

"Soon. But understand, anything you see will be an illusion, so even if you *could* see me, you wouldn't strike out, despite your clenched fists. Like hitting a shadow, it would bring you no satisfaction."

Jebrassy tried to relax his hands. "What's going to happen?"

"In time, you will be set free to perform your duty. But for now we need to understand what you have become. You ring like a bell, young breed—a bell that no one in this time has tolled. Your vibrations are important. But for the moment, only half of you is in my presence in any way I can measure. The other half has to become manifest—events have to catch up. Until then, we will get acquainted, and I will teach you some useful things."

"Where is Tiadba? Is she here, or somewhere else?"

"It interests me that you already know the answer to those questions. She is not here in the tower. She was not taken back to the Tiers. Where do you think she is?"

Jebrassy hated being played with, but he *did* know. "She's in the flood channel, with the others. The marchers. I need to go to her."

"You would do her little good. As I said, events have to catch up. You must reach your full potential, young breed—and then you will be ready to join your friends."

CHAPTER 59

The Flood Channel

Pahtun gathered the nine breeds on the channel floor, beneath the looming double arch, and stood before them, solemnly gazing at each in turn. The trainer was at least a third again as tall as Khren, their largest.

"You are chosen because your blood urges you outward," he began, his voice deep and sad. "But whatever your enthusiasm, you will need help in your travels and a tempering to your urges. You are inexperienced, no doubt brave, but for now—foolish."

Perf squirmed on the sand, as if afraid everyone would look at him.

"Out there, no warden will carry you gently home if you get hurt. Out there, more than pain—worse than death. That is what the Chaos promises. Beyond the border of the real lies the greatest challenge ever faced by human beings—and in that grouping, I include even the Great Eidolons on high, damn their arrogance."

Pahtun looked around as if this might shock them, but these breeds knew nothing of Eidolons, great or small.

He waved his long-fingered hand, and Tiadba noticed that on the tip of his sixth finger—he had six fingers and an odd thumb, mounted in the center of his palm—there was a pink flower. Patient observation, as Pahtun spoke and waved this hand some more, rewarded her with the realization that this flower was in fact a cluster of six smaller fingers—

perhaps used in delicate tasks. (Though Nico later suggested they helped the Tall Ones clean their ears.)

"No one can know what you will see and experience. While there are features that are relatively fixed and can be described, even partly explained, most of what is out there is great *change* with no *reason* or *law*. Accept it. The danger is constant. Your training will never suffice. But it will have to do, for between the will of those who will things," he pointed over his head and back a bit, high above the three isles, "and your own blood instinct, planted in you and nurtured—bravery without sense," he took a deep breath, "you *are* going. You *are* traveling. You *will* march. You have no choice. *We* have no choice."

Tiadba spoke aloud an odd word: "Amen." The others responded likewise, then looked at each other, dismayed.

"So, let me introduce you to the tools that might keep body and soul together out in the Chaos." Pahtun sounded a humming, whistling note, and they stood.

The escorts guided the breeds into the silvery dome-shed.

Glistening and strange, suits hung from the walls of the shed like the casings of farm pedes, though more colorful. Of a size and shape to fit each marcher, they were shades of orange, red, blue, green, and yellow—which seemed strange if one wished to hide from things that hunted.

"These are the best that the Shapers of the Kalpa have ever been able to manufacture. Here, the generators of the city protect us—and in the Chaos, your armor will protect you, up to a point. Within these shells, the suits sustain the laws and principles that allow life, and they carry personalities as well—as one would expect from the Shapers who made them."

"What are Shapers?" Nico asked.

"Like me, " Pahtun said, "only different. I've never seen one." He did not elaborate.

The trainer introduced the breeds to their suits and suggested they try them on. Tiadba knew immediately which was hers. She stroked its outer shell—smooth, orange, and cool. The armor vibrated beneath her fingers and made a small, accepting noise.

Grayne had told them a little about such things, but she had not mentioned that the armor clambered over one's limbs and trunk with a life of its own. The suits practically put themselves on as the breeds danced and squirmed. Herza and Frinna tried to pull free and failed. Those who finished first expressed nervous amusement at the expressions of their fellows.

The helmets fell limp over their shoulders like split hoods until, at Pahtun's command, they rose up, stiffened, and sealed airtight. Yet from within, Tiadba felt no oppressive closeness. Her breath came easily and the air seemed fresh. She felt only a slight itching at the joints, which she soon learned to ignore.

"They become a second skin," Pahtun said, "only more subtle and talented. Your armor protects you from endless misery; it is an ancient crafting still wonderful to my eyes—and yet, it has limits. It senses any slip or slide of the rules, such as they are out there. Your armor will transform or translate sensora in the Chaos, so that you may see light and shadow, color and shape. It helps you stay rooted to something like a surface, or travel over something like a landscape—reliably enough to make progress in your journey, presumably to a destination where the Chaos is held at bay.

"The Chaos is not entirely without form or character. There is a kind of weather—some places are more transformed than others, some almost untouched. While there may seem to be, for ages at a time, a thin coating of consistency in what we observe, in truth, the rules are ever-changing. Failure to learn and adapt quickly will have terrible consequences. And so, your armor will adapt and learn, and so will you."

Two of the escorts carried out a flat egg mounted on a slim black tripod—a portable reality generator, able to place a suspension around their entire group for several wakes.

"Within the Kalpa, the semblance of ancient reality is maintained by our generators. If your armor should weaken or fail, these smaller units may protect you for a time."

However, surrounded by such protection, they could not make progress toward their goal.

Next he introduced their weapons—never to be used recklessly or aggressively, which might attract unwanted attention. They consisted of curved, glowing blades called claves. The blades did not so much cut as accelerate change, Pahtun said. "Claves goad the Chaos—accelerate its own tendencies. The effects are unpredictable—what they strike may or may not disintegrate or cease to function.

"There are no other weapons—except your wits."

Flight and hiding were always better choices. And so most of their training consisted of being taught how to be elusive—without any real clues, as yet, about what they would be eluding.

"Why do we not send you with vehicles—flying machines, space-craft, transports through and over the ground?" Pahtun asked. "There's a law of size applicable to our generators—a scaling law. To protect more than a small group of breeds, our generators must become un-wieldy. And for any generator of reasonable size, an object in the Chaos may not move much faster than you can run—for that would exceed its ability to remap. As well, moving too quickly, in too great a force, at-tracts vortices of contradiction and failure that we call 'twistfolds' and 'enigmachrons.' These can be awful traps. They devour and incorporate whatever they capture, armored or not, bonding it with the Chaos. You will no doubt encounter victims of such—recent, and ancient. The vic-tims of the Typhon fade slowly. Some of the monstrosities that once were human have been studied by angelins—Chaos watchers—in the Broken Tower since before I was made.

"And they're still out there.

"Your armor is particularly vulnerable in the zone of lies, just within the border of the real. These are the middle lands, where the Defenders, the last rank of generators protecting the Kalpa, gradually ease their protection, and then give way to the Chaos. Crossing the middle lands must be done cautiously. Your armor must not become fully active— competing fields generate unpredictable results. I will accompany you into the zone to monitor your progress. I have not lost a marcher yet, not at that stage. But many other trainers have seen their marchers snatched prematurely, caught up in an intrusion or a twistfold.

"There are regions in the Chaos which seem to possess a constancy even across long ages. One of these is the Necropolis—the remains of the Kalpa's nine lost bions. The Typhon has drawn up these ruins and com-bined them with the perverted remains of other cities. Here, the Typhon presents its warning of things to come—a cruel mockery of Earth's great-est citadels, which once spanned the globe. Now, their remains, or their essences—their imagos—have been gathered and rearranged within sight of the tower. Some of these ruins still seem inhabited—if that is the word—by hopeless phantoms. Those who once lived, do not, yet persist and act, and that which never lived takes on unexpected life.

"Let me now describe areas of great danger and opportunity. One is a kind of road or highway across the Chaos, known as a 'trod.' Trods appear and disappear, forming serpentine pathways or lanes through all regions."

"What are they?" Tiadba asked.

"The trods serve as paths of conveyance. Even in the Chaos there are hierarchies of rule or misrule, power or weakness, grandeur or pity. The highest and most powerful figures or shapes—we dare not call them knowing or intelligent—use the trods to move about. Among them are the Silent Ones that have caused so much damage to our marchers, and which even in Sangmer's day were active and powerful."

"What do they look like?" Nico asked.

Pahtun shook his head. "Many shapes," he said. "Some in the tower monitor their comings and goings. Unfortunately, they tell us little down here."

———

The marchers stood beside the dome shed, grimacing and stretching and still getting used to their armor.

"The old matter that makes you and fills the bulk of the Earth was once sustained by the suspension that kept the Typhon at bay—but when that pulled tight around the Kalpa and the reality generators became necessary, we had to abandon everything outside. Primordial mass in the Chaos ages unpredictably, forming pockets of geological change and destruction, no longer limited by the simple rules of gravity, physics, nor even old space and time. The Typhon seems to relish that instability—whatever amuses the Typhon stirs the Chaos and torments old Earth."

"You keeping talking about the Typhon as if it were alive," Nico said. "Is it really someone bigger and more powerful than the Eidolons—whatever they are?"

"I am as ignorant as you," Pahtun answered after a short pause. "Some humans once regarded the unknown forces of nature as magnificent enemies or implacable gods. To me, the Typhon is not part of our nature—neither magnificent nor an enemy whom one might respect. It is a scourge and a disease. But you'll soon live it for yourselves, and whatever theory keeps you alive, that's the one you should hold and cherish."

Macht and Khren seemed intrigued, but this didn't satisfy Nico, the philosopher. Perf, Shewel, and the other females looked lost or bored. Denbord and Tiadba just listened and tried not to voice their opinions.

Seeming to sense Tiadba's quiet skepticism, Pahtun knelt beside her on the sandy floor of the channel. His head still rose over her, even as she stood tall in her armor.

"You have a question," he said.

"We're going where we have to go," Tiadba said. "But who made us that way?"

"Shapers, I suppose, following the orders of an Eidolon. I'd like to meet the old twitch someday and give him my opinion." Pahtun wriggled his fingers and then touched his nose, breed-style. "Ages ago, when I was younger, to salve my own guilt, I snubbed the laws of the City Prince and sent outposters to study the Chaos." He stopped for a moment, his face crinkling, and Tiadba thought this was the first time she had seen such an expression on a Tall One. She didn't know what it meant—sadness, wonder, loss? "They will not report back. Whoever leaves the Kalpa must never return, for reasons good enough and simple."

"But you keep sending *us* out there," Tiadba said.

"Higher minds than mine made these plans, and I suppose we're all committed, whatever the consequences. You feel your instincts, I do my duty." He stood. "If any of my outposters are still out there, and still free, they might help—they might not. You have to exercise the same caution you would with anything else in the Chaos."

Perf looked back at the Tiers, lost in mist beyond the edge of the camp. Macht put his hands together, murmuring a song of calming.

Pahtun's face smoothed and took on a distant look. "I do believe this, because I must: if any of you succeed, a greatness will be accomplished, something that may make all the long sacrifices of your kind worthwhile."

―――――

"The old pede-kicker is resting."

Khren, stocky and quiet-footed, approached Tiadba. She turned and looked him over critically. She had been feeling miserable again. Not his fault, of course, but Khren and his friends were no substitute for her warrior, foolish as he might have been at times.

"We have a moment," he said gently, aware of her mood. Macht and Perf joined him.

"Please read some more from the books," Perf said. "Teach us."

Grayne's shake cloth and the old letterbugs could not guide her now. She had to riddle the words on her own, but she had become better at that. What she read, she tried to convey and explain to the others. She was sure this was what Grayne had intended. Strange that she could no longer remember Grayne's face or the music of her gentle, insistent voice. Jebrassy she remembered clearly.

Others gathered: Denbord, Nico, and Shewel, carrying their mats. They had come to prefer sleeping in the open, under the dark arches, rather than inside the flimsy tents, which flapped in the tweenlight breezes and worried them.

Tiadba sat and opened one of the books. The breeds' favorite passages tended to be about Sangmer the Pilgrim and Ishanaxade, the Librarian's daughter, but the stories were seldom the same, a peculiarity that didn't matter much to her audience.

Of necessity, she skipped or paraphrased parts with which she had difficulty, and many of the words were still obscure, but reading them over and over again was like seeing them with more experienced eyes, and she took away more meaning each time.

Other passages, spread throughout the text like chafe-seeds in a cake, still stumped them. Some were lists of instructions, *go here and do* this, *then* that—word-maps, Tiadba called them—and sometimes she read these for their calming effect just before the Tall Ones extinguished the lamps for sleep.

This time she chose a more familiar text while the breeds curled at her feet, staring out into the shadows.

" 'The story I tell is simple,' " Tiadba began, and her eyes filled, remembering the times with Jebrassy, just a few wakes past.

Once, half an eternity ago, the glorious new sun—so-named, despite its having burned for ten trillion years—was almost surrounded by the Typhon Chaos. Five worlds remained, and on Earth, twelve cities, homes to those gathered from around the cosmos after a long and wretched decline.

Greatest and most ancient of these cities was the Kalpa, and wisest, for this city constantly made preparations against the time when the Chaos would swallow even the new sun.

Defeat was imminent, many thought.

The greatest human of the age was a Deva called Polybiblios. He had traveled to the final far end of the aging cosmos, to live and study in the glow of the sixty suns of the Shen, a great civilization about to be absorbed by the Chaos.

The City Princes of Earth promised a rich prize if someone would go to those last far places and persuade Polybiblios to return. For as absorbed as he was in his learning, and almost walled in by regions filled with traps and snares, he could not by himself make the journey back to Earth.

The first to volunteer was the young Mender called Sangmer, already renowned and beloved for his many exploits and rare courage.

Sangmer gathered a crew and revived the Earth's last great galaxy ship. With his crew—selected for strength, courage, and wit—he journeyed along the single open course to that final far corner of the universe.

In all their adventures—and many they were, strange and difficult—only ten survived, including Sangmer, to return with Polybiblios. The Chaos raged and consumed and did its deadly dazzle, and many times nearly took their vessel—for none is so persistent and perverse as the Typhon, some say, and others, none so unlikely and difficult to plan against.

Sangmer also brought to Earth Polybiblios's mysterious adopted daughter, who most agree was less human than the Shen—though her form was very pleasing.

She had taken the name Ishanaxade—born of all stories—and espoused the Deva gens of her father.

Back on Earth, they were welcomed by the City Princes and there was great rejoicing, yet funeral rites occupied many families, who mourned their lost youths.

Polybiblios began his work in the high tower over the First Bion of the Kalpa, and using his Shen knowledge, soon helped design and forge the Suspension that protected the new sun, and kept the Chaos at bay for a time.

Sangmer did not sit idly, but continued with his restless ways, making other voyages and studying, measuring, and defying the Chaos, all of which heightened his fame—though these journeys consumed many more sons and daughters of fine families.

So many youths perished that Sangmer the Pilgrim also became known as Killer of Dreams, a title he did not bear proudly, and so, he promised to go into deep exile within the Sessiles, and not to return until he had studied Silence for an age.

Ishanaxade emerged from among the curious that lined the ribbon road to witness his penitent journey, and stood before him where he bore up under the discs of memory of his thousand lost comrades, which nearly bent him double.

None was so wonderfully fashioned as Ishanaxade, but that is not why to this day her images are forbidden or erased; none so beautiful in her father's eyes, nor in the eyes of the curious who watched her partake of Sangmer's burden, and help carry the discs to the door of the Sessiles, where Silence is peace.

Some say that it was in the Sessiles that their lines first twined and grew together. Others say their love began on the journey back from the realm of the Shen. No one objected that a Mender should take to wife Ishanaxade, for few dared displease Polybiblios, who had saved the last of humanity, and who sanctioned this union.

Upon their emerging from Silence, Polybiblios assigned them many great works to do, together and apart.

So it was, so it will be.

———

Tiadba closed the book and the young breeds curled up tighter. Somehow, the story had changed since the last time she read it—details were different, or their ears had become more sophisticated.

"It's not a happy story, is it?" Khren said.

"We're all going to die out there," Nico asserted gloomily. "I don't understand, but I still want to go. That's total frass."

Suddenly, through her exhaustion, Tiadba felt a sudden urge to speak of Jebrassy, to shout at them—that he was *not* dead, and would somehow be joining them, and that his presence would make this march different from all the others . . . But she turned her eyes to one side and fell back a little, doubting her companions would believe or take comfort.

"Let's sleep," she suggested.

The young breeds blew out their cheeks and pulled up their sleep mats under the high dark arches.

PART THREE

TERMINUS AND TYPHON

CHAPTER 60

Wallingford

At first the squat, hard-packed old man in the tweed suit refused to tell Daniel his name. He could act aloof, then turn gruffly assertive, as if he had always lived alone but was used to being in charge. His accent was difficult to place: English, like cockney, but Daniel was no expert.

Together, they had built up their courage and abandoned the house, leaving Whitlow on his chair, locked in jerky rigor—and now something like sunrise was spreading all around, a burning pewter light painted over the streets. The neighborhood to the north resembled a pasted-up collage, bands of light and shadow lying over dark, forbidding houses. The people left on the streets seemed intent on getting somewhere but were being given a very brief time to do it—and worse, they were doing it over and over. A few seemed to vaguely recognize their plight—like insects caught in congealing resin, all except Daniel and the squat brute, and how long could their freedom last?

"A Shifter who doesn't dream," the brute mused between rasping huffs. He struggled to keep up as they turned east on what had once been Forty-fifth Street, toward the freeway. The air was gritty. "I'd never have found you. Mr. Whitlow was primed, however. Even without the dreams, he could sense your stone. That was his specialty. Ironic he couldn't find shelter—when *she* abandoned us." The brute seemed pleased with himself. "Me, alone," he wheezed. "Riding the last threads. Pulling them down and sweeping along. And you, of course."

"Terminus," Daniel said.

The brute nodded—understood this word well enough. "Mr. Whitlow called it that," he said. "Never knew what it meant. Where the railway stops? End of the line? Don't know now. But whatever, I don't like it. It's sticky. It catches."

Daniel wrapped his fingers around the two boxes in his pocket and blessed the little freedom the stones gave him—them. The brute was also contributing, Daniel could not say how. Both seemed aware that without the benefit of the other's presence, they would be as frustrated—as obviously doomed as the mired, wild-eyed figures they passed on the sidewalks and in the streets.

"Who's the Chalk Princess?"

"The highest of high, in my line of work. But truthfully—don't know. Never met her. Dangerous, you know."

"The Moth?"

"Ah, the Moth—so he *was* here. So many tiny thrones for the Queen's servants. *Nunc dimittis,* I say. I doubt he would have killed you, such a curiosity. He probably wanted to rip you about, like a sheepdog."

Daniel grunted and turned his head forward. He didn't like looking back—the street behind was not the street they had just traveled. Time, he supposed, was bunching up like an accordion smashed into a wall.

They came upon a rise overlooking where the freeway had once been. Now there was just a long muddy ditch flanked on both sides by empty houses. In this part of the neighborhood, the bunched accordion had brought along material things—houses and funny old cars. But nothing living.

"No more people," the brute observed.

"What's that mean?"

"You tell me, young master."

The freeway was obviously not available—and that meant they would have to take surface streets, such as they were. It would be a long, difficult walk. They looked into a car but machinery was hopeless. It all seemed made of fused cinders.

"What are you, my sidekick?" Daniel shot over his shoulder, flippancy hiding real fear. "My butler?"

"Your *guide*, young master—taking you back to where I've been already. It's south of here—a green warehouse. I walked around the building, knew *they* were inside, yet had nothing to offer and could not hope to enter. After the storm, after the wreck—after the Queen fumbled like a frightened lover and dropped our prey, I knew I wouldn't be allowed inside, however desperate my situation. They'll welcome you, however. It's where you belong—not that you're grateful." The brute's thick fingers clenched. "It's getting worse. I don't mind saying—"

Daniel held up his hand and looked out across a long dark ditch at where the University of Washington had once been; and still was, after a fashion, its shrunken structures black and shiny, like anthracite. Only a few buildings seemed relatively unaffected.

The brute went on. "Libraries," he muttered. "Queen can't touch them—not yet. But the books are scrambling. Soon they'll be wiped clean. No protection after *that*."

The nearest houses were taking on a dull glimmer of translucence, as if carved from sand-blasted crystal. Others had been cut in half, showing jumbled interiors—but no occupants.

Daniel said, "I think we're passing out of the zone where people can even exist."

"I doubt I understand any of that, Professor."

Just hearing each other's voices had suddenly become an odd comfort.

"What can I offer, what do I *do* for us, you ask?" the brute said. "I'm a Chancer. There are Shifters such as yourself, with their stones and all, and Chancers. Chancers have a muse—Tyche. A modest sort of muse, but she's ours. Right now I'm dragging every bit of good fortune I can into our immediate vicinity. Bit of a knee-wobbler, actually." He grinned like a hoary old chimp. "Even with your stone, if you get too far ahead of me, I guarantee nothing. We need each other, Professor."

Daniel started moving south—if there were any points left on a compass now. "I'm not a professor," he said.

"You were—once," the squat man said. "Part of my work was being a detective."

"What'll I call you, then—Pinkerton?"

The brute chuckled. "Max will do, while we work out whether I want to stick here with you or just chuck it." He laughed at this unaccustomed freedom.

Daniel pointed southwest, into the muddle where the black sky lay heavy over land and city. "Do you see what I see, over there?" The greasy darkness was less intense, and if he focused, he could make out an actinic paleness, less than half the width of his thumb.

"I was there earlier," the brute said. "That same blue glamour is how I found you."

"What causes it?"

"The stones, I'd say. The warehouse has two of them, inside."

"Who's there?"

"Some women. Two Shifters. And a collector of sorts, though no longer a servant of our Livid Mistress. They are getting along better than us, certainly better than the other poor souls out here. *Still* . . . I wouldn't dare approach them—not without you."

"Why not?"

"I collected one of them—reeled him in like a trout, fair sport and square. Not welcome. Oh, Mr. Whitlow was *your* man—I feel no guilt about you," Max said. "But the game doesn't matter. We're abandoned." He puffed his cheeks in amazement. "Didn't think I'd ever escape. Thought that at the end of my service, the Queen'd just flick me off like cigar ash, right into the gutter." He drew his face into a bereaved scowl. "More lives in my bindle than I imagined. *Still* . . . Over there—the warehouse—last chance. They *could* be *your* friends, if you introduce yourself proper. They might even accept me in the bargain."

"What'll you do if we get there?"

"Make myself useful. As always."

"You'll tell them about me?"

"Oh, they *need* you, Professor. Sum-runners attract. Tough to keep them apart when their time is come—that's what Mr. Whitlow used to say. Don't walk so! Have pity on an old man."

Daniel slowed. The pace was more than exhausting. He could feel something leak away when he pushed too hard—opportunity, fate, perhaps his proximity to Max's hard-gathered luck. It seemed possible they *did* need each other. Of course, it was also possible that Max was making him think that.

"Such a sad town," Max observed. "Never thought I'd see such a thing. All trapped, doomed, ropes growing shorter!" He clucked his tongue, face flushed, short scraggly hair on end in the dryness, like an ugly Christmas gnome jolly with cold-blooded humor. Then, "Can we get there from here? Such a distance, bad air, hard to—" He fell back in a fit of coughing.

Cold sweat on his brow, Daniel looked along the direction where the freeway had once been. They could not just walk south—things were even more jumbled that way, like blocks of ice backed up in a freezing river. "This way," he said.

They headed west, retracing their steps.

The pewter glow came and disappeared again.

What was left of their part of the big world—their small portion of space and time—was rapidly shaking itself to pieces.

<hr>

They came to a large, long bridge, still intact but wavering and ghostly in the gloom. They started to cross. Daniel looked over the side. Below, water had turned to rippling mist, gray-green and ominous.

"This isn't the one with the troll underneath, is it?" Max asked.

"It is," Daniel said. "The Fremont Troll. Made of concrete."

"Don't be too sure," Max warned. "I hate trolls. Always have."

CHAPTER 61

I am informed, our two rivals have lately made an offer to enter into the lists with united forces, and challenge us to a comparison of books, both as to weight and number ... Where can they find scales of capacity enough for the first; or an arithmetician of capacity enough for the second?

—Jonathan Swift, *Tale of a Tub*

"What are these things, really?" Miriam asked. Her hand hovered over the two gray boxes on the table. "Everything seems to point to them, everyone seems to want them, but I have no idea what they are or what they do."

"It is not so much what they do as what they *will* do, given the opportunity," Bidewell said. "Possibly the best story is how they come down to us, yet even with that, there is no simple explanation."

"Of course not," Agazutta said.

Bidewell uncorked the second bottle of wine from Miriam's handbag. He did seem to enjoy wine. He poured the ladies glasses, but Jack and Ginny demurred. Jack had never liked alcohol.

Bidewell lifted a toast and the ladies did the same. "To survival, against all odds."

"To survival," Jack murmured, and raised his empty hand.

"We'd appreciate some certainty, Conan," Miriam said.

Bidewell spun his glass, eyes on the swirling red liquid. For a moment Ginny's vision seemed to blur—she saw the glass and the red wine as a swoosh.

"Every little thing makes its trace," Bidewell said. "That much is intuitive. We can visualize everything leaving a trail. Sometimes we call them world-lines. But world-lines flow into other world-lines, and some join to create an observer line, or fate. The fate of an observer spins together many lines that might otherwise never touch, and that creates difficulties—entanglements.

"More perplexing, not all world-lines or even fates link back to the beginning. For creation does not always begin at the beginning. Creation is—or was—ongoing, and new things appear all the time, some of them implying long, ornate histories. These new creations and their histories need to be reconciled with what has come before. And so it is that Mnemosyne becomes necessary. As soon as she came to be—a most remarkable event, but perhaps only an afterthought, who can say?—she began her work. She found lost lines, entangled contradictions, and began reweaving them—reconciling them back to the beginning. She swept up and cataloged and put things back on the shelf, so to speak, a monumental task which she no doubt has yet to finish, poor thing.

"The creation of new things always implies the destruction of the old. Not all things that are created remain in creation. Some are erased. And so, I believe that Mnemosyne must be supplemented by another, sister force, let us call her Kali, though I've never met her, thank goodness. Kali disposes of things that have been left loose or cut away, and which Mnemosyne cannot reconcile—objects, people, fates."

"My head spins just thinking about it," Miriam said.

"Is Kali white as chalk?" Ginny asked abruptly. Jack looked at her.

"Kali is often depicted as a shriveled old woman, her skin the color of plagues and death—black," Bidewell said, watching the pair closely.

"But in this role, she might be pale, white as chalk. After all, she removes excess detail and color. She *bleaches*."

"I don't believe a word of it," Farrah said.

Bidewell found this amusing. "I wish I had that luxury. But long ago I discovered I had a knack—I could slip free, for a while, of all the backward-sliding fates and world-lines that were being reconciled. I could see with a peculiar clarity things that no longer were. When I was young, I learned to watch for the signs—learned to watch doomed people, places, and things as they faded, about to become inconsequential—and yet remember them in detail. I have sharp eyes and an ironclad memory."

"Mind filled with useless junk," Agazutta murmured, but her eyes were languid. She was enjoying the frisson of so many strange possibilities.

"At first, in my youth, I was confrontational. I tried to trace lost and fading things back to the moment when they began to be erased—or forward, to the moment of their creation. An impossible task, I discovered—though I came dangerously close once or twice.

"Soon, I realized that the last remnants of things lost might be found in records—in the Earth, in geological layers, for example, but also in lost animals, stray children—and scrolls. Books. Texts of all sorts.

"Mnemosyne values texts above all things, and saves their editing and reconciliation for the last, perhaps to be savored. And so—I began to find the books she or her dark sister had missed."

CHAPTER 62

Daniel had to rest. The walk through murk and confusion left him with no energy, no sense of purpose or progress, and no clear view of where they might be in the city's jumbled geography. He had the horrible feeling they were retracing steps they had already taken.

He paused before a half-wrecked and leaning house, then pushed through a splintered gate to sit on a stone garden bench, in a place that could no longer properly be called a garden. The plants had become sad, brown-edged things, but before dying, the last flowers had run riot, growing into cancerous clumps of wilted blossoms.

Daniel's body was filled with a dull fire, which he could only guess might be chemistry struggling against shifts in physical constants. Soon enough he would simply cease to be—as a living human being, at any rate. He could almost see himself clumping and growing out of any sensible pattern, multiplying beyond any possibility of life, like the flowers . . .

They crumbled into powder in his hand.

He had lost track of the faraway glow. Pewter brightness returned, replacing the bleak umber darkness. Jagged upheavals carved serrated shapes against the southern grayness—not mountains. He did not know what they might be.

But worse than all that—

He felt a chill and looked up. Max seemed to squeeze into his vicinity, more sound and shadow than material being. He, too, looked up—at a certain cool sensation on their skulls and the backs of their necks.

The gnomish man's thin voice pushed through the freezing air. "Something's eating the moon."

Whatever had smeared out the pallid stars and rucked up the voids between had left the moon untouched. Now, the high ivory crescent was turning bloody red, like a half plug stamped in heaven's flesh. And rising in the east—or rather, blooming and bloating, since there was no apparent motion in that direction—a ring of fire arced almost from one quarter to the other.

Within the ring swam a diseased, turbid blackness.

Daniel's eyes stung as if brushed with nettles.

The bloody moon shivered, then streamed across the sky like molten, fire-lit silver. It spread and merged with the arc of lurid, pulsing flame, until nothing of it remained.

"Everywhere we look, the Gape swallows the world." Max dropped next to Daniel on the stone bench, tried to swallow, and choked out, "We're in *her* land! God help us!"

The garden grew colder as the arc of flame and its dark heart expanded. "I've been here before," Daniel said. "I jumped right out of my skin to get away."

Max spat and wiped his mouth.

Daniel felt in his pocket for the boxes. "We can beat it. Work harder!" He stood, grabbed Max's arm, and hoisted him to his feet. The air had cleared. In the deepening shade, tinted but unrelieved by the arc of fire, and squeezed up adjacent to the massive mounds of the two stadiums—steel and concrete walls, roofs, and arches shriveling like the leaves in the garden—Daniel again saw the bluish glow, faint as a firefly across a desert. He pointed. Max lifted his chin in acknowledgment and wiped his face again with a black-smeared kerchief.

They stumbled on.

CHAPTER 63

In the warmth from the iron stove, Farrah and Ellen had begun to nod off, listening to Bidewell's steady, droning voice. Miriam and Agazutta remained alert, as did Jack and Ginny.

"I collected books that reflected Mnemosyne's unfinished labor—mostly forgotten volumes, texts long unread, hidden away in libraries and often enough in old bookstores. When a book is read by many, those copies must be reconciled first. There are few surprises in best-sellers! I presume that if I had become a fossil hunter, or a geologist, I might have found similar curiosities. But I have always been a man of books."

"Why are observers special?" Ginny asked, diverting his slow, steady river of information back to what interested her most.

"A simple world-line—say, an atom zipping and vibrating through the vacuum of space—needs accounting for only when it encounters something else. Observers have eyes, ears, noses—fingers! Our senses gather and bind far world-lines in a most convoluted and inconvenient way. And of course we talk and tell stories and write books, conveying knowledge over great distances. We inherit some of our fates from our parents in a rather Mendelian fashion—but fates have less to do with our genes and more with where we will go, what we will see, hear, read, and learn. Always, words and texts confound the issue. Texts are special—any texts, any language, in fact, language itself."

"I can understand that," Jack said. "When I feel into the future—I only know about things I'm going to experience. Then I try to shift away from the slipstream of negative emotions. I don't actually know what other people are doing or going to do. Only how I'll feel, and a little of what I'll see. As if the emotions my future selves will experience are washing back along the world-lines."

Bidewell smiled his agreement.

Ginny was concerned with more immediate problems. "How can

history just come floating by?" she asked. "Wouldn't the pieces be too big? How can they slide around each other? If they're all strung out like beads . . . I just can't see it."

"Excellent questions. A cleavage can occur along and across fates that have reached a blunt or frayed end, sometimes uniting fragments across great times and distances, a 'sliding around,' as you phrase it. These rearrangements may be linked by the cords or strings on which your particular beads progress."

"So everything piles up like a logjam."

"It seems so. We have been protected by the texts—to a degree. But mostly we are sheltered by your sum-runners, kept in a kind of bubble, at least until the rest of the broken world dissolves away. Then, we may see horrors and wonders on an awful scale." Bidewell hunched his shoulders. "All beyond my capacity to comprehend. I am humbled."

"For once," Agazutta said drowsily.

Bidewell poured himself another glass of wine. "It is the second sister who has gone quite mad. The bleacher, the eraser. Cut loose from all future moorings . . . coerced or co-opted, enlisted in the hunt for all who bear these marvelous stones. We can hardly recognize her now, and she was grim enough before—but she always served, and now, she works that all will serve *her*.

"Your sum-runners have protected you against erasure—but they don't protect everyone. They do not protect all whom you know and love. I will hazard a guess that the two of you are orphans—and that neither of you has ever been able to find records of your birth, or of your mother and father, whom you remember so clearly.

"That is what the sum-runners do—you become difficult to trace, but in turn you are given the talent of fate-shifting. Finally, you dream—you reach out and connect with others who have been chosen, presumably far away—at the end of time, as we have heard. This much I've puzzled out, but of course many mysteries remain."

He looked down into his glass, almost empty.

Ginny sat in stunned silence, trying to remember her mother, her father. Her lip trembled at the thought that she was their last record. Everything else—gone.

"The second sister—" Bidewell resumed.

Across the warehouse space, a shrill buzzer sounded. They all looked up. Bidewell's teeth clacked—a tight, hard clack—and vessels strained at his temple. Jack stared. This was the first time he had ever seen the old man frightened.

The dozing women opened their eyes.

No one in the room moved.

"The last people on Earth sat alone in a room," Miriam said dryly. "There was a knock on the door."

CHAPTER 64

"Do not allow the ladies to see that we are nervous," Bidewell cautioned Jack as they threaded the aisles between the high stacks of boxes. "This does not come as a complete surprise. After all, we have only two sum-runners—and three is the minimum, I believe."

Jack followed him through the outer door and onto the ramp. Except for Ellen's Toyota, the parking lot stood empty. Beyond the fence stretched a flocking of coal-dust shades, fragments, and vapors, spreading like paint on wet paper toward what had once been the city of Seattle.

All Jack could see clearly was a single sooty finger reaching through the fence to push the buzzer's button.

Bidewell walked down the ramp. As he reached the gate, two shadows condensed from the mottled grayness. He stopped, hands folded, elbows out—reluctant to say or do anything. Jack descended to stand beside the old man. Both looked silently through the wire.

A dirty white face—a man's face, older than Jack but not by more than a decade—came forward in the murk, eyes first, then nose, cheeks, lips: soft, regular features hardened by fear and exhaustion—eyes sharp and quick.

"I see one," Bidewell said. "Who's the other? Come forward, both of you."

A broad, shorter silhouette emerged and stood beside the first: an older man, heavy and strong, his gray tweed suit filthy. Jack snarled and drew back. He could almost smell the reek of desperate birds and frightened children.

Bidewell squinted and said, "Mr. Glaucous? That is *you*, isn't it?"

"Let us in," the stocky one grunted. "For old times' sake, mercy on us both, we need warmth and rest. Is it Bidewell, sir? Conan Arthur

Bidewell, formerly of Manchester and Leeds, Paris and Trieste? For the sake of decency, of all the sorrow we've seen, let us in. We've just crossed hell, and I bring a man of value—along with news, discouraging news, it may be said, but news nonetheless!"

The younger man's lips twitched. He looked up and around, as if measuring the wire fence, the wall, the warehouse itself. His eyes bore into Jack's. "I'm Daniel," he said. "You have time here, real time, like a bubble . . . we could see it glowing from miles away. Tcherenkov radiation, maybe."

"Are you friends, or partners?" Bidewell asked, making no move to open the gate.

"Of convenience, perhaps neither," Glaucous said. "Please, Bidewell. It hurts to breathe. We've seen fates and places crammed like mince in a pie, worse at every turn. This is no longer your town, no longer our Earth, I fear."

Daniel removed a gray box from his jacket pocket. He puzzled open the lid and showed Jack and Bidewell the dull wolf's-eye gleam within. Bidewell's Adam's apple bobbed. "Jack, go up the ramp, reach inside the door—to the right—and push the button that opens the gate." His voice was brittle. "I fear our third has arrived."

"May I come in as well?" Glaucous asked, retrieving with an effort his street urchin's simper. "I am of service. I have brought what you need."

"Perhaps," Bidewell said. "How much longer we can extend hospitality . . . not to be known."

"Same old Bidewell!" Glaucous enthused, and clapped his hands. "We are grateful, sir. Many tales, a sharing of jinks and capers over all the sad, lost centuries! Jolly times, such as they must be."

"You know him?" Jack asked Bidewell, angry and suspicious.

"I do," Bidewell said. He gathered up what spit he could and expelled it in a thin stream.

Glaucous's eyes sunk inward like a shark's. His lips pressed together and his cheeks grew red beneath the grit. "Sir," he murmured.

"Open the gate," Bidewell ordered. "We have no choice. The stones have gathered, bringing whom they will."

FOURTEEN ZEROS

CHAPTER 65

The Broken Tower

The warm darkness around Jebrassy cleared in one direction, revealing a bright pathway edged in green. Down this walked a white figure—one of the Librarian's many epitomes, faceless but no longer frightening. The epitome waited patiently as Jebrassy dressed, then spoke in that familiar, elusive voice—the voice you've known forever yet can't quite remember.

"We are going to the top," the epitome said. "You are recovered and almost ready."

"Has she left?" Jebrassy asked, dressing more quickly. "Has the march begun?"

The epitome gestured for Jebrassy to follow, and guided him back through places both dark and empty, bright and filled—all attended by many more white figures.

Jebrassy had difficulty comprehending the architecture of the tower. When he looked up, he saw a roof of sorts, but he could make the roof seem to rise higher, or lower, depending on how closely he walked the edge of the path and how he moved his eyes. Were those supporting arches high above, or free-floating shapes of no apparent use—perhaps decorations?

Or was he experiencing a different kind of dream?

The epitome preceded him for what felt like several thousand yards—a welcome hike after his fitful, fact-filled slumber.

They approached a curved wall, high and lined with tall windows—much like the wall near which he had first met the angelin. Now the epitome assumed a face—the face Jebrassy from now on would identify as the Librarian, however incomplete that equation might be. The Librarian seemed to exist all around—spread everywhere throughout the tower, distributed among all the white figures, directing the angelins and probably others he had yet to meet. Were the white figures like remote arms and legs—and the angelins more like servants? So much yet to learn, and frustration that he was *still* incapable of even asking the right questions.

The Librarian spoke, using the same voice as before, but rooted—somehow more real and immediate. "You've been patient, a quality I admire."

"Easy enough. I sleep most of the time."

"You have recovered admirably," the Librarian said. "So much to heal. I once did myself an enormous injury, then slept, just to give myself the time to work out a problem never before solved."

"What problem was that?" Jebrassy asked, sure the answer would make no sense.

"How the universe will die, and what opportunities that death will present. I did not live in the Kalpa at the time, but far across the universe, where I was learning from other masters, not human but natural enough, though doomed . . . They refused transport back to the Earth. The Chaos ate them. And that's why we're here, young breed. Come closer and take a look at what lies outside our poor city."

Jebrassy drew himself up. All he had seen of the Chaos so far was the strange gray beam that flashed through the high windows.

She might be out there already . . .

They stood beside each other, much of a height, just able to peer over the lower frame of the window.

"It's frightening, but it won't harm you—not here," the Librarian said. "It's changed over the last few wakes—more fundamental change than any of us have witnessed since it surrounded the Kalpa."

There was a horizon of sorts—like the far line of the channel beyond the Tiers. But where the ceil would have faded off into shadow, something else rose up—a *sky*. The sky made no sense—a tight-scrunched bundle of fabric, its wrinkles burning with a dim, purple fire, dwindling here and there but starting up elsewhere like dying embers.

"It doesn't like being looked at," Jebrassy said.

"A fundamental truth. The Chaos is not fond of observers."

Below the horizon and the wrinkled, burning sky, if he focused hard enough, Jebrassy could make out jumbles of shapes, what might have been faraway, broken buildings, old cities, or perhaps just piles of stone and rubble. He had no scale for comparison—how big, how high, how many were these things, spread out so strangely? How far to the line between "sky" and "ground"? His eyes couldn't seem to focus—details presented themselves then flashed away, elusive as motes of dust.

The Librarian held his shoulder. "This is what your female will soon be seeing."

"Then she hasn't left yet?"

"And you will join her. But first we must learn whether we have solved a great problem. Against this problem, I am, and always have been, as humble and troubled as one of your beasts of burden down in the basement Tiers."

Jebrassy said, "You don't know how stupid pedes can be."

The Librarian touched his finger to his nose. "In my world, I can be *just* that stupid. Look. Ask. I will try to describe and explain."

"How big is it, out there?"

"In the Chaos, distance is difficult to measure or judge. That has been the chief obstacle to your pilgrims—how to get from where they think they are to where they think they want to be."

"It looks confused," Jebrassy said. "It isn't finished—feels incomplete. Doesn't want to be seen undressed."

"A fair assessment. Though we should not ascribe our own motives to the Typhon. They are not the same—if the Typhon can even be said to have motive. In the simplest terms—applicable to our experience within the Kalpa—we are looking out over a thousand miles, horizon to horizon. Down there—look toward the closer regions just below—you can see a narrow gray circle, stretching out to a broader black border. You might be able to make out a kind of maze, and a low wall."

Jebrassy followed the Librarian's pointing finger and saw a gray curve surrounded by what might have been a black smudge of wall, two hand-spans out from the great rounded, shiny shapes immediately below—the word came to him, *bions*.

The tower rose from the middle bion, which looked damaged. The other two bions appeared to be in even worse condition.

"I've seen this before," he murmured. "My visitor told me." His face wrinkled in frustration, but the Librarian seemed to understand.

"Go on."

Jebrassy tried to finish his thought. "There's a shifting place . . . I think it's called the zone of lies."

"Very dangerous," the Librarian said. "Many breeds have had their journeys ended there before fairly begun. I believe the Menders have improved your education and training since those times."

"You're talking about our *lives*," Jebrassy said.

"No need to get testy. Tell me you aren't already attracted to what you see."

"I am!" Jebrassy shouted, and tried to turn away, but couldn't. He was fascinated. He *yearned*, said almost in a whimper, "I always have been."

"I have my inclinations, and you have yours. Right now we're working together—but when you go out there, to join your mate, as you have dreamed, you will carry to her information no one else possesses. Information that might help you both survive, and succeed. And if you do not succeed, then my half an eternity of labor will pass away, without conclusion—without product—a failure.

"All that I am, then, rests on your small shoulders, young breed. The Typhon is absorbing the old universe, from beginning to end. Our time and history are being broken up, dissolved—look out the window. The Chaos is just beyond the border of the real, waiting."

Jebrassy forced himself to look over the curved, darkened, jumbled landscape. Outside the zone of lies, great high shapes stood up against the Chaos, difficult to make out, as if surrounded by fog. *Defenders*.

"Only three threads connect us to the broken past that will soon be upon us—your female, who will soon travel into the Chaos; you, and one other, a driven being, forced to abandon all principle, who cares little for any sort of existence—but who must *return*."

Jebrassy frowned, trying to retrieve an elusive memory of hatred and pity.

The epitome tapped the crystal window with a white finger. "The lives of you and your dream-partners are strung like beads on the cosmos's remaining threads—heading for a collision. If all goes well, that collision will happen in Nataraja. That is where you will go—where all marchers have tried to go. There is no other destination.

"You must succeed where Sangmer failed."

Jebrassy thought of the books and stories that Grayne had guided them to. "You're the one who put the shelves in the Tiers—aren't you?" he asked.

"One of me," the epitome said. "Not very long ago."

"How long?" Jebrassy asked, defiant.

"What if I said a hundred million wakes—could you count them, remember them all, even begin to understand how long that is?"

Jebrassy tried to stare a challenge. Finally, he glanced aside. "No," he said.

"We are adapted to our time as well as our space. Even this epitome can hardly conceive of a hundred million wakes without external assistance, so don't be embarrassed. And it was longer ago than that."

CHAPTER 66

The Border of the Real

She was always going to do this.

She would always be doing this.

Tiadba had wanted to join a march long before she met Jebrassy; long before Grayne had instructed her to recruit the young breed warrior, long before she fell in love. And long before she lost her warrior.

And here she was, wearing a suit of supple orange armor, feeling no fear, only that ache of grief and loneliness that would never go away— and the realization that this was what she had been made to do.

To leave the Tiers, the city itself, and cross over the border of the real, beyond the reach of the Kalpa's great generators . . .

To cross the Chaos and see what lay on the other side.

Pahtun took Tiadba and Khren aside and told them they were group leaders. "I'll go as far as I can with you. But I will not go beyond the zone of lies. I must return. Our final battle is upon us."

Tiadba looked to Khren and saw that he was intent on the trainer's words. No sign remained of Jebrassy's buffoonish young friend. He, too, was always going to do this. She wondered: Had all breeds been made this way?

Assisted by the four escorts, the marchers prepared to roll out the small wheeled cart that carried their claves and two portable generators.

Pahtun got to his feet and repeated what he had said earlier, so often it was almost soothing in its familiarity. "The beacon from the Kalpa is perpetual. From its pulse you will always know where lies the city. There are moments when the Witness seems to interfere with the beacon—perhaps deliberately—but you will regain the signal if you persist. All your suits possess the means. There can be no communication sent *to* the city, ever—you must not alert the Chaos to your presence. There are vigilants, of all sizes and strengths, always changing but constant in their watchfulness. The Chaos is hungry."

Khren stood beside Tiadba and glanced at her through his golden-colored face pane.

"And now—the time has come to tell you your destination," Pahtun said. "It is the destination of all pilgrims since the time of Sangmer—the only other point on Earth where sense may still rule and where there may be help for the Kalpa. It is the rebel city called Nataraja. There, if all goes well, you will connect with whomever remains free of Typhonian rule. You will work with them and tell what you know, and follow their instructions. Believe me, young breeds, if I could go with you, I would."

Tiadba brushed the leg pouch that contained her bag of books.

Pahtun seemed nervous, even guilty. He was repeating his instructions. "No one knows what awaits you. Your armor has reactive protection—it can learn faster than you, and will do all in its power to adapt and to protect you against the Typhon's perversions. Your face panes will convert whatever passes for radiation into photons you can see, and that will do you no harm. Sometimes they may fail to find anything they know how to convert—and so you will see darkness or approximations based on recent events. The closer you are as a team, the more your suits can communicate and coordinate. It is unwise to straggle or scatter too far—but distance out there is difficult to judge, even with the best equipment.

"Temptations may exist. The vigilants will try to get you to switch off your generators and strip away your armor. Should you find their temptation irresistible, you will no longer be a breed, but become part of the Typhon's misrule—an atrocity like those exhibited across so much of the Chaos. And some who have failed—even the greatest, the bravest—are used by the Typhon against the Kalpa."

Pahtun struggled for words. "It is possible that the Defenders will fail, and you will lose the beacon's guidance. The last option then is destruction. The armor will bestow this mercy."

Tiadba's suit no longer itched or chafed. She could not feel her skin—the furry bits that had bunched here and there and itched seemed to have been soothed. No doubt the armor was taking charge of all her sensations—perhaps she would soon become just a suit and not a living creature.

What would Grayne think, seeing them now? How could they have been better prepared, better educated?

"We need to get moving," Pahtun said, one hand touching his shoulder. The four escorts straightened and held out their staffs. "We have a brief opening, and we must pass through the gate before it closes."

They began.

The halves of the marchers' helmets swung from their neck-pieces with the rhythm of their steps. Their boots made soft, flat clicks. Together, they sounded like farm pedes crawling over dry, hard dirt.

They walked for long miles beneath the huge central arch, one side illuminated by the wakelight of the far ceil, the other . . . not. The quality of sound changed in a way difficult to describe. Tiadba had spent her entire life in the Tiers listening to the hive-hum of voice and echo, all her fellow breeds speaking, moving, *thinking*. That now fell off into stony quiet and a new quality replaced it: destitute hollowness, bereft, lonely yet somehow proud—and more ancient than any of them could conceive.

The Tiers had always stood apart within the Kalpa, lower than any other level, yet special, *different*. How many marchers had performed this journey already, as scared as they were, as lonely and far from all they had ever known?

"It's quiet," Khren said.

Miles to go—hundreds, thousands. Who could know?

We're leaving the Tiers behind forever.

We're crossing into the Chaos.

———

Whether their eyes adjusted to the gloom or the air here was clearer, Tiadba could not say—but suddenly she could make out square, regular shapes lined up on each side of the arch—taller than the tallest of the blocs of Tiers.

"What are those?" she asked, keeping her voice soft. Out here she felt it might be even more important to show respect.

"The inner rank of reality generators," Pahtun said. "They become active if the outer ranks fail."

The floor was uneven, broken by periodic ripples as if it had buckled under awesome pressure. Here and there, scars and parallel scuffs marred the otherwise smooth surface. Perhaps intrusions had slipped through this way, touched down . . . and burned.

Ahead, Tiadba could just make out the far edge of the vault and something else—a slowly shimmering barrier.

As minutes of walking passed into hours, the shimmer did not seem to get any closer. Still, her energy did not flag. The suit's effect was energizing, electric. Grayne's words from the early meetings returned to her.

You could walk for thousands of miles across the roughest, most forbidding terrain, yet you'll remain fit and strong. It will be the fulfillment of all you are, the adventure of a lifetime. I envy you.

After dozens of miles and hours of marching, the dark vault overhead still seemed endless. Then—a change. The shimmer appeared distinctly closer. Despite her doubts, she could not help getting excited. *The sky. Pahtun said to be ready for the sky.*

"Helmets up. Seal them tight," the second escort ordered.

Tiadba looked around, took a deep breath. The air—the last *privileged* air of the Tiers—was already bitterly cold. Frost formed on her lower lip and around her nose. Then, as one, the halves of their helmets—which until now had lain on their shoulders like empty fruit skins—rose up and sealed with a hiss that made her ears pop. Her head grew warm and her vision sharpened. The shimmer ahead acquired a life and sparkle she had not noticed before.

"Wonderful," Perf said. "My ears aren't cold."

Pahtun brought them to a halt. The escorts lined up behind them, as if to block escape.

They don't get it. Pahtun understands—these others don't, not at all!

The marchers milled restlessly. They stood on the crest of a particularly high ripple in the Kalpa's outer foundations.

Suddenly, the shimmer fell directly in front of them, then bulged inward as if to push them back. The escorts raised their staffs. Pahtun leaned forward. "Wait for it," the trainer said. "Don't walk into it. Let it find you."

Khren glanced at Tiadba through his faceplate. What she could see of his face looked calm, resigned.

"Wait for it," Pahtun cautioned again. The breeds cringed inside their armor, as if they might be snatched up and eaten.

The shimmer did not move, but suddenly it was behind them. They had passed through without taking a step, and now saw more miles of uneven ground ahead, and beyond, a wall studded with huge shapes: the Defenders.

The final, outer rank of reality generators.

Beyond those tall, blurred shapes lay the middle lands, the zone of lies. Tiadba looked straight up. They were out from under the vault. The sky loomed.

Open sky.

She captured an impression of endlessly falling curtains, restless color she could not process or accept—no color at all, actually, and probably no motion. Her eyes suddenly lost focus. The sky worked them in ways they had never had to work before.

"You don't want to see everything at once," Pahtun said, "even through the faceplates. Look down, shut your eyes if they hurt."

Her eyes *did* hurt—they wanted to tumble in their sockets and face the back of her skull—but Tiadba did not look down, did not shut them. She had waited too long for this. She rotated on the pads of her boots and looked up along the great curved exterior bulk of the first bion, then left and right, trying to take in the other two huge, dark shapes, both split and cracked—in partial ruins.

The Kalpa—what was left of it.

Something above slowly came into view, pushing up and away from behind the first bion: a curving ribbon of painful fire, red and purple at once, fencing in a black, consuming nothingness, empty of thought and life. Tiadba's mouth hung open and her breath became ragged. It was instantly and obviously wrong—so strange as to push her beyond fright.

"Is that the *sun?*" she asked.

"Depends on what you mean by sun," Pahtun said. He had fixed his gaze on the ground. "It's certainly no longer the sun *we* made."

Tiadba asked her second question—on behalf of her visitor. "*Where are the stars?*"

"Long gone," Pahtun answered.

All their lives they had been protected by the warm, limiting light of the ceil, hardly varying through its pleasant, soothing cycles of wake and sleep—but no more. What lay beyond the walls and above the city was majestic but cruel, self-involved, producing not light but something that the transparent faces of their helmets had to *translate* for any sense to come of it.

The Chaos.

"Wait for it," Pahtun warned again, studying the ground. Tiadba had no idea what they were waiting for now. How could it get any stranger, any more challenging?

Something reached down, even though they were still within the border of the real—reached down and tried to casually flick them away, like brushing letterbugs off a table. Four of the marchers screamed at once, then fell and rolled into a shallow valley between the foundation's ripples, trying to hide. Khren and Nico crumpled to their knees and clung, leaving Tiadba alone beside the trainer, the only one still looking up.

The sky—what had once been the sky—seemed to know that it was being watched. It tried to reach into her eyes, plunge through her mind, subvert everything that defined her as a breed—as an observer, a thinker, a separate being.

It refuses to be understood—it will certainly not be mastered.

Tiadba slowly lowered her gaze to the uneven, fractured ground, then blinked, of her own will. Somehow she had fought off what lay above the Kalpa, fought it to a standoff.

Pahtun looked upon this young female breed with new respect. He took some small satisfaction in their distress, and professional interest in their slow recovery.

"That's just the beginning," he said. "No way to prepare you. No way at all."

———

They neared the outer rank of generators—high, narrow monuments sliding back and forth slowly along the perimeter—pale, shining, and indistinct, like towering glass giants surrounded by fog. Shapes buried inside these obelisks moved with slow deliberation, as if tracking outside forces.

Between the generators lay a misty darkness broken by a maze of low walls, barely knee-high to a breed. Tiadba could not believe those walls would keep out anything that really wanted to get in.

Pahtun and the escorts accompanied the nine breeds over the last five miles to the inner wall. Distance still meant something here, sixty miles out from the training camp in the flood channel.

They had learned to level their gaze upon the dark gray horizon and not look up unless they had to.

"There used to be seven bions to the Kalpa, and twelve cities on the Earth," Pahtun told them, his voice clear in their helmets. He walked ahead on the hard surface, crazed with cracks and crevices, his boots raising puffs from fine dust that had somehow streamed into tiny dunes. The dust lay over the ancient foundation like fine ash—perhaps it was ash. "The reality generators worked for millions of years to protect all the bions. Then—war. The Chaos took the spoils. Now there are only three bions—and soon, perhaps just two, or one. You might find the rest of that story in your books, young breeds. How the Ashurs and Devas and Eidolons fought among themselves, and the cities were sacrificed to their godlike stupidity."

"What's a 'god'?" Khren asked. Nico, Shewel, and Denbord walked on Tiadba's left, Khren and Macht on her right. Perf, as always, straggled behind with Frinna and Herza.

Nobody answered. "Just thought a Tall One might know," Khren murmured.

Tiadba felt no hunger, no pain—hardly felt the exertion of walking for long miles over the ancient, dead surface. She was beginning to feel beyond all real pain or care, all emotions except for curiosity, which never failed her. If Jebrassy were here, she knew he would be as curious as she, and as eager to see what lay beyond the border of the real.

Their only hope for freedom, they had once believed, lay outside the Kalpa, far from the stifle of history and tradition. The books, their trainer, the sky itself, such as it was—all told a different story. They were once again being used. As they had always suspected, they were just tools, means to an end. Still, Pahtun seemed concerned for their welfare. Now that the training was almost over, his gruffness had tempered to patient instruction about last-minute details. He repeated himself often, and this irritated Tiadba, but when she looked at the other breeds, she understood the necessity. Especially for Herza and Frinna, who never asked questions. They needed the stories told over and over for a reason. How could they possibly survive in the Chaos?

"The middle lands are most difficult," Pahtun said for the hundredth time. "The zone of lies is called that for a reason—intrusions can happen at any moment. You must cross quickly. Should the Chaos launch an assault through the sector you are crossing, the battle between the Kalpa's generators and the intrusion will create intense whirlpools of fractured time and space, almost invisible and deadly. Get caught in one and you will never reach the border of the real. Your suits will not become fully active in this region. Listen to them—they will tell you when an intrusion and its effects are near, and whether your perceptions, or your decisions, are being clouded."

Their own spoken words reached each other directly, right in their ears—but the way the armor communicated was difficult to get used to. It only rarely used audible words. Much of the time they simply "knew better." Tiadba was not sure whether she resented this subtlety. It could certainly prove useful beyond the gates and the border of the real—though Pahtun and the other escorts had warned them that the suits could not know everything.

Pahtun said, "Don't underestimate your instincts—you are *observers*, made of ancient matter, and observers are primary even out in the Chaos. The Typhon is envious of your senses. This is the first principle—out there, to look, to perceive, is to be *hated*. Later, when you've acquired direct experience of the Chaos, you will learn to rely more and more on your own judgment, above all things. But at first, and certainly in the zone of lies, rely upon your suits."

"How can something inside the borders be worse than what's outside?" Nico asked.

"Not worse—just treacherous," Khren said. "Like being bitten by a tame pede. You don't expect it."

"Oh," Nico said.

"A meadow pede bit me once, when I stepped on its tail," Shewel said.

"Pedes are all tail," Perf said.

"This one was all bite. Nearly lost a toe. Still hurts when I walk a long ways." Shewel's skin shone pale behind his golden faceplate.

Pahtun slowed enough that Tiadba could catch up with him, then tuned his voice to her helmet alone. "Some marchers think they've been betrayed," he said. "They think the Kalpa sends them out into the Chaos to die, or worse—for no reason. Doesn't matter what trainers tell them. Maybe it's the books they find back in the Tiers. Bad start, that sort of thinking."

She didn't know how to respond, so she stared straight ahead.

"What's most startling to the trainers is that even when the marchers start off badly, if they make it across the zone of lies, they seem to do well—as far as they can be tracked from the Broken Tower. It's true, young breed—you were made for the Chaos."

"But none come back," she said.

"Maybe they get where they're going and it's better there—for breeds. If I could, I would join your march and go see. Do you believe me when I say that?"

He seemed to care about her answer. She did believe him, but did not want to give him the satisfaction of saying so. After all, his kind had let the cities die, let the Chaos advance, let the intrusions in—and had taken Jebrassy from her, and she could not guess why.

More miles passed, and they came to a row of square gray pillars, each about a hundred feet tall and ten feet thick. They stretched off in both directions for as far as she could see—tens of miles.

The marchers gathered around one pillar.

Pahtun patted it. "These mark the outer boundary of the old city, before the Mass Wars and the Chaos. Back then the Kalpa was huge—bigger than I can imagine. The middle lands lie two miles beyond these markers. I'll take you a few hundred yards into the zone, and then we must part company."

Pahtun stood for a moment, hand against a pillar. Then he straightened and walked on.

"He's afraid," Khren said as he drew near Tiadba.

"He can hear you," she reminded him.

"*I'm* afraid," Khren said, and tipped his finger against his helmet, as if to touch his nose. "But I'm excited, too. What does that mean?"

The others tipped their fingers to their faceplates, and Nico stretched out his arms, folding them like a warden's wings, and danced over the cracked, dusty plain. His boots—all their boots—were gray with the ashen dust.

"Maybe we're going *aaarp*," Perf said. "That would explain a lot. We're not even there and already we're broken."

Pahtun and the escorts may have been listening, but just kept walking until the low black line they had seen for some while now grew into a glossy black wall, with a narrow gap cut through, barely wide enough for one breed.

"Do all marchers pass through there?" Khren asked.

"No," Pahtun said. "This gate opened a few minutes ago. The Kalpa has chosen the safest path—for now."

"Somebody up in the tower is keeping track?" Perf asked.

Tiadba felt the sudden urge to look over her shoulder. She knew— suddenly and completely—where Jebrassy was. He was in the tower— but he wasn't watching.

No need to turn around. No need to look back at all. She was done with the city. She would never return.

But she was not done with Jebrassy, nor he with her.

He's coming. But by the time he arrives, you might not care.

"Oh, shut *up*," she said under her breath.

"Sorry," Perf said.

"Not talking to you."

Pahtun turned sideways and squeezed through the gap. Tiadba went after him. All of the others followed, their armor brushing the exposed inner surface with an eerie, slick hum. When all were through, Pahtun gathered them once again into a tight group, and they stared out at the zone of lies—gray, jagged, broken; indistinct shapes mounded low along the horizon. "You'll cross quickly. I'll go as far as I can, but then you're on your own. The next barrier is another low wall, about as high as your knee—marking the farthest reach of the Kalpa's generators. These are the border of the real. And just beyond, you'll see what looks like a great gate welcoming you, but don't go there. It's a trap—it rises wherever observers try to cross. A Typhonian welcome—if you pass through it, you're lost. It takes you straight to the Silent Ones."

Tiadba saw Khren mouth *Silent Ones,* his eyes wide.

Tiadba looked up just long enough to see a sharp gray ribbon arc overhead, and realized the Witness was still rotating its searchlight beam across the Kalpa and around the Chaos. With every sweep, the beam intersected the Broken Tower. The Witness was looking for someone—for Jebrassy—had always been searching for him. But why the Witness would care, *could* care, and why Jebrassy might be there, rather than here, her unreliable inner voice could not inform her, and so she did not know, and refused to think about it anymore.

"Now, follow! Run!" Pahtun said, and he loped off to provide an example. The four escorts stayed behind, kneeling with staffs held out in salute.

The breeds did their best to keep up, but soon the trainer was far ahead. Tiadba could barely see him, clambering over broken rubble, then standing and looking back over their heads—raising his arms. He saw something—but Tiadba knew he shouldn't just stand there.

A warning—

Something dark covered the sky, and a sound like a hideous siren issued from the bions far behind them, pitched high and then low like mournful keening and growling—a noise that raised the fur under her armor and set her teeth on edge. She ran faster and pushed up against Khren and Nico, both dashing for their lives, but not as fast as Herza and Frinna, stumbling up and over blocks of heaved stone and mounds of heaped black foundation and thick drifts of slow, sucking ash.

The darkness dropped. For an instant Tiadba wondered if the Kalpa wasn't giving them cover—blanking the awful sky, distracting whatever might want to find them and tempt them. But then she realized the darkness came from outside, not from within—rolling back toward the bions in slow, oily waves.

An intrusion. Like the one that separated us and scarred the Tiers—like the one that took Jebrassy's sponsors. We were warned!

They were within a few dozen yards of Pahtun, still standing on a high block of gray stone with his arm outstretched, frantically waving them on.

"What's wrong with him?" Khren shouted.

"Don't stop!" Tiadba yelled. "Keep running! Cross the zone!"

The city fought back. A luminosity carved the landscape in simple, ragged patterns of black and white—no grays. The darkness spasmed. They dared not look up, but Tiadba glanced sideways at the block of stone, at Pahtun—and saw him caught in a burning coil of orange and empty black. She saw his armor break apart and blow away in rippling fragments. He shook free of the last scraps, then stood naked on the rock, and she saw—for an instant, but she would never forget—the bare truth of a Tall One, too smooth, too naked, and much too vulnerable.

And then he was gone. A cloud of sparkles rose from the block and flew off.

She swallowed a moan and kept running, head down, eyes burning with shame and fear.

It seemed just a few hard, thumping steps later they came to the low wall that Pahtun had described—the outer perimeter. The border of the real. They leaped over it with hardly a thought.

Looming before them, where nothing had been before, they saw a magnificent, arching gate, covered with monumental figures, all breeds, caught up in some beautiful golden substance, smiling and waving a frozen welcome—the gate stretching up and breaking through the flow of the warring darkness and the defending waves of luminosity from the Kalpa.

All nine marchers slunk around the foot of the arch, squeezing between broken, jagged rocks—rocks everywhere, big and small—and then, exhausted, they slid into a hollow and shoved up against one another, hugging and shivering.

The siren's keen fell to a grumble, then stopped.

Silence.

Tiadba wept. Herza and Frinna muttered prayers. Shewel and the other males lay still, but their eyes shifted to the broken shadows. The hollow was cramped but seemed a fair refuge—at least, it did not open like a mouth and eat them, which she could easily imagine, given all they had been taught.

They had survived the zone of lies. Their armor was hiding them effectively enough, something that Pahtun's had failed to do. He'd been caught up in the city's defense against the intrusion, just as he warned them—or so she surmised.

He sacrificed himself. For us.

This suddenly affected her deeply. Now, if they could believe their training—she could almost hear Pahtun's sonorous voice—they must not stay where they were. Yet they could not move; paralysis gripped them as each tried to sort through what they had been taught, what their armor was saying to their bodies, conveying the depth of their peril. They couldn't hear a thing except their own breathing and then Tiadba's soft, trembling words as she encouraged them to get up, to move.

"The Tall One told us to stay low," Khren said. "Did he go back?"

"He's gone," Tiadba said. Now wasn't the time to tell them what she had seen.

"We should stay here until he comes to get us," Perf said.

"He won't come for us anymore. We're on our own."

"Where exactly are we?" Nico asked, trying to overcome sudden hiccups. He tugged against his friends' gripping hands and pushed up, trying to see out of the hollow.

"We made it," Perf said, astonished. "We're still alive."

"We can't stop," Tiadba said. "We should travel as far as we can before we rest."

A pleasant low tone, languid and musical, sounded in their ears.

Herza and Frinna touched their helmets. "The beacon," Herza said. "We're on course."

"Time to go," Frinna said, transformed, and Macht echoed her, their enthusiasm surging, paralysis broken—too quickly.

"What if something's looking for us?" Perf asked.

"Something will always be 'looking for us,'" Khren said, with a buzz of sarcasm. "Let's move, like she says. We should take a peek first, of course."

"That's what I was trying to do," Nico said.

They could all feel it. They were in the Chaos, in the wild at last, and to Tiadba, the sudden excitement and anticipation were almost as frightening as Pahtun's destruction. They were much too eager.

But they knew that whatever came next, they were where they belonged.

TEN ZEROS

The Green Warehouse

Daniel and Glaucous stood silent and watchful by the warehouse door, too tired to speak. Bidewell had brought the new visitors inside, then left them with Jack and went off, he said, to make preparations. "Things will be getting worse sooner rather than later."

Glaucous dropped to the wooden bench beside the door, face swollen with fatigue, piggish eyes bleary, paying neither of the younger men a whit of attention, as if for now they were beneath notice. Daniel lowered his head and bent over, fighting nausea.

"I don't know you," Jack said to Daniel. "I *do* know *you,*" he blurted at the squat, gnomish man. "If you try anything, I swear . . . I'll *kill* you."

Glaucous stared up at Jack. "Well spoken, young master," he said. "You should know that I killed the pair that hunted the young lady. We all have our mixes of good and bad."

"How did you get out of the van?" Jack asked. "Where's the fat woman?"

Glaucous waggled his hand, demonstrating something flying off into the air.

"I wouldn't worry about him," Daniel said, pushing up again.

"What about you?" Jack asked.

Glaucous smiled. "So very tuned, so very sharp."

Jack worked to keep his temper. "I don't know why the old man let either of you in."

"You assume Bidewell's brought you here to protect you—to keep you safe from such as me. He hasn't told you his story, I take it?" Glaucous asked.

"You shouldn't talk when he's not here."

"Ah, we are in your charge," Glaucous mused, then dropped his gaze to the floor.

"How many of us are here?" Daniel asked. "Shifters, I mean. I'm thinking three, me included."

Jack shook his head, unwilling to give up information. "Where did you get that stone?"

Daniel winced. "I don't remember. Do you?"

Jack glared.

"From your family, right?" Daniel asked. "My family's gone. Not dead—just gone, forgotten, even before this—what's happening outside."

"A bad place," Glaucous muttered. "And no escape."

"That's what happens to us," Daniel said. "We get wiped out of the histories."

Ginny had come through the aisles and stood in the shadows, watching them. "You're not in my dreams," she said to Daniel. She pointed to Glaucous. "Who's this?"

"My hunter," Jack said.

Bidewell returned with Agazutta and Miriam. The two women inspected the newcomers with expectation and dread. Ellen and Farrah joined them, and Ellen took Ginny's arm. The circle stood in silence—except for Glaucous, whose breath came in labored, grinding snores, though he was not asleep.

"We have work," Bidewell said. "For the moment, there needs to be a truce. Mr. Glaucous, are you fit?"

Glaucous pushed to his feet with a whistling sigh. He rubbed his nose vigorously. "A dray horse most of my days."

"I remember you more as a bull terrier, sent down rat holes," Bidewell said.

"Do you still offer a workman's reward for a workman's labor? I remember you were fond of drink."

Bidewell turned to see that all the ladies had gathered and arranged themselves around Ginny, who stood trembling in their midst.

Jack found it difficult to restrain himself. "Where's your fat partner?" he asked again.

Glaucous smiled obsequiously. "I will miss her."

Bidewell startled them by clapping his hands. "Enough. The outside will soon become more demanding," he said. "We have no choice but to place our strongest defenses where they will do the most good."

Glaucous tipped open a box flap and fingered the corner of a book. "I do like a good read."

Bidewell flared, "Caution, Mr. Glaucous. These are not mere children. Tease at your peril." He motioned to the stacks. "We must move boxes and crates to the outer walls."

"Your servant, sir," Glaucous said, and inclined his head.

Jack approached Bidewell as the others headed off through the stacks. Daniel tossed him an enigmatic, measuring glance. Ginny was quickly hustled away by the book club ladies and did not object; they were off to form their own work detail, Ellen explained.

"I don't like any of this," Jack said to Bidewell when they were alone.

"Have you noticed, we are not the ones making the arrangements?" Bidewell asked.

———

The cacophony outside—like boulders grinding in a giant mixer—had grown louder. Every few hours, following a sharp crackling and slam like falling masonry, deep bell tones would ring, vibrating curtains of dust from the rafters.

Bidewell walked along the aisles, through the warehouse, saw that his people were sleeping—fitfully. He listened to the low voices of Glaucous and Iremonk in the storage room where they had pitched their cots, set apart for now, and with good reason. Jack could hardly stand the sight of, either. Bidewell mostly held back his own opinions.

In truth, though, he was puzzled. There was something unusual about Glaucous, very different from his experience of other hunters and servants of the Chalk Princess.

The voices of the two refugees softened and finally stopped, and Bidewell returned to his desk and the warmth of the iron stove, wide-awake. He truly slept perhaps once a month, to avoid the wretched things that passed for dreams. For Bidewell, a man who never forgot anything, who never shed his brushed connections with all possible histories, dreams were like sick spells or fits of unproductive coughing. The past, all of his pasts, refused to be expelled.

It was apparent that none of his assembled people—his chosen family—could understand why he had allowed Glaucous into the warehouse. Daniel Patrick Iremonk was more of a conundrum, a fate-shifter, after all, with his own sum-runner; but still unlike Ginny or Jack.

Bidewell felt the presence even before he saw the man, if man he still was. The hunter appeared a few steps away, wrapped in convenient shadows. "Getting uglier," Glaucous said, his voice almost lost in a rumble that rose through the floor. "Out there, I mean. You should get out and see. Quite an experience for such as us. Consequences and conclusions."

"Make no accusations. You are barely tolerated," Bidewell said. "I was never a cager of birds."

"Yet I've completed your *set*, Conan. He might never have come here without my guidance."

"It seems you need him more than the reverse."

"No doubt. He has never been caught, never come close to being caught—and until now, never attracted the attention of her hunters. But it seems Mr. Iremonk is made all the more crucial by his exceptions."

Glaucous found a chair, sat, and somehow managed to cross his short, thick legs. He had insubstantial feet, tiny for a man of such bulk, and the shoes he wore were narrow, with pointed toes abruptly squared. The effect was bitterly comic—grossness combined with delicacy, like a Cruikshank caricature. "Wish I'd brought my tobacco. You wouldn't happen to . . . ?"

Bidewell shook his head. One didn't offer a personage such as Glaucous anything more than was necessary, and Bidewell hadn't smoked in more than four hundred years.

―――

Jack did not sleep—could not find sleep. Something inside kept trying to connect with something outside. He sat up on the edge of his cot, fists clenching the blankets, and thought of all the people stranded in Bidewell's insulated fortress—people, cats, and what else?

What was Glaucous, really, or for that matter, Daniel?

What am I?

His muscles ached from moving so many boxes. He was not used to blunt, heavy labor. He stood, brushing down the rumples in his clothes. They all slept in their clothes. Asked himself when was the last time he had dreamed or been visited. A couple of weeks.

Maybe that was done with.

He listened to Ginny's soft, steady breathing on the opposite side of the wall of books. He peered around the crates, pulled aside the ragged sheet that served as a curtain. She had wrapped herself in one of Bidewell's old brown woolen blankets—army surplus, probably. But which army, which war?

Knees curled up, back to him, her shoulders quivered. She still dreamed.

Then she became still. He stood in that makeshift entry, his expression snagging on successive thorny branches as it fell: pain, exasperation, puzzlement, before it settled into a blank stare. So many expectations, so little understanding of *now, next, never*.

Ginny opened her eyes, turned her head, and blinked. Her lips twitched. Jack backed away, bumping into a wall of boxes, before he realized she was still asleep. Quietly, with great respect, he stooped over her, brought his head closer, turned one ear. Wherever she was, whatever she was experiencing—whatever she was saying, in a language that itched at the back of his head—she was not happy. He was powerless to help, *here* or *there*.

"What's wrong?" he whispered.

Her eyes looked beyond and through him, and her brows knit in supreme effort. Speaking English seemed difficult. "Following us."

"Who?"

"Echoes. I think they're dead. Walked right through him. He's gone."

She squeezed her eyes and curled up tighter.

Jack wiped tears from his cheeks. The rumbling had intensified—outside, under, around the warehouse. After a moment, he returned to his own space and took a swig of water from the plastic bottle he kept in his backpack.

Lay down, drew up his legs.

Tried to will himself to sleep, to dream, to cross over—go to where Ginny was.

Then, before he could grab hold and control himself, he willed another, very different sort of move—a shift. The effort rebounded from something incredibly hard and knocked him half off his cot. He felt as if he'd been slugged with a hammer. His muscles spasmed and he lay back twitching and sweating.

Stupid. Everything squashed, corroded, and trimmed down to at most two or three fates, rammed up against what Bidewell called the Terminus—Jack knew that, but still, his fear and disappointment were intense.

He was trapped along with everybody else.

All the ones I've always left behind. Fear leading to jumping leading to being forgotten. How in hell can I believe I deserve any better?

He sat up on one elbow, rubbing his neck and ribs.

At the very least he had confirmed something important.

Out beyond the walls of the warehouse, in the time-shivered, ash-fall gloom, Burke had become a helpless ghost. Needles lay over the soggy floor of their apartment like a pricking lawn of steel, and through the curtainless windows, the city-etched horizon curled up like an old rug, crimped and threadbare.

There were now *two* cities at the end of time.

Seattle was the second.

<hr>

"Can't sleep?" Daniel stood in the opening to Jack's cubicle, arms folded. Jack turned and stared at the plumpish, pasty-faced man. He had a soft nose and soft green eyes. What looked out of those eyes did not match the face—a feral sharpness out of place in an habitual expression of contented curiosity. "Feeling guilty that you survived, and they didn't?"

"No," Jack said. "Not exactly."

"Glaucous is talking to Bidewell. The girl's asleep. She doesn't look happy."

"Her name is Virginia." Jack swallowed his indignation that Daniel had looked into Ginny's cubicle. "You don't dream?"

"It's just black—maybe I dream of a big, deep nothing. How about you?"

Something seemed very wrong with this man who stared out of another's eyes, but how could he know that? Jack wondered. Just because
Daniel had arrived with Glaucous, more seabirds fleeing a storm . . .

"Ginny and I dream about the same place," Jack said. "That's why
we're here."

Daniel made an agreeing noise that also indicated he didn't much
care. "We should spy on those two, listen in, I mean, then go up to the
roof and see for ourselves. I've found a ladder."

Jack considered, then pushed to his feet. "All right." He could play
along—for now.

As they walked through the labyrinth of crates toward the sliding
steel door, Minimus fell in behind. Daniel looked down. "Cats are natural Shifters," he said. "Nine lives, right? I studied them when I was a
kid. They move fast, and they don't care what they leave behind. I don't
think this one likes Glaucous."

Minimus sat. They paused to wait, but the cat blinked and slunk off
through a gap.

Daniel brushed his fingers along the boxes. "I hate being surrounded
by books. Give me one or two—not thousands."

They came to the door. Daniel applied his ear to the cold metal. Jack
did the same, though he did not like being led.

Two voices sounded faintly through the steel. The deeper voice—
Glaucous—was saying, " . . . combined, might do what two could not."

Bidewell cleared his throat. "You've done me no favor, bringing the
bad shepherd here."

Daniel curled his lip and smiled at Jack.

Glaucous: "Three rooms. Three Shifters. As described long ago, my
friend. The role I play is positive."

A noncommittal noise from Bidewell, some words below their
hearing, then Glaucous, louder, setting the hook: "I've always asked
myself, what and why, what is it that produces these children, sweeps
up memory in their wake—and why put them through such torment?
We both torment them, Conan. You promise them answers we do not
have."

"And you hook them and reel them in," Bidewell said.

"And should they escape, on the bounce, they come to you."

"And if they don't escape, you deliver them to—"

Daniel pushed back from the door with an expression of disgust. "We can't trust either of them," he whispered.

Jack held his finger to his lips, ear against the steel.

———

"Whitlow once told me about your years on the continent, long before my time," Glaucous said. "What larks, tramping after mouse-nibbled manuscripts across the Alps and around old Italy—and no doubt seeking lost children."

"Whitlow hunted, not me."

"Well, no matter. He's out there stuttering to his doom in an old shipwreck of a house, beached and hove to. Best forgotten. Still, you rubbed shoulders with famous folk. Petrarch, past his days of young love, became devoted to the sport of resurrecting classics. You and Whitlow were with him when he died, weren't you?"

"I sought not the lost genius of antiquity, but the marvels of impossibility."

Glaucous snorted two nose-blows into his kerchief. "Whitlow's stories fascinated me." He raised his hand, snot rag draped from his palm, and poked a thick finger into the air. "Boccaccio, spinner of bawdy tales, redeemed himself searching for bits of Tully. A fine pair of noses for tales lost—or perverted."

"You date yourself. Tully is now properly known as Cicero."

Glaucous grinned. "I am surprised to find you confined to this box."

Bidewell got up to tend to the stove.

"Still fond of wine," Glaucous observed. "Always have been. Mr. Whitlow—"

Bidewell clanged shut the stove's iron gate.

Glaucous thinned his lips. His hand started tapping one knee and he looked up, pinched his nose, snuffed again, glanced sideways at Bidewell. "Whitlow set his trap for Iremonk. The Moth made an appearance. I have never had such tools at my disposal. Always on the margins, forced to catch the wax dripping from all the sad dim candles of our night, forced to trim their pitiful wicks. My partner . . ." His expression faded into gloom, and to revive his spirits, he struck his knee with a fist. "Came close to the prize, I did—snagging Mr. Jack Rohmer, fine young Shifter. Painfully close. Ever and always flashers with a net."

"Was your mistress too frightened to accept your gift?"

Glaucous changed the subject. "How solid is your fortress, Conan?"

"Firm foundations, carefully laid."

"I suspect you've prepared three clean, pure spaces. So much easier to find emptiness in this wilderness than on the old continent, where the very turf is thick with bones. How long vacant?"

"One hundred years," Bidewell said.

"Is that sufficient? Mr. Whitlow once claimed—"

"Conclusions are upon us, Glaucous. Much depends on your employer. Will she gather courage and return—as a shrieking *Harpy*, do you think?"

Glaucous scowled.

"Failed you, didn't she? Eater of eaters, hunter of the hunt. We called her Whirlwind's Bride, and some named her Whore of the South Wind . . ."

Glaucous leaped up at another shuddering slap-clap from outside. The walls hummed.

Bidewell poked a chunk of firewood into the stove. "Notice a thickening of motion and thought?"

Glaucous lifted an eyebrow.

"We'll soon be caught between the adamantine walls of Alpha and Omega. It's not just Terminus your Mistress was fleeing. There's little or nothing left between us and the beginning, or the end. All of history, eaten away. Skeins pinched to threads, stripped to fibers—compressed to points. I wonder what *that* will be like." He slowly squeezed his fingers—down to nothing. "A sudden brightness, I imagine, and great heaviness, as all remaining light and gravity bounce back and forth through a compressed pellicle of time—and the noise!—*shattering,* old nemesis."

"Do you suspect, or do you *know*?" Glaucous asked.

Bidewell nodded at his books. "I've absorbed bits and pieces of past and future, sorting and combining until they make an inevitable sense."

Glaucous flexed his hands and clasped his knees, rocking. "Joints ache," he said. "Cold, even in here."

"We'd better go up while there's still something worth seeing," Daniel whispered, and walked away. This time Jack followed, his face heating.

The ladder was made of boards hammered onto the close-spaced studs on an outer wall. Jack looked up into the darkness and made out the outline of a hatch below the roof. Daniel was already halfway up. The hatch was not locked. He shoved it open and clambered into a sloped shelter. A warped wooden door opened stiffly to an expanse of tar paper, sealed and repaired by stripes of uneven asphalt, and crisscrossed by walkways of weathered shipping pallets. The roof sloped from a low peaked center, bordered by a knee-high wall cut through at intervals with rectangular drains. Over the wall, outside, all around: what was left of Seattle.

Daniel stood silhouetted by the northern perspective, a lighter shadow against the rippling, ripping curtain. Jack joined him at the edge. Breaks in the curtain revealed a mélange of buildings industrial and domestic—houses, warehouses; to the west a forest of masts, and in the streets, dirt, ballast cobbles, brick, asphalt, wood, and concrete sidewalks. People dressed in dated fashions had been caught mid-stride, where they juddered like broken clockworks—going nowhere with painful slowness.

The torn curtain parted to reveal other streets, other buildings, a puzzle thrown together from ill-fitting pieces of time, poured from the box of the sky onto a half-seen landscape that surrounded the warehouse. The thick, chilled air was choked with grit—what sort of grit, Jack didn't want to know.

Daniel coughed and waved his hand. "Everything left behind finds its place," he said. "Just like you and me. I'll bet if we had picture books, we'd recognize neighborhoods from before this warehouse was built. People, too."

"What's happening?"

"Who knows? But think it through." Daniel gave Jack a wry grin. "We're ants clinging to the last gobbets in the stew. Most of the chunks have already been chewed and swallowed—most of our universe is gone. Otherwise . . . why *that*?"

He pointed through a luminous rip in the curtain at an immense, flaming arc, rimming a painfully black center. It stretched across almost two-thirds of the sky. "That's not our sun. And *that* is not our city. Not anymore."

NO ZEROS

Observers are like tiny muses. They process what they see, based on the logics they are given, but also on what they can assemble for themselves, what they think must be real, based on what they live and see and know, the truths they incorporate in their flesh.

Every group of observers establishes a kind of local reality. It cannot deviate too far from consensus, from what the muses have ruled must be. But that flexibility allows the cosmos a latitude that makes it more robust than any rigid framework, because it welcomes observers, welcomes their input. And sometimes, very clever observers can influence the muses and the cosmos as a whole, and so, Mnemosyne reconciles on a huge scale, those forward and backward pulses that we've already discussed.

We are not so much made by a creator as deduced. In fact, all creation is collaboration between the great and the small, always interconnected and dependent upon each other. There are no lords, no kings, no eternal gods of all, but there are forces that work across time and fate, and finally, outside our conceit, there is justice.

To be alive is to be blind. It is hard work to stay alive. And when our work is done and we are unburdened, we are rewarded with the joy of matter, about which only the wisest and the most foolish can know.

—The Chronicles of the Elders of Lagado
A lost or spurious work of Spinoza

CHAPTER **68**

The Chaos

Despite the efforts of their armor, light was a tricky commodity in the Chaos. Distances beyond a few yards tended to foreshorten or lengthen unpredictably. Nico in particular found this unnerving, and lost his balance more often than the others, until finally he lay down in a shallow dip and tried to be sick.

The armor would not let him.

Tiadba knelt beside him while Khren and the others circled the depression. All were woozy.

"If I could just throw up, I'd feel better," Nico said, wretched behind the golden transparency of his faceplate.

"That would be a mess, in your helmet," Tiadba said.

"I could take off the helmet for a little bit . . ."

"Too late for that," Denbord said, kneeling. "I'm not feeling so hot myself."

"Listen. I piss and shit inside here. Why can't I throw up?"

"Just don't think about it," Tiadba said. "And stop looking at the sky."

"I can't help it. It keeps changing. I look away, look back, and it's different—except for that *thing* up there. Always burning, but not in the middle, like a big hole. If it's on fire, why doesn't it burn everywhere? What's it trying to be?" His voice was getting shrill.

The fearful excitement of a few hours earlier was turning into a sour anxiety next door to panic. Their suits could only give them so much support, and weren't designed to interfere with their emotions.

Tiadba was beginning to think that Grayne's enthusiasm for the luxurious comfort of their adventure might have been overstated.

She swallowed frequently. Her face stung, her arms itched again, and her feet hurt, though they hadn't walked very far. She felt confined, trapped, lost, and it took real effort to keep from crying or, worse, screaming.

"You feel it, I know you do!" Nico called out, and rolled over on his stomach, grabbing at the rock, but the rock in the dip was solid, smooth.

Khren, Shewel, and Macht stepped down. Herza and Frinna flanked Nico and nudged the reclining breed. They seemed well enough, though still quiet.

"We haven't even started yet," Khren said.

Sad, Nico said, "Don't make it worse."

"We could swap. I could roll around and act scared for a while, and you could stand up here and be brave and try to see where we're going."

In their helmets, the beacon—a steady, low musical note—faded or increased in volume, depending on whether they kept to their course. But there had already been two broken walls high enough and long enough to force them off the course, and then they trekked about in nervous arcs and circles until they heard the beacon again at maximum melody. They had encountered crumbling barricades in the rolling emptiness, casting odd double bluish shadows in the reddish flare of the ring-fire sun. Tiadba thought it best not to climb over and investigate, and the others agreed—curiosity the first emotion to fade in that first mile. So they had walked around.

Now she worried they were already losing their will to go on. Swinging between extremes of exaltation and fear in so short a time—most unpleasant. And as yet they had met nothing particularly fearsome or frightening, just what they were trained to expect.

"I think I'm getting used to some of it," Macht said, but didn't sound convinced. "Really," he added. "Come on, Nico. Let's keep moving."

"We'll go on a few more miles," Tiadba said. She began gulping painfully. *We're being poisoned!* Yet she was sure nothing was getting in from outside the armor. Surely the Tall Ones would have equipped them better than that!

But the Chaos changes all the time. How could they know what kind of armor to make?

She looked sharply at Khren. He wasn't feeling the same symptoms. Nor were the others. Each was reacting in his own way.

Nico rolled on his back but kept his eyes closed. "Why are we still stuck here, if everything's so different? Why don't we just change the rules and lift up and float away?"

Tiadba suddenly felt a kind of love, and her eyes welled up. That was the sort of question Jebrassy would ask.

"It's called gravity," Khren said. "It's everywhere—even out here. Pahtun told us, remember?"

"Yeah, and where is *he*, now?" Macht asked darkly. "I don't even know what gravity is. Gravity *or* light."

"Light is what lets us see," Shewel said, echoing what they had been taught. He was certainly not the swiftest learner in the group, but what he learned stayed with him in perfect detail. "Gravity is what glues us down."

"Aren't you getting bored down there?" Denbord asked Nico. Khren and Macht reached down to grab his hands and lift him up. He stood on wobbly legs, arms out to keep his balance. "Let's go back. I think we could make it."

Macht climbed out of the dip. "Tiadba, you're the leader. Make us go."

Tiadba looked around, confused. She felt inside her for the visitor—any other voice giving advice, other than her own, so confused. But the visitor was not saying anything. And she could no longer imagine what Jebrassy might tell her.

Then she heard herself speaking, not good words, but words out of an angry little knot right in the center of her chest, above her stomach, below her lungs—she could feel the burning disappointment. "I don't know what we thought it would be like. Want to turn around and go back? How many of you think the city's going to last much longer?"

"Not me," Nico said. "I saw that thing take Mash. I don't want to go back. Out here—"

"Out here, we can see them coming," Tiadba said. "Back in the Tiers we die in our sleep. Or worse."

CHAPTER **69**

The Green Warehouse

The book group women sat in the chairs around the iron stove. They had been joined, with more than a degree of awkwardness, by Glaucous and Daniel. Glaucous accepted exile to the far corner, where he sat on a box, like one of Oxford's stony gargoyles.

Ginny stood apart from them all, and far from the room's southern door, her eyes downcast—steeled against another ordeal.

"Mnemosyne is special, and always difficult," Bidewell said. "A certain mental preparation is required before you meet her. I hope you have had time to consider what we've discussed."

"Is she a person, or a thing?" Jack asked.

"Neither. How old is the universe, Jack?"

"Billions of years, I guess. That's what I've been told."

Agazutta had become subject to fits of shivering and whimpering and now held her hand in front of her mouth. Miriam and Ellen stood on either side, firmly gripping her shoulders.

"And how old do *you* think it is?" Bidewell asked.

"Well, I was born twenty-four years ago," Jack said with a wry face. "That's how old it is for me."

"The beginning of a good answer. But we will not dive into solipsism. I wouldn't approve—more important, Mnemosyne would not approve. She responds best to a certain level of, how should we say, *skepticism* about the taught order of things. How old do you think these atoms and molecules are that you eat and breathe, that make up your body and propel the currents of your mind, your observing wit?"

"Same as the universe," Jack said with more certainty.

"A common error. Not all matter came into existence at the beginning. It is still being made, and will continue to be made for a very long time to come—if we did not face Terminus, of course."

"Of course," Miriam said.

"But that is beside my point. In certain parts of space and time, it is supposed that entire galaxies have appeared instantaneously, complete with hundreds of billions of stars burning, planets formed, civilizations alive and busy. Yet their histories have not arrived with them. Reconciliation is thus made an epic task."

Jack looked to see if Bidewell was joking. The highlights on the old man's lined face flickered in the warm firelight, but he showed no hint of humor. If anything, he seemed drowsy, wearily repeating an obvious and well-known truth.

"Appeared out of nothing?" Jack asked.

Ginny pulled up enough courage to say, "That doesn't seem possible."

Bidewell shrugged. "True, spontaneous creation usually delivers smaller units—particles, atoms, molecules in profusion. Virtual galaxies are difficult to conceive, I admit. But no less real. Once a particle or an object is created, it *has always been here.* It makes connections with all the particles with which it has interacted, and those connections—that connectedness—must be established, you might say after the fact. Literally," Bidewell smiled, "the books must be balanced."

"What about us?" Ginny asked with unexpected archness. "Human beings. Dogs. Cats. I mean, who keeps track of all the people on the streets?" She looked sharply at Daniel, and then at Glaucous, in the shadows.

Bidewell lifted one shoulder.

"How could anyone tell if I just popped out of nowhere?" Jack asked.

"As a rule, we cannot," Bidewell said. "Mnemosyne is the force that keeps it all from crashing into ruin and contradiction. She does her job, and she does it well."

Jack whistled. "Some lady."

Even this flippancy did not pique the old man. "You'll like her," Bidewell said. "But she is no lady."

"Sounds like a backward way of doing things," Ginny said.

"Perhaps, but it results in a cosmos of infinite richness and complexity. For this reason, logically speaking, the universe has no true chronological beginning, out of which all things flow. Every moment, until the end of creation, is a sort of beginning, somewhere."

"What's this I've heard about a Big Bang?" Jack asked.

"I'm not asking for belief. You'll see the truth soon enough—my words are preparation. Rays of light, you know, must be set in motion, already entangled, to complete the picture every observer sees or will see from that point on—and before. The wave of reconciliation passes back in time, and then forward again; pulse after pulse, until the refinement is complete."

"Sounds complicated," Jack said.

Ginny looked at the tall shelves of books, the opened boxes and crates whose contents had been laid out on the big table in the center of the high-ceilinged library. "You said some of the books you were looking for were odd, impossible, because they have no history. That must mean they were never reconciled, even before . . . what's happening outside."

"Good," Bidewell said.

"And that means Mnemosyne . . . well, she's been distracted, or something is increasing her workload. Or—she's sick. Maybe dying."

"Better," Bidewell said.

"Books, galaxies . . . What else?" Ginny asked.

Jack suddenly remembered the giant earwig he thought he'd seen scuttling between the warehouses. "Strange animals?"

Daniel looked both sly and sleepy. "What makes you say that?"

"I've seen them," Jack said. "One, anyway."

"Oh, my," Bidewell said, folding his hands. "Yes, those are indicators."

"Dreams sometimes come out of nowhere," Ginny said. "Are *they* indicators?"

"Mnemosyne can reconcile everything, everywhere, except in the heart and mind of an observer. That territory is forbidden to her. But observers die and their memories die with them—except for the legends, the myths of beginning times, the way things were before creation grew huge and complicated. Those are passed along in speech and dreams, and linger despite Mnemosyne's hardest labors. For that reason, Mnemosyne rarely concerns herself with dreams."

"When does she?" Daniel asked.

"When they come true," Bidewell said.

CHAPTER 70

The Chaos

"What are those?" Denbord asked. He knelt on the crest of a vast ripple in the sea of stone and looked down. The others joined him.

In the trough of the frozen, rocky wave, for as far as they could see into the reddish, murky light, row upon row of cylindrical shapes lay in rough parallel beside their dark cradles, like the broken rungs of a toppled ladder.

"They don't look that big," Nico said.

"Big enough," Shewel said.

Perf assumed a teacher's tone. "It's tough to judge size and distance—but if we went down there, I bet we'd be tiny."

Tiadba tried to remember Sangmer's description from the stories she had been reading to the breeds, to distract them from the long march, the brief rests, the strain of keeping to the beacon's line. Whatever these were, they blocked the path the beacon had been drawing for them. "They're boats," she concluded. "Like in the nauvarchia."

"They don't have sails," Denbord observed.

"They wouldn't need them. They're spaceboats. They travel across space—or they did, back when there was space to cross."

The others slowly understood her point. "Starboats," Perf said. "Back when there were stars."

Until now, the going had been steady though strange—over a monotonous gray landscape, dotted with tiny pores that pinched out pulsing green globules as the breeds approached, then shrank back into the rock.

All around, the rock sweated—the rock oozed light.

Tiadba looked both ways along the crest, then into the trough. "No way to avoid crossing," she said.

"What if those things roll over on us?" Shewel asked.

Denbord touched his finger to his faceplate. "Quick and easy," he said.

"What if the Silent Ones are down there?"

"Nobody's seen them," Nico said. "Nobody knows where they are or what they look like. Maybe they're gone. And the armor hasn't said a peep. We must be doing something right."

"At least we haven't stumbled over a trod," Perf said.

"I'd almost like to see that—or a Silent One," Denbord said. "Just to know what they are—what to expect, or avoid."

As Nico had pointed out, their suits had mostly kept quiet. On just one occasion, Perf was warned not to kick at the glowing balls.

Tiadba looked to the other side of the trough, the opposite crest, apparently two or three miles off. The clarity in the distance between the crests was increasing—something she'd noticed earlier, that the light could at times, unpredictably, grow stronger and more coherent, letting them see over a greater distance.

Perversely, the lower they were, the farther they could see. Light in this part of the Chaos apparently climbed around and over obstructions, then curved down to meet them—an effect among the most disturbing they had encountered since crossing the zone of lies. From the bottom of this valley, they might be able to see across the Chaos for many hundreds or thousands of miles. If distance still held, still mattered out here.

Nico moved up beside Tiadba, though they did not need to be close to hear each other. "What'll we do?"

"Climb down and cross over," she said.

"Can't we explore?" Perf asked. "I'd like to see inside a spaceboat."

Macht had walked off to their left. Now he rejoined the group. "They must be old," he said. "There are thousands of them."

"If the armor doesn't stop us, we'll look around," Tiadba said.

They spread into an optimized arc, to let their helmets see and process from a wider angle. Their view was now almost too crystalline. Beyond the trough, above the fallen ladder-rungs of the spaceboats, Tiadba saw the outline of edifices at least as large as the bions they had left behind—stark and caved, edged with a greenish fire that flickered as if still burning.

The others sucked in their breaths.

"What are those?" Khren asked.

"That's the Necropolis—isn't it?" Denbord asked, ever the studious one. "But I don't see any dead walking."

"We're too far away," Khren said.

Their armor responded, "There are many ancient cities, collected from many regions and histories. They should not be entered."

Denbord and Macht looked at each other, then at Tiadba. The others simply stared across the valley at the jumbled ruins, lying out there for no one knew how long.

How far humanity had been pushed back, how much had been destroyed . . . How little remained, compared to the vastness of the past—how little there was left to lose.

Just us.

"Is it dangerous to cross?" Tiadba asked. This time the armor did not answer. "I guess not," she said.

Denbord added, echoing her own irritation, "Kind of rude, isn't it?"

They began their descent.

———

The closer they got to the bottom, the hazier became the outlines of the spaceboats and their infrastructure, until they saw only a dancing puzzle of grays and browns cut through by dim arcs of green. However, the ruins of the cities beyond the next rise seemed to loom, and it was tempting to just stop—to halt their steady progress across the valley and contemplate dazzling visions of towers, domes, great rounded shells tens of miles wide, carved open to reveal uncounted interior levels, concavities filled with what must have once been urbs and neighborhoods, most collapsed and covered with irregular encrustations.

"Not tidy," Denbord said.

"Do not stop here," their armor told them. "Move on."

"What's wrong?" Tiadba asked.

"Unknown disturbances. We are being followed."

"By what?" she asked.

"Echoes are possible."

Tiadba tried to reason through to what that could mean, based on what Pahtun had told them in training. "We're following ourselves?"

"Unknown."

CHAPTER 71

The Broken Tower

Jebrassy looked up from the book he had been reading, stood away from his pretty golden desk, and saw the Great Door open.

Here, he could never tell what was an instructive illusion and what might be solid and real. Fear could not grip him, nor hunger, grief, or anticipation. He was comfortable in both mind and body. All was smoothed and welcome, small challenges and large explorations equally and curiously invigorating.

He was happy.

Sometimes the epitome of the Librarian walked with him, sometimes he explored alone, though he did not feel lonely. It was a new childhood, and it seemed to last a long, long time. He was learning much about the Kalpa, and some of the simpler secrets of those who lived within the upper levels of the city. Mathematics, for example—never his strong suit, beyond the shopkeeper's necessities trained into all breeds.

But always *this* door had been shut: the Great Door, more like a wall, easily as tall as a bloc of Tiers; curved like a crest or shield and covered with deeply engraved words, some of which he could read. He seemed to understand many more languages and signs now.

Jebrassy stepped through the breed-sized gap in the door, expecting something marvelous. He was not disappointed. He looked up and up at walls of shelves rising overhead and—he leaned over the parapet on which he stood—dropping down for as far as he could see. All the shelves were packed tight with books, too many to count, not uniformly bound, but a crescendo of colors leaping from the shelves, as if demanding to be inspected. Dark bindings neutral, untouched and unread; pale bindings touched once or twice; colored bindings, particularly blue and red, announcing greater degrees of interest.

These colors attracted the attention of many figures, small and slender, but not breeds. More like the angelins he had already met, but solid and dedicated. They flocked joyously up and down the spiral stairs, searching the shelves along all the levels.

"This must be a Babel," Jebrassy murmured to himself. "All of it packed inside a *minicosm*, a Shen invention, no bigger than a pebble. And these people are out exploring."

Up close—walking the parapet beside and around him, mostly ignoring his presence—their skin was smooth and eternally young, their faces serene or amused. Some glanced at their intruder with welcome but no speech. All here used signs, flashes of fingers and arms, changes of expression, to convey most of what they needed to say to one another.

Within the Babel, all was quiet, until a useful text was found, and then, throughout the immense spaces, along the galleries and the radiant walls of shelves stretching off forever, great songs and shouts would ring out, and all gathered to celebrate. Platforms expanded into circuses, and the searchers—members of the team that had made the discovery—would stand surrounded by admiring crowds. The readable text would be announced, and its binding color-coded.

The volume would then be cataloged, given a number—and that number would roll out like a dazzling silver ribbon across the plaza, only to be magically rewound and reduced to a folded paper octagon, soberly delivered to a shrouded, dark-robed figure that moved sometimes among the bright seekers . . .

The songs would fade, plazas empty and shrink, spiral stairs grow and reconnect.

All would return to what had been before.

Jebrassy understood this much: to live in a Babel was to be endlessly fascinated by the slow, steady drama of prolonged search. Still, his fingers itched to walk with these happy figures in their knee-length robes, to lose himself in the blessed anonymity of the greatest quest of all, in the greatest library of all—

The library that contained all possible stories. All histories. And all nonsense.

A Babel, a name as old as life itself, out of the Brightness, where all possible languages gathered. A place of confusion, seeking, and very, very rarely, illumination.

He tried to stop one of the searchers, clumsily signing a question: *How long?* But the seeker shrugged loose and went back to its search. So Jebrassy climbed a spiral stair, then hiked for what could have been days or years along a parapet.

Every now and then, he would stop and tug loose a volume, count through the thousand or more pages, and attempt to read—only to find the seemingly random text impenetrable. That did not disappoint him, not in the least. There was always the next volume. And so he would re-place the book and move on. Lovely work, peaceful, fulfilling.

But this existence was not for him.

When he realized he did not know his way back, would never be able to find the Great Door—which in any case might have already closed behind him—somehow, even that did not concern him.

He pulled from his own robes a number folded in an octagon and held the paper over the railing, then tricked it open, letting it unfold and uncoil, laughing as it dropped into the abyss between the walls of shelves.

A searcher approached, queried with signs: Who had assigned him the task of seeking this specific volume?

Jebrassy expressed some confusion. The searcher helped him read the first few digits printed on the long strip, then led him to that very volume, which had been discovered and cataloged quite early on.

Jebrassy pulled down the book, opened the sturdy blue cover, and read. At that moment, the dark figure approached and pulled back its hood and Jebrassy saw that it was the Librarian—the epitome he was most familiar with, at any rate.

"It's all an illusion, isn't it?" Jebrassy asked.

"I thought you'd appreciate the adventure," the epitome said.

Jebrassy scowled at the approaching end of this blissful adventure. "Why did I find this particular book?" he asked.

The epitome took the volume from his hands and seemed to weigh it. "A biography," he explained. "Not all the text is accessible. Some is garbled. Perhaps there is another volume that completes it—somewhere!" He waved at the endless shelves. "But no matter. This volume, for you—*is* you, for now, until we find the others—and thus holds great interest."

"Is it my story?" Jebrassy asked.

"Not precisely. And not completely."

Then Jebrassy understood. "It's *his* story, too," he said. "The one I'm entangled with."

"I wondered how easily you might find it," the epitome said, and waved a hand at the immensity. "You have excellent instincts."

"How does *anybody* find anything here?" Jebrassy asked. "I mean, is this really all compressed into something the size of a pebble? A small place, to hold so much."

"True. All these seekers—their greatest joy is to perform their task over and over, across lengths of their own special chronology so vast even my full self can hardly imagine them. But all this—within the pebble, as you say—is not infinite. It is limited. Like the Babel itself."

"There's a number called *pi*," Jebrassy said, proud of this knowledge. "It begins three decimal one four one five . . . and so on, forever. It isn't represented in here, is it?"

"Nothing infinite can be represented completely in here. There are segments of pi, of course, printed in a great many of these books—I suppose you could find them all, arrange them end to beginning, and then keep carrying some of the volumes to a place in the line, push them in— over and over again, but *that* would take you forever, longer even than time within the pebble. No. Pi is not contained here, nor any other infinite number or constant—not even infinitely long stories, which have been assumed to exist somewhere." The epitome again showed breed amusement, finger to nose. "A story in need of an infinite editor, no? But all the equations that can produce pi exist here. And if you desired, you could take one such equation—or all of them—and generate that number to whatever length, without further benefit of what is printed in these books. And that is both the glory and the sadness of this Babel. It is unfinished. The stories it contains are not alive—they do not reverberate with the unpredictability, the infinity, the repetition of a true existence. Even in its immensity, a Babel is only a seed. A map. As a master lost in the mists of the Brightness once said, 'The map is not the territory.'"

Jebrassy thought this over. Slowly, his face lit up.

The epitome appreciated his reaction, and took a book from the shelf, hefting it. "Actually, we do not generate such large volumes all at once. That would be wasteful. We generate much shorter strings of symbols—optimal lengths—and then we whirl them through analyzers that search for grammatical connections, using simple rules. That helps us assemble and spin out longer texts—and all their variants. Only then do we chart and catalog them. Suggestive texts—texts with extended meaning—have a way of being compressible, you know. They can be encoded and reduced, without loss. More random or meaningless texts cannot be so reduced.

"Thus, from my exterior perspective, the Babel within the pebble shows regions of density—and we seek them, though finding is just the beginning. Pi for example is completely random—I proved that myself some ages ago—and cannot be compressed, but only collapsed into an equation—and an equation is like a factory. Interestingly, pi at the circumference of minicosm is very simple—just 2. Can you tell me why?"

Jebrassy blinked. He had not studied these matters yet. The epitome went on without pause. "And of course, there is symmetry—many kinds of symmetry. For example, half the library is a mirror of the other half—the same texts, but reversed. We can eliminate those. There are many, many other techniques, some quite simple, others extremely difficult, devised over half an eternity, some by me, most by others whose identities have long since been forgotten."

"So much has been forgotten," Jebrassy said. "Why? If you can make Babels, can't real histories be preserved for all to find?"

The epitome was pleased by this question. "Perhaps. Though we should not underestimate that task—knowing everything, everywhere, is impossibly difficult. But the Shen did not reveal their techniques until long after the cities of Earth had found their records burdensome. Beneath the Kalpa, the ground-up libraries of Earth's history supply the foundations for the bions that remain—memories and records crushed and buried, no better than ancient bedrock. The only way to access parts of that past, tragically, is to watch it be digested by the Typhon, cut into pieces, and drift back toward our final moments—guided by the entangling associations between you and your visitors. Our dreamers."

"How sad," Jebrassy said. "But that means the Typhon serves a purpose."

"I see you would make an excellent searcher," the epitome said. "But you would not be happy. Indeed, I'm no longer happy here. Something is missing."

"Life?"

"Surprise. Unpredictability. The territory. All is laid out in these shelves, waiting to be discovered—but fixed. When the seed is planted and these texts become part of a new cosmos, everything will change. The nonsense will become as valuable as the stories. For a multiverse builds itself mostly out of unreadable nonsense, and none can ever know for sure which text is truly useless."

Jebrassy opened his book to read, but the letters began to blur.

The epitome cautioned, "Not yet, young breed. There is a true indicator, an unfailing marker of the real." All was beginning to swirl and blur, but the epitome's words stayed clear in his mind as he was swept back down the spiral stairs, as if by a great but gentle wind; along the shelves, down and down and sideways and down again, back to the Great Door, swinging shut just after he squeezed through.

The epitome's voice followed him to the small golden desk:

"When you open a book within a Babel, the text is pristine, pure—black marks on white paper. Nothing will mar the texts or interrupt your concentration. But out there, in what is left of the old universe and what will become the new, in the *territory* to come, you will open a book, you will read a page . . .

"And a living thing, tiny, surprising and perverse, will crawl across that page, that story, startling you—until you recognize it and smile. It is alive—a mere bogle, a bug, but it is thinking, living in its own way, and most pointedly, it is not *reading*. It is not part of the library. It walks over the text, unexpected and vital."

"Until I slam the book," Jebrassy said.

"Ah, but you won't. This creature is the ultimate symbol of she who reconciles, who allows memory and thus time to spin out. A friend of the mother of the Muses, Mnemosyne, and the first sign of a new cosmos.

"True creation unfolding—that which lives and walks over the words—that is quickened by the spider between the lines."

CHAPTER 72

The Chaos

There was no way to tell how far they had walked, but they could no longer see the Kalpa. The three bions and the Broken Tower had vanished, not visible even when they descended into the stony trough.

The return path would have to be different—if they could ever return, or would ever want to.

The gray, knife-edged beam swung overhead, causing a tingle in Tiadba's scalp. Pahtun had said it came from the Witness—something or someone to be avoided if at all possible.

The starboats—the hundreds and perhaps thousands of hulks they saw from the opposite crest—had also vanished. All they found, once they reached the bottom of the trough, were broken, jagged rows of blackened shards, outlines of oblong hulls almost obscured by drifts of gray and black gravel. So much for exploring and satisfying their curiosity.

They rested in the trough, setting up a reality generator and producing a bubble of warmth and protection while they unzipped their hoods, removed their armor, scratched where necessary, and tried to feel normal.

Frinna and Herza played a small game of leapcheck, scooping hollows in the drift and arranging circles of alternate gray and black pebbles.

Within the bubble of the small generator, their view of the surrounding landscape took a disturbing lurch. The broken cities on the other side of the trough swam like reflections in water. Only when they put on their armor and helmets again, and shut down the generator, did the huge hemispheric shells and their exposed levels return with any clarity.

Tiadba took some encouragement that the light-oozing pores had become fewer and many steps between; they did not have to deal with so many of the globules.

"I don't understand any of this," Denbold complained as they resumed their march.

"We follow the beacon," Khren said, pretending stoicism. Tiadba had noticed him rubbing his feet and grumbling quietly during their rest under the bubble.

"Where are those echoes?" Nico asked. His quiet had been almost unbroken, perhaps to hide disappointment at not being able to see the starboats up close. "We were promised dangerous echoes, right? And we'd learn something new."

No one responded to his poor jest. They walked over the top of the rise and turned to see, behind them, that the trough had inverted to become a high ridge—a long, continuous hill—and that the line of huge starboats had returned, cradles and all. Furthermore, looking ahead, the broken cities were gone, replaced by a glittering orchard of small trees dotted over low black hills.

"Too much," Denbold muttered.

The marchers formed a line a few dozen steps from the first of the trees, to consider their options.

"It doesn't look dangerous," Shewel said, squirming within his armor. He apparently hadn't found all the places that needed scratching.

"Is it dangerous?" Tiadba asked her suit. Sometimes the armor responded to a direct question—if it had an answer. This time, when she thought she saw small things moving between the trees, there came no reply for some uncomfortable moments.

"Evolution is occurring here," her helmet finally said. "This should be reported."

"Good luck," Shewel said. "Doesn't it know we can't do that?"

"What's evolution?" Frinna and Herza asked simultaneously.

"Adjustments that promote survival in changing conditions. Sometimes, the adjustments stabilize the conditions."

Macht snorted.

"What's that mean when it's lying down?" Shewel asked.

"There could be opportunity here. Conditions of reality and stability are being maintained without machines or tools. These could either interfere with armor and generators or strengthen them."

"That's definitive," Shewel said, and added his own snort.

"Turn around," Tiadba's armor said.

They all swiveled and saw figures some way off, armored marchers very like themselves—thirty or forty, coming down the ridge, but leaning forward as if to climb, not descend.

They approached—came within an apparent hundred steps or so.

"More marchers from the city!" Khren said happily, and began to jog toward them. Tiadba grabbed his arm.

"Prepare to flee," their armor advised. "The danger behind you is greater than the danger ahead."

"Echoes?" Tiadba asked.

"These are echoes," the armor affirmed.

The other marchers—whatever sort of marchers they might be—moved with slow, weary steps, yet seemed to make good progress toward them. Khren moaned. They saw quite clearly now that the armor worn by these breeds was falling apart. The helmets lay in shreds over slumped shoulders. The faces of the echoes were wizened, dark, sunken eyes exhausted and desperate—unfocused.

They seemed to be *blind*.

And they were getting nowhere—repeating endless motions. *Echoing*.

"Set up the generator, focus the bubble in tight, and huddle," Tiadba said, realizing that the armor was not speaking but she was receiving instructions nonetheless, quick images in her mind. Her companions quickly did as instructed, and came together within the small, shimmering hemisphere like newly delivered crèche-mates, as close as they could fit, clasping hands, arms, legs, staring outward.

The blind echoes passed around the bubble, then veered into the thin forest of low trees, where they met the glowing branches—only to pop like soap bubbles, leaving behind drifting, plasticky skins that hung from the branches, then turned to dust and drifted away.

"Where's Perf?" Shewel asked. They felt around their group, and Tiadba forced up through the clinging mass to look around. She had not seen him. They shouted and called, but dared not break the hemisphere.

Then Tiadba saw him, ten steps away, leaning into a cluster of blind marchers, waving his arms slowly as if swimming through thick liquid, trying to stay upright.

The cracked and broken armor of these gray forms, decayed as it was, clung to his suit wherever they brushed him, changing it from vivid red to dead gray, and then, peeling it back like the skin of a ripe fruit, spinning him about as each shred was tugged loose.

The breeds inside the bubble watched helplessly, frozen with terror, as Perf twisted and danced and finally stood naked on the black pebbled surface. More of the weary gray echoes passed both around and *through* him, sanding away his integrity until he became a translucent mannequin, shimmering and wobbling as if made of gelatin.

And then he simply powdered. His dust flew up, vanishing into the purplish black tatters of the sky.

"More coming!" Khren shouted, pointing to the ridge crest. Thousands of false marchers—dead marchers—echoes, whatever they might be, had gathered and were now moving in hopeless tides to join in the apparent destruction against the forest of glowing trees.

"They're the ones who didn't make it this far," Nico said. "Why do they want to kill us?"

"Pull in tighter!" Tiadba cried, seeing the image very clearly in her mind and feeling her muscles respond, feeling them all respond simultaneously, protected and controlled by their suits.

The hemisphere shrank and became silvery, sucking down around their forms, ringing against their suits. Tiadba felt herself shoved against the pole that supported the generator—saw sky, horizon, everything, tilt and whirl—no pretense at visual approximation through their faceplates now, all energy devoted to simple survival.

For the first time they came close to "seeing" the Chaos as it actually was. An impossibility, of course. It hurt so badly they could neither move nor make a sound. The armor replaced these incomprehensible perceptions with wandering blankets of color. Or at least Tiadba thought it might be the armor—there was no way of knowing, hardly any way to think.

Something, a scrap of concern, seemed to come from her visitor—in the wandering, comfortable sea of colors, she could feel her other, peering in as it were, saying, *Before you freeze and die, you feel warm . . .*

CHAPTER 73

The Green Warehouse

Glaucous buttonholed Daniel as Bidewell escorted Jack and Ginny to the southern door. "He has tricks. You were listening when we spoke— you heard him."

Daniel smiled. "You're warning *me?*"

"He wants something. He'll deliver you over, just as I would."

"Or will," Daniel said. "What happens if the Chalk Princess shows up right now?"

"Lost in the grayness, like Whitlow, like the Moth—but not for long, I see it now," Glaucous said, and jerked his eyes around nervously. "I can almost sense their return. This is becoming their country again. I need a partner," he added, more nervous still that Daniel seemed un-afraid. "We both need partners. When our Mistress does return . . . Alone, we'd be unbalanced, unprotected."

"You're the hunter, I'm the prey," Daniel said, lowering his head to Glaucous's upturned face, wincing at a musty reek barely masked by the scent of anise. "Remember that."

"I've let birds go, in my time," Glaucous said, wiping his mouth. "I've done good deeds in my time, I have."

Daniel shook his head, then turned back to the door.

Glaucous called after him, "I'm not the only hunter. And *she* is not the only danger."

———

Daniel joined the three at the door. "I hope your Mr. Bidewell knows what he's talking about."

Bidewell watched them together, resigned. "I'm sure Mr. Iremonk knows of these matters at a practical level." He pulled a ring of keys from his apron pocket. A black iron lock hung from the door's steel hasp. As the ladies waited some distance back and Glaucous moved closer, hands stretched out to the warmth of the small stove, Bidewell lifted the ring and jingled three keys.

"These are my instructions. Follow them precisely.

"Jack, go to the far wall and open the door on the left—the left, not the middle or the right. Ginny, you enter after Jack and open the door on the right—not the middle door and not Jack's door. Leave those be. Jack, left—Ginny, right. Daniel—"

"Middle door. Got you."

"The rooms should be comfortable—neither warm nor cold. A small window, just enough light to see. No one has been inside for a hundred years. No observer has witnessed anything therein. Except for an old chair and—I imagine—some dust, your rooms are empty and clean."

Jack looked at Ginny. An odd girl, she returned his look with wide, blank eyes, as if she did not recognize him—as if they had never met, and she wanted nothing from him. She was lost in the moment, it seemed, deeper than he was.

Daniel's look said: *We're all crazy, let's humor the old man.*

"Your time with Mnemosyne will be difficult to judge—but from our perspective, out here, it will go by quickly. A few minutes at most. For you—years may seem to pass."

Bidewell took a big brass key, green with age, and opened the lock. As the book group ladies watched from their far pool of warmth and security, surrounded by high shelves and ladders—the highest shelves lost in the receding gloom above the stove and the green-shaded lamps on the desk—Bidewell opened the wooden door. It creaked, and bits of paint flaked from the top of the jamb. Cold air slid past Jack's feet like the ghost of an impatient dog.

"You first, young Jack."

He felt the pressure of the eyes fixed on his back, and with a shudder, he passed through.

"*Bonne chance*," Glaucous murmured, as Bidewell closed the door behind him.

The high, long room beyond the door was dark but for a window-fed shaft of purplish sky-glow that crossed from his left, above his head, and painted a pale square on the far wall. The between-space was high and narrow and empty, the old boards ancient and gray.

Squinting, Jack could just make out the rectangles of three doors on the opposite wall. His eyes adjusted. The sounds outside seemed to fall from the sky, softened, less important.

Jack walked across and to his left and stood in that corner, considering the way the high walls and beamed ceiling in the long room joined. Normally, he could reach out and grab world-lines the way Tarzan grabbed vines, great clumps of them. But all the possible paths had been cut away or converged to *I enter, I do not enter*—an angular choice.

He had reached his zero point. The zero moment.

He took a step away from the safety of the corner. Laughed to himself, uncertain, but the laugh died and he almost stopped breathing. The between room was empty, but he was not alone. Something waited for a choice to be made. Waited, measuring the beats of his heart with infinite patience, and yet . . .

"What do you want me to do?" Jack whispered.

Three doors, six decisions.

But still—only two fates. Not really an answer, and it didn't make sense. What each of them did seemed disconnected, did not add up.

Still, he took the two steps necessary to stand before his door. The knob was crusted with verdigris. He inserted his key. Old brass—hard to turn. He gripped it tight, twisted from his shoulder, and after several attempts something let loose, the old mechanism broke free, and his door opened with just a small scrape.

Remarkable that there had been so little change all these years.

He could barely hear the dead or dying city outside, could almost believe he was on a ship sailing over a far, soft ocean, listening to a radio playing in someone else's cabin, tuned to an obscure indie station—he managed a grin—KRAK, Ragnarock AM.

Peace welled up, and all his guilt, indecision, worries, and fears vanished, leaving behind just Jeremy Rohmer. No need even for the pretense of *Jack*. Jeremy, the name his mother had given him.

The room behind the door was narrow, long and high. Bidewell had divided this end of the warehouse into three equal rectangles. High in the wall at the far end, a single window let in wisps of uneasy light. The way the light fell contradicted the angle of the source in the between-room.

Jack approached the plain white chair, thick-daubed paint on its flat seat and back cracked with age. He turned around, looked up, then slowly sat.

Folded his arms.

Raised his eyebrows at the high corners.

After a while he yawned. The sound of his ears hummed with the pressure of the yawn, and his jaw popped, obscuring a sound, a voice deep in his head.

—your first memory?

Jeremy jerked, wondering if he'd dozed off. But he was still alone, the door shut tight.

He jerked again at the sensation of fingers brushing down his arms. Then he pressed back in the chair. He could feel it beginning. His self was breaking up like a crust of ice, and memories gushed through like water.

Jeremy's father was driving them from Milwaukee, in search of a new place to live—six months after his mother died, three months after a brief and, as it turned out, final gig at Chuck's Comedy Margin—one month after Jeremy had broken his leg trying to juggle while riding a unicycle.

He had been fifteen.

"You ever hear of the Bleak Warden?" his father asked.

"What's that, a band?" Jeremy asked.

"Nope."

The land unrolled outside the windows: flat desert and low brown desert towns, sunsets tan and pink, afternoon sky dazzling with thunderheads, and between the storms, sheeplike clouds grazing on endless blue fields.

Broke my leg?

In the empty room, his leg suddenly ached. He reached down to rub it.

———

Bidewell opened the door for the second time, and Ginny entered. If he spoke, she did not hear him. The high hallway beyond stretched across the width of the warehouse. The air smelled cool and stuffy. She glanced at the leftmost door—Jack's door. Shut, quiet. Whatever was happening there, it wasn't noisy.

Bidewell closed the door behind her. With a short breath, almost a hiccup, she walked slowly to the right, inserted and turned the key, and grasped the knob, but hesitated before entering her room. Odd that she accepted that possessive without argument.

No one else had been through this door for a hundred years. What waited inside must be hers.

Outside, the low, hollow destruction continued to grind time and the Earth like wheat beneath a stone mill, and she did not care. In this room, she thought, it might soon be over. What she knew—the nightmare that her *other* knew—could not be reconciled, not even by a master muse or whatever Mnemosyne was supposed to be. God. Goddess. Demiurge. Housewife of the creator, sweeper-up of unresolved messes. Kindhearted sister to the awful Chalk Princess, who was white but should have been black: Kali, *ḳala*—Sanskrit for time, both bleacher and blackener. Ginny had read some of the books Bidewell chose for her, pulled from a bookcase labeled Nunc, Nunquam—Greek and Hindu mythology, mostly. But none of their tales quite seemed to match what Bidewell was describing.

Old time is at an end, or soon will be. New memories must be made. New time will be forged. Who will fire the forge?

Memory begins and ends with time.

These words or impressions, less than words but more deeply felt, suddenly made Ginny angry. Bidewell made her angry. Jack and Daniel made her angry. None of them fit into any sort of life she had ever wanted. She wanted *out*. She had to leave. She wanted to jump between the lines, cut them all loose—let them float away.

Instead of turning to run, however, she again grasped the knob to her door, forced it around—it stuck, she grimaced—and then the door opened and she looked across the length of the room beyond, perpendicular to the hallway, stretching to the back of the warehouse.

A window mounted high in the rear wall showed a curling, flaring lick from the broken sun that had eaten the dying moon.

In the middle of the room stood the old white chair, as Bidewell had promised. The paint on its seat and back had cracked after a century of quietly heating and cooling.

Ginny swallowed and said, "I'm here." She stood beside her chair, laying one hand on the curved back. Then she realized she had not closed the door, and turned to go back. But the door had never been opened.

A shade made way, removed itself from the chair . . . trick of the eyes.

She was the shade.

She sat.

Bidewell opened the door.

"Hurry," he told Daniel. Around them the entire warehouse rattled with the stuttering havoc outside.

Daniel felt supremely confident. Never more so. He could beat this. He could even beat Terminus. *Someone* would get through—otherwise, why would they all be gathered here, what would the point be of this rigmarole?

There were the two young people—younger than Fred—and in a pinch there was always Glaucous, ageless in his way, and no doubt a tough subject. But Daniel knew instinctively he could not transfer to Bidewell whatever happened. He did not want to be stuck in the warehouse, and Bidewell would not leave this place and likely would not survive its destruction.

GREG BEAR

Nor could Daniel choose any of the older ladies. With a twinge, he had seen one of their little green books poking from a handbag, the spine marked 1298. The woman in the doctor's coat, Sangloss, seemed to take a clinical interest in him. The others simply ignored him. He could almost smell their suspicion. In their way, they were stronger and perhaps more armored even than Glaucous.

Not for him.

Glaucous sat on a low bench, watching this little drama with a fixed smile. "Go on," he said. "There's nothing for you out here."

How right he was. Once the door was closed, Bidewell and Glaucous and the ladies might fade away completely. The whole warehouse might just lift up like a burning feather. Anything could happen, but he would survive.

Daniel walked through. Bidewell closed the outer door. The inner left-hand door and the door on the right were both shut and quiet. He could picture Ginny and Jack sitting in those two rooms, bored, waiting for enough time to pass so Bidewell would call them out and apologize. The old man clearly had no idea what was going on.

The warehouse hummed like a sympathetic string. It wanted to join in the vast crumbling. It wanted to die.

Daniel went to the middle door, turned the key, and grasped the knob. He made sure to latch the door behind him. Nobody would sneak in. He had to observe the forms.

In the long room beyond, he sat in the white chair, hunched forward, and waited.

Afraid.

The old Dodge was coming up on low hills, and soon there would be mountains, but Jeremy did not know where they were and did not much care.

He lay squished into the corner of the backseat, cast stretched almost full length across the old car. He was in a lousy mood. Not so much a mood as an unyielding concrete tunnel with no end, no exit. Ryan, his father, was dying, and that meant he would finally have no one, nothing but his rudimentary skills: mediocre patter and the poor, blunt magicks Ryan had managed to teach him.

"I had a dream about this Bleak Warden. It's a kind of flying robot,"

Ryan said. "It comes when you're dead. Takes you away. Kind of like a garbage man, I guess."

"Comes for *you*. Not for me," Jeremy said, and then wished he could take it back.

Ryan grinned like a raccoon. "Riiiight. There was this place in my dream, a kind of big cavern with a bright sky, filled with different people. Small ears, bushy fur instead of hair. I only remember a little. I've been there a couple of times. That's what they call death, the people in the dream—they call it the Bleak Warden. Pretty scary, except in this place it never takes the living—and nobody is ever sick. They fight, but they don't kill each other. They never steal. They raise kids, but they don't *have* them—kids are delivered like packages. Like storks leaving you under a cabbage leaf. Weird, huh?"

Jeremy sat up in the backseat, rearranged his cast, nudged by a phantom memory. Tried to remember where he really was. Could not grasp it—

His father continued:

"They hold festivals and what they call little wars, where tough guys get the crap kicked out of their system. Interesting, huh?"

"Dreams are showstoppers, Dad. You told me that."

"Well, this one is actually exciting. I keep wondering what will happen the next time I dream. And it's consistent—except last night, in the motel in Moscow, it changed. I was in a different part of the same place. Some of the people were taller. They were handing out these suits, red and yellow and green, like soft armor, to the smaller ones. Self-contained, like spacesuits, except not only do they give you air and heat, but . . . this is tough to describe. They *keep body and soul together*." Ryan's voice became reverent, as if he totally believed, was totally reliving that moment.

"You were having a nightmare," Jeremy said. "You woke me up."

"You whacked me in bed with your plaster club," Ryan said, glancing over the seat. "Humor me, Jeremy. This is a long trip. Now of all times."

That hurt so much, Jeremy thought it was unfair. "I'm listening, aren't I?"

"We're not going to have too many of these days, you know, so I thought I'd impart a little of what it means to be your dad, a little fatherly wisdom, however cracked."

Jeremy did not know, whether his father was feeling self-pity or ex-pelling a lousy joke. (Ryan always called telling a bad joke "expelling," like coughing out a piece of food or a gob of phlegm stuck in the wind-pipe: "You try to tell a joke and it makes you choke, but stop! Don't expel it. Wrong joke or wrong crowd.")

"Impart away," Jeremy said, preparing to suffer in relative silence, because Ryan *was* dying, he was pretty sure of that, though of course no-body would tell him anything right up front.

"All right." Ryan thought for a moment, frowning in concentration. "These suits keep them alive and together in a dark, nasty land where there are no rules. But the people with little ears—me, my friends—we're going out there, into the weirdness, and these *superior* people—the tall fellows—are suiting us up. They won't go themselves. Maybe they can't, but we can, the little ones. Weird, huh?"

"Totally," Jeremy said. "I never have dreams like that."

"When things change, dreams change. I used to have normal dreams. What do you dream about?"

"Roads. Toads and roads." Jeremy had worked out a pretty funny routine about toads crossing a road, grim and hilarious. "I want to dream about Mom."

"Right."

Ryan drove for a while without saying anything.

My father is fat. He wants to be a comedian. That's what he had told Miriam Sangloss in the clinic.

Jeremy's father had thin red hair and a round red face and the body of a carny roustabout—big muscles, big bones, boiled-freckle skin, Mom had called it, that memorable time when she painted Ryan up in flower and beast tattoos for a street parade in Waukegan. She was acting in a film then, a real paying job, and they stayed over for a few weeks after the end of the shoot, doing local theater and of course that parade, which had been fun.

Jeremy had been eleven. On his fingers, he counted the days after the parade, the days before she died. Four.

The Dodge had taken Ryan and Jeremy through Montana and Idaho and into Oregon. They had stopped off in Eugene, where Ryan had worked a small circus whose owner was once Mom's boyfriend. Ryan and the circus owner spent one night drinking and crying on each other's shoulders—*very* weird, Jeremy had thought.

They left Eugene for Spokane, crossing the eastern high desert. Their last trip.

"We all lose our mothers," Ryan said on that trip. "Every mother since the beginning of time has died. Memory is the mother of us all, Jeremy."

And now—*Nunc*—he was sitting in the chair.

Everything signifies, nothing is of itself. You call yourself Jack because it is a safe name. So many are named Jack, you can hide; but it is a strong name, universal.

The odd thing, as if there had ever been just one singular, odd thing in his life, was that sitting in this room, he had no difficulty believing that road trip with his father was his very first memory, his first experience of being alive. What went before—his mother's death, the beginning of the trip, breaking his leg—was like the sound of the dying city outside this high, empty room: there, but unconvincing.

There is a number, assigned to volumes arranged on a nonexistent shelf in a time far away from now, all waiting to be reconciled. Waiting for choices to be made. Where do you really *come from, Jeremy?*

Who is your real mother?

And why does she seek you?

———

Ginny closed her eyes. She was back in Milwaukee, then in Philadelphia. She was back with her parents.

They rarely stayed in one place more than a few months. And when they moved on, they arranged things so they left behind no impression—nobody remembered them. They could have circled back through the same towns, moved back into the same houses a few years later, and would have been greeted as newcomers. But they never did.

"We don't leave footprints," her mother had told Ginny as a child.

Ginny remembered her attempts to make friends, meet boys. But then, inevitably—exhausted, discouraged—her family stayed too long in one town and the whole memory thing doubled back on them. Her mother wandered off or just vanished, as if erased from a giant blackboard. A few weeks later, her father vanished as well. Maybe they were taken by collectors, like the man with the coin or Glaucous. Maybe her parents sacrificed themselves to protect her. She would never know. Her entire family might as well have never lived. There was no proof they *had* lived, other than the library stone.

Alone, carrying the sum-runner, her dreams began—and she learned she could shift.

She had come so very far. Her entire life became a long bad dream; both of her lives, *here* and *there*. It was curiosity about *there* that landed her in her present trouble.

A few weeks after her father's departure, Ginny boarded a Greyhound and stared out a smudged window at rolling wet miles of fields and hills. In Philadelphia, she lived on the streets for a few months. Street people forgot things under the best of circumstances. She decided that wasn't what she needed.

She soon hitchhiked to Baltimore, where she peeled a tab off a flyer on a bulletin board, and that same night carried her backpack into an old two-bedroom row house occupied by goths and ravers—determined to settle in, stay awhile, leave behind some footprints. For the first time since her parents had vanished, she felt comfortable, at home—for a while.

Then she left the house in Baltimore and called the number in the newspaper ad.

Ginny looked up at the blank wall, the peeling paint, the shadows moving slowly over the overlapping slats of wood.

Is this what you choose?

Is there a better past for you?

"Who are you?" she cried.

No answer. Foolish question. She already knew the answer—though it did not make much sense.

"What am *I*, then? I really don't remember anything before I called that number—is that it? Who were my parents? I couldn't just pop up out of nowhere, out of nothing, could I?"

A polite waiting.

"All right," Ginny said, angrily determined to test the limits. "You asked for it, here it is. I come from a country called Thule. It's a big island northwest of Ireland. The last contact with the outside world was . . . World War Two. The Germans occupied my island, but we pushed them out before the war ended. There were huge stone castles built on the crests of high hills and in the mountains. My parents worked in the royal palace on the southern coast, and I had the run of the hill-castles where the prince and princess were hidden, moving to a new castle every day. Everyone was afraid, but not my family. My brothers and I—

I had three brothers—we used to ride gliders off the cliffs, and I broke
my arm . . ."

Someone laughed—behind her, around her—delighted with her
presumption. Her arm suddenly ached, and with this pain, all the memories flooded back: broad fields below the stone castles, brown and purple with sweet prickle-thatch, the taste of comb-laden honey-of-Thrace
in the fresh spring air; her father's concern as the palace physician set her
arm without anesthetic, wrapped it in a poultice of lard and chalice-
herb, then in a temporary wax-soaked cast stiffened with clean white
pine slats . . .

She had been named after the Virgin Queen, who once offered the
hand of alliance to Thule to seek their aid in fighting off Spain. That alliance had soured in the days of James the First.

Ginny grinned—free to choose. She could actually feel that lovely,
brightly plumed tail of history and memory stretching behind her, a
thrashing, vibrant past filling out and coming alive, smells and colors
and tastes struggling to be made and fixed in place.

It was real—not just her imagination!

"Oh, my God," she said, and her voice echoed from the walls. "It *is*
true, isn't it?" She felt a lightness and liberty she had never known before. It made her giddy. She was shifting fates, in reverse.

And then a gentle remonstrance enveloped her.

*Wonderful it is—a beautiful stretch—but too far from where we are
now. It cannot be reconciled.*

Not yet.

After . . .

That beautiful history faded as quickly as it had come, but the taste of
honey-of-Thrace lingered on her tongue like a reward for her audacity.

"You're real, aren't you?" she whispered. "You're real and you're
beautiful. But you're sick . . . you're dying, because the universe is sick
and dying, right?"

No answer.

"But is it true—can I have another past? A better, happier past?"

No answer needed. Ginny felt for the box in her pocket. "When was
I *really* born?" she asked, suddenly catching on.

———

"I've been here a long time," Daniel said to the looming silence. "Thousands of years. Millions. I don't remember all of it, of course, but that's

what I've figured out. And I'm talking here just to pass the time, because this is all crap. In fact, I only remember a little bit about what happened before I took over Charles Granger. That's the problem—the things I've had to do to escape the bad places, the dying places—one big leap at a time. And now there's only one path, one escape." He sliced the air with his hand, then jabbed. "Go straight through Terminus, come out the other side, whatever that's like. So—who's going through, and who's going to get stuck here? Maybe you don't know, because that's not your job. But if anybody's going through, I'm your ticket, hitch a ride." The silence seemed to become deeper. "Are *you* the Chalk Princess?"

Daniel felt acutely uncomfortable. There was something in the room—it just wasn't responding. So sad. He just couldn't remember something important—something essential.

"I mean, this is my audition, isn't it? The others—they say they dream about another city. I don't. So why were those monsters so interested in me—the Moth, Whitlow, Glaucous—whatever *he* is. What have I got to give them? The stone? I don't even remember how it came to be mine. I think I killed somebody to get it. That's how it always comes to be mine. Somebody has to die."

He had stopped breathing for a moment, so he took a short breath, all he would allow himself, even if his head was starting to swim.

"I'm a madness that moves from man to man. I've betrayed and lied and ruined and been ruined, but I've always escaped. What does that make me?" He closed his eyes. Suddenly, his head hurt with so much longing and need.

"We're not going to find each other anytime soon, are we?" Daniel whispered to the stillness.

Paramedics were called to the motel after Jeremy found his father sprawled on the floor of the bathroom. Something small had burst in Ryan's head, paralyzing him and slurring his speech.

Ryan never again mentioned the Bleak Warden. In the hospital room, the last thing he told Jeremy was, "Save your mother. Always remember." No explanation.

Jack was making his choice—stubborn, as always. He'd *loved* his parents—had wanted to be very like his father.

Three days later another stroke killed Ryan. His father was gone. It was one thing to gull the shills, fool the audience—entertain them with the brightness of the game. It was another to build his life on a firm, wonderful foundation of memories both good and bad—life solid, painful, but real.

Jeremy had his cast removed just in time for the funeral. Magicians, comedians, buskers, and actors came from all over Washington and parts of Oregon and Idaho. He had never realized his father was so loved—which only showed how little he knew about anything important.

Before vacating the room in the Motel 6, he opened his father's trunk. Inside he found a stack of paperback books, mostly Clive Barker and Jack Kerouac (that was when he decided his new name would be Jack), three changes of clothes and five changes of underwear, none of which fit him—and the gray box, wrapped in a velvet bag. He opened the box and found the twisted stone, burned-looking but for a small, embedded red eye that seemed to shine even in the dark.

The sometime stone.

The sum-runner.

Ryan had never told him where he'd found it. Perhaps it had belonged to Mother.

Jack's luck changed. It did not get better, exactly—not in the larger scale of things—but it changed.

———

"I'd like to be—to have been a little girl with friends and a good school, good teachers, a normal little girl. I'd like to grow up normal and fall in love—without dreams. Are Jack and I supposed to be in love? Because it doesn't seem to be happening—not yet."

———

Outside, the sky grew brighter. Yellow and green light flickered through the high window, but Jack could not tell if dawn was coming. It didn't matter. No more dawns, probably. He did not need to get up and move around—he was comfortable, for the moment.

"How long should I wait?"

Now the window spread a diffuse silver glow on the wall opposite.

Still nothing. Then:

What is your other *first memory?*

Jeremy was stunned by how quickly he came up with his reply. "Something's carrying me. I'm young, I don't know too many words. A door opens—but it's an odd sort of door, it *melts* aside. And then—

there's my mother and father, but that's not what they're called—still, they're like my parents. They love me. They take care of me. They're going to be taken away from me."

He made a bitter face, crossed his legs, and tried to lean back, but the chair creaked, so he bit at his index finger. What he had just said made no sense, but it felt right, felt real.

"That's what you asked for. My *other* first memory. I remember being young. And yet here, now, I don't remember being young. I'm less real here than in my dreams . . . That's not right. This is wacked. Take my word for it, this is triple wacked."

Jeremy looked around, suddenly very frightened—more frightened than he'd been in the sack in the back of the van, or sprawled out bruised and wet on the transformed street, his hand sluiced by the storm's cold runoff.

"You're supposed to be Mnemosyne, right?"

A breeze blew through the room, cool but not unfriendly, pulling at his shirt, flicking his pants legs. Playful, sad. He blinked and shifted on the chair, then just listened. A quiet rushing hiss came from outside, more like falling sand than wind—and nothing else. Falling sand or endless quick, tiny waves on a beach. The room was dark. No dawn through the high window. Jeremy—no, he was Jack again—had no idea how much time had passed.

He looked over his shoulder. "Hello?"

The lone high window was more pit than window—he couldn't even see the frame or much of the wall. The room seemed much colder. "Everything I know is wrong." Jack smiled, crossed his arms. "I get it. I'm ready."

He would not just get up and leave the room. That would show them he was a coward, that he couldn't take their stupid test, which didn't mean anything anyway.

Hours later, "I jump away from bad things. Everybody would if they could."

Whom do you protect—and whom do you leave behind? Where do you go when you jump—into another you? How many of you are there?

Jack broke into a sweat. "I don't know." He wiped his forehead, then his cheeks. Someone, somewhere, had to be talking quietly through a hole or a speaker. Time to get real. He was willing to give up the illusion that he could jump—that had always seemed crazy—as well as the memory of the dark, crumbling world and what lay beyond the membrane—give it all up, no problem—forget about Glaucous and the huge woman and the wasps—fine by him. Forget about the frozen stuttering city outside the warehouse and the ladies and even Ellen and Dr. Sangloss and Bidewell. He'd dump it all—well, maybe not Ginny. But just don't ask *those* questions, because he had wondered about the answers for years. How many selves had he betrayed, just by avoiding their pain, by jumping to better, safer lines?

"I can't be all of us at once." He tried to laugh. "My head will explode!"

Maybe he was remembering the wrong things. Maybe he had never escaped from the back of the van. Everything between now and then could be a lie, an illusion. Glaucous was torturing him—they were holding him here by spinning out their wasp-winged fates—maybe that was the rushing sound and this tall, narrow room was surrounded by wasps, blacking out the lone window. Who could possibly know?

Jack tried to laugh again but only made a sound like crackling paper.

But admitting that Glaucous was real was admitting as well that Jeremy Rohmer—Jack Rohmer—was special, had special talents, dreamed special dreams. Glaucous was no more a sufficient explanation of where he was, of what he was being asked to do, than Bidewell or Mnemosyne—whatever she or it might be. Maybe they were all the same. Madness needed no sequence, no rules.

They had not remembered him at the Busker Jam—not even Joe-Jim had remembered Jack at first. That blank look—and then the click of memory.

"You reconciled me, didn't you?"

Jack was really sweating.

"When was I made? Really."

What is your earliest memory?

The waterfront, cranes looming, the last light of day falling like burning gold between the gray warehouses—not much different from Bidewell's warehouse, though not as old. He saw a bumpy asphalt road overlying bricks and patched with gravel and concrete, broken up by bands of light—light, shadow, light, shadow, warming and cooling his face as he rode on his bike. And still, in his pocket, next to the stone . . .

Jack pulled out the origami puzzle, let his fingers work around the edges, poke through a cupped fold, pull at a tab he had not noticed before.

The sometime stone had arrived first—a long, long time before. The stone tied up past and future, called forth protectors, invoked his card number, the number that Glaucous had asked for—probably written on the inside of the puzzle he had not yet learned how to unfold.

Jack was just a book on a shelf in a library.

"I'm with *him*—in the dreams. I'm with the Librarian. He has my catalog number—all the numbers to all the volumes in a library that goes on forever. The Librarian started this.

"He's the author of my being. No surprise."

He opened the puzzle cleanly, without a single tear.

One problem.

As the puzzle kept unfolding, the number rolled across the floor and curled up the walls, surrounding him with ratcheting digits—longer than time.

Jack laughed out loud. "I was on the bike, right? That's my real first memory—the first time I appeared. That's why everyone has such a hard time remembering any of us—we're new, and you're still filling in the gaps."

Between those who reconcile, and those who see and judge, there is only love. Without you, the muses would not be necessary. And after you give up seeing, there is the joy of matter. But now that fades to nothing.

Jack wiped his eyes, stared down at the bead of moisture on his fingers. He did not know what the tears meant. A loss greater than death . . . the joy of *what*?

The greatest secret of all, and he would soon forget he had ever heard of it.

———

Daniel sat in the chair until the silence seemed to swallow him, and still he felt nothing, heard nothing.

He stood and walked around, rubbing his hands, and for a moment a bit of Fred came to him—a chain of thoughts about mathematics and physics. *Sum of all possible paths is the most efficient, the most probable path. Use the entire cosmos to generate all possible strings in a matrix of permutated texts. A universal library will help generate the most probable path. It's obvious.*

Daniel smiled grimly. "Good for you. You're still figuring things out. But none of it makes sense to me. This least of all."

Fred's thoughts bleached away.

"I'm Daniel!" he shouted to the high ceiling. "I've protected these stones since the beginning of time, across *all* the worlds! *You must know me!*"

Silence.

"I had a family. I had a brother. Lots of brothers. I remember them— some of them. I think one was named John or Sean. I didn't just jump up out of nowhere. I can tell you about what's coming—there's worse coming—if you're even here. But you're *not* here . . . are you?"

Falling dust outside, everywhere.

He slumped in the chair. The others would probably lie and say they'd had a nice chat with whomever, whatever. All a sham. Bidewell was pulling a hoax to get control of their stones. Maybe the old man had locked them in and was going to let them starve.

He murmured to the still, cool air, "I know who I am, even if *you* don't."

But now he wasn't at all sure.

Something changed in the corners. Daniel stiffened and sat up straight, peering bright-eyed into the shadows.

Remember. Very far—farther than anyone. From the outer reaches, hidden from all searchers, until you were brought to the main cord.

Remember.

His eyelids fluttered, his eyes closed, and he clenched his teeth. He saw a place, a huge construction made of something like stone sitting in a crater on a vast smooth plain, silent—silent for millions of years, if time had any meaning there. He saw himself moving from room to room without actually walking—first as a child, then as an adolescent, feeling so very lonely and empty—his growth not continuous, but accomplished by fading at one age, reappearing elsewhere, older and more complete.

And outside the house—lining the far, worn hills—huge beings without face or feature, held captive, never moving. Waiting to be summoned.

The Vale of Dead Gods.

Daniel was being forced to remember the impossible. He had been re-created and then stashed so far from any main sequence of reality

that his earliest memories were an agony. He had passed through so
much destruction to get here—but it was his origin that pained him the
most.

Two stones. Why?

The room changed again, and the confrontation he had dreaded—
believed impossible—came and went, so quickly he had to reach back
with sharp discipline to even recover it.

Daniel was freezing. What he did not want to remember—what
fogged his will, his intent—rose for an instant into memory and dictated
his responses.

You know me.

"Yes," he said.

But not as I am.

"No."

I am changing.

"Yes."

I am lost.

"You're dying. But we'll meet again. We meet on the shore of a silver
sea. That's all I remember."

The cold reached down into his bones.

Daniel sat in the chair, too cold even to shiver.

On the wooden floor before him lay a small round piece of glass.
First green, then blue. Foggy with age, as if it had lain on a beach,
rounded by an endless surge of sand and water. Maybe it wasn't glass.
He couldn't tell what it was, really. He reached down and held it for a
moment, turning it in his fingers, then slipped it in his pocket beside the
puzzle boxes.

Daniel looked around the silent, empty room. "Good-bye," he said.

———

Bidewell walked along the high narrow hallway and opened the doors
one by one, and out came Ginny first, more at peace than he had seen
her before. Next came Jack, thoughtful, but with a new light in his eyes.

Bidewell hesitated before the open middle door, then walked to
Daniel's chair, where he reached out to shake the man's hunched shoulder. Daniel stirred and opened his eyes. They were sharp as knives—the
wrong eyes for that face. "I fell asleep," he confessed, then stretched.

The third shepherd was still an enigma.

"We'll convene in a while," Bidewell said.

"Pretty interesting—a question—" Daniel began, but Bidewell raised his hand.

"No need. It's all private." Bidewell nodded three times, eyes flicking at three different random points in the high room, before passing through the door.

The moment is over, Bidewell thought, for which I have prepared for a thousand years.

CHAPTER 74

The Chaos

They had no choice. Another wave of dark marchers—dead, dying, or echoing timelessly—swarmed down from the ridge.

"They are too many and too strong," their armor told them. "The generator will not protect you."

Tiadba pulled up the device. The field dropped back into the ovoid, which sparked and hissed before falling dark. "Into the trees!" she shouted.

"They're not *trees*!" Denbord protested. "They'll kill us—you heard the armor!"

But there was no choice. Tiadba pushed her group forward. Denbord took the generator, slung it over his shoulder, and booted the cart aside, then pulled his clave from his belt—the first time they had tried to use this weapon. Tiadba did the same. The mottled black notched blades fanned out, spun, and almost vanished. Two walls of force flashed outward, defined by the angles of the blades—translucent one moment, but where they coincided, silvering like a mirror. In the mirror, which curved and whipped, the ground behind seemed to clear and the dark marchers fell back, fell away.

"We can kill them!" Denbord shouted, triumphant. He continued to wave his blade. Its field whipped around upon them. Their suits fluoresced a pale green at the near miss.

"Keep that away from us!" Macht shouted.

The breeds instinctively pushed toward the shimmering trees—there were simply too many echoes rising and spilling over the ridge, thousands of years of lost marchers massing against those still alive. The more the claves cut, the more there were. Tiadba had sudden doubts their weapons were that effective. She saw that the claves fended off the 'dark marchers only temporarily—they broke apart, vanished, then seemed to rise again from the black ground.

Khren was the first to push between the trees, the pearl-colored balls of light on the branches popping and snapping as he brushed them. Yet the trees did not chew up their armor, in fact wrapped branches and trunks around them, causing great fear—until they saw the branches close up behind, projecting a curtain of glinting drops as delicate as dew. The dark marchers did not follow. This was completely unlike the generator's bubble shield, but apparently more effective.

Tiadba, Khren, and Denbord led the others deeper into the forest, until they reached a clearing. Tiadba tumbled over Khren when he stopped, and Macht over them. As they untangled, the others dropped to their knees, murmuring prayers, weeping, then collapsing on the soft gray surface, while all around the trees rose twice as tall as their heads, slender fronds growing up and over, forming a bower and giving them cover as they caught their breath.

Tiadba rolled on her back, still expecting to die—or worse. All her marcher training and instincts seemed unreliable, blacked out by fear that reached deep into the old matter that made her. What had they gotten themselves into? How many more terrors would they face, much worse than this?

Were they even safe here, with cover and apparent protection, the Chaos held back, frustrated?

Macht wept for Perf. "He went just like the Tall One. Just sparked away."

"He was slow," Denbord said.

Macht took offense and moved on him with fists clenched, but Herza and Frinna held him back, and together they all collapsed to the ground once more, coughing out little howls of misery.

Tiadba sat apart, too exhausted to join in. Nico recovered first and looked around through his faceplate, unable to believe they weren't still being followed.

"What is this place?" Tiadba asked the armor. No answer.

"The armor doesn't want to help us," Macht said. "It's useless."

"Maybe it can't talk about what it doesn't know," Shewel said.

"The armor didn't save Perf—it didn't tell him what to do!"

"Everything out here changes," Nico said. "The trainer said—"

"Then why let it speak at all?" Macht shouted. "What use is it to *any* of us?" He kicked and thumped his arms and hands on the gray ground, a crèche-born gesture of anger and irritation that they understood too well.

Denbord crawled over and flopped down beside Tiadba. "I don't know whether we're safe or just in the belly of something different."

Tiadba felt the gray surface and noticed that her armored fingers did not produce the faint glow of adjustment they had observed in the Chaos. "The suits aren't working very hard," she said. "Maybe there's a generator nearby."

"I don't see anything," Nico said. "Just the purple, and those branches. I don't like the way they glow."

Shewel joined them and lay on his back. They all seemed to want to stay low and not touch the branches, growing ever thicker.

One positive: they could no longer see the burning crescent.

"Nobody said this would be easy," Denbord offered, his voice quavering, not at all convinced a show of bravery was appropriate—certainly not false bravery. Macht stared at them all with large, round eyes. Herza and Frinna sat beside each other, clutching hands.

They all sucked in their breaths.

Silence—no more words—seemed best. Tiadba examined her gloved fingers, felt the suit drying and soothing her twitching, itching skin, the most comfortable clothing she had ever worn. The armor was still working, then.

Slowly she let her fear burn itself out, leaving only a hollow grief and, like Macht, disappointment. If the others looked up to her as some sort of example, a leader . . .

After a while the branches stopped growing and everything became still.

"If we're in a belly, there's nothing we can do about it," Tiadba said. "Better here than out there."

"We can't stay here forever," Denbord said.

"We know that," Macht said. "Just shut up and let us be sad."

"Maybe this is a mourning place," Nico said, ever the philosophical one.

Tiadba looked left, to the edge of the clearing, just a few yards away, between the smooth brown trunks that had so quickly branched out. The glowing tips gave off a dim yellow light. She wasn't sure they would be able to escape through that thicket.

No shadows, no motion, no threat—and no promise.

Then she thought she must be dreaming. The branches parted, the glowing tips formed an arch—and through them stepped a Tall One, wearing nothing but a kind of curtus—smudged, torn, mended with what might have been lengths of twig.

The Tall One approached close enough in the dim light that they could see him clearly. All of them stared in astonishment.

"What is this?" Tiadba whispered, but again the suit had no answer.

He looked a great deal like their trainer, Pahtun, but then, to breeds, Tall Ones tended to resemble one another. He approached and knelt, his dirty face impassive, eyes examining but incurious, as if he was not surprised to find them in this place but felt no immediate concern over their intentions.

"What is this?" Tiadba asked, louder. "Where are we?"

The Tall One shook his head. Then he spoke.

Their helmets suddenly split and fell around their shoulders, making Denbord cry out and cover his eyes and mouth, until he realized he was not dying.

The breeds gasped—the air was thin but sweet enough.

The Tall One said, "They recognize me and they follow my orders. Poor things." He stroked Tiadba's shoulder—not her, but the armor she wore. "Out of date. Obsolete, actually. Breaking down under the stress."

Khren said, "One of us has already died."

They stood and their heads were of a height with the Tall One's shoulders.

"I am Pahtun," he said.

"Pahtun is dead," Macht said.

"There will always be Pahtuns," the Tall One said. "Where did he die?"

"In the zone of lies," Nico said. They all nodded agreement.

The Tall One nodded. "A grand object lesson—don't you think? I made many copies and broke many rules to help the marchers. If breeds reach my cache, they deserve rest, instruction, better forecasts of Chaos weather . . . knowledge not available in the Kalpa. And we should re-fresh and upgrade your armor, don't you think?"

"That would be good," Macht said. "But I don't believe you—not one bit. Pahtun told us not to trust things like you." He spoke reason-ably, without anger, but his face was tense.

The Tall One reached up, touched his own nose, and made the sound Pahtun had made when amused—a rumbling, crackling exhala-tion, somewhat upsetting to a breed. "Good instincts," he said. "But if I were a monster, even your poor old damaged armor would have warned you. How are things back in the city? We can't see it from here, of course."

"Bad," Tiadba said. "Very bad."

"Well, it had to be. The Typhon grows restless, ever stronger, and wants to have done with us. Any more breeds coming after you?"

"We don't know," she said. "Maybe not."

"Then all the more reason to get this thing done," Pahtun said. "These shrubs will only last a short while. I trained them myself—grew them from old ground. They're primordial matter, just like you—and me. Good thing you broke through . . . if you had gone around, you would have crossed a trod, and the Silent Ones have been busy of late. Follow me."

He got to his feet, towering over them, and held out his arms. "Con-gratulations, one and all! You've made it this far."

CHAPTER 75

The Green Warehouse

Throughout the warehouse the book group women were arranging their own cots in preparation for the night that was not even remotely a night. For though dark had fallen, and Ginny could see two stars gleam-ing through the skylight, *they were the same two stars*. The Earth was not moving. Sun and moon had not changed their positions in the sky.

Ginny reluctantly arranged the blankets on her cot and sat, sur-rounded by her pitiful cubicle of stacked boxes, exhausted, ready for sleep—but she knew what would happen if she laid down and closed her eyes. She dreaded this part of the dream: the separation (though Jack was asleep just a few yards away—she could hear him faintly snoring); the journey through the . . . she couldn't remember what it was. Great gray walls and dusty floors.

If only I could put it all in sequence!

Minimus crept through a crack between the boxes and leaped onto the cot. Ginny let the cat lie across her lap, purring contentment and watching her with the royal concern only a cat can show—aloof, alert, curious only out of politeness.

With Minimus she felt safer, but the cat could not go with her into the dark behind her eyelids—the unwanted world that opened just a crack and rustle beyond.

Finally, she could stay awake no longer. She heard the cat jump down but did not care. She was so tired of trying to understand and take control of her life.

And so, for a few unclocked moments—a brief interlude in a slice of world bereft of real time—she gave up, gave in. She let the out-of-sequence existence she so dreaded wash over her, fill her up. Every time she closed her eyes—anytime she had to rest, to sleep—until her two lives were combined and *reconciled*—this would be her sacrifice, her misery.

Yes, yes—I've dreamed those things before. Move on!

Take me out into the Chaos—send me to the False City—abandon me— get it over with!

———

The women gathered around the stove. None could sleep. "How long do we have?" Agazutta asked Bidewell. She had recovered her dignity, but there were dark circles under her eyes, and her red hair was in complete disarray.

Bidewell handed them all cups of chamomile tea.

Miriam came last into the darkened, stove-lit room, having checked on Jack and Ginny, and—she murmured to Ellen—having made sure that Daniel and Glaucous were in their closet.

Bidewell held his answer until all the women had gathered. Most sat on the old wooden chairs—Agazutta remained standing. Farrah lay back on the overstuffed chair, languid as always, but her eyes flicked at every noise, and her hands clutched the padded chair arms.

"Not long," Bidewell said. "I haven't told the children. From this point, things will decay rapidly. I have deeply valued your company."

"But not our judgment," Farrah said with a sniff. "Letting those bastards in. Why?"

Bidewell stared up at the high rafters and shook his head. "The stones choose."

"How do you know Glaucous?" Agazutta asked.

Bidewell made a disgusted grimace. "Him I could have predicted."

"If he's a hunter, why let him in?"

"No answer I give will ever suffice . . . but the sum-runners pick their companions."

"More like *create* them, right?" Ellen asked, her hands making small lost movements to her cheek, her chin. They all jumped at another sharp crack and grind from outside the walls.

"Not to be known," Agazutta said wearily.

Bidewell looked down and there were tears on his cracked, rugged cheeks, which shocked them all. "I know this much. The shepherds as confirmed by Mnemosyne are by text, out of text—text is central. The sum-runners have mazed their courses throughout all the world-lines, traveling all possible avenues, even the most unlikely, and now they have arrived, summed—come to our attention . . . and out of themselves, vaster than anything we can imagine, they have made guardians. Even Daniel, though that is not certain."

"A false one, perhaps," Miriam said.

"We do not know that," Bidewell said. "Though his proximity to Glaucous—worrying, certainly. For centuries, there have been rumors of a bad shepherd . . . But I have never met him, or her."

"What's a bad shepherd?" Agazutta asked, combing her fingers through her hair.

"A traveler working his way forward, through other shepherds. Using them. Bringing more than just a stone—bringing something else, for his own motives."

"Sounds charming," Farrah said.

Bidewell held his hands over the iron stove, then examined his fingers. "As always, I apologize for my ignorance, ladies," he murmured. "But as you say, our time is limited. I sense restlessness. I can assure you the opportunities outside are very limited."

"They've made up their minds," Ellen said.

"Who is going?"

Agazutta raised her hand. "Children, grown and moved out—France, Japan, far away, but maybe they've left messages for me at home. Maybe there's still a way to speak to them. I have to try."

Miriam raised hers. "I need to get back to the clinic—if it's still there. My patients must be scared out of their wits. My staff . . . They've been with me for years."

Farrah stood and stretched. "I'm alone," she said. "But I'll go with Agazutta and Miriam, just to watch out for them."

"I'll stay," Ellen said. "Whether I'm needed here or not—no one out there needs me."

"Not even us?" Agazutta said. "Is this the end of the Witches of Eastlake?"

"It's been good," Ellen said. "You are all the best friends, the finest adventurers one could hope for."

"Well, it ain't over . . ."

"Until I sing," Farrah said.

The women exchanged hugs. More tears were shed. Then they took up their bags and purses, and Bidewell escorted them to the northern door.

"You have your books?" he asked. "Do not lose them. Keep them close at all times."

They gave him wry looks. "Slender tomes," Agazutta said.

"What does 1298 mean?" Farrah asked.

"They are your stories, dear ladies," Bidewell said, "penned long ago in Latin, by your obedient servant, copying from even older texts—scrolls that were burned at Herculaneum. So long as you keep your stories near, you will be afforded some protection. I do not suggest reading ahead or skipping to the end—not yet."

"Will we get out of this alive?" Farrah asked.

Bidewell lightly snorted, but gave no answer.

Miriam opened the door to the outside. The air over the city had cleared a little. "Oh, look," she said with a sigh. "It isn't raining."

"What will happen to the rest of you?" Agazutta asked, taking Bidewell by the elbow as they walked down the ramp side by side.

"*That* is well known," Bidewell said. "I am marked. I have been in the fray too long to go unnoticed, and so . . . I fear all our fates hinge on the outcome, and before that arrives, we must enter a kind of storage, along with this city—all cities, all histories, all times. The world out here is not the only record, and not the final version in the edit."

Agazutta shook her head in wistful irritation. "I've never understood you, or why we did all this."

"I'm a seductive fellow," Bidewell said.

"That you are," Miriam said, and kissed his cheek.

The gate was opened, and three of the Witches of Eastlake departed into the grayness, holding bags or purses, and their books, before them. They left their youngest, Ellen, standing beside the ancient man with wet cheeks, who looked even older now.

"We should go back in," Ellen said, peering after the figures. They were limned by barely visible halos, and the flickering of the sky—the leaning and grinding of the walls—slowed as they departed.

"It will not long matter where any of us stands," Bidewell said.

Ellen grasped his face and looked straight into his eyes. "You didn't tell them. You think things have gone wrong."

"In the short run, now equal to any long run, we are all together. There are only two fates, two paths remaining. We shall all be moved along one path or the other—to be reconciled and ordered in our conclusions by Mnemosyne, or played with by the Chalk Princess as she sees fit. And it is our visiting children who will steer us, ultimately."

He pulled himself straight and waved his hands at the curtain of gloom where the women had passed. "I wish them well," he said. "It is cold out here." He closed the door but did not shoot the bolt home. "We have been dealt all our cards."

CHAPTER 76

The Chaos

The branches swung aside as this Pahtun—he had no other name—led them deeper into the trees. Tiadba knew they would never be able to find their way out. The branches had parted reluctantly, and then tried to enclose them, perhaps as defense. And the armor no longer responded to her commands to close up and form a seal. Obviously, the Tall One was in charge, and seemed to know what he was doing.

Macht wore a steady scowl, and Denbord had frozen his face in a look of insolence, though he said nothing. They had already been through too much.

"Did you try out your claves?" Pahtun asked. "How effective were they?" The Tall One spun about, arms extended, and the tips of the branches overhead brightened almost into wakelight.

"We tried them," Denbord said. "They were hard to manage. But some of the old marchers fell back—the dead ones, I mean, whatever they were. They fell apart."

"Echoes, no doubt. They're thick around here."

"Were they dead?" Tiadba asked.

"Perhaps not dead, but most unfortunate. They might have been versions of *you* who made wrong choices and got trapped, their fates snared and looped by the Typhon. The Typhon uses whatever it captures or finds. Not a pleasant end. No end at all, from what I've seen over the past few tens of thousands of wakes. I work out here, save what I learn, and pass it along to such as get this far."

"How many breeds have survived?" Denbord asked.

Nico lifted his hands in a counting prayer.

"I'm not sure. A hundred . . . fewer." Pahtun touched the ground and a box rose up, about the size of a clothes box. Walking around it, he scratched his palms, spoke a few soft words, jerked his head. The box responded and its sides fell open. Within, thin branches spun and grew with dizzying speed, throwing sharp little sparks. They were miniature versions of the trees that surrounded and covered them.

"Take off your suits. Lay them out on the ground. Once they air out, we'll throw them in here." He pointed at the spinning mass in the box. "Your armor will be remade and improved—new knowledge, better guidance. And then you'll go. I'll be breaking this camp and fleeing myself. The trod is close, and I don't want to be caught by a Silent One. Besides, we're all much too near the Witness."

"How is that possible?" Tiadba asked. "We were let out into the Chaos far from there."

"Distance, angle, the metric—all changing, I'm afraid. And it isn't getting any easier to plan and prepare for."

He gestured with his hands, flower finger prominent, and one by one, reluctantly, they peeled off their suits—all but Macht—and laid them on the ground. Herza and Frinna stayed close to the box, as if comforted by its apparently benign mystery. Shewel joined them.

Pahtun gathered the suits and flung them into the spinning branches, where they sizzled and vanished. He waited for Macht to make up his mind.

"Tall magic," Denbord said, with a wink and a nod, and then touched his nose. He still did not believe, but what else could they do? The protection was obvious—if temporary.

"Just do it," Tiadba instructed Macht. He glared at her but finally handed his suit to this Pahtun, who dropped it into the silvery tangle.

———

The breeds lay mostly naked around the box and took turns telling of the last large intrusion, the damage to the Kalpa, their training, the end of the first Pahtun, the starboats in the valley that went away, the shattered ghosts of cities, the strange way light moved out here.

And the echoes.

"No doubt Perf is with them now," Macht said, and Nico knelt and tented his hands, a prayer of supplication—though to what, out here, no one could say.

Pahtun listened intently, though Tiadba suspected he had heard such tales before. "You've done well against all odds, young breeds," he said. "Good to know we can still shape such as you. But the city is ignorant about much of the Chaos—always has been. I can't go back, nor can I communicate what I know, because the city must not take such a chance. We might be products of the Typhon, after all, made to misinform."

"That's what the trainer told us," Macht said, and looked miserable.

"*Might* be," Pahtun emphasized. "Use your instincts—they are so much better tuned than those of any Mender or Eidolon. Closer to the primordial Earth, closer to the truth. Am I of the Chaos?"

"No," Denbord finally said, and Tiadba agreed. The others kept silent.

"Well, some believe, some are suspicious; all good. None of you can be right all the time. Here is what I can tell you. The trods shift and grow. There are any number of them out there, pulling in tighter—most of them pointing to a great crater, cut through by a vale that extends almost halfway around what remains of the Earth. I've seen a few strange things gather and grow out there—I don't know what they are, or what they might do. The Chaos lets them accumulate, for now. I've heard Eidolons call them 'Turvies'—singular, 'Turvy.' The angelins in the Broken Tower can sometimes see that far, tricks of Chaos light being in their favor. They surround your goal, Nataraja."

"Does it still exist?" Nico asked.

"Let's hope," Pahtun said. "If it doesn't, then all our efforts have been wasted. The Great Eidolons, in their wisdom, exiled important persons to that rebel city—and with them, I hear, they carried important tools."

"What?" Nico asked, eyes bright.

"Only they would know. The Librarian's tale—have you been told that one, young breeds?"

"No," they said.

"Not all of it," Nico added.

Tiadba lifted the books, which she had kept strapped within the leg pouch of her armor. "Maybe we don't need to know," she said.

Several times, Pahtun had glanced at the books with something like hunger. "I doubt that your ignorance would help anyone," he said. "It's part of the great story, the greatest story of all. But you, young breed—your name is Tiadba, is it not?"

She had not told him. Perhaps he'd learned it from her armor. "Yes," she said.

"Read for us, why don't you? We have time, and I haven't heard a marcher's story in ever so long."

She opened her book and found a passage by Sangmer that described his crew, and their journey in the starboat across the last winding reaches of space and time.

THE FIRST OF ISHANAXADE

Even surrounded by the beauty of the Shen necklace-worlds and the clever arts gathered in past times from all the living galaxies, my crew could only feel pity at what we had seen—and dread at the thought of traveling back through those ruined spaces. Whatever we brought back with us—whomever we transported—the return journey would be even more difficult.

While Polybiblios made his preparations—shedding his Shen selves and returning to Deva unity—I walked along the grainy margins of the basin wherein the Shen had stored their discoveries. Here, glistening like a soft jade ocean beneath the banded glow of the greatest ringstar, lay the pooled fate-logs of Shen travels during the Brightness, before the end of creation, their information long since scrambled and irretrievable—but still beautiful.

I sought quiet, a lonely kind of peace, but better than contemplating our almost certain oblivion in the Chaos.

My crew was amusing itself by visiting the shrines of Shen accomplishment—erected by human students from worlds long since eaten by the Chaos. The Shen acknowledged no gifts, accepted no reverence; not even to the extent of refusing or demolishing these tributes. Abandoned in scenic disrepair, the monuments rose or fell at the shivery whim of this huge pseudo-planet.

The Shen had been the first to map the five hundred living galaxies, the first to link the ancient barren whorls of dying suns into ringstars, the first to do so many things. And here was that dead, glistening sea of exploration and knowledge, lapping on a beach of whispering grains, a mockery of all who have ever sought glory.

With only my dark thoughts as company, I stripped my garments and walked out onto the vectors, feeling them coil like jelly-crystal, cool and silver around my ankles, seeking the glow of my order—but unable to share or partake. They fell back with lost whispers, a muddle just on the edge of sense, as if they might still be capable of retelling lost tales. Melancholy to match my own—and no one else's, I thought, until I saw what at first I took to be a small young female, walking toward me from a mile or so farther along the strand.

This was an impossibility: a human-seeming figure on a world where only my crew claimed humanity; my crew, humble Menders all, and of course the Deva Polybiblios.

The girl could have been a young Mender, but none of my kind had been born and raised in such a way, through incarnate infancy and youth, for tens of trillions of years.

As she grew close, I waded to the shore, then knelt on the margin to caress the tiny, rounded bits washed up there, glowing with a soft green radiance. I watched this girl-child from the corner of my eye, helpless—feeling that a truly irreversible moment approached.

But there could be no retreat.

"Are you the Pilgrim?" the child asked when her voice could be heard above the whispers.

"Some call me that. Who were you?" I thought she might be a ghost of vector history, brought back by some contribution I had made to the bright-roiled sea—a bit of shed skin, tricked up by forces far beyond Mender understanding.

"I am, not were. I have no finished name. The Shen have bequeathed me to a human I will call Father. He has gathered my parts in this sea, like these pieces on the shore, and helped shape them into what you see now."

"Are you human?" I asked.

"Mostly," she said. "My father pledges me to Gens Simia through Deva lineage."

Close as she was, her features had not yet settled. She showed many graceful possibilities, yet seemed neither hurried nor embarrassed by this multiplicity.

"How are we to be introduced?"

"I have a Shen name, but that is little better than none."

"What else are you, besides human?" I asked, trying not to sound rude.

"I'm not sure. Polybiblios assures me I contain elements of the forces that once helped shape and resolve creation. The Shen found them, collected them, and deposited them in this sea, for Father to rediscover and shape. How he could fit such large ideas into this small form, I don't know. Can you see them?"

"I don't see anyone or anything clearly."

She assumed a determined face, and her outline sharpened, but then she grew larger, too large, rising above the vector sea many times my height.

I looked up, charmed by this metric naiveté.

"It must feel important to be a vessel of creation's glory," I said, shading my eyes against the brilliant light of the ringstar.

"Most of the time, I can't feel it," she admitted. "But sometimes I lose control and try to fix things, or bring logic—to correct. As I mature, I'll control myself and take reliably solid form, like you, I think. Your form is pleasing. That's what Polybiblios tells me."

"Are you a reward, then? A gift from Shen masters to Deva student?"

"My father does seem to bear me great affection." She had fallen in altitude and was now just a little taller than me, and already appeared more mature. "I think he wants to study what I will become."

She dipped her toe into the vector sea and rose-red waves spread outward, as if by herself she could revive all that had ever been lost. "If I stay here, the Shen can't or won't give me what I need. I will become another abandoned memory, like this sea. And then—what's left will perish when the Shen succumb to the Chaos."

My melancholy evaporated. She breathed out newness, freshness—radiated a potential for joy unlike anything I had ever experienced. This glamour had its own adaptive properties, no doubt, but what could she ever be to a Mender?

She drew close and extended a star-bright hand. "Polybiblios says the captain of the twistfold ship must extend an invitation to join the voyage back to Earth. He tells me there are dangers. It is your decision, Pilgrim."

I could feel the ancient forces like a fire heating my eyes and skin. What had once been abstruse history and theory—a lost muse, condensed and scattered at the end of the Brightness—stood before me, real and vivid, though transparent.

"You're still a kind of ghost," I said. "You probably won't take up much space, or consume many units of support."

"I don't eat at all—yet. But I will. I might eat you, Pilgrim." She seemed very mature now, with eyes bold and deep and golden. "Perhaps I will learn my true name on your ship. Perhaps you will help my father find it for me."

I was already more than half in love.

———

Exhausted, mind spinning with things she could not possibly understand, Tiadba glanced around the circle of marchers. All looked puzzled, struggling with mysteries and words far beyond their experience. The Pahtun made a low grumbling noise, then shook his great head. "It's a very old tale," he said. "Not sure I believe any of it."

"That's the way it reads," Tiadba said, defensive.

"Oh, I don't doubt that," the Pahtun said. "So many marchers, so many tales. I've often wondered how the Eidolons came to be the way they are, and how Ishanaxade came to be what *she* is . . . but those are other stories, and maybe I still don't know the truth of it."

"It makes a sort of sense," Nico said valiantly. "We'll have to read the books later. See if the stories change."

"I don't know that the stories change," Tiadba said, not for the first time. "Maybe my understanding changes."

"Time to teach us all to read the old letters," Denbord insisted.

"We'd like that," Herza and Frinna said, to Tiadba's surprise.

"Fat chance," Macht said, and yawned.

"If there's time," the Pahtun said. "The armor will be ready soon."

———

Something like a drowse—but far from sleep—came over Tiadba for the first time since they had left the training camp to cross the border of the real. She could not be certain she was having a dream, or finding a strange kind of memory. She thought she was in a large room surrounded by shelves of books, two or three times taller than the shelves in the upper Tiers. She saw four women—large women by her standards, but how was she to judge? She was small—they were large. They moved around her, talking among themselves—deeply concerned.

———

She broke her trance with a gasp and looked up to see the Pahtun pulling pieces of armor from the spinning branches at the center of the bower and assembling their new suits. He placed them in standing positions, knitting limbs to trunks using a small sphere gripped by his flower finger. He was blowing air through his lips with a musical succession of notes, not what Tiadba would call a tune. Observed, he finished what he was doing and winked at her, then touched his nose. But he looked worried—if she was any judge of the expressions assumed by Tall Ones.

As the others gathered beside the reassembled suits, Pahtun—so like his namesake, she decided she could not detect any difference, other than the smudges and ragged apparel—walked around the circle and passed his hands up and down, making each suit glow.

"They're finished," he announced. "Fresher, more informed, as promised. Now, put them on quickly. There's no time. The trod is shifting, and we will soon find ourselves right in the middle."

The marchers quickly donned their new suits, moving about to try the fit. They felt little difference at first; Tiadba's seemed slightly stiffer, that was all.

The Pahtun confined the spinning branches. The box reduced itself until he could pick it up, and he slung it in a piece of fabric that hung from his shoulder.

"You don't wear a suit," Tiadba said.

He waved one hand. "The bower is my armor. Watch yourselves—it's about to collapse, and I will vanish with it. Stand aside. We will not encounter each other again, I hope. If we do, we will all have failed. Your armor will be more responsive and informative and even stronger, but remember, there is worse to come. Above all, believe I am real. Don't think I was never here."

The bower burned away, exposing the rucked-up sky and the long red-purple arc of fire. Tiadba's helmet rose around her head and the faceplate colored, tinting the scene orange as all about them the branches broke into violet flame, too bright to look upon.

They stood on rolling black ground, and she heard the others stifle cries of dismay. They were back in the Chaos. For a moment Tiadba thought she saw a tall, slender figure move rapidly away, a flash of white limbs—a nimbus of glowing, spinning branches surrounding a Tall One—a lone Mender.

"Marchers on alert," their armor warned. "Listen for your beacon."

She heard it now—a steady musical pulse, stronger as she faced in one direction, weaker in all the others. And she recognized the armor's new voice.

It was Pahtun's.

Denbord and Khren approached her, and then the others. They formed a circle, facing outward, and realized each could see what the others were seeing, allowing better judgment of their surroundings—many eyes combined at once, a strange sensation.

"Did the Tall One squeeze himself into all our suits, or did he just pick up and leave?" Macht asked.

"Let's hope he was real," Nico said, "and we're not laid out on this black stuff, naked, dinner for monsters."

"Follow your beacons," the armor insisted. "Much distance to cover, and quickly. All this region is uneasy. Silent Ones always seek what defies the Typhon."

"March!" Tiadba said, and with greater confidence and greater alertness, they followed the pulsing tones, forming a wavering line that soon drew straight, Tiadba in front, Khren taking up the rear.

All of them could see what she saw ahead, around: a low green light that flickered and rose in spikes, as if to touch the sky.

Their steps slowed and they felt oddly heavy. From their right, something loomed and passed too quickly to see—something huge, broad, and flat, flying past on high, slender pillars that pulled up the ground ahead and behind—and then it was gone.

"It had a face," Khren said. "A human face. Bigger than a meadow..."

"Move quickly," the armor instructed. "Distance will close in, light will move in unfamiliar ways, and things will seem to burn. Above all, follow the beacon."

Off to the left, Tiadba saw a swinging gray sword of light, brighter than before: the glowing beam sent out from the Witness.

"We're right under it," Nico said. "How did we get so close? Wasn't it on the other side?"

"We should set up our generator and wait for it to go away," Macht said.

"No!" the armor insisted. "You are being hunted. There is no shelter here. There is only escape."

CHAPTER 77

The Green Warehouse

Jack knelt beside Ginny's bed and put his hand on her arm. She had been sleeping for hours, even after the pewter light of whatever passed for dawn touched the windows beneath the warehouse roof. At his touch, she shifted on the cot, then opened her eyes and looked beyond him. The peace after her time in the room had passed. The gnawing worry and fear were back—especially in sleep. She was sleeping so much now. Jack, on the other hand, was mostly wide-awake. His dreams since being in the empty room had been brief and uneventful.

"They're huge," she murmured. "They're like stingrays, but they have faces on one side. Arms and legs make dimples in the road as they skim along, like water striders on a pond. They shoot by too fast to see, unless they see you first—and if they catch you, it's over."

Jack wiped a tear from his cheeks, feeling emotions that were not his own, not yet. "Where are you?" he asked.

"We're miles from the city—I don't know how far. It's always night out here, always dark. The sun doesn't cast any light—it's just a glimmer on the edge. We don't even have real shadows. The armor says the Chaos here is thin—some of the old rules still survive. We can even take off our helmets and breathe the air. But it freezes your lungs if you suck it in. Fur on the nose—good thing." She looked around, as if trying to locate his face, seeing neither the warehouse nor Jack. "Is anything coming?"

"I don't know," he said, his face contorted. "You're way ahead of me."

"The beacon still sings in our helmets, so beautiful . . . that's the only thing that guides us. Distance is tricky, but we keep walking. I think it knows we're here, it just doesn't care. It's stuffed full. It's eaten almost everything . . . but we're giving it indigestion. It's won, but it's keeping an eye on us—a big, big eye. The Witness is always there. God, I hope we don't get too near it."

"What's that?" Jack asked.

"No words for it. The other city isn't . . . It isn't the same. There's something awful in its place. I know that, but I can't tell her. Jack . . . *She doesn't know*."

Jack laid his head on Ginny's chest, put his hand over her eyes. That searching, distant gaze . . .

"I'll be there," he whispered.

"Too late," she said. "They've found us."

She fell back on the cot. Jack stroked her forehead, then stood. He couldn't bear watching her suffer and being so powerless. He bumped the boxes on his way out of the cubicle.

Bidewell was sitting in a chair near the stove, reading a slender green book. The old man's face looked ethereal, as if it might turn to mist or glass. Ellen stepped out of the main warehouse, carrying a knitted bag with the outline of her own small book weighting one corner.

"Where are the others?" Jack asked.

"There's nothing they can do here," Bidewell said. "They're trying to reach their loved ones."

"I thought they were alone," Jack said.

"Only you are ever truly alone," Bidewell said, with a strange twist of envy. "Our time is almost over, for this cycle. Yours is just beginning."

Ellen looked at Jack, at once hopeful and stricken. He saw that both of them had been crying and felt uncomfortable, so he moved on and found Daniel sitting under the almost bare shelves in the annex room, paging through a large, thick book. Daniel looked as exhausted as Jack felt. Somehow, that made him more sympathetic.

Daniel put the book aside as Jack approached. "I heard the door open," he said.

"Three of the women took off," Jack said. He examined Daniel's expression, looking for any sign of strangeness, but could not find anything to dislike or even be suspicious of. That was Glaucous's doing, he suspected. He recognized the symptoms, more subtle but still the same. Why would Glaucous protect Daniel?

Shaping him as a new partner, perhaps?

"I don't hear much outside," Daniel said. "And there's certainly nothing new in here. Let's go topside for another look."

For the moment, the curtains and wrinkles above the city had parted, leaving an inky blackness and a sky full of stars, but something was very wrong. The stars, like the moon, had smeared, twisted, wrapped themselves in rainbow-colored rings—and were growing dimmer.

One by one they were winking out like spent fireflies.

"They're being eaten," Jack said. "The moon, the stars . . ."

"You got that right," Daniel said. "But we have to think it through—*what*'s being eaten? *When* is it being eaten? I can believe the moon being sucked up by whatever *that* is, that ugly sun-arc thing—we'd see that almost right away, but the stars are too distant. Unless . . ." He wiped his forehead. "Unless the past was chewed up first. That would mean everything behind us has already been eaten, space *and* time . . . Those stars are already gone, the last wave of their light is bouncing off the Terminus—and now *it's* fading. We're like the core of an apple, the seeds, being saved for last."

"Seeds," Jack said. "That's what Bidewell calls the stones."

"None of what he says makes sense, Jack."

Jack persisted. "Still, things are reaching back from somewhere."

Daniel thought this through, brow wrinkled, plump cheeks growing pale. He gave Jack a pinched look, part disbelief, part envy. "Okay, magic boy. You know something."

"It's obvious. We're being messed with—someone sent the stones back, like Bidewell says."

"Like he *hints*," Daniel corrected.

"And the thing that controls the hunters—the Chalk Princess, Glaucous's Livid Mistress—that could be from the future, too. But what's messing with us is no longer *in* the future. We're being shoved up *against* the future—what's left of it. Right?"

"With you so far," Daniel said, intrigued that Jack was suddenly engaging in theory.

"So we're just getting the last ripples of aftereffect. Whatever's going to happen, *has* happened—here. Except for the warehouse—and us."

"Because of the stones, or Bidewell's weird library?"

They both stared at the fragmented city, beyond shock, even beyond wonder, and then stared at each other, expressing their only remaining surprise: that they were still alive, still thinking, still speaking.

"Maybe both," Jack said. "We're saved—for the moment. But that moment is going to be awfully short. And then we're going to have to do something."

"What?" Daniel asked.

Jack shook his head.

The cityscape around the warehouse had congealed into a bleakness of broken buildings, sluggish flows of muddy water, torn, ragged clouds barely obscuring the battered sky. The last limb of the hideous arc of fire dropped below the horizon and the clouds glowed blood-red, then dimmed to somber brown, their undersides fitfully illuminated by curling wisps of orange and green.

"The whole city is a grab bag of past and present," Daniel said. "If you're right, it could mean this Chalk Princess is still out there—waiting for things to settle before she comes and gets us. Glaucous has a weird confidence."

"He's protecting you," Jack said.

"Is he? How strange. I don't need protecting." He poked and rubbed one temple with a thumb. "I don't see any sign of the women who left. Your friends."

Glaucous made sure Daniel and Jack were out of the way, then approached Ginny's cubicle. With batlike acuity, he could hear her moving about from across the warehouse.

Ginny blinked and looked confused as he drew back the flimsy curtain. "I don't want you near me," she warned, her tongue thickened by the long, hard sleep. "I'll call for help."

"Abject apologies for my crude appearance and manners," Glaucous said. He glanced up. "The young men are on the roof, satisfying curiosity. They seem to be learning to trust each other."

"Jack knows better," Ginny said, still blinking—whether from nerves or irritation, she couldn't tell. Everything felt gritty. Everything seemed to be running down—even her brain.

"Perhaps. At any rate, I am no threat," Glaucous said softly. "In fact, I eliminated the ones who came here to hunt you. The man with his coin, the woman with her flames and smoke. A dreadful pair. I have my allegiances, of course—and they may not match yours. But with no leadership, I am no more a threat than one of these warehouse cats. You are not *my* mouse. Whom would I deliver you to? And why?"

"Please go away," Ginny said.

"Not before I salve my conscience. You have misplaced your trust, and now I fear the worst. Bidewell has hidden himself for many decades, but we—my kind, hunters all—knew him long before that. He was legendary among us."

"He's been kind to me."

"We do have that ability, to be charming when we wish, despite all other appearances. Can you feel that between us, even now?" He looked down, raised his hand to his forehead as if ashamed. "Pardon. It's an instinct, misplaced no doubt. I will withdraw it immediately." He shut down the treacle ambience.

Ginny stepped back, even more confused.

"I will come no closer, and I will leave soon. But I must tell you . . . in the spirit of an honorable hunt, which must soon resume. Bidewell brought you all here for the same reason I attached myself to the one who calls himself Daniel—a strange fellow, don't you feel it? Not what he seems. Very ancient. We call his like bad shepherds—but no matter. Whoever possesses a stone exudes an atmosphere of protection, and provides others a pass to the next level of this astonishing endgame. As do you, young Virginia. Here's the pattern, the picture of our next few blinks of time. I will complete my part in the game, and Bidewell will complete his. He will deliver you to his mistress, and I will deliver Daniel and Jack to mine."

"I don't believe anything you say," Ginny murmured, but her eyes indicated otherwise. She had never been good at trust.

"Pardon me for speaking truth," Glaucous said. "But even among my kind, there are rules."

Glaucous backed out and let the curtain fall, then returned to the storage room, his face stony and gray.

CHAPTER 78

The Chaos

Under the Witness's eternal gaze, the Silent Ones had almost skimmed down upon the breeds when the entire land seemed to erupt with geysers and fountains of sooty darkness. The huge, flattened faces with their darting, ever-searching eyes—reminiscent of Tall Ones, breeds, and other varieties unknown to the marchers—had suddenly pulled away, leaving Tiadba and her companions spilled on the black ground, waiting for doom . . . doom delayed.

Tiadba withdrew her arm from her faceplate and saw that Khren and Shewel were already up on their knees. Herza and Frinna had risen as well. Still vibrating with shock, Tiadba managed to push into a crouch, and listened to the shrieks and wails shooting skyward from all around. The compressed ruins of a dead city had either risen around the Witness or been pushed into place like a pile broomed up for burning.

"Where are we?" she asked. "Has the Chaos shrunk?"

Khren and Macht crawled beside her. Nico had found another wall with better footholds.

"There has been movement," the armor's voice announced to all. "Distances have been reduced."

By now the marchers had found vantages to all sides, less interested in the city than in what had happened to the Silent Ones and where the Witness was now situated, almost on top of them.

Tiadba studied the Witness with a frown. The huge, distorted head—as tall as three or four blocs stacked on top of each other—had been erected on a massive scaffold of old buildings. Its expression seemed frozen in weary despair. Perhaps that half-melted visage revealed its emotions over times longer than the life of a breed. With everything shifting and changing, perhaps the Chaos would accelerate and she could actually *see* the agony come and go across those ruptured brows, accentuating the rotation of that huge, protruding eye, dull green glimmers winking within its dark pit of a pupil.

The sweep of the beam had been interrupted, but now the glimmers were focusing, re-forming . . . and the beam lanced out again over the Chaos, returning to its slow, inevitable rotation.

Khren and Shewel pulled Tiadba to her feet. None of them had been hurt—yet. They were left untouched in the very shadow of the Witness, wrapped around by labyrinths of broken walls and toppled structures— spirals, towers, ornamental facades.

The walls had grown up in no time, while the sky had turned a sickly metallic gray and something like wind had rushed over the Chaos, carrying fanned-out clots of black dust. And now the fountains, shooting into the sky, suddenly joined into spinning funnels, then curved over and swooped toward the distorted horizon.

"Here!" Herza and Frinna called.

Tiadba pushed Khren back and climbed the opposite angled wall to see. They all watched as the Silent Ones maneuvered on their tracks, hunkering, collapsing their stilts to avoid the funnels, now like thick fingers, with the marchers in the middle of a giant palm. A kind of living smoke shot through with gray and silver rose all around, and the Chaos erupted once more—this time bolts of red light rose up and spread against the wrinkled sky.

"More intrusions," the armor explained.

"I *see* that," Tiadba said, and then reached to make sure she still carried the bag in her pouch, with her books. *Their* books.

How could Jebrassy ever find them, ever make his way through *this*?

"Where's the beacon?" Nico asked. "I don't hear anything." If they lost the beacon, then it did not matter whether they were alive or dead.

"It's stopping," Khren called.

The fountains fell short, the geysers sputtered, the continuous bedlam of screams and whoops dropped in pitch and intensity to low rumbles.

"We have to move across the trod," Tiadba said.

"There's something out there, on the other side," Nico said, pointing.

Their suit faces magnified what he had spotted and showed them a different kind of ruin, blocky cubes and rectangular structures laid out in a grid and topped by a lighter swirl of sky.

Tiadba closed her eyes and tried to remember what her visitor would have called them.

Streets. Roads.

"I know a place like this," she said.

"We'll have to make it fast," Nico advised, and Khren agreed.

They pushed over the rubble and ran over the dimpled trod, its pale surface spongy, then mucky, like a fallow swale. Behind them the nearest Silent One began to rise up on its thin legs, the mouth in the flat massive face twisting as if in pain.

"Faster!" the Pahtun-voice commanded, and they pushed, tugged, braced against the suck, and crossed the trod to step out on glazed black crust, dust beneath, and then—

A road made of square red stones, covered with black ice, but hard—they could run! They could flee as the Silent Ones pulled up their stilt-legs and began to reach out with fluorescing grapples. But the marchers were now out of reach.

———

They walked in silence, moving what might have been miles through the ruins. The small generator had been sucked down into the rubble on the other side of the trod, pinned between collapsing walls. They had only one clave left between them.

And Tiadba had her books.

"Is this place new, or old?" Khren asked.

"Very old, I think," Tiadba said as they increased their distance from the both the Witness and the trod.

"What kind of place is it?" Herza asked. Usually she was the least curious, less even than Frinna, and never asked questions.

"I think it's called a 'town,'" Tiadba said. "Like a bloc, but laid out flat instead of stacked."

"Some of the buildings look like they might have been taller," Khren said. "Maybe something mowed them down."

Twisting curls of feeble blue light arced from the Chaos into the flat cityscape, dancing down the roads and caressing the shattered walls. Nico asked what the loops were.

"Entangled matter," Pahtun's voice responded. "These are ring fates, interactions between particles that are the same, once separated by time and fate—but no more."

Ring fates. Tiadba shuddered. She had not heard that phrase before, not even from her visitor, but it sounded important, even crucial.

"Are they dangerous?" Khren asked.

"Unknown," the armor replied. "They cannot be avoided. You are made from primordial mass. There may be more entangled recognitions between matter from the past, now joined to itself in the present."

They tried to focus on the words they almost understood. Tiadba thought that her and Jebrassy's visitors might have spoken to them out of just such a past. Did that mean they were connected—made in part at least of the same matter?

She told the others that they needed to find something like shelter, and stay alert. The Chaos had been crunched, compressed—that seemed to be the simplest way of expressing what they had experienced—and perhaps that meant this past had caught up with them, colliding and merging with everything around the Kalpa.

"What's next?" Herza asked, her second question of the journey.

CHAPTER 79

The Green Warehouse

Jack leaned over the edge of the roof, looking for people and finding a few still out in the open. But he could not recognize any of the bookgroup witches, and no one else out there moved. They had become obsidian sculptures locked in attitudes of walking, running, or just standing, arms held up as if beseeching someone, something—anything. "Are they all like that?" Jack asked.

Daniel had no answer but felt a twinge . . . an unwelcome jab of concern. He could see through many of the buildings, as if their reality had been frozen mid-collision. Some of these were slowly fading, crumbling—turning to more black dust.

He rubbed his temples vigorously, then bent over, fighting off a headache. "I'm not smart anymore, Jack. This has me squeezed flat. Every secret, every bit of knowledge—it's right before our eyes, and we don't know what it means," he said. "I used to be an arrogant bastard—from what I remember, which isn't much. Maybe I belong with Glaucous, and you should stay away from both of us. I'm sorry I brought him here with me."

Jack could say nothing in response. Their past was gone—literally gone, deleted, absorbed, powdered away. What could they be responsible for now? What sort of freedom of action or choice could they possibly have?

———

Ginny took just enough time to pluck her stone out of its box, throw the box between some heavy crates, and pull a bundle of clothes and a can of beans, all she thought they could spare, from under the bed. Enough was more than enough. She couldn't sit still another second—couldn't waste any more time waiting for the others to finish their enigmatic preparations.

She had slept through the departure of the three witches. She did not see Ellen in the stacks or near the outer door. She did not want to see Jack or Daniel, and she certainly did not want to encounter Glaucous again.

Or Bidewell.

She was going to do what she always did best: turn left, move on, make the wrong decision. Leaving the security of Bidewell's warehouse—if it *was* secure, which she had always doubted—seemed foolish, but now more than ever she couldn't stand the thought of falling asleep again and dreaming of her lost other.

She worked her way through the stacked boxes, smelling their dry mustiness, feeling the strange new cold that wafted through the lofty old building, winding like an invisible vapor down the aisles and between the rooms, chilling the steel doors like frozen hands, reaching in, searching . . .

The stone felt warm and heavy in her pocket. All the lightness after her hours in the empty room, the time spent with Mnemosyne, had collapsed under the weight of troubled sleep, and now she felt only leaden desperation.

She pushed open the outer door, cringing at the squeal it made, and pulled the mechanical lever that released the gate lock now that the city's electricity was gone. The cold on the ramp was stranger and more intense than in the warehouse, and the brown, dusty darkness beyond the gate more forbidding than she had imagined while making her preparations.

But this was the way it had to be. Separation, escape, in the hopes of a new uniting—when they were ready, when they were *mature*.

Whatever they could have time to grow into.

With damp fingers she rolled the stone in her jacket pocket—the jacket that Bidewell had given her, a heavy woolen British Air Force coat, sixty years old or more—and used her other hand to pull the wire gate inward.

The last scatter of writhing clouds were lit with arcs of pale green and yellow flame that flickered and passed overhead, like the northern lights, she thought, but more intense—and not at all lovely. Above the clouds, the sky had become a vault of nothing. She should not look up, she decided. Yet looking at the streets outside—the shaved, dissected, rearranged buildings, covered with crawling black ice, the few people left behind by Terminus, petrified, contorted, filled with that same waxy, crawling ice—awful! So she kept her eyes on her feet and walked as quickly as the thickening air allowed.

She seemed to fill a kind of bubble, an unseen protected volume that pushed ahead and around her. The bubble might be an effect of the stone, but she couldn't know for sure. It was like a pocket of air dragged below the surface of a pond by a diving beetle. It might give out at any moment, and the waxy dark ice would fill her veins and then something else would peer out through her blind eyes . . .

She looked back, a bad idea, but she couldn't help herself. The gray air behind could not completely obscure the sharp bluish glow rising from the warehouse, the only building she could see that had not been destroyed or rearranged like a child's set of blocks. She wished them well.

The warehouse grew smaller too quickly, as if each step she made were a dozen. A new way to walk: tattered running shoes turned into seven-league boots . . .

Ginny lifted her arms, wondering if she could will herself to fly, but nothing happened. She kept walking. The ground changed from cracked cement and asphalt to soft gray dirt, then to something blacker and harder—a kind of ropy crust like old lava, but thin and crunchy. She hoped the fine gray dust that puffed up from beneath the broken crust would not swallow her feet, or swallow *her*.

Some of her thoughts as she performed this odd journey were taken up with the protests of a rational, practical young woman who told her that leaving the warehouse was worse than suicide—but who also told her that none of this could possibly be real. In the broken, flat, and listless world of Terminus—a thin coat of paint between life and doom—there had to be an answer to the madness, an escape, a door or hatch through which she could crawl and pull herself into real sunlight, real night, walk under real stars, real moon—

Real sleep, normal dreams. And a real city, not this broken-down jumble.

But then she looked up from her blur of feet, looked around again. She was no longer in the city. The brown and gray air was reddened by the rise of the flaming arc—all that seemed to be left of the sun, wrapped around a cindery disc. This was accompanied by a deep rumbling and trembling beneath her shoes, the black ground itself rebelling against what now passed for day.

And off in the distance she saw the ghostly hint of a sweeping beam, not precisely a searchlight, more like the blade of a huge sword cutting through the sky.

I know that. The Witness.

This made her stop. She found herself actually wringing her hands, a story-time gesture she never would have believed herself capable of. But she took some solace from the repetitive motion and the pressure of her strong, curling fingers.

Her frown deepened, wrinkles and seams growing across her forehead and cheeks until her face felt like an old, old woman's. The air seemed to be aging her. Terminus might be pulling her up short, abruptly snipping her world-line like a grim, silent Norn.

Anything could be happening.

And so she had to keep walking.

From the middle of the roof the shelter door creaked and slammed open. Ellen kicked the door again as it swung back, then stepped out onto the wooden pallets. "We weren't watching her for just a moment . . . !" she called, and then stopped, sucked in her breath, and lifted her hand to shield her eyes against the aurora glow.

Jack didn't say a word, just broke into a run over the wooden path to the shelter. His shoulders bounced from the walls, then he swung onto the ladder and scrambled below like a monkey.

Daniel followed, more deliberate. Trying to figure an advantage, he thought with the smallest pang. Ellen stared at him as he walked past. She focused on his face—she did not want to see any more of the sky and landscape than she had to.

"The girl took off?" Daniel asked.

Ellen's face was white with accumulated shock, and now this. She folded her arms tight and nodded. "We were supposed to protect her."

"We'll go find her," Daniel said. "This place isn't going to last much longer, anyway."

CHAPTER 80

Downtown

The witches could not find any street they recognized.

The whole downtown area had been fractured and then tossed into a mishmash chronology. The only structures that seemed familiar were bookstores, some shuttered for decades, yet once again presenting faded signs to empty streets; but their interiors were deserted, empty of both books and readers.

Agazutta, Farrah, and Miriam moved on in a tight huddle, exchanging quiet, hollow jokes—the last little encouragements they could muster—but unable to hide their fear at the appalling state of their once beautiful city.

"I never imagined it might be like this. I thought I'd die in bed," Miriam said.

"Alone and unloved?" Agazutta made a wry face. "Maybe this is better."

"Speak for yourself," Miriam said.

"Always have."

"Girls." Farrah nudged them around a gray, jagged corner. "This is Fifth Avenue."

"My God, have we walked that far?" Miriam asked.

"I'm not sure what 'far' means now," Agazutta said.

They stood for a moment, the dusty breeze chilling them like a soft, dead hand.

"That's north, I think," Farrah decided. She wiped grit from her eyes and intensified her frown. "What now?"

"I recognize something up the block a ways," Miriam said. "It's the central library."

"Haven't we had enough of books?" Farrah said.

Miriam said, "I think it's our little green books that have got us this far. Maybe we can climb to an upper floor and get our bearings."

"I say we go east, that way," Farrah said, pointing. "I think that's still east. The freeway isn't far, if it's still there."

"My house would be north," Agazutta said.

"I don't know if we can make it," Miriam said. "It's getting much too cold." She pulled up the collar of her sensible gray wool coat—the sort of coat one wore for many seasons in Seattle.

Agazutta turned toward a window crusted into the wall beside her, its frame cracked, pitch-dark behind the dusty glass. Palm- and finger-prints streaked through the dust, as if people had walked by with hands out, touching the walls, the window, anything solid to guide themselves through the murk—before they vanished.

She stared into the glass and realized that the reflection staring back was of another face entirely, not hers—and not a happy one. With a little cry, she backed away, and the face faded.

To the southwest, around Bidewell's warehouse, a pillar of swirling cloud seemed to be gathering, piping out a thin calliope whistle—the voice of a mad mother crooning to her children.

"Let's get off this street," Farrah said. "Anyplace will do, even a library."

They walked through the fragile rubble, crunching like burned meringue beneath their shoes, in the direction that had once been north; toward the big library.

————

Inside, the library was remarkably intact—deserted, but only loosely touched by the changes beyond its high, staggered glass and aluminum walls. Quiet filled the lobby and stairwells leading to the upper levels—empty quiet.

Agazutta leaned against a desk and coughed into her handkerchief. "We'll get black lung out there."

"Dust of ages," Miriam said, and reached into her cloth bag to pull out her book. She held it up, showed it to her fellow Witches.

They produced their own volumes—the books that Bidewell had given them years ago, when they began working for him.

"Books are special," Miriam said. "They mean something beyond any value I ever gave them. Not that I don't love books. I mean, look at this place . . . it's hardly been touched."

Agazutta fumbled with the brass latch on her book, but Farrah reached out and stopped her. With a sigh, Agazutta slipped the book back into her bag.

"Whatever protection books give didn't seem to mean much to the people who worked here."

"Maybe they left," Miriam said doubtfully.

"I'd hate to think that we're all that special," Farrah said, and when the others looked her way, puzzled or irritated, she added with uncharacteristic sheepishness, "I don't want to be the last of anything—especially the last old woman."

"What's old mean, here?" Agazutta said.

"I want to be in my clinic," Miriam said.

"Time's over, except for us," Farrah said grimly. She pointed to the high, broad windows. They were frosting, black crystalline rime creeping up like a cold shadow.

Farrah had made her way behind the abandoned information desk and held up a thick volume from the *Cambridge Ancient History*. She opened it and flipped through the pages. A dark silvery fluid spilled out around her feet and gathered into a shining pool. Miriam bent to examine the spill—touched it with her fingers, lifted them. The tips were covered with dark iridescence, alphabet rainbows—hematite words. "Uh-oh," Agazutta said, and backed away from the nearest flight of stairs.

From the elevator doors a thin dark liquid gushed through the crack, while another, more copious flow cascaded down the steps. The women retreated.

The streams joined on the concrete floor.

Behind the desk, Farrah shook a few last drops from the book of history, then held it up. In the dim light its pages were as pristine as untouched snow.

Miriam's expression turned from astonishment to resignation—almost to understanding—but then held firm at acceptance. "Keep your things close," she warned. "It's what Bidewell has been saying all along. Without readers, books do unpredictable things."

"Waiting for new characters, new stories," Agazutta said.

"*Us?*" Farrah asked, her voice as frightened and gentle as a child's.

"No, dear," Miriam said. "We've never been very important."

But Farrah had laid the book on the counter and, like a librarian, was smoothing her palm over the blank pages to press them open. At her touch, letters returned, apparently random, unreadable—embryonic history waiting to be made. This was what had softened her voice. "Are you sure?"

"Oh dear," Miriam said.

CHAPTER 81

Ginny

Ginny stumbled as she ascended a low ridge of blackened stone, and then, beyond, saw a thick stream of something iridescent sliding toward her, then curve off to the right—flowing uphill, not down. She would go around that curve to avoid crossing the fluid—whatever it was.

She hadn't brought much real water—just a plastic quart bottle bumping around in her pack. But she wasn't thirsty and she didn't feel hungry or tired. Only a few minutes seemed to have passed, and yet she must have walked many miles.

A practical part of her mind now asked a key question, and Ginny wondered why she hadn't thought of it earlier: What was guiding her?

She reached into her jacket pocket and touched the stone, felt it roll in her fingers—a new freedom. Yet when she tried to pull it back behind her, even in the narrow confines of her pocket, it resisted.

It had a tendency, a preference.

It pulled in the same direction she was walking.

"I am the stone, the stone is me," Ginny sang in a hoarse whisper, and felt a kind of reassurance, a counter to her fear.

The flaming arc passed beyond the horizon again. She looked down from the not-sky to keep her eyes from aching. Then it occurred to her and she let out a small cry. She had left the last place on Earth that was not already part of the awful dream.

I'm walking into Tiadba's Chaos. Where's her city?

Where's the Kalpa?

As she held the stone, words streamed into her head—very familiar, that voice she had never heard yet knew so intimately—awakening what she had been made to know all along.

You are here.

You are in its heart.

Find me.

Find your sister.

CHAPTER 82

The Green Warehouse

In the small storage room, surrounded by collapsed cardboard boxes and piles of broken-down crates, Glaucous lay back on the narrow cot, thinking over all he had seen and done, all those he had caged and put to an end. Birds sold or tossed to the rats; children delivered by the dozens to the Chalk Princess.

In the long run, in the undoubtedly stellar perspective of someone like the Mistress, it came to no difference. He did not feel guilt so much as imbalance. He did not seek understanding—Daniel might understand a little of what was happening outside, but Glaucous worried that he was too old, too much a living fossil. His intellect had been whetted to a dedicated edge more than a century ago, and then blunted by hard use. He could manufacture a semblance of cleverness, summon a pattern of behaviors in response to a more or less familiar challenge—

But not to this. This was a young person's game. He could only contribute what he had added to the mix so often before: the fog of promise, the taint of lies.

When the three had been isolated in Bidewell's back rooms, he had *felt* something moving through the building like a subtle breeze— Mnemosyne herself, he supposed. For a moment his memory had sharpened, put itself in order. Quite the opposite sensation of being around the Devil's whirlwind, the Queen in White.

His lips moved. In the lowest, softest voice, he tried to remember his story differently, to speak of a young boy treated well—not showered with riches, but trained to fulfillment and not servitude, his potential shaped by firm, gentle, if not expert hands—fine propensities nurtured, bad tendencies discouraged . . .

Maturing into a normal life. A homely but honorable woman might have taken him to be her husband. Children might have come that he—they—would protect and never, ever deliver up to *her*. He could not imagine love, not after all these years, but he could summon a vague picture of mutual respect and understanding.

He clenched his teeth, got up from the old cot, and put on his jacket. The door opened.

Daniel and Jack stood in the gray light.

"The girl's gone," Daniel said. Behind them, ice grew over the boxes and crates, up the walls and ceiling. Near the concrete floor the ice was slowly staining black.

"Ah," Glaucous said, head inclined, eyes mere cracks. He rubbed his hands against the cold. He was used to moving in the dark.

"We can't find her," Jack said. Glaucous searched the boy's face and found only nervous excitement. A fog of promise. He would unite these two. They would become like brothers. His last contribution to the game—perversely, the creation of a bond of trust.

"I heard three of the women leave," Glaucous said. "Where's the fourth?" *She stayed here for you, Jack. Do you care?*

"She's with Bidewell in the office," Jack said.

"If we are here," Glaucous said, "and we do seem to be *here*, and moving about and speaking, then I assume Terminus has . . . I'm at a loss for words, young masters. Has Bidewell navigated us through that impassable barrier?"

Neither Daniel nor Jack answered.

Glaucous pushed past them. "*She* will come soon," he said. "The Chalk Princess hates bookish sanctuaries."

"Doesn't matter what the Chalk Princess does now," Jack said. "We're where we're supposed to be."

"Ah, did Bidewell tell you that?" Glaucous asked.

"Jack dreams, remember?" Daniel said with a sharpness that made Glaucous uneasy. "He might know more about what's going to happen than we do."

"Then by all means, we should go after the girl, and Jack will guide us," Glaucous said.

They will take their stones with them—all will be gone from the ware-house. Our Livid Mistress will come to claim Bidewell—his books alone can-not protect him here.

And then, what has always been promised to her *servants . . .*

That promise had been revealed to him just once, over a century be-fore. He could hardly remember the details, only the lingering aura of a glorious triumph, control, wealth—unimaginable victory over all ad-versity. A complete absence of guilt. And what would he be, then? Per-haps not even Max Glaucous anymore.

For the first time in decades a note of a conscience played somewhere in his chest, sharp and painful despite its tiny size. He peered at Jack, then at Daniel, and felt the muscles in his face turn waxy, freezing his expression into an amateur parody of a smile.

How ugly I am, he thought. *How old and cruel and full of lies.*

CHAPTER 83

The Kalpa

In the tower, waiting . . .

The fusillade of intrusions had scorched deep into the Kalpa, high and low, practically destroying the two outer bions and leaving the first bion—and the Broken Tower—in a highly unstable condition. A third of the Defenders had dissolved into fiery clouds. It was apparent that the conclusion of the Typhon's vendetta would not long be delayed.

Ghentun had put his affairs in order, surveyed the damage in the Tiers, and determined what could be done for those ancient breeds that still lived, who did not require the ministry of the Bleak Warden—a small remainder cowering in their niches, moaning songs and prayers, watched over by the few samas brave enough to walk the hallways.

Nothing more could be done.

He had left the Tiers for the last time and returned to the Broken Tower, not at the bidding of the Librarian, but for the sake of his own conscience. Even then he was well aware that any course he chose was likely already embedded in the scheme of one or another Great Eidolon, and he was filled with loathing for them all.

Enslavement. How could you enslave a dying cosmos? What could any of these Eidolonic schemes mean to a being like himself, no longer capable of the evanescent noötic shimmer, much less of passing signal and sense from epitome to epitome, incapable of even approaching what passed for thought among those powers who still claimed to be human?

Waiting to be noticed by the servants of the Librarian.

Ghentun looked down from a high window cracked and smoking, blackened at the edges, rimed inside and out with crystalline densities that crawled and rearranged, trying to heal the crack on this inward side, while on the outer, black otherness crept and sought a point through which to pry entry.

The angelins finally appeared and filed into the wide, once empty chamber—not one this time, but thousands of many different shapes and sizes, all blue, all cold, settling themselves in concentric curves with Ghentun and the high window at their focus.

He glanced back at them, unmoved, then returned to his contemplation of what now lay beyond the border of the real. Few in the bions below would ever witness what he was seeing; Eidolons and Menders and Shaper alike preferred ignorance to the certainty of this swiftly approaching doom. The Chaos had fundamentally changed, no doubt about it. Nothing like what surrounded the Kalpa had ever been seen before.

How the ancient emotion of curiosity had declined to a deathly, classic superiority—the triumph of blind satisfaction! This must have been what it was like for so many across the five hundred living galaxies during the last of the Mass Wars . . . awaiting transformation or destruction by the Eidolons. Not so very long after, many of those same Eidolons were now giving way to the Chaos.

The Chaos had even less mercy for Eidolons, so it was said. Ghentun took grim satisfaction in having this history lesson pressed home so vividly. It stung him deeply that he had once abandoned his primordial mass, given up his Mender heritage for a few thousand years of hopeful integration into the upper urbs . . . A betrayal of high degree, he thought.

The only higher betrayal—

He contemplated the still vague outlines of the deep knowledge given to him by the City Prince. Not to be trusted, of course. And when that knowledge did emerge, would it transform him into the Kalpa's avenging agent?

The angelins did not move—did not disturb his thoughts. Perhaps the Librarian was preparing for his final moments as well.

The Keeper wondered what had become of the young breed male he had delivered. Analyzed, partitioned, dissected by a crazed Eidolon with an intense and pointless lust for telling detail? Or kept in seclusion, a prize lost among all the other failed and cataloged experiments?

What Ghentun was seeing, outside the border of the real, visible through the broken, leaning sentinels that still tried to surround and protect—

The Chaos had burned through almost all of Earth's old reality, twisting time and fate into blackened cinders, but along the way, choice bits had been perversely encapsulated, preserved, and now trophies were being arranged as if in a bizarre museum. The shattered artifacts of ancient times and ancient cities terrestrial and otherwise had been collected, somehow transported, and laid out around the last bions of the Kalpa, closer than ever before, as if for the horrified awareness of the next victims—soon to be melted and disfigured and distributed in their own turn across the dark lands of the Chaos.

Who could doubt that the Typhon hated all that lay within this huge broken circle of protection? Who could ever doubt that the Typhon's entire existence had consisted of dismantling and rearranging—but always failing to understand—the secrets of creation?

The Witness lay sprawled like a gray, ghastly mountain in the midst of this heap of murdered history, its gigantic battered head and slumped features still pushing forward the prominent, slowly rotating eye that swung a gray beam across the heights of the tower.

Ghentun could only acknowledge at his core a vacancy of emotion. To learn the nature of one's lifelong enemy—the enemy of all the scattered galaxies, all those who had once called themselves human—the enemy that had shaped and distorted his life, and yet had provoked the creation of the creatures he so dearly loved, yet now had to abandon . . .

Vacancy.

Only vacancy.

Ghentun looked for the channels that had always wormed through the Chaos's reactive scablands, spread around the Kalpa: the trods, along which, it was said—if you watched closely from the city's sheltering heights—you might see Silent Ones skimming and darting, huge and swift, no doubt seeking breeds, marchers; dispatching or delivering all they caught to those awful repositories: the Necropolis, the House of Sounds, the House of Green Sleep, the Fortress of Fingers, the Vale of Dead Gods, the Wounding River, the Plain of Pits . . . or any of the other stations of mutation and doom that had been gouged, erected, morphed from the landscape beyond the border of the real over the times since the tower had been shattered.

How do I know these names, these identifications?

Ghentun looked back again at the angelins and realized he was being played with. Was this the City Prince's gift? Or were the Librarian's servants sharing some of their knowledge? Either way, the Keeper was being given a lesson in Chaography—what he needed to survive in a land without law.

A single angelin broke from the ranks and drifted forward. It extended a slender, tiny blue hand to caress Ghentun's cloak. Jewels of singing snow fell before his face.

The runners have summed. They are all here.

The dreamer is ready.

The angelins parted and a white epitome escorted the young male breed into Ghentun's presence. The breed approached the high window and stared out, eyes bright with fear and longing.

He knew what Ghentun knew, saw what he saw.

Jebrassy looked up at the Keeper, then turned back to the Chaos. "You sent her out there. I have to go find her."

"Not alone," Ghentun said.

CHAPTER 84

The Green Warehouse

Another kind of slowness and darkness was approaching. Bidewell peered up at the skylight as he pulled on his gloves and walked between the aisles to his library and the fitful heat of the stove, the last bottle of wine. Ellen was waiting there, his final companion in this cosmos, he presumed. And bearing down upon them both—something he could only sense, not explain.

Another part of the broken chain—as usual, out of sequence.

Or something worse. Perhaps the wall of Alpha, come to squeeze them against Omega. If that was the way of it, then they had not failed. There had never been any way to succeed. Dark thoughts indeed.

Ellen sat and stared at the dim orange glow within the stove's isinglass window.

"Perhaps you should have gone with them," Bidewell said. "The women, I mean."

"I thought Ginny would want company," she said.

Bidewell made a sound at once dubious and sympathetic and sat across from her.

"Are we done? I mean, there's nothing more we can do?"

"Not at all," Bidewell said. "Assuming there is still a move to be made in this endgame, we are making such a move now."

"Care to explain that to me?"

"Of course. The Chalk Princess will come to collect a former servant, now a turncoat. That desire for vengeance might delay her in the pursuit of our young shepherds."

Ellen peered at him, beyond fear—almost beyond curiosity. "What would it be like, to be collected?" She looked deep into the isinglass. "What is the Queen in White?"

"An awful force. A multidimensioned storm of pain and fear, carrying a retrograde wave of hatred."

"What is it that hates us so much?"

Bidewell shook his head.

"Satan?"

"Ah."

"What's that mean?"

"How often have we asked ourselves that question?" Bidewell said.

"Is there an answer?"

"Worse than Satan, is my guess. Worse than anything we've ever imagined. A malign embryo that will never be born, much less achieve any sort of maturity. A failed god."

"And this female . . . is she that failed god?"

"No. She serves, but I believe her servitude is forced. Sometimes I almost recognize her . . . I've dreamed and guessed and thought about it for long centuries now. Perhaps when she arrives, I'll know what questions to ask."

"Something's coming," Ellen said. A new intensity of darkness and cold was closing in, and something else was in the air—something that made her want to weep. A loss far beyond the loss of a world—the loss of all history.

"Do you have your book?" Bidewell asked, getting to his feet.

"I thought the books were spent."

"Not these. They still tell our stories."

"What do we do—read them aloud?" Ellen removed her book from the bag.

Something moved through the fallen, frozen crates and boxes—not a cloud, not a figure—swirling around corners that did not exist, turning in directions no eye could follow, radiating a dark spectrum of emotions.

Bidewell gestured—a quick jerk of his fingers—and they opened the books, pushed them to their breasts, leaning toward each other, heads and hands touching.

A sound came in soft gusts, like a cry out of deep caverns—Rachel, weeping throughout eternity for her lost children.

"She's blind," Ellen said. "She's blinded by grief."

"Do not feel sorrow for her, not yet," Bidewell said. "Everything about her is obverse. Grief is joy, and even her blindness is a kind of seeing."

"Is that *her*?" Ellen asked as the shadows fell and the room seemed suspended over an abyss.

Bidewell opened his mouth but could not take a breath. There was no need for an answer. The Queen in White was upon them, and in her way, tried to love them as they deserved.

CHAPTER 85

Ginny

Ginny settled into a hollow in the crusted ground and pulled up the hood of her parka, then drew the strings tight, hiding most of her face. That weird sun was in the sky again. When it burned overhead, she could feel her small bubble of protection shrink, could almost feel it wither—just as when the deathly gray beam passed over. No doubt about it—this sky and what lay beneath did not like her.

The stone in her pocket had turned cold, but she didn't dare let go. It protected her, of that she was certain, and it didn't matter how it did so—not yet.

Then she had a thought: What if leaving the warehouse had put Bidewell and the others in deeper danger? There wasn't anything she could do about that now. She had made her choice, half hoping someone would follow her, argue with her; and then, reasoning it through, she understood that it would have to be someone carrying his own stone, Jack or Daniel, perhaps both—but would they bring Glaucous, too? That seemed bitterly incongruous—a strange team indeed.

After a few minutes of rest—at least, it felt like a few minutes—she peered over the edge of the hollow and experienced another connection to Tiadba, this time while awake. They were closer. She had known that for some time now but could not understand what it meant; *closer* in what way? Their worlds had merged. She had guessed that much—doubted it, but could find no other explanation. Not that it was any sort of explanation.

Despite all her foolishness and "bad" decisions, she had always primly asserted her rationality—and now pondered for the ten thousandth time the reasons none of this could possibly happen. Her doubt was like tonguing a jagged, painful tooth. All the rules had been broken. What remained? Magic? Strength of will? Some effect of whatever science or knowledge had created the sum-runners?

Ultimately, she knew there could be no explanation, only survival and completion. Results. In most ways, she had lived her short life—perhaps shorter than she was happy to consider—in clueless ignorance, wrapped in the baby blankets of culture and surrounded by the poor theories of fellow travelers—all of that amounting to another kind of protective atmosphere, off which the smaller, plunging impossibilities bounced or burned away before reaching her. Consensus reality.

Another kind of bubble, equally inexplicable.

Well, out here that was gone, too. She was alone.

She ducked back into the hole. Something huge swung past nearby—a glimpse of sparking shadow accompanied by a thin, strident howling or weeping, penetrating the bubble and hurting her ears.

Ginny slowly gathered enough courage to look out again and saw that the shallow dip in the land lay beside a kind of road, colorless, neither bright nor dark—like something half seen by moonlight.

The road stretched to a sawtooth horizon.

"Stay away from the trods," she murmured. "Whatever rides them might be strong enough to break your little bubble. Or *see* you—and collect you."

She understood that inner voice. Tiadba again. So close!

Despite this warning, Ginny walked alongside the trod, a dozen paces away—such as her paces were, difficult to judge—and descended a grade onto a broad, grayish-tan plain. The mountainous walls to either side were lined with a dim audience of monuments, strange, seemingly dead and still. Twice she had to hide behind rocks or in dips as huge, flat, elevated shapes glided past on the trod. These made no sound and gave no warning. She did not want to know what they were—her glimpses, from a distance, might have shown heads big as buses, twitching, sweeping eyes pointed down, searching.

But they did not see her.

Ginny realized that she needed to think less and act more. Going mad out here would be less than pointless—like lighting a match inside a supernova.

She kept walking. The wrinkled, purple-black sky, devoid of stars, did not bother her so long as she did not look up. Strange, that feeling of silent resentment, like a fly flicked from the hindquarters of a sleeping horse. Whether or not she made any real impression, this place tried to repel her and negate every assumption she brought with her.

Still, she could not ignore a deep curiosity about the nature of the valley. Wherever she looked, the horizon was always curved. Perhaps light behaved differently here.

"I don't know what that means. *Stop thinking.*"

The plain between the mountains . . . the monuments or statues—part of her had seen it all before. Tiadba had been here, was here now.

Or would be here.

Maybe they would meet.

"I'm not sure I'd like that," she whispered, still walking. "I'm already stretched thin." She dropped again as something on the trod skimmed by, like a huge dinner plate or a squashed crab with a human face. After it passed, when she got to her feet, she noticed a curved, shining green blade stuck in the black ground directly in front of her. A small handle on one side made it look like a baker's dough-cutter. *A weapon, I think. Why was it left here? Who dropped it?*

She decided against touching the blade, much less picking it up. Could be a trap. Then the hair on her arms pricked—something was *watching* her—and she swung around, dizzied as the entire horizon seemed to careen this way and that—

And faced her first ancient breed. There wasn't time to look away. A male, she guessed.

Not alive. Not dead.

And not alone. There were hundreds just like him, crawling or walking over the ridge into the valley, a river of figures, each smaller than her—this one barely up to her shoulder—and festooned with scraps of what might have once been thick clothing—armor? Red, orange, green, and blue, now faded, ripped and hanging like tissue.

They were *marchers*. She was sure of it. Their faces drooped like soft wax, their eyes—

She could not look into their eyes. Failed, lost, changed. Like ants they flowed into the valley, trying to reach something in the center, a structure hidden by a trick of the light, unless—as she did, frightened—you spun around twice, flinching and leaping between each spin to evade those who trudged past.

And after the second rotation—she *saw*.

Like a huge house or castle, it rose from a shallow crater in the center of the valley—could it actually be that many miles wide, that many miles high?—shining and cold, like hoar-frosted green glass. Every bend of her head or twist of her gaze made it almost impossible to simply *see* the structure again. Still, with effort and focus, its detail grew—and its true immensity became more apparent.

It had to be a city.

The line of failed marchers were indeed like ants, flowing toward the bowl and the city at the center—where they would slide in and be pinched up by a predator, like an ant lion, while all around the arena the silent sculptures formed a nightmare audience, caught in mid-hope, mid-stride, frozen into something like stone.

A history lesson, she thought.

She moved along with the marchers. It was time.

Time to go down there.

Into the False City.

CHAPTER **86**

The Kalpa

Ghentun's relief at leaving the Broken Tower was clear even to his young companion. They said very little on their descent to the upper urbs, and Ghentun made no attempt to hide the city's dismal realities—such as they were—from Jebrassy's bright, curious eyes. If the Librarian could educate them in his selective way, then the Keeper could supplement that education from a more grounded perspective—by taking the long way down, and showing how dire the city's situation had become.

Jebrassy said little as they moved through the highest urbs and levels of the first bion, carried along and between and around the sinuous tracks and channels that formed a silvery three-dimensional web. The web was cut through with complicated surfaces studded with spheres and extrusions that moved slowly like great boats on a fluid sea, though many stuck out sideways or hung upside down from the curves. He cringed at what must have once seemed supernatural power and arrogance—now fallen victim to extraordinary failure and disaster.

The intrusions had broken through to all levels of the Kalpa. Many of the tracks and channels had been sliced away, whipping around to snap and cut across other tracks, shedding their miles-wide neighborhoods— now tangled, blocked, and studded with embedded, flickering debris.

"I don't understand" was all Jebrassy managed as they descended below the Eidolon urbs and approached the ruins of the crèche.

"Welcome to all our lost worlds, high and low, young breed," Ghentun murmured. "I'm more at home down here."

They walked through the Shaper's domain, now a shambles—barriers broken, machines collapsed in blackened piles of molten slag, but fortunately, no evidence remained of the lost young themselves. The many-armed Shaper had made an attempt at cleaning up after the most devastating intrusions. Clearly, however, there was no longer a crèche, and the umbers would never again deliver young breeds to the Tiers to be raised in the old way.

They stood silent before the Shaper, who gave Jebrassy a brief caress with one long, warm finger. The breed drew back in shock and embarrassment. But he could feel new knowledge filling his insides like a rich and energizing meal. It spread a cool, speedy lubrication throughout his being. He liked that sensation—but he did not enjoy the following awareness of how badly wrong things had gone, nor how ignorant he had been of the foundations of his existence.

He felt small, but not diminished. So much to tell Tiadba when they finally met again. Of that eventuality he was absolutely convinced, despite the gloomy presence of the Tall One—which puzzled him. He would almost have rather made the attempt alone.

Could a breed and a Tall One—a *Mender*—ever act like equals? Jebrassy felt up to the task. But he wasn't so sure the Keeper could actually keep up once they were in the Chaos.

Ghentun issued his final instructions to the Shaper—using words Jebrassy could not understand, though he suspected they were not so much elevated or inaccessible as simply specialized.

"The last generation," Ghentun said as they departed the crèche. "It saddens. But it's long since time this was done with."

"Why?" Jebrassy asked. "Weren't the breeds worthy of being made?"

Ghentun looked down with puzzled respect. Perhaps the Librarian had been liberal with his information, or at least his allowance of sophistication. Either that or they had all underestimated the facility of their smaller charges—in much the same way Eidolons dismissed the abilities of Menders.

———

The worst part of this start to their journey came when they passed through the Tiers. The Keeper had given Jebrassy his gift of invisibility.

A few breeds had survived. They wandered among the smoky ruins, dismayed at the destruction of their blocs and their meadows, yet still trying to put their lives back in order—but clearly that would no longer be possible.

While Jebrassy could hardly have understood the destruction wrought upon the upper levels, this hit him hard. This threw a dark pall over his sense of challenge and adventure.

There would be no coming home—that had been clear to him from the beginning. But now, very likely, there would be no home to come back to.

"I feel sad," he told Ghentun as they descended to the flood channels by way of a hidden lift. "How can sadness make you free?"

———

The hike along the black-streaked channels past the outer ends of the three isles—in the final, flickering glow of the partially collapsed ceil—seemed to take no time at all. But the long walk to the camp where the marchers had once been trained and equipped gave Jebrassy too much time to think, and his confidence plunged, until they came upon the huts, the tents, the scattered footsteps in the sand and dust.

He crouched. Someone had knelt and then sat in the fine sand. He bent to sniff. "She was here," he said.

"No doubt," Ghentun said.

"How far?"

"We've come thirty miles. We have forty more to go before we pass between the inner generators, then exit the Kalpa into the middle lands. This is the last time we'll actually know how far we are from anything. The last time distance makes any sense."

Jebrassy understood. "What will happen if the Kalpa falls—will travel be meaningless everywhere? What will happen if we can't mea-sure—"

"Best not to worry about those problems yet," Ghentun said. "Just grieve for your dead and enjoy their memories." He knelt beside the young breed, sad and proud at once. *Like a father,* he told himself.

After a while he escorted Jebrassy to the silver dome and introduced him to the last three suits of armor. There was no longer a Pahtun to train them, but they managed.

Jebrassy chose a blue suit and put it on with only a little assistance. He seemed to be a natural. When Ghentun commented on this, the breed shrugged. "I don't remember it until it happens . . . don't really re-member it at all. But maybe my body does. Or . . . maybe the Librarian is still reading me my story, but skipping ahead."

That comment unsettled Ghentun. Who would be the leader, and who the led? Distances had changed in more ways than one.

Ghentun tried on one of the trainer's outfits. It seemed to adapt well enough to his bulkier frame. He left the gloves unsealed for the time being.

"Someone's coming," Jebrassy said, and pointed across the channel.

Ghentun saw a small, pale figure glowing against the black smear that had cut through the sands and marred the channel floor. The figure moved with an awkward, erratic lope.

"It's not a breed," Jebrassy said, beginning to feel alarm. "And it's not big enough to be a Tall One."

Ghentun extended his vision as far as a Mender's ability allowed. The figure was an epitome, part of a Great Eidolon.

They stood their ground and waited.

"I know that one," Jebrassy said as it drew near. "I recognize the face."

"It showed a face?" Ghentun asked, astonished.

The figure moved swiftly enough, despite its odd gait.

"I've gone through a dreadful ordeal," the epitome called, and joined them on the sandy floor of the channel. "Made myself primordial. Still not entirely knitted, I think." It held up a small, pale hand and turned it this way and that, inspecting its fingers as if for the first time. "Limitations have their limitations, that's becoming more obvious," it said, then glanced with envy at Ghentun's flower finger. "Is that actually useful? It looks useful."

Ghentun grimaced at the memory of his own return to primordial mass—then clenched his hand in embarrassment. Flower fingers were seldom referred to openly in polite company.

"I'll be annealed in a few hours," the epitome said. "Out there . . . I'll be able to survive for a time. But I'll need some sort of protection, just like you. How marvelous."

"How should we address you, Eidolon?" Ghentun asked, confusion bringing out a perverse courtesy. The old forms were definitely being shattered. No Great Eidolon had ever gone primordial, to his knowledge. It seemed an affront—both a sacrilege and an imposition on the privileges of the low.

"Please call me Polybiblios," the epitome said. "I shall be a male—by tradition—and so I shall be known as 'him' and not the more appropriate 'it.' Though real sexuality seems lost to us all—with the possible exception of our young breed, here."

Now it was Jebrassy's turn to be embarrassed.

"In a way, I am probably the best part of the Librarian—or at least I will suffer that delusion until I am proved wrong. May I join you, young marchers? I promise to be humble, in my way. And possibly even useful—like that wonderful finger."

Ghentun sealed his gloves and put his hands behind his back.

The epitome sat in the sand and with an expression of delight, lifted a handful of the gray grit, then let it fall through soft fingers to the channel floor.

Jebrassy had grown strangely fond of the fragment of the Librarian that had offered companionship and teaching in the tower. But seeing him solidly incarnate, similar in size, and out *here* . . . very confusing.

"How *can* you be useful?" he asked.

"I brought this," Polybiblios said. He held out a gray box. "Without it . . . nothing will happen. Nothing important, at any rate. Things will just come to an end. And after so much time, that would be a pity."

CHAPTER 87

The Chaos

They might have been marching for years. Lifetimes.

The marchers were adapting to the Chaos bit by awful bit. Asserting a new sophistication by breaking the rules, they had become expert at crossing and sometimes even following trods. Trods, it seemed, had a kind of predictability. When there were no travelers about—for there were other and even stranger users than the gliding Silent Ones—the trods were hard and slick, like glass. When travelers approached, and long before the marchers could be seen, the trods would go all gummy and start sucking at their boots. There was usually more than enough time to scramble to one side or the other and hide in the broken rubble.

The entire Chaos was like a garbage heap. Wherever they went out here, stuff had been tossed about, disrupted, discarded—and most often, left in a crumbling, blackened state, its vitality sucked away. There were lots of places a breed could hide.

None of them had been lost since Perf—but that only meant they were lucky. They had seen more than enough evidence of the destroyed, the transformed.

During their short periods of rest, if the Chaos was not too badly mangled and some of the old rules still applied—and if the armor advised them it was safe—they would remove their helmets and breathe what was left of the ancient atmosphere of Earth.

It was not pleasant, but it was different enough to relieve the dragging boredom of the ever-changing, the unpredictable, and often enough the indescribable.

Their journeys had taken them around some of the largest monuments to the Typhon's dementia. The marchers created their own names for what they saw: the Awful Bumbles, Great Burning Pile, Last Chance Ditch, Glider Dumps. That last had been a kind of miles-wide cemetery of worn-out, discarded Silent Ones, their eyes glazed and probably blind.

But still alive.

No finality, no mercy, no sense.

———

How many times the marchers had been pursued by things they could not see . . . beyond count. Their armor—and the Kalpa's beacon, still pulsing and singing—guided them through ditches and around chasms filled with sluggish, churning liquid. Things seemed to swim or drown deep in that oily ooze. They walked on the flat margins of lakes of blue fire, casting long shadows against brownish cliffs like puppets backlit on a screen. The enervation that had come over them was not so much physical as mental.

They were made of old, ordinary matter. Such matter—configured into a breed—could not absorb too much strangeness without throwing it out of memory, or stopping to rest. But there was no chance to stop.

And so much of what they saw, they promptly forgot. Another mercy.

CHAPTER 88

Glaucous grabbed Jack and Daniel and pulled them back into the red-rimmed shadows. "Stalkers," he said.

Large, sinuous shapes slid over the cobbles and through the streets. Jack squinted to see, first making out what seemed to be several beetles dragging long, bloated worms. Blinking, he saw something else—

snakes wagging spadelike heads, their eyes black and deep, crawling on a cluster of appendages and trailing long, bloated bodies. The bodies looped and coiled until these monsters passed out of sight around an eroded corner, yet still, afterimages danced in his eyes, light being what it was out here.

Daniel hugged the wall, fingers rubbed raw against the brick and mortar. "What are those?"

Glaucous shook his head. "I've never seen their like."

"Ugly," Jack said.

"We didn't escape after all, Jack," Daniel said. "The bad places have caught up with us."

They were about to move on again when from another direction, over the shattered walls, they saw seven large, manlike creatures in procession, heads bowed, dressed in robes that fell behind them in pools of blood-colored fabric—but the shapes that bumped and protruded against the fabric could not have been legs, not two legs, at any rate. Their faces were dark, smooth, with long red vertical slits for eyes and slick ropy hair writhing on their shoulders.

Glaucous gave his companions a curious, almost fey look, as a hungry man might look at a banquet he is sure is poisoned, or as someone about to hang will regard his approaching executioners. "They'll search the ruins of the old cities, wherever they can," he said. "These places may still be unfriendly to them—not completely digested."

Daniel covered a disgusted cough. Jack waited for the streets to clear, then jabbed his hands into his jacket pockets and walked ahead on the cracked, twisted roadbed.

They followed.

"Where do they come from?" he asked Glaucous.

"I'm as ignorant as you. The Mistress employs the Moth, and I presume the Moth employs ghosts and such I've never seen—not even in a Gape. If they're the same things that gathered up the shepherds—the children brought to our Mistress—they never revealed themselves, never came out into the open."

Daniel asked, "Would they recognize you—take orders from you?"

Glaucous laughed into his fist and shook his head, a very amused no. "I am low, very low. If they hunt, they hunt everything that survives and moves about. I presume they are searching and clearing before our Mistress goes out for another tour."

CHAPTER **89**

The Chaos

Thrusting up hundreds of feet from a cleft that stretched from horizon to horizon, the building was bigger by far than anything the breeds would have thought of as a dwelling, a house: a crystalline heap of shapes and angles, crusted over with what might have been broken pieces of other buildings, and those parts decorated with the petrified remnants of people and animals. The awful whole glowed with a pallid, putrid light that played tricks even through their faceplates, bending and warping, making their companions seem farther away, or looming close, huge and menacing—and then lulled them into a desire for senselessness, isolation—to run off and be alone, find a trod, just sit and wait.

The seductive green emanation seemed to penetrate even their armor's strongest protections.

As they moved in two close groups along the edge of the cleft—avoiding a particularly broad and spongy trod—Macht and Shewel could not help but stare at the ugly, angular pile, as if trying to make sense of its madness.

"Are those *people* all over it?" Shewel asked, squinting, his eyes reflecting the twisted, cluttered image.

"They might be carvings," Macht offered without conviction. "Too big to be people of any kind we know."

"Well, what *are* they, then?" Shewel asked sharply, as if angry at the armor's quiet.

Pahtun's voice echoed in all their helmets. "This is the House of Green Sleep. If you must know, they are the shells of victims gathered from long-dead galaxies, swept up on waves of shrinking space and time, then carried heedless and hated to this last place, to be displayed without pattern or thought."

Macht grumbled, "You had to ask."

"Oh," Shewel said. "Well, now I know."

Nico glanced back from some distance ahead, walking point with Herza and Frinna. "No more stupid questions," he said.

"Ignorance is bliss," Frinna agreed.

They found a small, dry pit deep enough to hide them from both the trod and the sickly light of the house, and paused long enough to rest and set up the portable generator. They pulled aside their helmets and huddled close as Tiadba took a book from her leg pouch.

"Read," Herza insisted. The sisters were the least critical of the marchers, most enthusiastic about the odd, wandering bits of story Tiadba found or deciphered.

"Yes, read," Macht said. "Take our minds off that thing out there."

"I'd prefer softer stories," Khren said. He'd developed an aversion for these difficult tales and all their odd words.

"This is what I can find," Tiadba said.

"Just read *anything*," Nico said, and closed his eyes, lying back on the dark earth within the protection of the generator.

Tiadba opened the book.

We chose our vessel, the *Intensity*, from the last great fleets parked in huge yards all through the twelve cities. She was reputedly the fastest of transports, faster even than the cosmos-spanning portals of the middle Trillennium, but in poor repair. She had not flown for a hundred thousand years.

During the Reduction, all these ships had ferried refugees to Earth and her sister planets, as well as to the orbiting web planes, spiral ribbons, and shells set twisting and spinning around the re-newed sun. They had carried back to Earth survivors of the Chaos's desolation, a pitiful fraction of our cosmos's former glory.

Dealings in my youth with a diversity of Mender ship clans and the more rooted portal clans had taught me the ways of all transport, some outmoded and even then becoming impossible as the Chaos altered the fine anatomy of the cosmos—the swifting ways by which travelers flew.

I found my crew among young rebels, deviant Shapers and Menders. In contests, I tested and winnowed from the thousands who volunteered.

And chose my twenty-five, about to become philosopher-adventurers all.

All past science had to be adapted, or abandoned, to get around the Typhonic perversions. Nearly all hyperdetics and means of communication and transport were blocked. Superluminosity, transfate reassembly, dark-mass portals—the technologies of almost a hundred trillion years no longer carried us across the cosmos. Only one reliable engine of spatial motion remained—bosonic threadfold, itself rumored to be Shen in origin.

We converted the *Intensity* to threadfold. By itself, the method puts tremendous strain on any crew, for you do not arrive what you started out being—whatever your matter. Fates curl back, traits and lives mix—for a time, the crew becomes the ship, and then the journey, and later, it is difficult to rebuild what once you were.

We would become intimate in ways none could foresee. We accepted this. It was better—to our way of thinking, a unanimity among the perversely disagreeable—than becoming noötic.

And so we departed the ports of Earth.

Familiar to all is our passage through the realm of the Spectrals, who first learned to recharge, train, and breed galaxies.

Displayed along the inward-closing membrane of the Chaos, the last of the Spectrals had been enslaved by the Typhon, studied—if that is the correct word—and then vitrified: trapped in a slow, constricted bosonic glaze across millions of light-years while their boundaries were dissolved—an awful end for one-time masters, to whom the Trillennium owes its very existence.

Less familiar because less clearly explainable, even by those of us who were there, were our encounters with the enigmachrons, where fifth-dimensional fates lie spread out like thin bones beneath the rotting flesh of space-time. The *Intensity* found itself caught in a swirling storm of dead futures, tiny whirlpools of despair and repetition, and four of our crew lived horrible lives in scant hours before our eyes, aged in misery, mercifully died—and could not be revived by any recourse to ship memory. Some of their names remain forgotten—their fates erased even back to the Earth.

The Shen, it seems, had accepted their destiny with maddening calm. As we were welcomed to the sixty green suns—and as we were shriven of our Chaotic taints, cured and reborn in ways that both agonized and refreshed in the old, simple, cold stone rooms of the Final School, we met with Polybiblios, a simple figure, plainly made, unusually small for a Deva.

Among the Shen he had become known as Curiosity embodied.

The Shen exemplified in all their ways and histories the exalting humility of correcting error, and followed in all their days the smoothly prickled course of knowing one's blind stupidity. Polybiblios had been among them for a million years, had watched them react—or not react—to the harrowing of the Chaos. When presented with our case, he consulted his Shen teachers, and without ceremony they prepared to cast him out, after a brief, enigmatic explanation. "You will create more error and more confusion," they told him. "We cannot allow you to remain on the necklace-worlds, beneath the Green Suns. All should end soon, but because of you it will not. Cosmos will follow upon cosmos, challenge upon challenge, out of any thinkable sequence, but forever and ever nonetheless—for you will misuse what we have taught you. And so it must be. For we are again in error. Perfection is death. For us, that is good—but you reject our purity."

Even so, they allowed Polybiblios to keep what he had sought for so long, their last and greatest discovery: the secrets of budding minicosms from the quantum foam, finite but incomprehensibly vast seed-sets of new universes.

"I can leave now," Polybiblios said, and briefly bowed his head and laughed in Shen-like acknowledgment of his joyful grief.

Our return took us through regions briefly unveiled by the Chaos's cruel recession, the Typhon proudly pulling back its cloak, leaving nakedly visible and scattered over the withered geodesics those systems and civilizations that had not retreated eons before. Billions of contorted suns—the great human fields of the Trillennium—lay across the darkness like embers of burning lace. Signals from these regions came to the Intensity, difficult to translate, but when Polybiblios—against our experienced recommendation—analyzed them, we saw once more how deep and perverse the Typhon's ruin could be. To the poor monstrosities surviving in these corrupted regions, the roots and laws of former nature still seemed consistent.

They still believed a future lay before them, and reasoned that we were the monsters to be hunted and destroyed.

Perhaps we were.

We doubted everything.

Our threadfold engines faltered—the Chaos gnawed at the last technique we could use to spend less than eternity on our return to Earth. Polybiblios applied all his Shen learning, and we proceeded in a dreaming bubble squeezed out of the necrotic flesh of the cosmos, defying predatory shreds that whipped out, breeding insanity and mutation even within our isolation—and forcing us to kill nine more of our crew.

The twisting corridor of our passage, the last geodetic of the old cosmos, constricted tight.

We gave up whatever hope remained.

I entered my own darkness, defeated, maimed in my soul.

But Polybiblios, with his quiet, steady way, saved us. His unceasing ministrations to the *Intensity* pulled us through. We awakened cruising through clean space, alive, saner than we had been for long years—surrounded by our ship's humming regularities.

We neared Earth's sun.

Our rescued Deva, who had rescued us in return, celebrated the passing of his masters and teachers, the Shen. We stood with him and listened to his words, though they meant little to us at the time, and even seemed to contradict what we had learned before.

"They will not give in to the Typhon," he explained. "Nor will they commit suicide. They will reverse their genesis, and return themselves to the libraries from which they were patterned—never to be retrieved by any intelligence, in this or any subsequent cosmos.

"For they have made a pact with the handmaiden of creation, who reconciles all."

Perhaps he referred to himself more than the Shen. Poor Shen!

After this, Polybiblios retreated into contemplation as we entered the last open gate to our legacy system, returning to the ports of ancient Earth—and mourned our dead, those we could remember.

———

Tiadba closed the book and thrust it back into the bag.

"That's Sangmer talking again, isn't it?" Frinna asked. "He doesn't mention the female, the one on the silvery beach."

"Maybe she's part of the secret," Macht said. "Maybe she's that hand-maiden."

"No, she became his wife," Herza said.

Shewel pulled his ear and rolled over.

"How many times did he write this story?" Nico asked.

CHAPTER 90

"The Defenders won't last much longer," Polybiblios said as the three marched through the pitchy, uneven middle zone. The snaggled line of remaining obelisks diminished into darkness on either side, spinning fitfully. The nearest leaned and groaned and sparked under the long night.

The epitome's armor made halfhearted attempts to fit but had been fashioned for a breed and did not seem in the mood to adapt. Polybiblios walked at first with a jerking, puffing gait, until, in frustration, the suit seemed to take control and march *him*, and finally he squatted beside a heave of dark reddish stone and looked at his companions through the fogged faceplate with a reasonable simulation of perplexity. "I designed these. I should know how to use them."

"What else don't you know?" Ghentun asked, in no mood to pause—or to be generous to a former Eidolon.

"Oh, much, no doubt," Polybiblios murmured, then concentrated on pushing at the suit's joints, poking, tugging, muttering some more, and finally requesting their help. "Push this here . . . and this segment, pull it out, there."

From both sides, Jebrassy and Ghentun grabbed at his arms and legs, then pushed and tugged until the suit glowed green at the joints and sighed around the epitome's slight form, fitting as well as it was going to.

"At least now I can walk," Ploybiblios said, standing and shaking out his arms and legs. "Well, let's move away from here—this place is dan-gerous."

"How much longer?" Jebrassy asked.

"Until we're in the Chaos—or until the Kalpa dies its inevitable and horrid death?"

"That," Jebrassy said, swallowing.

"It should have happened already," Polybiblios said. "The Typhon has failed at building a foundation of rules. It exists only as a foul shadow, a catalog of thefts from the old cosmos. If it absorbs the last bit of our world, it might simply—pop!—cease to exist. Everything will go to nullity. If we fail . . . well, there is no word for what nullity does or does not do."

They walked more quickly now, across what seemed like many miles to Jebrassy, following Polybiblios as he cut through the tight-packed clutter of the condensed and amplified Necropolis. Jebrassy struggled to see where his feet were going—the ground seemed to curve up to meet each bootfall. Soon they were within sight of a great poly-form dome of crazed and warped architecture. To Jebrassy it resembled many bridges set on end, spun about, then dropped, smashed, and fi-nally, as an afterthought, hung with long mossy ribbons.

"Does Nataraja look like that?" he asked.

"Unknown. This particular structure has been here since before the tower was broken, carried from some far galaxy, I seem to recall . . . There are many such scattered here, there." He stabbed about with a finger. "Meant perhaps to draw curious marchers. The Typhon . . ." Polybiblios looked down at his trembling hands. "This body reacts with revulsion. How interesting. I had thought myself beyond such feelings."

Polybiblios guided them along another dark, crusted path winding around the ruins.

"Of course, without the generators, the Eidolons will cease their ex-istence within the Kalpa—or outside, for that matter—but the Ancient Breed and most of the Menders might still survive."

Ghentun understood the implication of that. "What about other marchers?" he asked.

"Not to be known," Polybiblios said, shaking his head. This gave Je-brassy a twinge—he had heard that phrase before . . .

They crossed many more apparent miles. Ghentun inquired as to whether the epitome knew where they were.

"On the outer boundaries of the Necropolis," Polybiblios said. "Everything *is* tighter, shrunken—drawn in. We're moving faster than we should. And soon . . . ?" Polybiblios closed in, peering at the breed. "What will we soon come to?"

"You're like a teacher," Jebrassy said. "Always testing."

"The houses," Ghentun answered for him. "Ten of them, at last count, cutting across the strongest path of the beacon."

"And beyond them?"

"The Vale of Dead Gods. Beyond that, all is conjecture."

"Just because I am with you, do not think you can let down your guard," Polybiblios said. "Great men and women have been lost out here, with more ancient conviction and experience. So many marchers, but others as well—Menders. Pilgrims. Many have been sacrificed while we waited."

"You sent things back," Jebrassy said. "Now they're returning."

"Emerging might be a better word, like something rising from the depths of an ocean."

"I don't know what an 'ocean' is." Jebrassy lowered his head as if in pain. "Upside-down rocks . . . ice and mountains in the sky. That's where the dreamers are going. Is that an 'ocean'?"

"No," Polybiblios murmured, but he did not sound completely convinced. "Worlds falling together. All a desperate gamble, and how many times did we fall into that splendid quag of despair only Eidolons can feel?"

Jebrassy clenched his teeth and pushed ahead.

CHAPTER 91

Denbold and Macht tested the trod with their boots. "It's firm," Denbold said, returning to Tiadba. Herza and Frinna stepped out on the surface together. "We can cross here."

"The beacon gets weaker that way," Khren said. "It's strongest on this course. That's the path we should be taking. We should follow the trod."

"It's a long, wide one," Shewel said. "It won't stay firm. And there's a peculiar bump ahead—we can see over it, or should, the way the light works here, but there's only darkness."

"What he calls a bump looks like a . . . what's the word?" Khren asked. Tiadba had been reading other stories from her books. Some described features of land and water that the breeds had never experienced.

"A *mountain*," Tiadba said. "Lots of them—a mountain *range*."

"Well, whatever—that's where we're supposed to go."

"What's out there at the end of the trod?" Tiadba asked the armor.

Pahtun's voice responded. "Once there was something called the Vale of Dead Gods. It was a broad-floored rift with ten houses, including the House of Green Sleep, held in a kind of countertwist bowl at its center. Many marchers were lured there and enslaved in a chronic noose. The tower changed the arc of the beacon to avoid the vale. But the last update said there was only shadow—a lack of detail."

"How long ago came that update?" Nico asked shrewdly.

"Kalpa time, a hundred thousand years," the armor said. "But out here, in a countertwist, how we approach changes everything. Away from the guidance of the beacon, circling in from another direction, there may still be the vale. The House of Green Sleep is or was a strong lure. If the vale and the house have changed, then there may yet be other traps—or a clear path."

"Typhon's lies?" Nico asked, squatting beside the trod and poking at it again with a tripod leg. The surface seemed hard as glass.

"Perhaps," Pahtun's voice said. "The trod passes close to the vale. If the beacon guides us along the route of the trod, it might still be safe."

They all looked to Tiadba. Her weariness had grown. She sensed a cycling sadness in the back of her thoughts, as if she were leading the marchers into a trap even worse than the echoes, worse than the twitching glider dumps and churning graveyard bogs they had already seen. But the beacon was strong. There was nothing else they could do; they had no other guidance.

"We could stay on one side or the other," Khren said. "But it's getting rough and there are lots of cracks. Take us much longer."

They all dreaded the possibility that the Kalpa would fall and the beacon would be silenced—or worse, deceive them, though Pahtun assured them that was not possible.

"We'll use the trod," Tiadba said. "Khren, stay as far back as you can and still see the rest of us. Herza and Frinna, go ahead an equal distance. Any sign of softness . . ."

They spread out and moved toward the "bump" in the land ahead.

———

They walked on for what seemed a very long time before they were forced to abandon the trod. They then hid in crevices that radiated from the roadway and watched the passage of Silent Ones by the dozens—wave upon wave of gliding monstrosities, moving with even greater speed over the broad milky surface. More time—long, slow, boring time—passed before the surface again became glassy, and they resumed.

The Witness's beam curved and whipped through the sky. Something was happening again far out in the Chaos—thick scuts of darkness shot up and then fell back like ghostly, smoky heads popping out of the ground.

After another long spell of travel, and another smoky eruption, Khren saw a change in the sky to their left, well off the vector of the beacon's greatest intensity. None of the others could duplicate his sighting, hard as they tried. "My eyes must be going," Khren said, downhearted.

"You and me both," Shewel said.

"What did it look like?" Nico asked, boring in with an angry tone.

"Enough," Tiadba said. "We'll force him to make up stuff."

"I wouldn't do that," Khren said, indignant.

"We'll stop here for a while . . ."

"It's out there again," Herza said, and Frinna pointed—they had both seen a blue glow in the dip between two heaves of brownish, crackled ground.

The armor now spoke. "It may be another Pahtun, or this far out, someone else from the Kalpa—older."

They thought this over skeptically. "A deception?" Nico asked.

No answer. Anything could be a deception—except for the beacon, nothing was certain.

"I'll sortie," Macht said. "I'm tired of this monotony. A little climbing and jumping is just the thing."

CHAPTER 92

"Does he look different to you?" Glaucous asked Daniel. Jack forged ahead through the ruptured and redrawn streets, walls, buildings. His concern was obvious—there was no way to tell what could happen out here, nor how things had changed since Ginny passed.

Or whether they were even following her trail.

"He's standing straighter," Daniel said.

"He's looking *older*," Glaucous said. "And bolder. He takes risks, leaving us here. What does the stone tell you?"

"Still tugging," Daniel said. The urban rearrangement around them muttered and groaned like deep ice settling over a rocky slope. "If the girl feels the tug—and if it's the same tug . . ."

"It is," Glaucous assured him. "Have you seen the like before?" He waved at the dismal scene, apt to change unpredictably, like a show of lantern slides planned by an idiot.

"Once," Daniel said. "Jack might have seen it, too."

"Fleeing our Mistress?" Glaucous asked.

"Something like that."

"*She*'s back there. Near the old warehouse. I can feel her."

"Will she use you to find us?"

"If you ask am I notching branches and overturning rocks . . . no. But the Mistress is ever and always aware of the disposition of her servants. At least, she was on Earth. Here . . . maybe our oddness blends in."

"This *is* Earth," Daniel said. "Bits of it. Look. You're old enough—maybe you recognize these buildings."

"Asian, I'd say." Glaucous blew his nose, inspected the rag—more streaks of slick black—and shook his head. "I never journeyed to the East. We left your city miles back."

"Bidewell said it was all getting cinched in."

"Did he? I missed that."

"It's all burned or corroded. Broken time seems to act like fire or acid."

Silence between them as they worked around a mound of bricks and stones. With a dour twinkle, the stones became shards of concrete and steel—part of a newer wall, but still a jumbled ruin.

"Like a battlefield," Glaucous said. "I walked the trenches around Ypres, almost a hundred years ago, looking for a particular gent—a fine, strapping fellow and a poet. He dreamed, so I was led to believe, of a place he called the Last Redoubt. He'd written a book before shipping out, detailing his dreams . . . But the war had already blown him to bits. Lean years for hunters, during wartime."

On both sides, streets and buildings ascended steep inclines, as if a city map had been draped over another, rougher country. Some of the structures looked more intact than any they had encountered before, despite leaning at awful angles.

Glaucous saw Jack ahead. He was passing under a precarious arch formed of steel and glass.

Daniel shook his head and his eyes darted. "How far does this go on?"

"Don't know," Glaucous said. "Just tagging along."

"You've done more than that," Daniel said. "You scared Ginny. You might as well have pushed her out here."

"That concerns you?" Glaucous asked.

"I don't know why you're with us. Jack knows what you did."

"Does he?"

Glaucous looked up as they reached the arch, then felt his shoulders draw down and his thick neck stiffen at the thought of thousands of tons choosing to fall at just this moment. "No shame," he said. "Shifters may have more charm, more romance than Chancers—but what we do is all the same in the end. We grab at happenstance and care little about stealing luck from those around us."

"I never claimed to be righteous," Daniel said.

"Well, then," Glaucous grumbled.

"Just stop trying to make me *happy* to be here."

"Apologies. Old habits."

———

For Jack, listening to the voices behind him, the dread sense of approaching conclusions made the shadowy ruins fade to insignificance. He had seen this before—or something like it, less dead. Only now that it was *all* broken could he piece together a picture of what his cosmos— his small part of the cosmos—had been like, and how he had managed to skip through it with fewer consequences than most; and fewer advancements, fewer of the milestones of common life.

His inability to feel strong affection—that puzzled him. In the dreams, there had been an almost surreal, childlike passion, but for Ginny, only a *liking* . . . and nothing more he could pull to the surface. He was less a man in all this than the figure in his dreams.

Jack never dropped anything, because he never held anything for very long: Ellen, who settled for a few hours with him, had been content with his ghost of affection. But before her . . .

His mother—a pale outline on a pillow under the bright spot of a hospital lamp. His father, even less defined—big, tried to be funny, tried to love him. How could those who controlled their destinies settle for so little? Ginny was like him in that regard. Fate-shifters did not seem capable of great things. They wandered, but left attachments, love, even memory behind.

How could he find fault with Daniel or Glaucous? They were all alike, selfish in the utmost. Both those who held the stones and who sought the stones were diminished—shriveled to points of darting consciousness, without breadth or depth.

Not even the favor or Mnemosyne had lifted Jack's gloom. He stalked on through the guttering relics of human history, blackened middens revealed one after another like images sketched in ghostly embers. Where was he going—where could he go?

After Ginny. A dream-sister. Who was chasing what?

And along the way, they would meet with—

Daniel called him back.

"Slow down. We're leaving the city stuff behind." All three gathered, and their protection merged with a hollow smooch. Jack looked around and pressed his temples with two fingers.

"Do you remember anything like this?" Daniel asked.

"Do you?" Jack asked, still pressing.

"My fate was chewed to pieces, so I jumped closer to your lines. You probably came up against the corruption before it actually closed in. All different. This is all that's left now—fallen bits, colliding chunks."

"Memories of history?"

"Oh, they used to be real enough . . ." Daniel's lips worked, as if he were trying to stifle another voice. "Sorry. I've got a frightened, curious landlord to deal with."

Jack stared at him, not so much shocked as disgusted. "Putting it politely, you're a hermit crab."

"Putting it crudely, I'm a tapeworm, a leech," Daniel shot back.

Glaucous watched both through red-rimmed eyes.

"But I'm not useless, and I'm not so cruel. What did you leave behind for Bidewell and your woman friend?"

Jack shook his head.

"I thought about giving them a stone of their own," Daniel said. "I have two. Something to protect them when the Chalk Princess comes."

Glaucous's eyes grew wide. "That's impossible," he said. "No shepherd has *ever* carried two."

"No shepherd has ever been as monstrous as me," Daniel said. He swiveled his head to watch thin blue arcs loop between gray rocks and scattered ruins. *Always in pairs—a kind of cosmic handshake.* "In the end, I knew Bidewell would turn down the offer. Three is the minimum—four is safety."

Jack turned away. He had no idea what this information meant. "This *is* like where we go in our dreams," he said. "Where Jebrassy goes after he leaves the city."

"Who's Jebrassy?"

"I think we're going to find out soon enough. We're supposed to meet."

"Past and future self? How's that going to work?"

Jack shook his head.

"I'm not going to meet anyone," Daniel said. "More or less of a puzzle . . . can't say."

"We're living in text-time," Jack said.

"Something Bidewell talked about before we arrived, presumably," Glaucous grumbled.

"Maybe," Jack said. "Can't you feel it? We're just shells filled with explosive. When we land—we're done with. This text is finished. Close the book."

"And open another," Daniel said.

CHAPTER 93

Ginny walked with the waves of haunted marchers into the valley, observing them with pity and wonder; they hardly seemed solid, much less alive, their armor in strips, feet worn and bloody, the blood long dried—like walking corpses, yet they spoke to each other in high, sapped, tinny tones of triumph and enthusiasm, though harsh with fatigue.

To them, she might have been a wisp, a vapor. Yet one or two stopped to watch her pass, their pale eyes weak and blinking. She could barely make out their words, but some of Tiadba returned to her, and she began to recognize the breed speech of her dreams. What little she could understand told her they were happy, that they thought they were arriving at the conclusion of a long-destined journey, and for a while, surrounded by their shambling, rushing forms, she wondered if they were right; perhaps the dark green edifice rising from the bowl in the middle of the valley *was* where they all needed to be.

The journey had been hard, the marchers were simply worn down; but in the dreams, Tiadba had never heard of *thousands* joining in a march. How could they all arrive on the edge of the valley at once, all together?

One of the marchers, a female breed—not Tiadba; Ginny would have known the connection—tried to watch her more closely. She had a broad face, large eyes, and a blunt, simian nose bearing a scut of fine fur, now crusted and patchy.

"Something's there. Is it a monster?" another asked.

"I'm not sure," the female answered. "The armor's silent."

"The armor's dead. *We're* dead."

"Hush with that! It's as big as a Tall One. If it's really there."

"It's a monster. Stay clear."

The female tried to reach out and touch this apparition. "*Are* you a monster?" she asked.

Ginny did not trust herself to answer. What would her voice sound like to such as these? As if she could be any more real than everything else between the statue-lined mountains. And why couldn't she *see* and comprehend those statues? Gigantic, twisted, motionless . . . might as well be dead . . . That much she could be sure of.

A substantial number of marchers—dozens—had slowed and matched their pace with the one that seemed able to keep her in view. "Is it still there?" several asked.

"You!" the female shouted, rushing in again to touch her—but the bruised, broken hand was gently repelled by Ginny's bubble. Something bright arced out of Ginny and formed a ring of pale blue between them, then winked out.

Entanglement. They shared a little matter; they were made of some of the same stuff. But not much of it.

Ginny looked away, blinking back tears, and concentrated on the broken, stony path. There was nothing she could do and they frightened her. She did not want to end up like them, but she knew Tiadba would suffer a worse fate.

"You!"

The female muttered to those around her, and they suddenly stopped and formed a ring, blocking Ginny. She could not pass—she tried and was pushed back. She could not leap or close her eyes and move ahead or do any of the things that might have seemed possible earlier; they had confined her within their circle.

"What is it? I can barely see it."

"It's a Tall One."

"Another Pahtun?"

"No—don't break the circle! Keep it here until we know what it is."

"We should move on."

"Doesn't anyone *remember*?" the female cried. "We keep trying to get across the valley and into the city. We keep being sent back and starting over."

"That's not what *I* remember. We're almost there. It's beautiful and bright and close—look! We've crossed the Chaos. We're going to make it . . ."

Ginny hugged herself and studied the wan, peeling faces. Some of the figures were little more than wisps floating above the jagged, crusted surface. Who was more or less real here, and what did it matter?

She finally tried her voice. "I understand you. I know what you're saying." Those words startled them—drove them back and widened the circle. Even now she could not be sure what language she used.

She looked up to the green structure—the city. It seemed closer and much larger, but something about its outline, its margins . . . it might have been a high mountain viewed through a living, smoky haze, deliberately closing and then revealing. Endlessly teasing, jealous, disappointed, angry.

Tormenting.

"It speaks. I hear it," several figures murmured, and they all closed in, reaching out to touch the bubble. Several more elliptical arcs of blue pulsed between them, wreathed their hands and arms, pulled away in slips and curls, and vanished.

The marchers withdrew, paler and less defined, as if the interaction had weakened their very existence.

"What are you?" the female asked. "Where are you from?" Her weary, filmed eyes glanced one way, then another. She could not see

Ginny—couldn't see anything clearly. "Tell us we're on the right path. Tell us we know where we're going."

Before Ginny could answer, a wave of grainy darkness surged outward from the base of the city. The marchers flinched, hunched their shoulders . . . then dropped and tried to hug the rugged ground, as if this had happened many times before. So familiar, like a delivery of fresh fire to the damned.

The wave spread and lifted all, seemed to haul up the very earth. Ginny closed her eyes and rode within her bubble through the wave.

It shook—spun the sky, then moved on.

Fell back onto a dark, syrupy foam.

The foam soaked down into the black surface, hissing.

After a sickening wait, the ground seemed stable again. Ginny got to her feet and looked around.

The marchers were gone. On the threshold of what they seemed to think was their salvation, within sight of the place they had been created and trained to reach, they were snatched, shoved back. Tricked. The valley was a place of endless temptation and disappointment.

"For them, a trap, the wrong city," Ginny said, shading her eyes against the rising arc of fire. But the green edifice was where she needed to be. The stone tugged her in that direction. This deceptive jumble of walls and shapes, watched over by legions of frozen giants—

If Tiadba was not already within, then perhaps she soon would be. *And what can I do to help? This can't be real. My nightmare has sucked me in.*

Ginny's hand had never left the surface of the sum-runner. And the stone's strong pull had never lessened or wavered—until now. It tugged her sideways, on a different course than the marchers—into the valley, perhaps to circle around and approach the bowl from a different angle.

She did not dare look behind her. The marchers would be lining up on the crest of the rise, memories spun back in a barbed circle. They would look down into the valley, filled with relief, sure of their victory, then run forward once more in a ghostly, decrepit horde.

There was nothing she could do for them. Not here, and not yet. If she was too afraid to move, the same female might repeat their scene and dialogue all over again.

Ginny walked on alone, drawing closer to the stony giants that looked down from the peaks of the surrounding mountains, locked in perpetual silence—always watching but never seeing.

CHAPTER **94**

An awful suspicion grew within Tiadba. They had come so far, lost only one of their company—Perf, near the beginning of their journey—and yet she felt no closer to Nataraja and could not escape a terrible sense that disaster was looming. Worse, she was coming to distrust the beacon—the musical note that pulsed out of the Kalpa and sang in their helmets when they were on the true path, and faded when they deviated from that path. Some shade of knowledge pestered the back of her weary thoughts—a phantom of foreboding.

The marchers rested now in the protection of the portable generator, on the top of another inverse ridge—a hill from one side, a valley from the other, light sweeping in devious curves from whatever direction they chose to look; mirages everywhere, only slightly corrected and straightened by the faceplates of their armor. From the inverted valley side, they looked out over a wide, lightly traveled trod that led straight into an enormous, sandy plain ringed by high, jagged mountains. A few travelers, swift and low to the ground—a variety of the Silent Ones—swooped along the trod and vanished behind outcrops. None could be seen to travel all the way out onto the plain.

On all sides, nestled among the mountains like carelessly dropped toys, great frozen things towered, facing inward toward a greenish architectural mass—if such could be said to have faces.

The Pahtun voice suggested this might be the Vale of Dead Gods—occasionally seen from the Broken Tower. No Pahtun had ever explored this far. The mountains surrounded the House of Green Sleep—though that had likely changed, compressed into an illusion or disguise wrapped around the ancient rebel city of Nataraja. They might be near their destination after all, if Nataraja was still worth finding.

Once, while they rested—or dragged their feet, more truthfully—Khren said he saw motion on the far side of the vale, at an unknown distance, like a horde of insects swarming over the rim of the vale—perhaps more echoing marchers, lost and pitiful. And when Tiadba stared in that direction—trying to see through the tricks and deceptions of the light—she caught a brief glimpse of something pinpoint brilliant, blue—almost hurting the eyes, even through the filter of her faceplate.

Sometime later Khren saw it again—exactly the same—and Macht, Nico, and Denbord all agreed it must be more echoes, captured and distorted marchers repeating their frustration by the tens of thousands. It was a sobering prospect that even now, having come this far, breeds just like themselves had somehow become imprisoned in an illusion of triumph; or so Nico speculated. "They might even think they've succeeded. Over and over again. A twisty prison."

Herza and Frinna listened without comment. They had said little for some time now—many cycles of the flaming arc. Yet even those cycles were slowing. No way to calculate how long they were gone, how much distance they'd covered—not even Pahtun's voice knew.

"We've walked halfway to nowhere," Nico said, slumping in a split of black rock, holding his gloved hands to the sides of his helmet. There had been no chance to breathe outside air for many cycles.

"What are those things in those mountains?" Shewel asked.

"Nightmares," Denbord said. "Perf was lucky. He wouldn't have liked any of this."

Tiadba sat between Denbord and Nico, who had a thoughtful expression, as near as she could tell through the dusty golden glow of the faceplate. The armor was not offering much more in the way of explanation. "I think I understand," Nico said cautiously. "It's like a shelf of prizes—trophies from a little war. Only much bigger."

"How's that?" Khren asked.

"Who's collecting?" Macht asked simultaneously.

"We've seen a lot since we left the Tiers," Nico said. "We've met Tall Ones, and things out in the Chaos that might or might not be breeds . . . We know that people don't always look like us, not now and certainly not long ago. So . . . the world outside the Tiers was once bigger than we can imagine. If we just stretch out and think about all the people . . . so many peoples, all different, all strange but somehow *us*, like in the stories in Tiadba's books, if the stories are real . . ."

"They seem real," Khren said.

"They contradict each other," Shewel said.

"True," Nico said. "But imagine . . . for once, do more than a breed can do and think *outside*. Think of all the time and all the people, how different they must have been, and think of the Typhon burning and shrinking everything, playing and destroying at the same time—filled with hatred . . ."

"Or filled with nothing," Khren said.

Nico nodded. "The emptiest of empties. Think of all the times past and all the stories we haven't heard, and all the people who lived those stories and didn't look anything like us, big and small—giants bigger than the Tall Ones, smaller than anyone we know, and stranger than anything in the Kalpa, wakes and sleeps beyond count between them, but still *us* . . ." He let out a sad, soughing breath. "Maybe some of them *were* like gods. But all were defeated. Their stories were stripped away, mangled, burned, but their images and maybe even their bodies might have been collected and carried here, put out on the mountains as prizes, or maybe just to scare us. But if we think of it this way," he concluded, "they're not dead gods. They're just people. They're us."

"We might be stuck out there right beside them," Khren said. "More trophies."

"We'd be with family," Nico said.

Tiadba felt her chest fill and her breath catch.

"They're still scary," Herza said softly.

"If they get up and scoot around, they might not remember we're kin," Frinna added. "Do we have to get close?"

Tiadba sat up and tuned her faceplate to define something she saw gathering over the vale—a cloud that blurred the arc of fire, a mist that dropped from the ruckled sky. "Do you all see that?" she asked.

They gathered in the harsh, high rocks, and their helmets took multiple points of view and worked to discern a pattern, an image, above the greenish mass at the center of the vale.

"It's like an upside-down mountain, just hanging there," Khren said.

"A mountain made of ice," Denbord said.

"A Turvy," the Pahtun voice said. "This can be dangerous."

"What's a Turvy?" Tiadba asked.

"No one in the Kalpa knows much about them. They jumble positions in the Chaos. Turvies are dangerous because all the forces in the Chaos will concentrate around them—new trods will form, the Typhon's servants will gather, and prisoners will awaken to a new level of slavery. It will bring rapid change and great unknowns."

"More monsters?" Frinna asked, drawing close to Herza, and then dragging Denbord toward both of them. He did not struggle.

Macht had turned to walk a few paces away from the group, looking behind at the land they had crossed.

"Everything's shrinking again!" he called. "I can see the Kalpa. The Witness . . . there *it* is, too!"

Tiadba turned and felt herself go dizzy. Light was bending in screw-like loops, and it was certainly possible—even likely—that the Chaos had begun another great deflating, like a toy balloon. If they had all waited . . . would they have had to walk so far to get where they were now?

Frinna screamed, "We're on a trod!"

The rocks smoothed and become sticky, trapping their boots with shocking speed. They seemed to plummet with the flat, pale surface to the level of the floor of the vale. All around the vale, gaps were opening in the mountains and trods were flowing down toward the greenish mass in the center.

Khren lifted their one remaining clave, but before it could activate, a whip shot out and grabbed it away.

No escape.

Already shadows loomed over them, half-blind eyes sweeping and twisted, bruised faces spread flat beneath high, arched bodies . . . and surrounding them, the slender limbs that glided, pulling and pricking at the surface of the trod.

Tiadba watched, paralyzed, as the others were grabbed and raised one by one in flickering, half-seen talons, then held clutched and squirming in the air.

The strangest and largest Silent One of all—three joined faces, sharing four whited, frosted eyes with black pinprick pupils—moved up to bend over her and leer. An arm with a hand like a thorn bush snatched her.

From the center of the vale—the frosted, uncertain green edifice and the icy mountain now hanging over it—came an awful, squealing trill, like millions of things lost beyond hope of rescue, all forced to demonstrate their joy, their happiness . . .

Forced to *sing*.

From the mountains all around, the huge frozen shapes quickened in a way that did not involve life, beyond a breed's understanding— reluctantly juddering down from the mountains, gathering as if by decree to watch and perhaps participate in the Turvy.

One by one, as Tiadba watched, her companions were stripped of their armor. And then came her turn. First the Silent One with three faces and four eyes exposed her arms and legs, all the while the eyes vibrating and shivering, and then thorn-claws pulled at her helmet, which split and gave way just as the Pahtun voice spoke its final message:

"This is not the destination. The beacon—"

Tiadba felt no pain. Yet a kind of vacuum sucked all hope from her mind—then searched, cut, pushed aside . . . and found what it was looking for.

Your sister.

Not a voice, not a presence . . . the emptiest of empties, the quietness of a thing that did not have a voice, but used thousands of other voices to express its message.

You shall not be joined.

Your stories shall not be told.

Her companions were not dead. They were very little changed, in fact still struggled despite the loss of their armor—dangling and squirming, moving their lips without being heard. The Silent Ones swifted these tiny burdens along the new trod toward the center of the vale. Tiadba spun slowly, saw in flashes of spiraling light the giants gather, saw the central greenish mass resolve, take on rough edges and serrated shapes beneath the hovering whiteness . . . an ancient, shimmering illusion now profaned, and mocked, its translucent jade towers and domes spreading throughout the vale, and she *knew* it, recognized it for what it had once been and was no longer.

I've been journeying here since the beginning.

The marchers were carried into lost and haunted Nataraja—the False City.

CHAPTER 95

This was a dream, Ginny was sure of it—a dream someone else was having—and it was lovely.

She was two people in one form, standing under a cloudy sky with patches of brilliant blue, and rolling hills stretched like great swabs of a brush to a definite and pleasant horizon. She was in fact in Thule, the great island just a hundred miles north of Ireland, rich with history: the place she had imagined while being visited by Mnemosyne. The place she had been patiently denied.

It was not quite fully formed, of course. She had to stare hard to make things assume a visual, tactual truth. She could look at the foliage near her feet—a rough kind of bush, heather or gorse or something with purple flowers—and with an effort, the flowers would suddenly *pop* and become real.

Her lips said, in vague tones, "This is wonderful. I've never seen anything like it."

Behind those lips, Ginny asked, "Who's dreaming whom?"

"Maybe it's you. You must know about sky and hills and bushes—I don't."

"What I know, you know. But I don't remember your name."

"We don't have names—for now. I'm in a terrible place. But sometimes I can sleep. So we're together again. *Come for me, find me, before it's too late.*"

———

Ginny shook her head and pushed up from a crouch. She felt refreshed, maybe even encouraged—until now, she'd expected only sadness and grief and pain at the end of her peculiar stroll. She rubbed her cold hands and reached out to test the limit of the bubble.

Thus far and no farther.

More real than the dream, and much less pleasant.

She stood before a great opening in the mountains, guarded by two giant figures she did not want to examine too closely. Made for other places, she guessed, and made of other matter, substances that did special things under special circumstances. *Whatever the hell that means.*

She turned on her heels twice, like a slow top, as she had when faced with the Gape, and felt the dark gritty landscape pirouette. Now she stood before another cleft in the high jagged rocks, guarded by another pair of frozen figures—just as strange, but different. Spinning twice again, she stood before a third opening and a third distinct set of guardians that didn't seem able to do much in the way of guarding. Like colorful ceramic figures decorating a door—*but this time, let's fire the decorator.*

Trophies, all of them. Preserved and mounted after something had enjoyed an awful hunt through the galaxies, collecting specimens.

Ginny shivered.

Spinning twice again—a total of six spins—brought her back to the first gap. She recognized the first set of figures, though she still did not want to examine them up close and personal.

Personal might mean something very different here.

Without doing anything more difficult than spinning on her toes, she was making the entire valley revolve like a lazy Susan platter in a Chinese restaurant. Imagine that. Such power.

There were three entrances to the Vale of Dead Gods. She could imagine them evenly spaced around the bowl formed by the mountains, points on a weird kind of super-triangle.

Typhon space. Or the kind of space a dying universe falls into.

Which entrance should she take?

Each, she knew, would lead her on a unique and separate spiral course into the False City where her dream-sister waited. Other people could enter through other gaps and follow other spiral courses, but they would never meet, never see each other, separated by Typhon-time as well as Typhon-space.

That thought bothered her. All along, since she had left the green warehouse, she had hoped that Jack and maybe Daniel would come to save her from her persistent foolishness—always deliberately choosing the worst path, leading to disaster. Jack seemed the opposite, shifting toward a pleasant sort of survival, if not genuine fortune.

Daniel . . .

Daniel she couldn't figure. *Not a whole number. Irrational.*

He has an irrational set of decimals.

Ah. What's that mean when it's lying down?

But they would no doubt enter the False City through other gaps, and that meant they'd never find her.

Ginny squinted at the guardians, forcing herself to see them for what they were—a matched pair, each with a circlet of ten or more eyes wrapped around otherwise human faces, lips and cheeks skewed in some strange emotion—the head set without a neck above powerful, many-limbed bodies, each limb configured to do something that she could not begin to understand.

She gave up her inspection. No sense adding confusion to madness. She decided that she would call this set of guardians the Welcome Wagon Committee to Hellgate One. She spun around again and named the second pair: WWC to Hellgate Two.

The experience could be repeated. Very scientific. Bidewell would be proud of her.

Spinning again, she found the WWC to Hellgate Three.

Shouldn't just do this all day, however long a day is. Make your choice, Ginny. Even if it's the wrong one.

That was her inner voice, nobody else's. The other had fallen silent. She was alone.

Alone, Ginny knew she could always be relied upon to take the wrong path—except when she decided to go to the green warehouse. And even then, she tried to undo her good decision by venturing out. But now it wasn't just *her* choosing. The sum-runners drew each other together.

So where were the others? Were they out searching for her in the mash-up, their stones tugging them along like eager terriers out for a run?

CHAPTER **96**

The longer Jebrassy marched with Ghentun and Polybiblios, the more he realized what it was like to live around a Great Eidolon—even a fragment of one.

Polybiblios seemed to radiate knowledge. Some new and significant collection of facts or visions flowed into Jebrassy's awareness every hour, filling him with history and science until his old self felt misplaced and overlooked.

Ghentun knew the epitome's influence as well—and spoke his concern. "You're leaking," he told Polybiblios as they paused, helmets off, to rest and assess a new disposition in the Chaos around them.

The epitome squatted beside them. His movements had grown more certain and less awkward, far from the support of the Broken Tower and all the Librarian's servants and selves. He was acquiring his own kind of agility, a grace that reminded Ghentun of an angelin—no surprise. "I apologize. I will try to be less generous."

"I don't mind much," Jebrassy said quietly, staring at the changing ripples of stone. "I just need some time to catch up. I have to think about things and make them my own."

"Of course," Polybiblios said. "Long ago, philosophers would have played a game of questions with their students—or their servants. Each question, so the philosophers claimed, would coax out prior knowledge, natural instincts born into them. What you feel may not be just my 'leaking.' It may be your own quality, emerging right on schedule."

Ghentun looked aside and shook his head. "You've taken us away from the path of the beacon. Why?"

"We will find the beacon again," Polybiblios said. "It was perverted long ago, you know—shortly after my daughter vanished, and Sangmer disappeared in search of her."

Jebrassy's face crinkled in dismay. "Why?" His innermost voice still told him the beacon must be inviolate—the only thing that could guide them to Nataraja, their ultimate goal—their reason for being made in the first place. "That's impossible. Who would do that?"

Polybiblios met their obvious anger with resigned sadness—an easy enough expression in an offshoot of one so old. He did not give them an answer right away. "I hardly remember my own child," he said. "As much as she *was* my child, so many had a part in her making."

"We know the story," Jebrassy said.

"There are so many versions of the story," Polybiblios continued. "The truth may lie frozen and buried in the rubble that shores up the foundations of the Kalpa. So many versions to compare with the fragments of memory that I've managed to retrieve."

Jebrassy lowered his voice and his head and circled the epitome, his anger burrowing deep. Polybiblios followed the breed with calm yet not precisely fearless eyes. "My people are out here, dying or worse—*for no reason?*" the breed growled. "Because an *Eidolon* has forgotten, and others have been careless?"

"Not at all," Polybiblios said. "Between Eidolons, all things have a purpose, sometimes more than one. My greater self knew the lineaments of change the Chaos would undergo over time—its gradual reduction. The beacon now points us to where we need to be. It is finally correct. Sit here." He patted the ground with his gloved hand.

Jebrassy looked between the epitome and Ghentun, his fury undiminished—but controlled. Did this mean all the previous marchers had never had a chance? That they had been sacrificed to distract, provide cover, and prepare for a future time when only a select few would succeed?

With a supreme effort, Jebrassy sat and stared down at the black dust and sharp, ancient stones.

"The path we are taking fits the best version I've pulled from all the stories," Polybiblios said. "Draw from your emerging qualities—think of Ishanaxade, making this same journey. Think of her long sacrifice, that things will come right again."

"You had us search for the stories, then take them with us. You wanted us to find the real story by testing them *all*. Because you had lost the truth. You were *careless*."

"I don't deny carelessness," Polybiblios said. "But putting the past—even could it have been perfectly recorded and stored for tens of trillions of years—packing all that into a microcosm, would have taken far more time and energy than creating and searching a Babel, practically speaking. And had we made that choice, preserving one history—or an ambiguous few—would not be enough to quicken a new cosmos. Not enough to seduce and distract Mnemosyne and awaken the Sleeper."

"Sleeper?" Ghentun sat across from the epitome and the breed. "That's an ancient idea. The Sleeper is supposed to have died at the end of the first creation."

"The Father of Muses," Polybiblios said. "Brahma, some called him very long ago. Not dead. But bored—and so, sleeping."

"That sounds like nonsense," Jebrassy said, fighting his own growing comprehension. He did *not want to know* anything that would blunt his anger.

Tiadba was out there. They might never find her—

But Polybiblios was still overflowing, and this time they were brushed by the emotion of a Great Eidolon.

Ishanaxade.

Jebrassy and Ghentun looked at each other and felt a kind of sadness they had never known before—not the sadness a breed or a Mender could ever feel, but loss and betrayal that could only spread and age and mellow and sharpen all at once, among thousands of millions of epitomes and angelins, through the heights and inner recesses of the Broken Tower . . . across half a million years.

"The City Princes. They reset the beacon. They betrayed *you*," Ghentun said.

"They betrayed my daughter," Polybiblios said, looking away from them, as if he could not bear any kind of mirror. "We may have all betrayed her. What she must feel, after all this time—hiding out there, waiting. Or worse—captured."

"If you know all the stories, then you know all the endings," Jebrassy said. "Which one is true?"

"There are far more endings to a story than there are beginnings," Polybiblios said. "The best stories start in the middle, then return to the beginning, then come to a conclusion that nobody can foresee. Sometimes, when you return to the middle, the story will change again. At least, they did when I was young."

His voice seemed to hypnotize them. They saw a whirling lattice of fates surrounding a tiny and indistinct shape, barely remembered after so many ages.

"The City Princes," the Keeper said, making it a kind of curse.

"They agreed to send Ishanaxade on a secret journey, without your knowing," Jebrassy said. "But why?"

Ghentun placed his hands together as if in prayer. "Ishanaxade offered herself up to save the Librarian. She carried away the key to the most complete Babel the Librarian had created in the Broken Tower."

"That much seems true," Polybiblios said. "Whatever our disagreements, the Astyanax and all the other City Princes knew—"

"That a complete Babel, with all its parts brought together, would dissolve what remained of the old cosmos," Ghentun said—and then saw that this knowledge did not come from Polybiblios. This was part of the image the Astyanax had placed inside his mind. "The muses, what little was left of them, would revive to examine the greatest wealth of stories—all possible stories, and all possible nonsense."

"Both nonsense and story necessary for any creation, though, as always, there is a vastly greater proportion of nonsense," the epitome said, and got to his feet. "My daughter sacrificed herself, when others wished only to see my project come to an end, incomplete."

Ghentun said, "The Great Eidolons wanted to live whatever sort of life was left to them, trapped in the Kalpa, repeating their amusements, lost in decadent boredom but also extraordinary comfort—they wanted this to go on *forever*." He stood, fists in the air. "*You* wanted to jump-start creation. That would have been the end of us all."

Polybiblios looked between them, guileless as a child—an exceedingly old child. "That was my expectation."

"The Eidolons allowed Ishanaxade to cross the Chaos," Jebrassy murmured. "But they knew Nataraja was already dead."

"The City Princes made a deal with the Typhon," Polybiblios concluded. "We were all betrayed. But that does not mean we failed. Far from it."

The air in this part of the Chaos was growing stuffy and unpleasant. Together, as if in silent agreement that there must be a pause in this conversation, they sealed up their helmets and prepared to move on.

Jebrassy asked after they had resumed walking, "What is the Typhon, that it can make bargains?"

"Not to be known, young breed," Polybiblios said. "But the Kalpa should have fallen long ago. It has not."

"You knew this—yet you allowed me to send out marchers . . ." Ghentun was greenish-black with anger. He could no longer express himself in words.

Polybiblios looked around the changing landscape. "My daughter carried crucial parts of my creations, took them to Nataraja . . . Away from the reality generators. There was never any choice. But before she left, she asked both of us—Astyanax and Librarian—to join together and remake the oldest form of human being we could conceive of, in primordial matter. She asked that we assign their upkeep and education to the Menders. Of me alone, she asked that sum-runners be made and entrained—the most sublime of Shen technologies, more subtle even than the reality generators or this armor. And of me alone she asked that I place my fragmented Babels within the sum-runners, as a contingent plan—sending them back to course forward from the beginning of time, whispering to each other, and connecting all who touched them. Ishanaxade was mother to the ancient breeds. And she is mother to all who dream."

"It *is* the greatest story of all," Ghentun admitted. "She left her city, she left Sangmer—everything and everyone she loved. And she thought she served even as she betrayed."

"What about Sangmer?" Jebrassy asked. "How could he possibly understand? Did he ever find her? What happened to *him?*"

"We live that story, young breed. We echo its flesh and bones, that we may tempt it out of hiding. And then, when it is finished, we move on— or come to our own abrupt conclusion."

CHAPTER 97

Ginny felt something go out of her as she passed under the frozen gaze of the inner ring of giants. Her bubble of protection seemed to thin and breathing became difficult. The stone no longer tugged in a specific direction, but instead pulled her one way, then back, then another, its insistence growing weaker, until finally she stood as still as one of the statues, within sight of the defile where she had entered the valley.

There was only one conclusion she could draw from the stone's reluctance to offer guidance. Either she had moved too far or traveled too fast . . . entering a place where one stone by itself could not protect her.

Why lead her on at all, then?

She wiped her eyes and noticed particles of soot floating above and around her, made more obvious by contrast against a rapidly coalescing mountain of ice that hung upside down over the valley. Needles and flows of sapphire blue grew from the floor in complete silence while she watched, her head cocked and neck growing stiff. They formed a ring of columns around the valley's perimeter, as if to cage the False City, the central jade structure. Mist draped the mountain rims, thickening into clouds like clouds back home—if home was anywhere now. If she had ever grown up, ever lived, if any of her memories could be said to have been real . . .

Out here, the ice pinnacle and pillars possessed an eerie beauty more terrestrial than Chaotic, like the bottom of an iceberg, maybe, or the Alps inverted. Strange that something impossible would look more convincing, surrounded by things only very unlikely.

Her exhaustion became dark and profound, and she lay down on the uneven softness of the bubble, but her eyes would not close. She could not sleep—had not slept since leaving Bidewell's warehouse.

But if she could sleep—and if she could dream—then she knew that her visitor, her other, was already inside the ghostly green city . . . and that Tiadba had also come to the wrong place.

Both had been misled.

Both had been betrayed.

Ginny thought of the awful, stocky old brute and his insinuations. She had not even spoken with Jack or Bidewell before leaving. Or Daniel. What would either of them have told her?

They might have told her to *wait*. And so, that was what she was going to do now that she had no choice. She would lie here just a bit above the valley floor, surrounded by mountains and paralyzed giants, with an upside-down mountain of ice waiting to fall at any instant— and she would *wait*. She would stay here forever, if necessary, growing more and more tired, until she simply floated off like a bit of weightless ash.

The moment of rest stretched on. She tried to roll over—felt the bubble closing in until she could no longer move. She lay on her back, watching the ice mountain block out the rim of fire. The fire had turned dusky orange, the darkness within faded to grayish purple. The wrinkled sky beyond the ice mountain was slowly obscured by blue mists, clouds edged with glorious gold. The sky itself was shrinking.

It was frightening and beautiful.

All she had seen so far was frightening and ugly.

"Something *new* is coming," she murmured with numbed lips.

By which she meant something *old*.

CHAPTER 98

The three—Jebrassy, Ghentun, and the epitome of the Librarian—saw the paleness over the center of the vale.

They had walked many miles, approaching at times the innermost of the so-called Dead Gods that watched each other across the uneven plain. Their faces—if they could be called faces—seemed locked in a quiet, reflective arrogance, shaped by trillions of years of self-determined change, intelligence in control of all evolution; a variety of visages and shapes both handsome and incomprehensible, monstrous and beautiful at once, like so many sea creatures spread out on an immense, eternal reef.

"Will they ever live again?" Ghentun asked. Polybiblios seemed about to answer.

"No more time for lessons and leakings," Jebrassy said. "Move on."

The epitome listened with patient humor. "Time is indeed shorter. But time for others will not flow over this vale with the same speed, nor cover the same instants. This is a Turvy. Every pass, every gate, sends its entrants onto a different track to the center."

"I thought there were only two fates left," Ghentun said.

"Fates, yes—but in a Turvy, those paths can be swirled until they seem to lie parallel. You can jump from one to another—but they are the same, part of a spiral. In many regions of the Chaos the rules of the very tiny have been writ large. You have to spin twice just to face the same direction. Here, it is even more complicated. We can see behind us—there seems to be a way back, a retreat—but if we reverse course and try to leave, we will fail."

"We could jump to the other track and get to the center faster, couldn't we?" Jebrassy asked.

"No," the epitome said. "We are where we need to be."

Ahead, the gathering cloud had hardened into an upside-down mountain of ice, its edges like scalloped blades.

"The tracks will merge soon enough," the epitome said. "The cosmos is in its final moments. The revolt of the very small is about to begin—and I don't mean *you*, young breed. The pressure on the Typhon is growing. Out here, the former master does not know *how* to change."

"What pressure?" Ghentun asked.

"This is all that remains. The Chaos has shrunk to two circles. One circle surrounds this vale. The other surrounds what is left of the Kalpa. There may still be a path between them, sprinkled with bits and pieces of the past. I don't know. Maybe that's closed, too. Outside lies nothing. That is the Typhon's legacy. For all its power, it can leave no mark— only void. It tried to be a god, and it failed. There is no nowhere left for it to go. No escape."

"All the stories left unfinished?" Jebrassy asked, unsure, then disgusted.

"No. If we succeed, what comes after, not even the whole of my self could understand. We will be as children before wonders. There is a greater force, who thus far has paid little heed to most of our trillion centuries."

"Hmph. The Sleeper?" Jebrassy was tired of being ignorant until taught. He wanted to teach himself—learn on his own. Learn what had happened to Tiadba.

He was almost afraid to know.

"The Turvy will be the Typhon's last chance," the epitome said. "It will need to capture us and prevent the sum-runners from being joined. Watch for trods. Gliders, Scouts, Ascendants, Silent Ones . . . If they have nowhere else to go, they'll come hunting here."

They moved on toward the bowl and the green center of the vale. Ahead, blue pillars of ice grew to meet the upside-down mountain's gleaming edges.

"Something's coming," Jebrassy said. "Not trods. Not monsters. Something else—I can feel it."

"So can I," the epitome said. "So can they all."

They could hear a thin, shrieking bellow now—pulsing in from all around, an awful nastiness, like strangling, screaming, and shouts of warning commingled.

The giants lining the mountains were struggling to speak. Some seemed to struggle to move—shivering and stiffly casting off soot and rubble from around their bases.

"They've seen this before," Polybiblios said. "It's this vision that filled their blood and marrow and turned them fossil. It's what the Witness has tried to warn us about for half an eternity.

"The Typhon has nowhere left to hide. It is coming here with all its servants—all those it has captured and tormented. Here we will find my daughter."

CHAPTER 99

The seeing had not gotten any easier. There was an optical perversity that no manner of twisting and squinting could set right. Even within their protective caul, which Jack hoped he would never need to explain—he felt maligned by the views that somehow crept into his eyes.

Any living place showed both decay and growth, like the jumble of dead and living trees in a forest, or even a city burned, booted, crushed by war. Here there was only shoddiness, a despondent dull-ness of wit, will, and enthusiasm—in short, a lazing failure to keep and maintain.

This place showed only decay.

Not much comfort to be had from resting his eyes.

Jack was aware that Glaucous had been trying once again to hook his affection and trust, to consign these little fish to one or another bas-ket—his, or failing that, Daniel's. Daniel was a fake, of course—with-out actually slinking, he slunk, and without saying anything, he lied. Even the truth from his lips was deceptive, because they were not *his lips*. Glaucous was little better—honest in shape, but that shape worse than lies.

Still, they all had to stay close. Their bodies rejected what lay beyond the bubble. One could fall back just six or seven paces—no one dared more—before all suffered exhaustion, closeness of breath, headaches, sneezing—blood from nose, ears, fingertips. They were filthy with soot and streaks of wiped blood. The bubble did allow something like smell—phantom scents, madness and burning, sour and sick.

Nobody was supposed to be here. *Here* did not tolerate intruders. Now they could see almost nothing—a kind of spot of dim glow for some distance, restless darkness on all sides, a tumbled blankness, gray invalidity, the wholesale lack of anything and everything, only slightly less disturbing than the more defined things they had already seen.

Sometimes the tumbles and wrinkles assumed the crooked aspects of a landscape, then just as easily gave it all up—a bad piece of work—and resumed *void*.

Something seemed to surround the void and briefly spin, like being caught inside a wheel or a gyroscope. But then it vanished.

It might never have been.

The design on the box.

Jack had almost given up hope for Ginny. They hadn't found her or her trail—the surface beneath their shoes mostly felt like old but solid rock—but their sum-runners had pulled them along with precisely the same tug as Ginny's. Or so he assumed, since Daniel's two stones be-haved just like Jack's.

The dead, empty cities were now behind them—incomprehensible hulks floated ashore from far, severed times, beached and then subjected to perverse inspection, angry dissection, and finally—Jack tried to imagine and reconstruct it—a restless, angry rejection.

Whole cities cast aside like broken cadavers, marked and scattered with hatred and confusion. All that wreckage worked over by a starless, pitchy, unhappy thing, totally powerful, yet completely clueless within and without.

His fancies grew.

Glaucous's rough voice knocked him out of his fugue. "While you two slept, I kept watch. We've come around some things like hills or mountains."

"How could we sleep?" Daniel objected. "We were walking."

"You sleep, walking or not."

Jack wrinkled his nose. "Nightmares without sleep," he suggested.

"Lies without reason," Daniel countered, and looked left at Glaucous. Their shoes made an unpleasant sound falling on the bubble and pressing it to the uneven black rock—a squeaking *trunch, trunch*.

"Gentlemen," Glaucous said, as if urging civility. Then he halted and stared ahead and his eyes grew wide. "Couldn't be."

Jack and Daniel moved two paces by reflex before stopping. "Couldn't be what?" Jack asked.

"I am a sensible fellow," Glaucous insisted, sleeving sweat from his cheeks.

Now it was Jack's turn to see movement ahead—small, dark shapes, low and sleek, with long curls rising and twitching. Not unfamiliar, certainly not frightening in and of themselves. And yet—here!

"Cats," Jack said. Daniel turned.

"Amazingly capable, cats," Glaucous said. "Excellent and powerful Shifters, and some are Chancers. Gods and masters of those who diminish and gnaw."

The shapes had faded.

Glaucous took a deep breath. "Now, as to those hills and mountains," he said. "They've been described to me. They enclose an unhappy place." He made as if to dig a furrow in the air with his spaded palm. "I've been told this is where the Moth delivers shepherds and their stones. A long, shallow gouge—like a valley ringed with high peaks, surrounded by unspeakable things taken prisoner in far places. And in the center of it all, a shallow bowl with three fate-braided entrances, confounding to Chancers and Shifters alike.

"This is where the Chalk Princess rules."

CHAPTER 100

The False City

Tiadba had been wrapped in a cocoon of dust and fiber, like sweepings neglected in a corner. Her eyes stung and pricked but she did not dare lift her fingers to wipe them—hands and skin were both crusted with sharp grit.

Often enough, over hours like beads strung on endless necklaces, she had felt the grit crawl on her skin as if alive . . . Could not imagine what it might be.

Living, consuming decay.

Did not much care.

Here, beyond exhaustion, trapped—one bead of the necklace cold, the next neither cold nor warm—drained and burned to a crisp yet still capable of pain, not caring whether there was pain, only now and then could she rouse memory of her companions—her fellow marchers— and when she did, the grit jabbed all the more sharply. Memories and regrets had become tiny shards, sharp and glassy, caked on her skin and jabbing into her eyes.

Tiadba had seen her marchers carried along the glowing, fluid trod through a hole like spreading lips rimmed with sores, into a great dingy hollowness . . . had seen bloated, slavering things, long and malevolent, hurry from far walls to dangle from squirming legs and stab with scimitar jaws.

Jaws that smoked and sparked.

Grabbing, piercing, and burning, then scurrying back into the hollowness.

Tiadba curled. If she curled tight enough, perhaps she would simply fold into herself and vanish. Anything could happen here.

She opened her eyes long enough to lift her hand, crusted over by dried blood. Bits of glove—shreds of dead armor that no longer protected or spoke—tried to glimmer on her fingers. But memory and betrayal pushed the shreds apart, finished the task of peeling them away, leaving her totally naked.

All were naked.

She could not tell how long it had been before she was lifted and her eyes were brushed clear. She blinked at the immensity of gloom and shadow and dust.

She stood or had been propped stiffly on what might have been the side of a hill under a great canopy. The limits of the canopy seemed to waver, to rise and fall, uncertain not just in color or brightness, but also in distance and dimension. Still, something was arriving, something coming near promised to give what she was seeing proportion and perspective.

Something—or someone.

"Hello, crèche-born."

Drops of cool, soothing liquid fell into her eyes and then froze them in place—to stare unblinking at a triangle of unformed whiteness.

A cool, crystalline voice of immense beauty and sadness whirled up and lay on the porches of her ears, then introduced itself word by word, languid, stroking. The words filled her ears and caused a dull, stretching pain.

"I compelled Shapers and Menders to make you. Do you know me?"

The shape within the triangular cloud coalesced. Above the middle arrived a face—well-shaped, eyes large and deep—beautiful and sad and commanding. An emotion rose, swelling within Tiadba: *deep* recognition, built into her at birth, ordained for all her kind ages before. She suddenly wanted to feel glad. This was reunion, what should have been a time of joy. "I know you," she said.

"And I know you. I am proud, young breed. You are rich with dream. You have brought time forward . . . as you were designed to do. But now your connection with what has gone before is a curse. There is only turmoil and torment to come. But in this, our last moment of peace, I am allowed to ask one question of all who are brought here. That is *my* torture—an instant of anticipation and hope."

Tiadba tried to see more clearly the dazzling white face like softly mobile stone, malleable outlines surrounded by other pieces whirling up and falling back again on chill, dust-laden wafts.

The face drew close.

Tiadba tried to pull back—shrink away.

"Do you know what has become of Sangmer, called the Pilgrim?"

The voice, so close to Tiadba's face, carried no hint of breath or moving air—but a strange sweetness surrounded her all the same in that sensual desolation.

Tiadba felt a stinging shock. She thought of lying beside Jebrassy on the bed, making love and trying to riddle the ancient stories . . . of moments in the Chaos, reading from the ever-changing books to soothe and inform the marchers—but there had never been a conclusion to those stories, and the words were often obscure.

However, before this cold, frightening beauty, Tiadba could not help but offer hope. "I might have seen him. Maybe I wouldn't know," she said, lips numbing even as she spoke. "Tell me what he looks like."

"I don't *remember*." Sadness and zeroing cold fogged between them. "No time remains, no time at all . . ." Words like falling and dying insects. "You have brought me nothing."

"I'm sorry . . ." Tiadba searched for a word, found it in the memory of her other. "I am so sorry, *Mother*."

"I am sorry, as well, crèche-born. You cannot know my sorrow. It would be a mercy if we both could die."

CHAPTER 101

"We're never going to find her," Daniel said. "We're crazy to even be out here."

"Where would you have us go, young master?" Glaucous asked.

"Everything's different," Jack said. "It'll keep getting more different. Maybe it will get better."

The gap between the monstrous statues—the gap that opened into the bowl where stood the most unlikely city of all—had closed behind them as if it had never been.

"Three choices," Glaucous said. "This is the best."

"You said the Chalk Princess is just around the corner, right?" Daniel said. "Why doesn't she swoop down and take us?"

Glaucous stopped. His breath pumped and hissed like a steam engine losing its push. "She's here," he said.

"What do you think will happen?" Daniel asked.

"She'll release me," Glaucous said. "No reward, no punishment. Just put me to an end. I deserve no more—and no less."

He resumed walking like a long-suffering beast.

Daniel could hardly breathe. A feeling of heaviness, and compression, like bricks on his chest . . . he tried to understand what was going on in terms of physics but only made a bad job of it. "Vacuum energy heading back up toward zero," he muttered. "Higgs field collapsing. Too small."

"What?" Jack asked.

"Nothing. We're lost."

It did look as if they were out of options.

The land had never made sense. Now it was little more than a succession of silhouettes, trains and trails of pointless shadow. They had long since passed out of the neighborhoods of compressed and crunched history, through mad playgrounds of whatever passed for time outside their bubble—and now they were simply nowhere.

Fortunately, that nowhere was becoming smaller.

Daniel faced them. "The stones still tug. There's still direction."

Jack shook his head and took the lead.

They still had up and down, forward but not back, a kind of sideways . . . the limited movement a blessing in territory otherwise devoid of any particular quality. There was no going back and starting over. Something would not allow it.

"Whole numbers," Daniel said.

Jack walked into deeper shadow. For a moment Glaucous and Daniel almost lost sight of him, just two or three steps ahead.

"Jack!" Daniel called.

They caught up. Glaucous chuffed and staggered.

"You're a whole number," Daniel said. "An integer."

"Whatever," Jack said. His fingers tightened on the stone.

"Your call number," Daniel said. "However long it is, it's an integer—it's not irrational, and it's not infinite."

"We always ask for their numbers," Glaucous affirmed, looking between them. "Not that we know what we're asking for. Too long to speak aloud, all folded into trick paper. First seventy-five digits crucial, however."

"I've been thinking about it," Daniel said. "I don't belong in any library. Books make me uncomfortable. I don't have a call number. Never did have a folded piece of paper. Or if I do, it's not an integer—it's irrational. I don't have a story. That's why you didn't hunt me."

"Interesting," Glaucous said.

"I've had a long time to think it through," Daniel said. "I don't belong. Someone or something sent me back, stuck me there, but I just don't fit."

Jack disappeared into the murk.

Again, something spun all around them—the vanes of a gyroscope—and faded.

"Slow down!" Daniel called.

CHAPTER 102

It took Jebrassy a while to realize that he could no longer see or hear the others. He paused and waited. Drifts of sharp grit slid over the rippled black rock. The ripples had grown deeper—they were now channels in a curved maze that stretched to either side as far as he could see. Ahead, the edges of the ripples had risen up, curled over, and joined—creating a low wall of tunnel entrances, and beyond that, another higher rank, and still more beyond them.

He sat on the rim of a channel and waited some more, but neither Ghentun nor Polybiblios seemed anywhere near. Maybe they had gotten in front of him and already entered the holes. He could not wait. This might be another kind of trap—an eternity of indecision. Tiadba was still waiting.

He made up his mind to try one of the closest entrances. Only when he was some distance in, stooped, did he think that now that he was committed, the tunnel might be blocked ahead, and if he turned around, it would be blocked behind. It caused a moment of terror—he ran and pushed deeper into the tunnel, wanting to get it over with, to learn for sure that he was trapped, finally and irrevocably.

But nothing in the Chaos ever repeated itself, or was ever what he anticipated. The tunnel continued, growing a little in girth, and finally debouched into a larger space; how much larger, he couldn't tell, even after his eyes had cleared of sweat.

Jebrassy stood at the edge of an interior volume so large he could not see the other side. The only way he could know there was a roof was that the flaming arc was not visible, nor the ice mountain, nor the seethe of the shrinking sky.

Tentative, he stepped away from the wall of tunnel exits. Dimly, larger objects took on detail, then smaller. He seemed to be surrounded by immense piles of things he could not identify—huge spheres strung on massive cables, smooth but dusty round lumps rising from the ground between the spheres—more spheres perhaps, half buried—and jagged parts of things that were almost certainly manufactured but looked as if they had been treated badly—dropped, shattered, and then piled up.

Discarded.

He approached one of the suspended spheres, many hundreds of feet in diameter and floating no more than a breed's height above the floor—and reached out with his gloved fingers—only to be pushed back. The longer he looked, the more he saw on the sphere's surface, until he realized he was looking at a *place,* a planet, highly developed, covered with cities, roads, things he could not identify—outside even his dream experiences.

He turned slowly, wondering how these spheres and heaps had come to be brought here. Everywhere, the lost and discarded. He was beginning to think the Chaos was actually a giant litter bin.

Determined to keep a line of retreat in sight—if you could still see things, and kept them in periodic view, they didn't go away as often—he ventured farther into the rubble.

Polybiblios was waiting for him, sitting on a low wall that divided several larger and taller piles. "Good to see you," the epitome said. "I was beginning to think I had lost my companions."

"Where's the Keeper?" Jebrassy asked.

"Somewhere back there. It's humiliating, how much of a puzzle this is. A wasteland of failed efforts. Consider all these worlds, stored here like shrunken heads in a dusty box. But I might have found something— or someone—more interesting."

He gestured for Jebrassy to follow. With some misgivings, he did so. Was it possible, having lost sight of the epitome, that a duplicate might have been conjured up, completely different?

"I've spent a pretty long while exploring this space," the epitome said. "Making maps and then adjusting them for changes—not as many changes here as outside, interestingly. Something seemed to want to keep track of whatever is piled up here. Including . . . this."

They came to a glassy wall. Embedded within the wall, near the surface, was a figure roughly shaped like Jebrassy—but larger, more robust. He wore no armor and a very different style of clothing than that found in the Tiers.

Farther along, other figures—some much the same, others very different—also lay embedded, caught in moments of shock or anger or surprise. Jebrassy walked from one to the next, then put his gloved hand up against the smooth surface.

"A fate mire, I believe," Polybiblios said.

"What's that?"

"Not so easy to conceive of, but perhaps you've had enough preparation and training. Tell me what your instincts say."

"They're all like my visitor," Jebrassy said, thinking so hard—and feeling so many strange emotions—that his head hurt. "But there's too many of them."

"Definitely ancient forms," Polybiblios said. "If we had been able to access these when we were designing the breeds, we might have done better. Though they do differ in significant respects."

Jebrassy saw no signs of life in the embedded figures. "They're from the past?"

"Many pasts, more likely. How they got here—that's harder to conceive. I wonder if my full Eidolon self could solve the riddle. At any rate, that one there . . . Get closer—hold up your hand. Make as if to touch it through the transparency."

Jebrassy stepped up to the body closest to the shining surface and rubbed his glove against the smoothness. Thin bright ribbons of blue light—hundreds, then thousands of them—curled between the outstretched fingers and his own, penetrating his glove. He could feel a tickle, a slight shock, moving up his arm.

"Dreamers, all of them," Polybiblios said. "The same matter—in large part—from many times and many different branches of fate, eager to be rejoined."

"We're made of the same stuff?"

"I'd say so. Entangled atoms are reacquainting, exchanging particles of entrainment, which leave photonic traces—faster than the fastest velocity possible in the Chaos. Or anywhere else, now."

"Then none of the visitors have survived? We've failed?"

"Where is that Keeper? He might be able to help us judge the extent of this collection."

"There are so many—I don't think I've dreamed about all of them."

"Part of my plan was that shepherds and sum-runners would evolve together. But remember, there used to be many world-lines, many pathways leading to the Kalpa. Not to put too fine a point on it, but your visitor has failed to make a connection with you many times before now. Just as marchers have been snared and trapped out in the Chaos. Now the pathways are limited to two. There may be just one opportunity left."

"Does that mean you've come out here thousands of times before, and failed?" Jebrassy asked.

"Excellent question. Would it even be possible to remember?" The epitome considered this problem with apparent relish, then smoothed his face and said, "Most unlikely. This is my first and only path."

Jebrassy again spread his hand close to the fingers of the embedded other. The ribbons of blue continued to pass. "It doesn't hurt," he said. "It's almost pleasant."

Polybiblios pulled him away. "That's enough. We don't want to entrain you with the lost. We need to find the one that is still free, still alive . . . or arrive at a place where he can find you. I doubt very much he would be here."

CHAPTER **103**

Ginny walked and then crawled through the tunnels, feeling the stone in her pocket nudge with a gentleness that seemed almost to speak of understanding and sympathy. Or perhaps a touch of apprehension.

She was in no mood to be strong-armed. She knew she was close, but she was beginning to feel a deep anger, not at the prospect of failure, but at having achieved some measure of success, having made it this far on her own—yet without actually making a decision. She had never *chosen* any of this. It had all been forced upon her. Stronger persons and circumstances had always directed her, misdirected her, all her remembered life. Others were no doubt trying to find her and save her—from herself, from bad decisions.

But they had never actually been *her* decisions.

Maybe that was because she could not be trusted. She always turned the wrong way. Always stumbled into a path of disaster.

Yet she had come this far, ahead of all the others.

The tunnel had branched so many ways, and she had always gone to the left—gauche, sinister, awkward, but the best way out of this sort of maze. And how could she know that?

She'd always been awkward—had *always* turned left.

Now she crawled out of the tunnel and squatted in the gloom of a cavernous space, listening.

Silence. Neither disapproval nor applause.

Completely alone, in a place no one could call home.

"I'm worn-out," she said. "I don't want to be a guided missile anymore." She felt the stone through the cloth of her pants, then took it out and looked it over in the dim light. Its tug had faded almost to nothing. It turned and rotated freely in her fingers. The knobs and ridges were smooth and cool under the roughened flesh of her fingertips.

The red wolf's-eye gleam had also dulled.

"If you give up on me, I'll be stuck here, won't I?" she asked. She stood and felt the bubble draw in so close it might have been a layer of paint over her skin. The game was running down. There might have been some sort of excess of unexpected energy—Bidewell might understand. But now the entire universe, even the dead and dismantled parts ruled over by the Typhon, was closing its books, leaving the final accounts in disarray . . . because it was all going to be zeroed out anyway.

She moved slowly on numb feet toward a gleam in the distance. Ignored the weird stuff piled all around—not enough energy to pay attention, to show curiosity.

Alone. Good. She would make her final wrong turn without anyone clucking their disapproval. Out of the maze, straight into . . .

A long wall of smoky glass stretched out of sight on both sides. Within the wall, she saw dozens, hundreds . . . she looked both ways—*thousands* of contorted, floating, still figures . . . all young women.

"Too much," she whispered, but pressed her bubble in closer, trying to see. Blue lines whipped from her cheeks, chin, and fingers and touched the nearest body locked in the smoky, translucent hardness.

Familiar. Eyes blank, hopeless, set in a slack face with an expression neither of pain nor despair but of neutrality. A lot like herself, seen in an awful mirror.

"Is this my other?" she whispered. "Is this Tiadba? She's trapped somewhere—and this one's trapped, too."

But the figure looked nothing like Tiadba, as Ginny remembered the dreams. No . . . it was a version of herself. And . . .

The body was holding something in its hand. Or rather, suspended within loose fingers, not quite touching or being touched, the grasp having been loosened in despair or surrender just before the embedding, this floating, timeless preservation.

"You turned the wrong way, you got tired, you gave up," she said to her alternate self, beginning to feel a kind of attraction, a familiarity and warmth not just with the figure, but with its fate. So comfortable, never thinking or moving or feeling again. No more stupid decisions. A gentle conclusion. Not what she would have expected out here in the Chaos, on the outskirts of the False City.

Not so much cruel as just neutral—blank.

The blue ribbons of light streamed from her fingers and face, caresses of energy. They tingled. She could get used to that tingling. It was friendly. She was close to the family of all her alternate selves, all the ones who had failed and then . . . had been forgiven.

She had found her way here to reacquaint.

Somehow, there was a style about this that separated itself from the blundering cruelty of the rest of the Chaos. A kind of pity.

She recognized the sadness, the gentleness combined with the power and strangeness. This was what she had felt when confronted by the whirling storm in the woods, the great, desperate, swirling triangle of seeking.

This was where the Chalk Princess took her captives. Or where they came of their own accord, to join with their lost selves in continuous, never-ending self-pity and empty satisfaction.

The ribbons grew brighter. The wall seemed to soften.

The figure directly before her—inches away in the smoky substance—seemed to recede, and Ginny's last bit of unhappiness was painted over with a cool, complacent acceptance of all she had ever been: all her failures, her losses.

This was her story. Her life finally had a conclusion, however unsatisfying.

Perversely, the farther into the glass the other girl receded, the clearer her features and circumstances became—as if the ribbons of blue light were completing her, filling her out.

Ginny could easily make out the nature of the object in the other girl's hand. It was another stone—its gleam extinguished. A dead sumrunner, its course through all of time aborted, its shepherd snared.

The ribbons became blinding in their intensity. With them, something essential was being transferred, carried away, grounded against the frozen girl inside the smoky glass, useless, finished.

Ginny drew back her hand. Not quickly—not with revulsion or fear. She simply pulled with all her remaining strength. All these girls—young women—were just like her. But they'd had the luxury of multitudes. They could all fail and it would not be finished—more might come and join them.

Not her. Not this Ginny.

"I'm the last one, aren't I?" she muttered to this gentle and accepting tomb of hope.

If she were another type of shepherd, with another type of story, she might have entered the city through another opening into the bowl, crawled through the tunnel labyrinth in another instinctively natural fashion, making other types of unlikely and wrong turns . . . and found another smoky glass wall, infinitely deep, trapping another multitude of lost alternates.

There might be a wall of Jacks out there, a wall of Daniels—perhaps not Daniel—

Ginny now stood several paces back from the glass. The force of blue leaking from her skin, piercing the bubble and sucked into the suspension, faded. The ribbons curled back in livid disappointment.

"No wrong turn this time," she said. "I've got friends who need me. I'm alone, but not for long."

She spun around again, then turned the *other* gauche—not adroit, not her style—and made her way through the rest of the incomprehensible, accumulated garbage ransacked from a dying cosmos.

She knew she was making the wrong decision yet again—toward more misery and challenge—but for all the right reasons.

CHAPTER 104

Jebrassy walked with a slow step beside Polybiblios, his strength like a guttering fire. He felt less than half the breed he had been before he and Tiadba were separated.

Ghentun rejoined them beyond the fate-mire, on top of a high wall angled up against other walls that seemed to form an immense octagon. Below the walls: sharply curved perspectives relieved only by faraway glimmers of blue light—as if other beings made of primordial matter were being tested and compared.

Captured marchers. *Tiadba!*

"What's wrong?" Ghentun asked.

"A premature encounter," Polybiblios said. They paused to allow Jebrassy to recoup some of his strength. The armor seemed barely up to the task.

"I've reconnoitered," Ghentun said as they looked out over the cells beyond and—presumably—a multitude of enclosed fate-mires. "There's still some semblance to the Nataraja of old. The Deva quarters are almost unchanged—though deserted."

Jebrassy lifted his head. "The Mass Wars," he said.

Polybiblios reached out to touch his shoulder. "Not our concern. Histories lost and buried."

"Your kind—Devas—were forced to become Eidolons," Jebrassy said. "Many fled to Nataraja . . . Why didn't you?"

"You're still leaking," Ghentun accused the epitome. "He needs to rest."

"I can't help it," Polybiblios said. "My parts have been bathed in knowledge for a billion years."

"When did it ever work right?" Jebrassy asked. "When did anyone ever respect the heritage and birthright of others?"

"Often enough, for very long periods," Ghentun said, glancing at the epitome, as if competing over who knew the most history.

"But then, in all our memories: collapse, reversion, strife," Polybiblios said, unaware of any competition. "The cosmos has become tainted. History has been distorted by the corruption of the Typhon. In the depths of the Brightness, some might have called it original sin. But it was not original. It creeps back from the end of time. We refused to let the universe die gracefully. We allowed the Typhon to latch onto a weakened and overextended chronology. Brahma still sleeps. Not even an Eidolon will ever know the shape and disposition of the original creation. We gain some insight when we contemplate the joy of matter—now almost lost."

Ghentun was baffled. He had never heard of the joy of matter.

"We should move on," Polybiblios insisted. "Our moment is brief."

"Jebrassy needs to rest, to get back his strength," Ghentun reminded the epitome, though his motives for saying so were not selfless. Clearly, here were deep and ancient curiosities that deserved to be answered. And he was willing to give up his envy or resentment to learn.

"Not here," Polybiblios said. "If this Turvy or whatever it is truly does still have some of the old lineaments of Nataraja, there will be a better place . . . a preserve the Typhon cannot touch. And there we may have time for some explanations."

"Not bad from the beginning?" Jebrassy asked as Ghentun lifted him to his feet. "Bad from the end?"

"What is lost is lost, young breed," Polybiblios said. "Let us work with what little remains. The metric is greatly reduced. We've already traveled faster than any of our marchers. We can use that to our advantage."

———

Like most of the last great cities of old Earth, Nataraja had been a monument of efficiency—not spread out over thousands of miles, but concentrated in a high interlinked erection of spheres intersecting and carried by flowing sheeted curves, neighborhoods and urbs for those of different constructions and persuasions—the entirety enclosed by many different shields to defend against the threats of ages long past. With the passing of those threats and the coming of new ones, the shields had been transformed, incorporated into the city's matrix, just as cities in the early Brightness had grown and enclosed their old siege walls.

Between his education in the tower and the epitome's continuing outflow, Jebrassy found renewed strength in the realization that his curiosity was being met—he was learning much of what he had always wanted to learn, secrets withheld from his lower kind. Simply to be where so many breeds had been created to go, in the fabulous city of Tiadba's storybooks—however dark and awful parts of it were—seemed for a moment at least splendid beyond measure. If Tiadba were still with them—

Then together they could complete the stories, solve the mysteries. The Librarian's epitome was telling them that things had not always been so bad . . . and that meant there might be dreamers who would come to them, who could spin such beautiful tales, if those lost pasts could be patched together, refreshed . . .

All a wonderment of wishful thinking, of course. But his body felt the renewal. Hope for Tiadba—but beyond that, hope for all breeds . . .

He struggled to understand.

Hope for every type of human being or living thing that had ever been. *What we live now—what has been lived for more than half an eternity, perhaps* all *of eternity—is not the only way!*

———

With the combined skills and knowledge of Ghentun and Polybiblios, they climbed up from the hive of fate-mires and stood overlooking the center of the great bowl, under layer upon layer of collapsed shields and roof, the rubble studded with ruins, but also with crudely remade arenas, boulevards, even neighborhoods where—using the tricks of Chaos light and the concentrated cooperation of their helmets—they could make out the Typhon's most centralized and concentrated horde of captives.

Not just marchers. Those the Typhon seemed content, for the most part, to leave out in the Chaos, reenacting their failures—but representatives of all the great civilizations and reaches of human endeavor across the five hundred living galaxies.

A deathly museum.

"I have friends down there," Polybiblios said. "I see the Typhon gathered some of the Shen. And across the lake and sea cores, up against the old gravidity forests—"

"Stop, you're making my head hurt," Ghentun protested.

"Enough, then. It seems that the Typhon is gathering all its trophies into one location—hoarding them. Let's visit. In their sad condition, I doubt they'll even notice us."

CHAPTER 105

Despite the risks, Jack forged ahead of the others. The collapsed walls and buttresses and huge, shattered spheres of the interior of Nataraja offered a warren of passageways. The others would have to keep up—but he was not sure he wanted them to.

He needed to find Ginny. Felt responsible—and something more. He missed her. There had never been a girl he felt at ease with. Those moments in the warehouse had been special. Something he could not have—

A center.

Glaucous could still see Daniel, but not Jack—the consequences of separating seemed less here than out in the wastes beyond this double-Dutch jumble.

He was thinking a great deal now about the old bird-catcher, the slow quelling of their catch in the dawn light as the lurching cart rumbled back through the lanes to London. The clangor of the heavy iron stars in their baskets at each jounce. The smell of bird shite a sour urgent note over the green gassiness of fresh dung and the wet, rank coal smoke pooling in the cool air. Guilt meant nothing to the hungry and the desperate—no more than to a wolf biting down on the neck of a lamb. A merciful shake, snap of the spine: food.

Businesslike arrangement.

Now he was concerned with larger things. Even as a child, Glaucous had been dimly aware that nothing was what it seemed. The pretty scrim of seeming was freshly painted each hour for those with money and position, a facade for the privileged, a mask over the cruelty beneath. To the poor, the hungry, the rule of privilege was an acid spew between rotten teeth, hardly worth a hoot in a legless fuddle. War and you go die in a ditch. Lift a loaf to feed your sibs and the rozzers poke you in the ribs and you squat all ashiver in stir, each breath a stab.

Death and pain and privilege, out of one's control, keep your eyes on the gutter before the rats bite.

I know this place. Here is where privilege ends. My luck: the doom of the birds.

He stopped to catch his breath. A wonder any of them could breathe. Magic in the group, Daniel didn't call it that—but so it was to him. And yet he would have sold magic Jack into a cage, and then the Gape would have taken him here, along with the girl and so many others—and all hope would have gone.

Catch the birds. Bite the neck and bleed the lamb. Never my chick. Never my lamb.

Businesslike.

But this . . .

Even back in the lanes, bobbing on the tail of the cart, even then young Max could draw fortune, steer the cart to the quietest, least hunted fields beneath the biggest, darkest flocks. Even then he could fume out a cloudy seeming of happy birds and berries and bugs, piles of seeds surrounded by safety. An illusion of plenty with no hawks, no hunters.

Something pushed on his shoulders and he hunched, waiting for a blow. Breathing became more difficult. He might strangle. He couldn't see Daniel or Jack now.

But one was never alone.

Glaucous looked up, wincing at what he knew he would see. Instead, a brown muddle presented itself—like a sky filled with coils of coal smoke: curls and spirals and curves and slow, desperate flashes like drugged lightning. The smoke chunked down like hazy stones caught in the plunge of a landslide, trying to catch and pin the lines and curls. All in utter silence. Through it all flew wide, dusty wings and a wriggling wisp of a man who wasn't there.

Glaucous fell to his knees, as he always did in the presence of bad power.

The Moth.

As well, a thin man with a club foot dressed in sooty black stepped from the murk and held out his arms. "Last call," Whitlow said cheerily. "Hell hath no fury like a woman scorned, Max. *She* has been harsh, blaming us. But you—*you're* in her glory and grace. Brought in the pretty birds all by yourself. And one extra. My prize. The bad shepherd."

Glaucous swallowed his fear. "About them—"

"No apologies, and no going back, Mr. Glaucous. Time to receive your reward."

The clouded, whirling rocks spun away from an open center.

"Come with us," Whitlow said. "The Moth leads the way, as always."

CHAPTER **106**

Which of you dreams of the past?
Who carries the book?

The marchers tried to hide Tiadba—and one by one were firmly shunted aside. Khren and Frinna clung with the most conviction. Then they, too, were whisked away.

Paleness and sadness descended upon her alone once more. She was surrounded again by the procession of female forms that just eluded clarity. The sadness settled. The females, like jewels carved from different stages of the motion of a real being, folded together, combined—

Became one woman, her face illuminated from within like a lantern. Skin white as ice, eyes silver and gray and green, her body lost in something that wrapped her like a map of golden rivers and green fields— limbs long, graceful, fingers tipped with gripping flowers, and between these flowers, letters, symbols, numbers, written in flame, always changing, casting glows on Tiadba's face, writing with warm but not consuming fire.

The woman still seemed familiar, though they had never met.

Tiadba had already called her *Mother*. *Mothers* were a kind of parental—females who come before you and directly pass along their stories, which have recombined to make your own. Great chains of past experience—mistakes made in terror and joy, loss and triumph—all conveyed to the next experiments in the line of time: children.

Writing on and within the female, other partners—in some cases males, in others teams of male and female—sometimes just other females, sometimes sexual designations outside Tiadba's experience— Shapers, adjuvescents, conscribers, genesens—created many delicate flavors of offspring. Once, even entire cities had submitted their stories to quicken a female, then gathered to celebrate the birth of a single child, raised up and cherished, then doubled, tripled, and sent out to other cities as magnificent gifts . . .

A city like the Kalpa: woman, mother.

Ashurs and Devas—different varieties of human—all had their own ways of becoming partners and mothers, more than could easily be counted. In all the possible ways found over a hundred trillion years, stories combined and were sent forth to be read by others, to shape new stories.

Compared to Tiadba, the woman was tall—taller than anyone she had ever met in the Tiers, much taller even than Pahtun. And her shape was lovely, though challenging. But Tiadba was not frightened.

Only I am allowed to remember. It is my punishment for trying to destroy the Typhon. Once, I was so much more.

This, then, was what remained of Ishanaxade—born of all stories. A dreaming vastness flowed out of her, into Tiadba, more than any book could carry—and yet still made of words.

Child. You are my last. My father made it so—the circling bands that pass around and through. The end is here. Our lives echo, and I am lost.

Once, Nataraja had been beautiful—more graceful in its antiquities than any of Earth's other cities, rich and lovely with its acceptance of the human past. Nataraja sat out the Mass Wars until the very end, welcoming all, trying to stay neutral, until the City Princes of the remaining cities—and most of all, the Kalpa—forced her to choose sides.

The Chaos was swallowing galaxies, worlds and stars—and still, humans fought humans.

Nataraja, seeing the folly, had cut loose of the last alliances, accepting all who fled the noötics and the Eidolons—until the Kalpa drew in and concentrated its defenses, leaving the other six cities stranded.

Five cities fell.

Nataraja—as if saved for last—faced the advancing front of the Chaos alone.

Ishanaxade had been sent there just before the city was overcome. Those had been dreadful days, when all seemed lost, yet the citizens went about their lives—Devas, Menders, Shapers, Ashurs, and even a few noötics of conscience.

The Librarian's daughter had watched Nataraja and its people do what they could to defy the Typhon, that unknown quality—powerful, simple, perverse—which had transformed the rest of the cosmos. They had set up their own barricades and shields—had surrounded the city with all of its ancient texts, hastily engraved on stone, written in light and stored in the metric that underlay all energy and matter—scribed onto molecules and atoms and all other known varieties of matter— projected into the skies against the advancing membrane of misrule— all that remained of the libraries of a hundred trillion years of history.

Not enough.

————

Memories changed. That was the first symptom of the Typhon's triumph. The Ashurs and the few noötics disappeared almost immediately. Records and texts throughout the city faded. People began to misremember their lives, then to lose them—distortion of the fate-lines, forgetting, then falling away into gritty black dust, a final kind of mercy for a blessed few.

Until the last instants of freedom, Nataraja's philosophers tried to comprehend the new order, but there was nothing to comprehend, only a boil of ceaseless disorder. Change without purpose.

Human senses seemed to cause the Typhon both puzzlement and pain.

The Typhon probed the remaining minds, the memory stores, the souls of all living things, posing questions that in themselves tilted some into madness. To see was pain. To remember was a new kind of forgetting.

To the Typhon, this was simple curiosity. Even after trillions of years of effort, it had not found its recipe for cosmos. This made it redouble its efforts—and quicken its failures. The Chaos was a piecework, poorly conceived and poorly assembled—failing everywhere except along its vast membrane of change, the many-dimensional front along which the old cosmos was being gnawed and absorbed.

Ishanaxade alone—as her father had anticipated from the beginning, from his time among the Shen—was spared to remember all.

CHAPTER 107

Ginny thought it might have been a gigantic flower. Much taller than her, it rose from a cracked, rolling pavement in the shadow of the dangling, treacherous remains of the heart of this city, hanging like gigantic, moldy Christmas trees left behind by a receding flood, tossed into an awful heap, somehow still wearing their ornaments. But these ornaments seemed wider than entire towns on Earth. And no lights, of course.

The power had long since gone out for these ruins.

The flower—or was it a mushroom?—asserted a ghastly kind of independence below the architectural deadfall. As she walked around it, she noticed that it was made of elongated arms, legs, bodies, with an occasional head poking out. The anatomies within the stalk shivered and the heads opened their eyes, not to see—the eyes were blank, blind—but to express discomfort.

These were not marchers—not like Tiadba. They were more like Ginny. Contemporary to her. And there were many more flower-mushrooms, she saw, sprouting up beneath the hanging ruins.

Something had gone about gathering the people, the survivors who had been so unfortunate as to find themselves delivered along with a cross section of endtime.

That's why all the old parts of the city had seemed deserted when she left the warehouse. There had already been a sweeping, a mopping up. And something—perhaps the servants that moved along the trods—had brought a few or all of them here, where they had been arranged to form awful warnings.

Scarecrows.

This gave Ginny both a frightening chill and an odd sensation of encouragement. You didn't set up scarecrows unless you were afraid something could come and take what you had.

She glanced at the towering base of the mushroom, looking for faces she might recognize, anybody she'd known: friends, the witches.

Miriam Sangloss.

Conan Bidewell.

She recognized nobody. But there were so many. Maybe the ones she'd come in contact with had been reserved for a particularly painful punishment.

"*I hate you,*" Ginny said, eyes narrowed, growling her contempt at whatever might be listening. "*I am not afraid, and I HATE YOU!*"

She leaped aside with a small shriek as a velvet softness rubbed against her ankle. When she had gathered enough courage to come out of her crouch and actually look, she saw a small shadow . . . watched it approach her again in a low, cautious slink.

The shadow resolved into bright and dark splotches against the uniform murk.

It made a soft grumbling sound.

Ginny felt her eyes fill and tears spill down her cheeks, slipping salt into the corners of her mouth. She reached down and scooped up the blotchy shadow, rubbed its furry head against her cheek, and began to cry.

It *was* Minimus, six toes on each front paw, and small, ecstatically flexing thumbs! The cat rumbled and climbed and rumbled some more and settled into her arms.

"How?" she managed between childlike sobs. These sounds might or might not have ever left the bubble, might or might not have reached far enough to be heard by the human mushroom-flowers, but it seemed for a moment as if the whole awful foundation of the False City shivered.

Something new had arrived. There would be change.

Minimus squirmed and strained his head forward, looking down and around and issuing another urgent meow.

She was surrounded by cats.

Hundreds of them.

Thousands.

Ginny was not afraid. "What *have* you been hunting?" she asked in a wheedling tone, still oddly certain of the relationship between human and cat. "What *have* you been eating?"

Minimus regarded her with a slow, wise blink, then made a considerable effort, lips contorted, and spoke in a soft, hissing whisper: *"We're Sminthians, remember? We're gods of mice and things that gnaw."*

The cats milled in a gray eddy of fur.

Of all the impossible things she had seen and experienced, this broke the mirror—this totally popped the cork. Ginny narrowed her eyes, blinked—hard—and pinched her finger until it hurt.

Reality had just finished its long dying.

CHAPTER 108

Tiadba drifted in and out of the ancient story. She closed her eyes and again imagined words printed in their books. This took her back again to her last solace—remembered moments with Jebrassy, the letterbugs, the shake cloths, their rolling and combining.

The female was not allowed to forget the time when she had fallen in love. She could not leave behind the hope of memory itself.

On one of the far necklace worlds of the Shen, Ishanaxade was found by Sangmer. They spoke on the shores of the silvery vector sea:

"I am not truly anyone's daughter. Many have given me what form I have. I call Polybiblios father because he has been most patient with me, and in his way has loved me."

"Where did they find you?"

"I have been gathered from all the inhabited worlds for longer than anyone can recall—some say since the end of the Brightness. Bits and pieces—a gleam here, a quality there, a suspicion or speck . . . All treasured, transported, traded, by many, and then collected by the Shen, who amassed so much that I would have bulked larger even than the necklace-worlds or the sixty green suns around which they whirl."

Sangmer found this unlikely, and said so.

"Look at me. Do I appear likely? Am I like any other you have seen?"

"No," he admitted. "But I am young. How did you become so much smaller?"

"The Shen are very old and exceptionally curious. They worked for a long time to distill me. What was most essential they kept. But then they tired of the puzzle. When Polybiblios arrived, he resumed the task—and made me as you see me now. He believes he understands what I truly am. I do not judge his beliefs."

"What does he think you are—or were?"

"A muse," Ishanaxade said.

"Like, an inspiration?"

"Muses were once very important to the cosmos. They labored for a hundred billion years, cleaning up after Brahma, who could not stop creating, could not stop the outpour of his kind of love. The muses allowed memory and the flowering of all the little observers, so beloved of Brahma, who was careless, but vast and full of passion.

"And then, creation stopped. The Trillennium followed—nothing new, just clever rearrangements of the old. Some say Brahma slept. And while he sleeps, there is no need for any muse. We condensed out like snow or rain, a flurry of jewels spread over the dark light-years."

"An old name, Brahma."

"Old is not an adequate word. I don't know whether I served and failed, or was rejected as no longer essential—but I seem to remember scattering everywhere people still lived. After that—until I was brought here—I remember nothing."

"And now, you're almost human."

"Why do you stay and speak with me? Am I attractive? None of the Shen seems to find me attractive."

When she spoke, her breath was like a refreshing wind, cool and moist, yet when her eyes fell upon him, he was warmed, kept dry and secure. Sangmer studied her some more and considered for a while, on the shore of the great silvery vector sea. "You seem to like helping, taking care of people," he said. "That is admirable."

"You enjoy being nurtured?"

"Well, that isn't all you promise. When you touch me, I feel a fire at my center. You want me to grow and find my true story, my purpose. You seem to want to be there when I see new things. You want to share and enjoy my discoveries."

"I discover what anyone discovers," Ishanaxade said. "That's a truth. But if I become human—what you see now is not all that is left of me. I am two."

"What other is there?"

"She is always with me—not separate. Polybiblios might have warned you."

"He did not."

"The Shen did not mention this?"

"They mentioned nothing about you. My crew has had a difficult journey—perhaps they did not want to alarm us."

"Well, some of the Shen find me most alarming. They would be happy to see my puzzle resolved—or to send me away. I not only inspire, I correct."

"What's so wrong with that?"

"Some things cannot be corrected. Those things, I make disappear. As if they had never been."

Sangmer watched her closely—what he could see of her—and thought he spied a shadowy other-self within the beautiful and changing margins. "Then you should make the Chaos disappear!"

"Oh, my destructive side is no more effective than my inspirational side, so long as Brahma sleeps. So I have been told, and so I believe."

Sangmer frowned. "Well, whatever you are, you're the most extraordinary, almost-human female I've ever encountered. And I've known some wonderfully different females—and many that were not female at all, like the Ashurs—"

Ishanaxade seemed to condense more as he spoke. "Tell me about them," she said. "You thought they were beautiful. I'd like to learn how they pleased you."

This hurt. A shriek of eternal despair filled the vast dark hall, and was lost without echo in the smother of wreckage.

Where is he? Why does he not come?

CHAPTER 109

Jack looked over his shoulder. For some time now he had been trying to stay ahead of Glaucous and Daniel, and simply follow the tug of his stone. Whether he trusted them or not—he did not, of course—simply didn't matter. He wanted to test himself and see what he could accomplish on his own.

The endless miles of wreckage had its own silence, a quality deeper than simple lack of sound. Here, for a moment alone, he tried to think and remember where he'd been, what he'd seen and heard—and fit it all together without distraction or interruption.

Somehow, that made seeing and thinking easier as well.

A low tuneless whistle found its way between his lips. He held the stone out before him, trying to interpret its subtle tugging. And gradually, over a time of no time, he was guided beneath a huge, vertical sheet that stretched up into high shadow—a warped, bumpy sheet that might have been the size of Manhattan, turned on its nose and hung from a hook, covered with huge, broken ornaments, each with its own distinct cast, a grayish-silver sheen.

What would it mean if he believed that he was actually walking through—or beneath—the suspended ruins of a future city? That people had once lived here, and that what had invaded and sucked the life out of Seattle had also sucked away their lives, squeezing it all together, making them equal . . . ?

Jack had never been much for philosophy, but this was a poser. He could walk, whistle, see—wonder—but there wasn't really anything, including time, that made sense in the old way. There was *his* personal time—he was still making memories—

And wasn't that how one defined time anyway?

He kept walking, kept whistling, but decided that thinking was almost useless. Humility was easy when mystery threatened to crush you at every turn.

"I am that I am," he muttered. "I think, therefore I am. I remember, therefore I am. I've chosen my own name, therefore I am. I'm hungry, therefore I am. I worry about my friends, therefore I am. I'd like to see what's about to happen, therefore I am. I want to go on and finish my story—make more memories—never enough memories—therefore I am."

I am alone, and things haven't just winked out.
Therefore I am.
I want to set it all right again, therefore . . .

Far away, he heard a terrible sound—not exactly human. A banshee wail of despair and pain that seemed to drizzle down from above.

"Ginny," he said, and licked his lips to keep them from cracking.

Something touched his ankles—whiskers or feelers. Thinking of giant earwigs, he jerked and looked down, almost dropping the sum-runner.

A cat rubbed his leg, arched its back, looked up—and opened its mouth as if to make a sound. But the cat, too, was silent. He thought he recognized it—him—one of the cats in Bidewell's warehouse, and for once did not wonder for an instant what he was doing here. There could be nothing more improbable than Jack's own presence. He knelt and stroked the soft head, palmed the closed eyes and pushed back the velvety ears, and immediately felt a surge of comfort, normality, self-assurance. Cats could do that. Despite their apparent aloofness, or because of it, simply by their acceptance one acquired solid value.

"Well, maybe I don't hold everything together all by my lonesome," Jack said. "Maybe you have something to contribute, too." The cat purred agreement, then lightly nipped his finger and ran off a few yards, stopped, sat on its haunches; waited. Jack consulted the sumrunner, holding it over his head.

The cat ran off.

Cat and stone agreed. Both were leading him in the same direction.

CHAPTER 110

Nataraja was disturbing Daniel's deepest pools. How did he remember that name? Bidewell had never brought it up. Glaucous had never mentioned it. Neither had Jack or Ginny.

But he could see it all with a strange clarity, as if he had witnessed its end with better eyes, connected to a deeper and more subtle brain.

For Daniel, the disposition of the False City was strangely familiar, overlaid by the pattern, if it could be called that, of its awful defeat.

He clambered up an immense curtain-wall, leaning at about thirty degrees to the rest of the rubble: thousands of acres shot through with cracks, rippling tears, wide chasms, and faults. Spheres and stretched, twisted ovoids, bent cylinders and curving sweeps, still clung to the sheet, interconnected by thousands of silver walkways or transportation rails, some still supporting what might have been mobile constructs. When it was alive, when it all worked together, Nataraja must have been a marvel . . .

Of course it had been a marvel. He could see it. The picture was sharp. After all, coming to Nataraja had made a tremendous impression . . .

As he climbed, he (and a bit of Fred, still curious) tried to imagine the awesome power of something that could discard the rules of reality—and what that would do to a human construct, relying as it did on engineering, gravity, the basic balances of matter and energy. He did not have to imagine much. The results seemed to pop into his head, more vivid than any recent memory. The city had died like an animal set upon by much larger beasts: smashed down, torn open, shooting out gouts of itself—and then collapsing, squished out around its edges as if stomped by huge boots.

A hole big enough to push a small mountain through now let in a shaft of gray light from outside. The shaft moved with a will of its own, touching on great heaps of wreckage, merging with other stray shafts, cutting through thin screens of glow falling through huge rents in the crushed outer skin. The angle and intensity of these cheerless lambencies were never the same.

His own mind—what was left of it—had been scrupulously separated into thick, fluid layers, hot and cold—and now, from depths almost frozen with age, upwelling contents seemed ready to help him reconstruct what he could never have actually experienced.

"I don't dream. I don't dream of this city or any other."

Still, recollections of a multitude of historical cities came forward—linked by what circumstance, he did not yet know. Lost to siege or plague, burned to the ground, reduced to rubble, the rubble raked over and sown with salt: moving from fate to fate, and even from life to life and body to body, he might have actually experienced those things—who could deny that possibility?

But not the end of this place, not the doom of Nataraja. That made no sense at all.

But he knew. He felt. In its own way, Nataraja had been the greatest city of its age, greater even than the Kalpa . . . wherever and whatever that was.

"Tell me who I am!" Daniel shouted as he climbed the fallen curtain. "I don't dream. I never have. When I sleep, there's just blackness."

The Chaos had washed across the surface of the Earth in a wave of many dimensions, surrounding the last enclaves of humanity from above, below, and to all sides, cutting off their lines of fate as well as access in space and time. That was how the Chaos transformed, took control—and reduced its conquests to a misery of confusion and lies.

It burned through most of the threads of causality.

And then, as if exhausted—or uncertain what to do with its new domains—it withdrew, concentrating its efforts on the probing wave front, that membrane which intruded and cut across and around the chords, and which Daniel had experienced so often.

What the Chaos had left behind was the hulk of a city charred not by flames, reduced not by physical destruction—but crisped by lost history and eaten through by paradox.

Those who lived here had suffered most. The structures that once supported them in security and comfort had struggled to rebuild, or at least to maintain some part of an upright pile, yet were punished over and over again—dying, rotting, resurrecting in awful new ways—and finally the city had given up.

The legacy of everything the Chaos touched.

———

Daniel climbed to the massive edge of the curtain-wall. The pain and exhaustion this body felt did not matter. The upper portion of the curtain—several miles of it—had bent over and broken off and now lay sprawled across and through other structures, the bottom lost in shadow, all the way to the foundations.

Where his hands and feet touched, a few faint blue sparks sizzled from skin, bones, and muscle. Atoms, particles—matter astonished, recognizing itself and attempting to correct a perverse bilocation. But this was not the great recognition his new/old memories, his new instructions, told him to expect.

He had come very far, over a very long period of time.

A greater moment of reunion was out there in the ruins.

Daniel sat on the edge, ignoring the small blue lances and sparks, and took his two stones from their boxes. As always, they would not fit together. One looking older than the other, if that was possible. Similar in shape, but destined for other combinations. One of the stones tugged strongly to the left and then down. Simultaneously, he heard a savage, nasty sound, like a beast in pain, echo from all around, and then—perversely—swoop up with a Doppler howl to echo again.

The ruins seemed to enjoy this. They played with that sound, tossed it back and forth. Hanging structures shuddered and sifted corrosion down the slope of the curtain-wall, and then made an attempt to move, as if in response to that unknown command. They managed to shift a few dozen yards along their silvery connecting rails—and then ground to a halt, dropping chunks the size of the old houses in Wallingford.

He suspected this was not the first time Nataraja had echoed with that pain.

Daniel replaced the dormant stone and put the box back into his pocket. The other he kept in his hand, where it grew warm and then hot. He hung his head. Everything hurt. The wail . . . not a beast.

A woman.

The stone tugged again. For now, it was the only part of him that showed decision and direction. He had killed and pushed aside so many to come this far. A meeting was coming—a meeting that would resolve nothing.

Never would.

Never had.

CHAPTER **111**

The tangle of old Nataraja quivered above them, and the dreaded, all-too-familiar sound of collisions—mountains falling, caverns collapsing, dust swirling and sifting—announced another compression.

Glaucous felt his body cramp inward, as if he were being pinched between a huge finger and thumb.

Whitlow continued to lurch ahead, feeling his way through the city's deadfall like a cockroach through a festering forest—with the occasional guiding touch of the Moth, a presence of gray authority but no real substance or location. Glaucous finally followed him again, breath stacked upon breath, eyes stinging at the way light and shadow torqued through the high, snarled skeleton of the corpse city.

Whitlow stopped and touched finger to chin, scratching stubble. He examined Glaucous critically, as if blaming him. "Smaller still," he said. "Less of everything. Distances change, and directions. Do you feel it?"

"Yes," Glaucous said, hunching his shoulders as he imagined miners might in a cave-in, their candles fading, air turning to poison.

"Not done yet," Whitlow added, shaking his head. "Might squeeze us to the size of a pea. What then?"

It was obvious to Glaucous that all they had to do—Whitlow and the Moth—was lose him in this tangle, and none of his skills would save him. That might be their intent—yet he had no choice but to follow.

"I bear no resentment for being left behind," Whitlow said, watching his face with darting eyes. "New circumstances, new codes, not to say new honor. Indeed, not to say *that*. I might have left *you* behind, had it been the other way."

"The Mistress brought you here before?" Glaucous asked.

"Such a question!" Whitlow said. "She might have done so, and I might have forgotten. You might as easily forget that we are here now."

"I recognize some things," Glaucous said quietly. "Narrow escapes. Seeing what lay beyond."

"When I was younger, I imagined this was a sort of afterlife. Didn't you?"

"Never thought on it much," Glaucous said, and that was mostly true.

"I had some feeble excuse that our prey might find a satisfactory existence here—render their own extended service, no worse than what we endure, or what the Moth endures, perhaps. Mistakes also deposit themselves. Hunters clumsy enough to fall into a Gape. Many such, over the ages. No going back when that happens. You've lost partners—would you like to reacquaint with a few?"

"No thank you, all the same," Glaucous murmured.

"We may pass them on our way to the Crux. We are the only survivors. Of all the thousands—tens of thousands, I imagine . . ." Whitlow looked around. There had not been a touch, a guiding blink of gray authority, for some time. He whistled low and steady, as if summoning an invisible dog. "Where is that creature?"

"Does *she* reside in the Crux?" Glaucous asked.

Whitlow slowly turned, larger booted foot thumping, looked up, and lifted his hands, fingers feeling through the dark spaces as if he might grab a line and haul them up into daylight. "Not hers. Moth found it. Bigger game, now smaller and weaker, everything coming to its minimum. The small will loom large, Mr. Glaucous. Our last chance."

"I do not know what you mean, Mr. Whitlow," Glaucous said wearily. "Bad riddles always."

"You wouldn't say that had not all this brought me low. You would listen and smile, obsequious, and I would know there was an understanding. But the chain of command, broken . . . chain of authority, knotted and clanking. The Moth . . ."

"I don't feel him," Glaucous said, drawing closer to Whitlow. "Where has he gone?"

Whitlow regarded him with momentary apprehension—and then a mask of wry humor. "Tell me about your friend, the bad shepherd, before you decide to take your revenge, Mr. Glaucous."

"You found him. I followed you."

Glaucous drew back at another round of creaking and settling. Whitlow held up his fingers, separated by the distance of a pea, and shook them in Glaucous's face, grinning his threat. "It was rumored ages ago that some shepherds, tormented by the hunt, might acquire certain understandings, certain efficiencies. Threatened, they might leave their personal silken cords and attach to others. Become those others for a while. A desperate ploy. This would disrupt the track of their dreams—and so they would forget. Yet they would still carry sum-runners, still be guided by them . . ."

Glaucous felt the breezy touch of a huge, soft hand on his back, accompanied by a scent of dry, sweetly irritating powder. The Moth had returned.

Whitlow resumed his off-kilter step. "Better. Shouldn't wander off like that. What we have found is puzzling," he said to Glaucous. "Curtains have been pulled aside. Powers have shifted. We suspect the Chalk Princess is no longer actively engaged. We have need of another opinion."

Glaucous dropped his head.

"She may not know as much yet. More has been reduced than walking distance," Whitlow said, and pulled Glaucous close, then whispered in his ear, "This does not bode well for the Moth, of course." He winked and held his finger to his lips.

The Moth moved them again—a wrenching passage, swift but no more brutal than was strictly essential. Glaucous felt the change as a burning, as if his skin were crisping away. That subsided—and then he felt as if he were merely being tattooed all over his body. The pricking sting of predatory fates was something with which he had no previous experience. One normally lived one's fate; these lived *him*. Their examination was swift, impersonal, basic. Glaucous had never before been so close to the basement layers of his being, and he found it both terrible and exhilarating. He had also never been so close to an explanation for his life, his existence, and to a last moment of hope—the hope that perhaps there might still be room for correction.

An impersonal offering of grace—a remote and pure shriving.

The pricking passed. Now he was his own powdery thing, still standing, but falling apart and being put back together each split second.

The Moth protected them as best as he could.

"Welcome to the center of the universe," he heard Whitlow say or think.

Their eyes—they no longer seemed to have bodies—saw in some manner a deep black pool in which two large needles churned a thick liquid. The needles met beneath the surface of the pool and spun like the shaft of a gear in a jeweled movement.

"The Crux has no center and no radius," Whitlow said. "Brace for a nasty residue—a powerful thing once focused its heart of frustration and misery here. It ate our world and spat it out in nasty chunks. You'll feel it."

"The Typhon?" Glaucous asked.

Whitlow shrugged. "These steel threads are the last two fates. In one, the Typhon fails and we all pass into nothingness. In the other . . . there is a kind of success. Who can say which would be better? Now—

"Tell us where we are—draw up the proper thread, and tell us what remains for us to do. That is your talent, is it not?"

Glaucous could not shut his eyes, could not find any private place in which to make his decision—but that did not matter. He had decided long ago.

Fifty years and more had passed since he had decided.

Somehow, in this abstract heart with no center, and without the Moth's help, he chose the best fate—the last remaining good fate—and drew it down like a fortunate hand of cards, the one lucky flip of a coin.

And—always deferent to his employers—he made sure both the Moth and Whitlow approved.

Far away, an awful sound echoes again throughout the False City.

And the Dead Gods begin to move.

CHAPTER 112

The False City is quivering, snapping, shrinking. Jebrassy does not know why he is still walking, still seeing.

He looks down on Polybiblios, who has inexplicably collapsed, and then kneels beside him. Some steps away, Ghentun has also fallen. Both are wavering in substance and outline.

"The Kalpa is reaching its end," Polybiblios says. "The City Prince's bargain means nothing. I cannot last much longer than my stored fates within the city. All my fate-lines will die with the Kalpa. Finish it well, young breed. You have all you need—but for this."

The epitome reaches out to give him the thing he has carried since their journey began. Jebrassy holds the small gray box. The epitome of the Librarian winks at him through the armor's faceplate, then lies back on the black surface.

Jebrassy then moves to Ghentun and lies down beside the Keeper, to hold him as best he can while the Tall One—the former taskmaster and protector—stares up into the ice-crusted darkness.

His eyes sink.

"I chose to become noötic," the Keeper confesses. "When I was young. My only betrayal. I reconverted when I became Keeper. But my fate-lines were cut and remade, and tied up with the Kalpa. I won't be going any farther."

Ghentun touches the breed's hand, feeling Jebrassy's solidity, then moves his fingers to his own nose and makes that strange, explosive sound that signifies humor. "Let me see what he gave you."

Jebrassy holds out the box.

"Open it for me. Show me."

Jebrassy touches the top and turns it one way, then another, shaking it. He knows instinctively how to open it. The lid pulls away, and within there is a new, bright twist of gray metal, cradling a small reddish stone. The stone gleams within, like a star growing on the tweenlight ceil.

"Four is the minimum," Ghentun says, and his sunken eyes turn away. "Some say three. But it *is* four. Enough. They have had enough time and power. At the very end, the City Prince wins all."

Dying eyes now focused on the young breed, with his last strength the Keeper pulls the stone up and away from Jebrassy's suddenly frantic, grabbing hands, and smashes it against the littered floor. It does not break but makes a strange squeal and tries to pull away from the Mender's armor. As if remembering something obscure, a last bit of instruction, Ghentun nods, then with his other hand reaches for the lid of the box—and examines the design engraved there. "Why play Eidolon games, young breed?"

Holding both away from Jebrassy, he lurches to his feet and clasps them to his breast, then closes his eyes.

There is nothing Jebrassy can do. He turns between the Keeper and Polybiblios, like a child caught in a tormenting game played by cruel adults.

The incarnate fragment of the Librarian seems at first to share Jebrassy's horror, then holds up one hand, as if waving good-bye, or dismissing all further effort. Polybiblios crumbles to gray dust within the armor. The armor falls inward, shrinks to a wrinkled pebble.

No more words, no more information.

Trillions of years of memories—gone.

The Keeper turns white eyes upward, and then passes—becomes dust. His armor likewise shrinks, and pieces roll on the ground, sparking, sizzling around the box and the stone.

All crumble.

Jebrassy tries to gather the remains in his gloved hands, but at this touch, the destruction begun by Ghentun's passing is complete. Nothing but fine sand sifts through his fingers.

All pointless.

Jebrassy gets to his feet. He is learning for the first time what it means to be utterly and completely alone. The False City, like his heart, is filled with a terrible screaming. He knows that voice, recognizes it from his dreams—from his origins.

Someone throws a rock. The rock continues on its arc to a destination. So long as it flies, a life goes on—a fate remains in play.

But now the purpose is gone, and there is only the fate.

Why play Eidolon games, young breed?

One last glance at the piles of sand.

Something new has formed there—a larger, polyhedral shape with seven sides and four holes, made of the same substance as the gray box.

His fingers twitch. He touches it—the armor does not interact. It is inert.

Jebrassy picks it up and carries it with him, as a pede carries nesting material even after its clutch of eggs has been stolen and eaten.

He walks the last remaining distance under the deadfall, through a storm of whispering shadows—

The central shape of his most hidden dreams is gathering, he can feel its motion—a great revolving, spinning thing, like the design on the lid of the box: the symbol of the Sleeper. This geometric fortress will hold back the end for one last moment, until Brahma decides whether or not to awaken.

Jebrassy passes through just as a great rotating band swooshes behind him. There is no going back, of course.

He has stepped onto a lake of translucent blue-green, the same color as the pieces of the muse collected by the Shen and gathered into humanlike form by Polybiblios.

The final part of his journey begins.

Toward the screaming.

CHAPTER 113

Jack has reached the center of the city. It looks like a center—everything spins out around it—though the scene is cockeyed and difficult to define, and so he turns, looks back over his shoulder, then bends over and stares between his legs—through the last iridescent film of bubble. The stone is hot in his hands, quivering with its own excitement. But everything else . . . very cold.

The center is a circular, emerald-green lake surrounded by revolving and whirling circular bands: the ever-moving, ever-slicing and parsing bars of a special prison. He is inside them. Somehow he has passed through the cut and slice. The bands are flat, of no thickness, and smooth, reflecting light with a brazen, defiant sheen.

A cross formed of two straight ribbons meets above the lake. From one angle the revolving bands move behind the cross—from another angle they surround it—and from a third angle they whirl in front.

This is very like the symbol carved into the puzzle box. So he is where he should be, finally.

And the others?

All he really wants now is to find Ginny. If she's here, he's certain she's very afraid—that seems to define Ginny. Courage through fear. Jack—just a little afraid, but not like Ginny. Even this little fear comes close to paralyzing him.

Time to see things better. He turns around again, refreshing the polarity of his perception, and this creates a kind of clarity.

Curls of pale gray dart down and around, forming particle-chamber tracks through the distance above the frozen green lake, like greenish snow—all the snow in the world, summing to a peculiar blizzard here at the end of time.

The lake might be made of ice—greenish, glassy ice.

And at the center of the lake—

The Crux or heart . . .

A blurry black point. Too far off, too small to see any details from where he stands—just a foggy, dimensionless darkness. Nearby, another hollow opens up, carved out of the ice. Within the hollow he sees a lovely actinic glow—a billion arcs of brilliant blue. Vague shapes move there, small enough to be human—all but one, a nacreous cone with a brilliant luminosity at its apex—a face. Even from here he sees it is the face of a woman—or at least some sort of magnificent female.

Looking through the blue light at that shape, Jack shivers. He knows where this is—and what *that* is, or was. The icy surface of the lake is scored all around, as if giant skaters have carved deep pathways, gouges that would rise over his head if he went down there and fell into one.

The tortured tracks of the Queen in White.

And so he *is* going. The sum-runner is hot and pulls him along. If he doesn't hold on tight and go with it, it seems likely to just skitter down by itself, leaving him behind, and he will freeze, like all those giants he now sees gathered just outside the whirl of the bands—the ribbon sections of so many spheres—an armillary. That's what they're called. He saw something like it in a museum once.

The armillary paradox is the symbol of the sum-runners—broad, interlaced fates rising forward and slipping back.

Now about those giants. Were they there before? He sees them on the opposite side of the whirling bands, gathered like extraordinary chess pieces, waiting in timeless judgment. They are horrifyingly beautiful—he is inadequate to the task of assessing their grandeur, their former power. Seeing them carries by itself a kind of knowledge, access to what had once been a tremendous future history. Once, they were judges, he guesses, builders and movers of galaxies—and then they became prisoners, held in thrall to witness the fumbling, inane destruction of everything they had ever lived and loved.

Now they are gathered to await another judgment, another conclusion. The mighty and glorious await the arrival of the tiny and insignificant.

He has an audience.

He holds onto the sum-runner despite all of its enthusiasm. Jack never drops anything.

As he steps onto the slippery surface, white and black shapes move around his feet, precede him onto the green ice—a river of silent, vengeful fur.

CHAPTER 114

Whitlow is triumphant as they approach the Queen in White in her abode. Above, the magnificent confusion of the armillary makes a humming backdrop.

The Crux lies within the black point around which pivots this stately gyre. Whitlow exults. They were just there—at the center. They are powerful and privileged. They will be rewarded magnificently for their success. All that was promised will finally be attained.

The Moth is above, around, everywhere—guiding them with a silken, dusty enthusiasm.

Ahead Glaucous can make out, through a lattice of ever-changing shadows, one of the shepherds—the girl Virginia, walking carefully across the ice. She is attended by a few cats. He and Whitlow will soon be upon her.

Glaucous steels himself.

"A brilliant conclusion," Whitlow tells him. "We need to present just one shepherd, one sum-runner to the Typhon itself, the master of the Chalk Princess, to gain our passage. Oh, such a prize, at such a time!"

Glaucous moves cautiously. All around, the grooves and cuts yawn in expectation of the clumsy. He is wondering how they can remove the girl and deliver her—before the cats do what the cats must do.

The Moth brushes past, alerts them. Other visitors are crossing the circular green lake. Even at this distance Glaucous recognizes his own prey—Jack. The boy is following a much larger contingent of felines, like a fuzzy gray blanket.

Cats, ever the friends of books and stories—ever ready to attend to the reading of stories by sitting in a lap and purring. The death of all stories would not make them happy.

The Moth touches his shoulder again. A third is now on the lake. It is Daniel, the bad shepherd. There are no cats with Daniel. He moves alone.

"Consider the depths of time," Whitlow natters on reverently. "Beyond our understanding. And yet here we are—among the few, the last. It makes me *proud*. All of our pains, justified. All of our poor deeds."

Glaucous nods absently, focused on the Crux, the center—still working to draw down the last, best strand of fate.

Beyond the spinning cage, hauntingly familiar from all the puzzle boxes they have captured and tossed with their shepherds into the Gape: an awful audience, giants out of his worst nightmares. That a nightmare like himself should experience nightmares seems only just.

The worst nightmare of all, being thrown off the back of the bird-catcher's cart, rolling across the cobbles in a tangle of feathers . . . and then hearing the scrabble of rat claws out of the mud-and-sewage-caked gutters.

CHAPTER 115

Across the lake of green ice, from three directions the travelers move toward the center of the armillary fortress.

Jebrassy in his armor steps out carefully on the slick surface. The Kalpa has two final voices—the voice of his armor, and his own. "There are watchers," the armor tells him, something he already knows—the giants from the vale of Dead Gods. They remind him of point-minders in the little wars, presiding over the endgames but forbidden by certain rules to intervene, possibly because they actually *are* dead.

That doesn't seem to stop anything else in the Chaos. But he is just as glad they come no closer.

"There are Silent Ones closing in," the armor warns him. "They may be held back by the armillary. Sum-runners have gathered—the spinning fortress is their birthing shell."

Jebrassy is not at all sure what he can do about any of that. He is intent on the shimmering dome sketched by the arcs of blue light. That is where Tiadba must be; he is sure of it.

"There are no intact suits of armor in this vicinity. But there are breeds. And others."

Jebrassy is aware of those others, moving in, like him, on the center. "Who are they?" he asks.

"Pilgrims."

"Like me?"

"Very like you."

"My visitor?"

"Unknown."

He nods and pauses to think that over. He would have said, in any other place, at any other point in his young life, that there were ghosts out there—but now reality travels along a sliding scale. These pilgrims may be less real than himself, but more real than the Silent Ones or the Dead Gods.

One came to him in dreams. And is this any more real than a dream? Yet he suspects there are still rules of a sort. Not just anything will happen. Fewer things might be possible here than out in the Chaos.

Teamwork. Do your part.

The voice of his other brings him some relief. They are near.

"Where's Tiadba?" he asks.

"Unknown," the armor says.

"Is she alive?"

"Unknown."

"Everything's closing in."

"Yes."

"Am I doing the right thing?"

"There is no going back."

"Will I just crumble away like the Keeper?"

"Unknown."

Jebrassy shakes his head. They've all come so very far—he can't begin to understand how far. Yet he does not feel small. For once he feels

quite large. Bigger even than the Dead Gods, and certainly more powerful. More powerful than any Eidolon. He tries to imagine the Kalpa—
but all that is gone. He tries to imagine what Nataraja was once
like—now reduced to the deadfall and, at the last, crushed against the
spinning and whirling that wraps and protects a hard, slippery, very
cold lake.

Not for the first time he tries to imagine what the entire cosmos was
once like. "It's going to end in a few moments, isn't it?"

"Unknown."

"Anything else you care to tell me?"

"Yes."

The armor's voice becomes a gentle rush in his ears, like sifting sand.
He does not want to be completely alone out here. The lake and the
whirl change perspective whichever way he turns. So he looks straight
ahead at the blue light. He still clutches the small piece of sculpture
given to him by Polybiblios.

Barely audible, the armor's voice says, "You have arrived. Finish the
journey naked."

"Won't I die?"

No response.

The sandy rush fades to silence.

He squats on the ice, takes a deep breath behind the faceplate, and
begins to remove his armor, first the helmet, then the torso, and finally
the sleeves and leggings. It comes off easily, like peeling an overripe
tork.

As he strips down, a creature unlike anything in the Kalpa walks
up to him. It is barely as long as his arm and has four legs and is covered with black and white stuff that looks as soft as the fur on Tiadba's
nose.

"I've dreamed about you," he says. "You're name is . . ." His lips and
tongue struggle. "*Catth.*"

The creature slowly walks around him, inspecting, and then runs
off. Not what it was looking for, apparently.

Jebrassy stands up wearing only the clothes he had with him when
he left the Kalpa. The ice is cold under his feet. Everything is exceptionally cold. Worse, he feels his weight diminish. This makes him queasy.
He hopes everything won't just drift up and float away.

But he doesn't know why it shouldn't. Obviously, the last of the old rules—imitated, remade, and finally ignored and abused—are passing.

CHAPTER 116

Jack can barely hold the stone, it's become so hot. But he won't let it go. It can burn his fingers to char for all he cares. Ginny will be holding hers, he knows—and what about Daniel?

Blue veins rise in the green ice, begin to cut and churn.

There are two paths—there have been only two paths for some time now, at least since he rode the bicycle on autopilot and saw the earwig in the warehouse district.

But he doesn't know which path this is.

He's working on autopilot again.

Seeing with other eyes.

Staring down at different feet, naked—and watching a cat walk away with its tail held high.

"*Catthh,*" he says, his lips numb.

CHAPTER 117

Tiadba feels almost nothing. She can no longer see her companions— they lie at the edge of her vision, black crumples of flesh and abandoned underclothes, not alive, not dead, not even asleep.

Best if they were dead.

The female presence spreads like an enveloping cloak. But there are now *two* presences. She can feel them both—

One is cold and frightening, crying out in the darkness, seeking her lost children only to destroy them, surrounded by this swirling prison that is more felt than seen.

And the other—ancient, filled with potential.

The prison will keep one and set the other free.

Animals brush by—sniff her naked feet, rub against her arms, then move on. They are hunting something small and weak.

"Catthh," she says, then tries the word again. "*Cats*."

CHAPTER **118**

Ginny is paying so much attention to the other layer of vision and experience—lost Tiadba—that she does not feel the touch on her shoulder until it is too late.

CHAPTER **119**

Whitlow comes upon the child, kneeling on the ice as if to catch her breath. She does not turn, does not hear, apparently does not see.

Delight perverse and damp gleams on his pale, wrinkled face. He stumps the last few paces. The Moth is everywhere, a gray mist radiating its own triumph.

"For our Livid Mistress," Whitlow says matter-of-factly as he lifts the girl high with one hand. "A final delivery. Our greatest triumph."

Glaucous agrees.

With all of his strength, he holds out his fists and plays this game as no game has ever been played, pulling a single steel thread down even through the whirling of the spheres—and with the greatest of grunts, the grunt of birth and death and voiding, the grunt of victory and defeat and infinite pain, this squat gnome, hunter of birds, gambler's friend, hunter of children, *inverts* Whitlow, not just his heart but his insides—liver and lights, blood and ouns.

Through the messy cloud, heedless of the thin wail of the dissipating Moth—Whitlow was always his ground and root—Glaucous reaches out to grasp the girl before she simply flies away.

He has pulled down as much of this chosen cord of fate as he can: penance and game, set and match. This is the greatest thing he has ever done, and almost his last—almost.

The fate he has grasped and pulled forward is not a good one, not for him. He knew that from the moment he saw it, near the Crux. He sets the girl upon the ice, oblivious—still seeing with other eyes. "You're welcome," he mutters to no one, then crosses himself—an old habit—and kneels beside her.

As the avengers approach, Glaucous uses his thick, ugly hand to gently push her aside.

The wave of cats breaks over him. He is their first prey. Only right, he thinks—one terror of birds to another. Glaucous curls like a hopeless child and with all his remaining will tries not to add to the screaming. His blood spurts onto the ice. The gray tide moves on before he is finished, but the darkness closes in as his pain is chilled and pinched into a single, drawn-out throb.

Something else is about to die.

The cats have found other, more important prey.

CHAPTER 120

The Typhon knows neither time nor space. It exists without thought in a condensed shapelessness, smaller than the smallest imaginable point. In most ways, it can be described—much as we might describe the muses or Brahma—only by negatives: not this, not that.

But let us simplify things and use human words, ascribing such motives, activities, and emotions as are familiar to humans—much easier to convey, however incorrect.

When the Typhon first became aware of our aging cosmos, it sensed vacancy—and opportunity. The old cosmos had few defenses. Its observers were many but scattered across an immense and thin geometry, worn by long and decadent eons. Like a great tree that falls in a forest, lives on for a while, then slowly leaks away its sap and its will, the cosmos's heartwood was beginning to crumble.

The Typhon was young, as timeless things go, and untried. Even the smallest, most formless aspirant to rule must prove its quality. This was its chance to take root like a seed falling onto a nursery log. It would rise above the dying realm and grow—and grow—to full nobility.

To Godhead.

It did not expect resistance. This was its flaw. It did not know how to use and incorporate confrontation and defiance, necessary skills for any god. The push back of creation—the freedom of unbridled will—engenders love.

Not for the Typhon. Whenever it encountered things that saw differently, it ended them—with great fear and loathing.

And then with something like amusement.

It *enjoyed* hating, and there was nothing to stop it—for many trillions of years.

It had found its quality.

But now, in all possible dimensions, conclusions are arriving, consequences are falling into place. It is no longer a young god or an infinitesimal point, everywhere and nowhere at once. It has acquired a kind of limitation, an unwanted substantiality condensing out of the ur-nothing, the monobloc beneath all possible creations—rising out of the smallest virtual foam of the tiniest imaginable volume of vacuum.

The Typhon acquires dimension and shape—it becomes bloated and sprawled. In its awful, pointless passion for deconstruction and destruction, it finally loses whatever focus it might once have applied to its whims or tasks at hand.

The overextended cosmos—the old, crumbling nurse log—has deteriorated to such a degree that it has turned into a trap. The blades of Brahma's armillary spin. It is now a very bad place for a bloated, undisciplined god.

All the Typhon can do is flail within the whirling prison, using up the last of its strength to cause more suffering and frustrate any possibility of good outcome. It has stretched its contamination backward across time, perverting creation, causing endless cycles of directionless pain. It is now pressing our cosmos toward a nasty end, dissolving space and time back to the beginning—eating away and corrupting almost everything we could ever possibly know.

We might speculate about what would have happened to the Typhon in more fortunate circumstances. Perhaps we should extend pity, those of us who have felt its corrosive touch—every one of us.

The bad that traveled from the future, not from the past.

Final sin.

But we are inadequate to such speculations. We are inadequate to feel pity for a failed god.

And so—

Let's not. Let's not feel pity.

———

The Typhon—formerly without thought or viscera, without conscience or sympathy—realizes that its puffy carcass can now *feel*. What it feels is a kind of apprehension—even fear. It is no longer more powerful than those it once crushed.

It has become a small, brownish-gray thing, lying in the center of the last of the universe like a metaphysical abortion, pitiful but for its history. And soon there will be no history. No trace of its works, its conclusions.

What it had done its very utmost to stop, to prevent, is advancing. Even the tools it forged across eternity are turning against it. It can feel the last two threads, swirling and twining and trying to cancel, competing and summing against all the Typhon's efforts.

One of those threads is finally dissolved.

The Typhon experiences another unfamiliar emotion.

A dire, dreadful sense of *hope*.

Only one thread will survive. And that in itself is not a healthy condition for any cosmos.

The Typhon may pass into true nothingness, but it will at least have the satisfaction of taking every last observer with it—blinding forever those outrageous eyes.

No more memories.

No more stories.

No more.

CHAPTER 121

Jack sees Ginny half swimming through the snow and fog and the rising chunks of ice, toward the blue gleam. With supreme effort, propelling along this last cord of fate, all the other possibilities being pinched and cut to pieces by the armillary shell, he catches up with her. The stone helps—a little.

"Hey," he says.

"Hey." She glances at him. "Watch out for the cats. They look pretty mad."

"Yeah—didn't think I'd make it."

"Thought you'd forget about me," she says.

"Never."

She reaches out, he reaches out, their hands meet, and then they hug and feel their combined warmth, and something joins them together— far sexier than anything either has experienced—and gives them strength. The sum-runners clink against each other, squeezing their fingers between them, and then separate with a reddish flare.

"We need at least three," she says. "I remember that much."

"If the third one isn't here, we lose everything—right?"

"I guess so. Who's that?" Ginny asks, pointing at another shape in the fog.

CHAPTER **122**

Jebrassy has come to the edge of the brilliant blueness, naked and shivering, his feet and lower legs frozen into stumps. Two tall people—he assumes they are people, mostly enclosed in fog and snow—approach. One reaches down to lift him up by his armpits.

They are tall but not Tall Ones—not like Ghentun. He stares through the greenish storm into a familiar face, and then another. He sees himself through the other, and allows the other to see him, but actually it's very hard to see anything at all. Constant streams of blue light shoot between them, obscuring outlines but igniting an even greater sense of renewed will—perhaps even energy.

They're speaking but their words are difficult to understand. So he offers up all he has, like a child gifting a toy to new friends, old acquaintances: the sculpted polyhedron with four holes.

The piece almost explodes with blue arcs.

The two bring up their own twists of rock, dim red eyes buried in the gnarls, brighter now against the blue. These must be—

The sum-runners jerk inward, lock on, and fit into the sculpted piece, which completes and fills their own puzzle twists. They have traveled across billions of years, then tumbled through a dying universe to find their way back.

But two holes remain unfilled.

———

Daniel walks past the gory, crystallized remains of Glaucous and Whitlow, and does not know what happened here—or whether it is still happening. He is interested now in what the cats have set upon, just a short distance away. He follows a trail of bloody paw prints steaming on the green, glassy ice.

The armillary is cinching in, the bands tightening and whirling faster. A kind of snowy fog covers his feet, his knees, and then his shoulders. The ice is crazing—rising up in chunks. He pushes through, fingers warmed by the sum-runners.

The cats are at the center, that much he thinks must be true—and for a brief instant, with a fanning of his hands, he looks down to find them hissing and scratching and biting.

The cats are killing a small squirming thing in a pit. The process is slow. The thing keeps shaping itself anew, but it can't escape. Sizzling, steaming pieces of chewed-over theophany skitter across the ice, drawing etched curls of virtual particle-trails.

The light is failing. Daniel can hardly see. Inside, Fred is wondering how anything can exist at all. They are inside a diminishing spore of space-time, reality pushing its final push against nothingness—that which cannot be seen, thought of, spoken of.

Not this, not that, not anything.

"We're here because we *will* it, and always have," Daniel says, and that's that.

The unpleasant shrill vibration in his head abruptly stops. The brown, twisted thing has been destroyed—shredded.

If the spore shrinks to nothing, then the death of the Typhon— Daniel is sure that's what is down there in the tiny blur of a pit, covered with hissing cats—will mean nothing. It will not be recorded.

It will not be reconciled.

The Typhon may randomly return, unexpected, illogical, but just as real as before.

Cats push away, many with missing paws and limbs, distorted heads, burned fur, empty eyes. This deed has cost them dearly.

Daniel steps back as well. All this is very familiar—though not always with cats. The stone is tugging him away from the pit, the cats, the remains of the failed, would-be god.

Seconds tick with each swipe and whoosh of the shrinking armillary.

He reaches into his pocket. He always does this. He always passes along what he is given, to save everything that must be saved, and that ends his chances of uniting with the being he loves more than the entire world—the one he has traveled all this way to be with.

Who—or what. That was always our question, no? What could we ever be to each other?

I crossed the Chaos. The rebel city was dying—surrounded by the Typhon, betrayed by the City Prince. Despite everything, I joined her. And I did what I had to do. We agreed. I had to go back to the beginning with a piece of the Babel, the final piece—and at the Librarian's insistence, a second, a backup against further betrayal, in case another piece was lost—

And so I flew back with the last sum-runners, and found by brute force a path into the earliest intelligences of the young cosmos.

The only shepherd who never dreams.

The bad shepherd.

Jack is there beside him, hand on his shoulder.

"Do you know what this is?" Jack asks. "I sure as hell don't."

"It's a mess, that's what it is," Daniel says. "Take these." And gives him the two stones. "I'm done, this time around."

CHAPTER 123

Tiadba is in the warm embrace of someone she has never known, never met, and yet about whom she knows a great deal. How she was found in pieces around the dying cosmos, and brought by the Shen to a single place, where a brilliant thinker assembled her into a sentient form, which somehow chose to be female.

She has met the Pilgrim sent to retrieve her would-be father, and has spoken with him—and made a key decision, to become flesh and journey back to Earth. And there—

The fear and bitterness have gone—but the grief remains.

The young breed squirms in this embrace, uncomfortable, restless. Someone she knows is approaching. She only half sees what lies around her. Other eyes see from another position—and then Tiadba's skin erupts with piercing shafts of brilliant blue.

The entire volume around her becomes a sphere of glorious, blinding blue.

Her visitor is very near.

Her visitor sees—

Jebrassy!

CHAPTER **124**

The armillary accelerates inward at an astonishing rate. But within instants of the end, of infinite compression, squeezing down to zero and then echoing to less than zero, and vibrating that way until all is pulverized—the metric has suddenly expanded.

Something huge is stirring.

The armillary is now miles wide, spinning much more slowly.

The lake of crushed, turbulent ice rises and cascades out in melting waves to fill this new volume.

The Chalk Princess has gone—passed away forever with the Typhon. The armillary is no longer a prison.

It is the shell of an egg.

Within, as if a breath is being held, there is waiting.

Another presence—missing or held down for ages—returns in stunned bewilderment to find herself surrounded by some of the very breeds she ordained to be made, long ago. They have found her, as they were designed to do. They have snared and brought others with them—kindred shapes of primordial matter.

As they were designed to do.

There is reunion. Her father's goal is almost attained.

One thing remains.

She holds the tiny female breed in her naked lap like a mother and child. The breed writhes in a halo of brilliant blue, some of which leaps out in long arcs to pierce the fog, the mist.

"Have you seen the Pilgrim?" Ishanaxade again asks the breed, who barely hears.

CHAPTER **125**

Daniel has never seen anything so beautiful.

He has fought and clawed through countless adversities and fates, and countless bodies, to return to this beginning point. He carries the small rounded piece of green stuff that Mnemosyne left for him in Bidewell's empty room, an impossible time and distance behind him now. Back then the muse gave him a catalytic remembrance, a trigger of transformation, as if in the future they would meet and know each other again.

What shall he do?

The glowing female pushes through the fog and his knees go weak.

All are here. Who are you?

The face is so lovely—the shape, compelling and impossible, alien and comforting at once; so many shapes, so many limbs, so much power. Something very old, long suppressed, a condensation no more or less mysterious than the time-worn piece in his left hand, rises up in him.

Daniel tries to speak.

I am Sangmer.

You?

Then,

Where have you gone, Pilgrim? Husband? And what have you brought with you?

Daniel holds up his right hand, empty.

You have delivered them?

He nods.

Then it is done. A quorum of shepherds has arrived.

That time-tumbled ovoid in his other hand is like a hardened and constricted piece of the lake that churns and quakes beneath them. Like the pieces that the Shen gathered from all the galaxies they visited, after the Brightness and the end of creation.

A lost piece of Mnemosyne. It will quicken Ishanaxade and return her to what she must become. He can withhold it, deny it, and claim the woman he sought across the Chaos. Or he can present it and lose her forever.

CHAPTER 126

Ishanaxade looks down upon his sad, ancient body, surrounded and filled by so much pain, travel-worn, cruel, determined to finish his task and return—whatever the cost.

What have we done? she asks him.

What we always do. What we promise to do. Rebirth.

He holds out his left hand.

Ishanaxade unfolds his fingers and takes the fragment. It is not glass, of course. It is a piece of the mother of all thought, of those who see and think, including Daniel—and Sangmer. It is reconciling, which allows memory, and shapes the creation of the Sleeper, when he chooses not to sleep.

If I take this—I will become what I was. What will we be to each other then?

The body of Daniel is pitiful with fear. Already the lake is rising through the base of the glowing triangle, through her blur of feet and glowing legs.

Every few rounds, out of all infinity, we will meet, he tells her. *For me, that has to be enough.*

The armillary expands again. They cannot see its boundaries.

CHAPTER 127

Ginny and Jack feel the nightmares pass away. They know that no one will forget them unless it should be so. They see Jebrassy and Tiadba nearby—and together they make four points within the storm as ancient matter reacquaints, according to old rules that come into play only within the Sleeper's spinning fortress—and just for this moment.

Tiadba and Jebrassy have joined in so many ways, Ginny and Jack are confused—and envious.

Jack and Ginny collect Daniel's two sum-runners. Daniel is not with them—they do not know where he is.

"Should we?" Jack asks, and holds up the stones and the polyhedron.

"Bidewell would say we should," Ginny says. "So much pain and effort."

Jack juggles the remaining pieces, smiling at Ginny. He is thinking of the last words of the Keeper. "I'm not asking Bidewell. I'm asking *you.*"

"Don't be arrogant," she says.

"That's what I am," Jack says.

"I do *not* find it charming."

"The old gods watch. They'll forgive us—won't they?"

"I'm not so sure . . ."

Jack continues to juggle. His smile is infinitely sweet and distracting. "You choose," he says.

ENTR'ACTE

This is the unexpected moment. Gods will never be predicted or judged, their motivations will never be known. Ishanaxade enjoys a brief respite before her own tasks resume. Sangmer is there.

When they part, it will start again—her labor and his solitary quest.

The Sleeper will take over soon. Until then the children will play, all of them, and their play is crude and primal and sweet, the stuff of which dreams will always be made.

———

Out on a formerly gray domain, Ginny is taking advantage of this *interludium*, the malleable between-world, and has shaped a vision of Thule. The snowy crags and sun-pinked clouds, the green and yellow and purple fields, the immense patches of bird-haunted heather, the shore-scattered string of ancient castles between which the children can flee and find refuge . . . her own place, their own adventure.

Jack is content to let her lead.

Jebrassy and Tiadba find this open land enchanting, with its wide blue sky. They particularly love the lingering times between night and day, dusk and dawn. There are no stars, of course. But the sun is bright and full and warm—when clouds don't gather and rain isn't falling. The rain is unexpected and delightful.

They have built a small hut in a hidden valley, and have learned how to gather berries and make a *fire*. Jebrassy, of course, is learning to hunt—after a fashion. There is usually bread on the hearth, should he return empty-handed, which is often, since there are so few animals, and those not very convincing.

Tiadba is growing rounder. They wonder: What happens when a child is born between creations?

Throughout Thule the detail grows. There is a town, with its own library—and a bookstore, already filled with books and a few cats, some with burned toes and singed ears. In the bookstore, five green books appear. On the spine of each is the number—or is it a year?—1298.

One day Ginny opens the first of the five books to read, and notices that the tiniest spider is crawling across the page. She is about to brush it away, but realizes it is the first spider she has seen here. It is not part of the text, and it is not paying any attention to the words beneath its little legs.

The spider between the lines.

In the library, on a windowsill, sits a small round piece of wave-tossed beach glass, the color of pale jade, refracting the changing light of each new dawn.

Then it is gone.

Memory is returning.

———

Some say, even now, Jack travels with Ginny on all the roads anyone can imagine. Some say you will find them on every street corner, accompanied by two or more cats, asking those who watch what they should do next—how should the puzzle pieces fall?

All stories forever, shaping all fates, until the end of time—or is one story, one life filled with love, sufficient to rekindle time and make paradise?

Waiting for the Sleeper to finally awake.

To this very day, Jack juggles. He never drops anything.

Others say—

In the beginning is the Word.

Lynnwood, Washington
September 28, 2007